Beloved of the Pack

The Stars of the Pack - Book IV
N.J. LYSK

I0634690

Palm Hearts
PalmHeartsBooks@gmail.com
ISBN: 978-1-916630-17-8

For all the people who write me to talk about these people who live in my head. Special shout out to my editor, Proofyourlove, and to the Beta Wolves and the Alpha Readers for continued support, encouragement, and telling me when I mix up the babies! (Five is a lot, and my dad has never been able to keep four names straight, it's realism!)

Your kind words are *so* worth the weird looks I get on the train!

I hope you like this one,

N.J. Lysk.

The Stars of the Pack series (Chronologically)

0.1) Midnight Encounters*
1) Omega for the Pack
1.1) Simpler than Most*
2) Alpha for the Pack
3) Protectors of the Pack
4) Beloved of the Pack
4.1) Shock Therapy*
5) Betas Aside
5.1) Around the Hearth*

= Interludes/extras that don't need to be read to follow.

Companion series:
Runt of the Litter
Paper Kisses

Also available in German, French, Italian, Dutch, Spanish, Portuguese and bilingual learner editions.

Caveat lector: Warnings for suicidal ideation, panic attacks, depression, as well as discussion of past sexual trauma and body dysphoria.

Part I: Josh

Prologue

All kids thought their parents were invincible, but Ray had had more reason than most. Not only were his parents werewolves and immune to disease, they were protected by an equally strong pack that grew larger by the year. Wolves knew the world was a dangerous place, but pups, like children, learned from the environment they grew up in. That was how you eventually got dogs tame enough you could rest easy letting them sleep in your child's bed.

And, of course, the higher you were, the harder the fall. And at thirteen, Raymond Halley had been at the top of the world. Josh should know; he'd been nearly as jealous of Ray as he was of Ray's attention.

Ray had everything Josh wanted: a loving mother who was always home and always listened, an equally devoted father who worked hard but made time for his kids. He even resented Ray for his younger siblings, even though it meant Ray had started changing diapers at nine and got more responsibilities as he got older. But even if the little ones could be annoying, their existence meant that Ray could never be truly alone.

Josh was. Because his parents loved him, they made sure he ate dinner and did well in school and had friends. They asked him questions about all those things and they spoke freely in front of him. But they didn't make Josh want to go back home from Ray's house after he ended up there most days after school. And when he said he wanted to stay over during the weekend, they let him do it without a fuss. It was probably intended as a kindness, but Josh couldn't feel it as anything but a slight. He'd never let someone he loved spend all their time away from him—not without at least arguing about it.

And then Ray's dad had been killed in a car accident. The other driver hadn't even been going fast—a little over the speed limit, but they did live near a major motorway—and neither had Ray's father. The police had concluded one or both of them had been blinded by the sun in a vital moment before the crash. In an unexpected twist of fate, the human had survived and the werewolf had died when he'd been thrown from his vehicle and hit the rail guard hard enough to nearly detach his head from his body. Josh still couldn't think about it without feeling sick. Ray had demanded his mother tell him, refusing to believe his father was gone until she'd finally broken down and taken him to the woods to tell him away from his siblings.

Ray had lived as a wolf for a month after that. Josh had tried to join him, but his parents had insisted *he* had no excuse to miss school. He'd spent his free time with Ray instead, helping him hunt and bringing him fresh meat from the fridge when they couldn't manage.

Ray hadn't been able to speak—and not just because he didn't have the right kind of mouth for it—but he'd let Josh hold him up. He'd curled up next to him and, when Josh was in human form, let him rub his ears for hours. Josh had already known he wanted to kiss his best friend, but it'd taken the worst thing that had ever happened to Ray for him to realise that he wanted a lot more than that.

He'd told himself that Ray wasn't ready to hear something like that, that Josh wasn't sure. Not sure enough to talk about it anyway, and that they had nothing but time... But the truth was that admitting how much Ray meant to him made it all the more impossible to risk losing him.

And yet, he'd lost him anyway. He could see that much now. Ray was in pain and instead of reaching for Josh, he'd pulled back as far as he possibly could.

Chapter one

"I'm fine," Ray said again. He wasn't even lying. Maybe he'd said it so many times since that terrible night when he'd been kidnapped that he'd actually come to believe it. Maybe it no longer meant anything to him.

Ray wasn't fine. Josh didn't need to hear his heart skip a beat; he'd known Ray all his life. Sometimes it seemed like he'd loved him just as long.

And then he'd gone and signed his heart away to be torn to pieces by becoming Ray's alpha and committing not just in soul but in body to protecting and caring for him. If he'd thought it was intense when he'd been in love with Ray the human way and too afraid to fuck things up to tell him... Well, asking his wolf to join the party and actually having sex with Ray had done it for him.

He couldn't blame Ray for pulling back when he was going through the worst time of his life since the tragic loss of his father. He couldn't ask for his attention and his devotion when his best friend was barely keeping himself together. But it hurt. He missed what they'd had. He'd have given up sex with Ray any day for a movie marathon, or a day in the sun watching Ray draw while pretending to nap.

He had tried to give it up anyway, and he'd failed even at that because his inner wolf didn't care that the man was the love of Josh's life and he'd have rather died than hurt him, the wolf was an alpha that needed to prove again and again who its omega belonged to.

And now it'd stopped.

Only the price was too dear to ever be worth it. Josh looked away from Ray at the sole thought, feeling his claws grow as his wolf reacted to his barely repressed fury. It didn't matter that Josh wished he could kill Nicholas himself because he loved Ray and the wolf only wanted to eliminate a threat to their pack, they were in agreement. Without any strong emotion of his own to keep the wolf down, it took almost constant focus to keep it from unleashing its aggression. Josh knew Nicholas was dead—Gabriel hadn't been descriptive, but he'd left no doubts—but that only left his rightful anger without an object, and the wolf wasn't capable of believing it when it hadn't seen it.

The wolf only knew about one thing: Nicholas' scent all over their mate. Josh had seen the scrapes on Ray's face; the wolf had smelled Nicholas' seed.

"You got the list?" Ray asked, snapping Josh out of his dark thoughts.

"Yeah, you sure you don't want to come?" he asked.

It was pointless and they both knew it; Ray hadn't left pack territory since he'd returned after being forced to. He'd only agreed to leave the house at all to look at the fence when Josh had promised he'd stay in the living room with both Alec and Iesu to look after the babies.

It was a step in the right direction, Josh reminded himself when Ray shook his head.

"Okay, see you in a bit."

His fingers clenched as he pulled his hand back without punching Ray on the shoulder.

He chose the time carefully to be sure he'd find her alone at home. It was pretty rude of an alpha to show up at an omega's home unannounced, especially one from what was now technically another pack. But he was sure Ray's mum wouldn't think twice of it.

She made tea without asking and made him catch her up on the kids' latest accomplishments and misadventures, and the progress with the construction of what they all called the beta wing by now. It was all empty talk and they both knew it. Maybe she just wanted to reassure him that she wasn't angry at him—although the moon knew he deserved her anger and more.

"I need your advice," he finally said when she'd poured for them both. "I can't... He might never forgive me for telling you this," he confessed, his fear bleeding freely into his voice. Because he was afraid; if he crossed a line with Ray that Ray couldn't forgive... If he lost his friendship even when he could never really lose him in reality... He wouldn't be able to bear it. He'd leave. It'd hurt every second of the rest of his life, bound to Ray as he was, but he couldn't...

She interrupted his thoughts. "Why are you telling me then?"

He exhaled and made himself take a sip of his drink. "Because he needs help, and I can't— I don't know how to give it to him." He drank again, trying to distract himself from the bitter words with the sweetness of the drink. And failing. There wasn't enough tea in the world for this conversation. Not enough werewolf-grade vodka, either.

Martha nodded. "Then you are doing the right thing," she decided. It was stupid, but hearing her say it almost *made* it so. Josh's own mum wasn't the affectionate type; she loved him, indubitably, but she was in love with her work. She didn't have time for the minutiae of daily life, the little problems that had seemed so overwhelming when Josh had been a kid, a teenager even. Martha did. Josh wasn't her son, not even a distant cousin, but she'd been there for him too.

He'd learned to believe her.

Even so, he knew that she would put Ray first. It was only fair, he was her son, after all. Josh *wanted* Ray put first. Ray needed to be put first.

This was for Ray's own good, he reminded himself once again. It didn't stop it from feeling like a betrayal. "You know about... you know he was taken."

"Yes." There was fear in her voice, but she was keeping it back from her scent somehow.

Josh swallowed, hands folded in his lap, fists clenched carefully against his own claws. "It was... He killed him. The alpha," he clarified. He didn't want to say the bastard's name. "But... it was too late. He—" He stopped, body tightening in a dizzying mix of fear and fury. "He made—" He choked on the next word, feeling tears brim from his eyes.

Martha leaned across the coffee table and took hold of his arm. "Enough."

He was silent, looking at the space between their feet, torn between pure undiluted agony and revolting shame. He, more than any of the other alphas, had taken on his role as Ray's mate to protect him. He hadn't been able to make Ray happy with his situation, but he'd known that going in. Ray had made it abundantly clear he did not relish his role as an omega, but that wasn't something Josh could fix. He could make the most of the cards Ray had been handed though. He'd been working on it. They all had. He had thought— But then Nicholas had come, and Ray had started thinking about it, and what could Josh do? Tell Ray that he not only had a terrible choice to make for his pack, but that Josh would take away his right to make it?

He should have, he realised now. He should have confronted Ray with his concerns, insisted that he talk it over with his mother before making any decisions, moved heaven and earth to keep Ray from saying yes to something that would destroy him in soul if not in body. But he'd been too afraid. Too selfish. He didn't want Ray to be angry with him when his best friend had already pulled so far away already. He was meant to be the stone against which Ray tested his mettle and he'd gone soft on him.

He'd failed him because he'd treated Ray as an omega, exactly what he'd promised him he wouldn't do. He didn't know if it was instincts or love, but Ray was paying the price either way.

Josh had to fix it before he really lost Ray forever.

Even if fixing meant he lost Ray forever.

"Tell me what to do," he begged. He kept his gaze down, unable to face the judgment in the beloved face. "Anything. I—"

The hand on his arm tightened. "Shhh..." she said. "Keep your head, Josh. Nothing is lost while you are still alive to make amends."

He jerked in her grip, a reflex he couldn't control. Because for a moment he'd thought about Nicholas doing more to Ray than just... And then he realised she wasn't talking about her son; she was talking about her husband. He looked up then, uncertain, but her face was just like it had always been—she'd barely aged in the last decade—there was no sign of her pain on her skin. But it was there in her eyes: a pain so great it'd never stop aching, a loss so immense nothing would ever fill it. She nodded like he'd said the right thing. "I don't think he'll be ready to talk, at least that explains why he's been so vague with me on the phone. But he needs to keep busy; I know Ray, he always kept busy, made sure everything was done and then double checked. He doesn't do well with idleness, and he probably needs to keep his mind off... the incident."

"Maybe he can paint," Josh suggested timidly.

"Good idea," she nodded. "But you are a new pack, I'm sure there's useful work to be done. Ray loves to paint but he doesn't think of it as work."

"Oh," Josh said. It was true, he saw it at once. There he went again, thinking of Ray as an omega meant to be doing light work. But Ray wasn't pregnant anymore, he didn't need to take it easy. He was a strong, capable guy and even with the betas, they could use every pair of hands they could get. It would be wasteful to keep Ray entertained with his hobby when he could be helping the pack and... "You really think he'd want that? I just... If I ask him, it's not like he can say he won't, I don't know, help with building the beta wing."

"Josh," she said, slapping his arm and letting go. "He can make up his own damn mind. It's not your job to think for omegas, just to give them the options you can afford. Ray is an adult; if he is too distracted to notice his pack needs help, he'll want to know."

He rubbed his arm. "Damn, sorry, you are right."

Martha shook her head. "Don't be sorry, make it right," she said firmly. "You are his mate, not... It isn't your job to decide what he can handle."

Josh nodded. "Thank you, Martha. I appreciate it. I don't... I don't know what I... we'd do without you."

"Just take care of my boy," she answered. "And let him take care of you too, you look like you haven't slept in a while."

Josh couldn't say much to that: it was true. It was hard to fall asleep when you were always wondering if someone would come and take what you loved the most in the world from you.

Chapter two

O f course the one time Josh wanted Gabriel around, the other alpha was doing a 12 hour shift at the site—some deadline or other that the werewolves on the crew had agreed to help the company meet in exchange for some serious cash. It wasn't fair to resent Gabriel for it; after all, they needed money almost as badly as they had needed betas. In fact, they needed more money now because even though more people were a sound long-term solution to childcare in the numbers they required, the construction of the beta wing had drained their bank account even further.

Josh wasn't that naïve; he knew he wasn't really annoyed about Gabriel's absence. He was angry with Gabriel because when Ray's uncle had told him that he could help choose the alphas for the new pack, Josh had gone straight to Ray's older cousin. They both had liked him as kids and Gabriel had admitted he was gay when Josh had asked him about it. He'd been fourteen and already so in love with Ray, he felt like he could never look at anyone else. He had, of course, and he didn't mind sleeping with girls, or guys. It just wasn't... He'd never got to kiss Ray before he presented and of course he'd only messed around with humans and betas, but in his heart of hearts, he believed what made all the difference wasn't a part of his brain that lit up when his nose got a faceful of the right pheromones. It was Ray. It had always been Ray. It would always be Ray.

He'd trusted Gabriel with the one person who mattered the most to him.

And Gabriel hadn't made Ray happy, anybody could tell that. Josh had tried to hint, but an alpha could barely point out a spelling mistake to another without starting a fight. And Gabriel had so easily taken over as leader of their little pack—barely held together by their omega—that it would have been even more of a challenge to try and tell him how to treat Ray.

And he'd thought it wasn't his place. He wasn't more important than Ray's other mates. He wasn't Ray's choice any more than they were.

And then Gabriel had left them to go after Ray—exactly what Josh's wolf was desperate for him to do—and that had been the last straw. Josh wasn't one to judge others harshly, but he would not stand for anyone who didn't protect his pack or who let them come to harm.

Gabriel's actions had had no obvious consequences; all the babies were safe, as were all of them. The invading alphas had been dealt with, too. But it didn't matter; Josh didn't trust him anymore and he didn't think he'd ever trust him again.

So he was stuck living with a guy he had once admired, even crushed on, and who he now thought might be a danger to them all. And he was stuck—an alpha's claim was forever; they were bound to Ray as long as they lived. Technically, Gabriel could walk out but it'd hurt him to and Josh couldn't think of any reason compelling enough to make someone do that to themselves if they didn't have to.

He shoved thoughts of Gabriel aside and went in search of his friend. He was slumped on the sofa, watching as Iesu tried to teach Sergi some more Romanian. Sergi answered hesitantly, but it made Iesu clap and grin like a lunatic. Ray's lips were upturned, but he didn't laugh at the display like he would have before.

Everything about him was toned down. It made Josh ache to shake him, beg him to come out of his head. It didn't matter how awful whatever kept Ray's eyes dim was; Josh wanted to share it with him. It was his burden too. It was his... Except, of course, he couldn't ask Ray to do anything he didn't want to do.

"Hey," he greeted.

Iesu replied in Romanian, a word they all recognized by now—apparently, the babies could pick up the language easily if they just heard it spoken between two or more people regularly. Sergi made a face and tried to imitate his lover. Iesu didn't correct him but gave him an amused look that had Sergi huffing in exasperation. "I told you my tongue doesn't move that way!"

"Now, don't go insulting your tongue. You know I really like it," Iesu replied, just short of leering.

Josh snorted. They had never tried to hide their relationship—perhaps aware scent would give them away faster than any terms of endearment or lingering touches—but lately, they had been getting outright exhibitionistic.

Or maybe Josh was jealous. He looked at Ray again and found the omega had closed his eyes. He was sleeping too much, except when he woke up screaming. Josh didn't need to be an expert to know what it meant; anybody with eyes would have seen Ray was depressed. He'd taken his presentation hard and the pregnancy maybe worse...

Josh couldn't blame him. He blamed himself; he could never forget that he hadn't told Ray what he felt in the forest when they still had time. Instead, he had led Ray to the other alphas. He had been given authority only to choose them and weed out anybody who would cause trouble, nothing more. If he wasn't such a coward... If he'd just *taken* what Ray and he needed...

He had convinced Ray it was for the best and he thought Ray believed him, but he wasn't completely sure that they couldn't have simply disappeared for a few months and then returned, bonded and with their first child.

It was stupid to think of it now. They couldn't take it back, and Josh knew neither Ray nor he could wish the rest of their children to disappear, no matter how dearly they had cost them.

He took a seat on the armrest of the sofa, then slowly pushed the tips of his fingers through Ray's soft blond hair—longer than he'd ever kept it before and curling at the edges in the same way Michael's did. Ray didn't move for a very calculated moment, then turned his face to encourage him. Josh pushed his fingertips against his skull and massaged, soft but firm.

Josh's pulse was too fast. Stupidly fast, but so was Ray's. For Ray, it had to be the fact that he found it hard to let anybody touch him after what had been done to him. For Josh, it was the fact that despite everything, Ray wanted Josh to touch him.

A part of him hoped it was just him. But that was just the instincts talking, really. Ray needed to let them all back in, to make it easier when the moon rose and want became need.

"It's my mum's birthday soon," Josh said. "And, well, I'm a bit short on cash." Ray's eyes blinked open, curious and patient. For once, he seemed present in the moment. "Could you maybe do a portrait of the babies?"

Ray frowned a little and sat up, not seeming to notice when he dislodged Josh's hand. "But that's... I mean, that's like a primary school present."

"What's like a primary school present?" Iesu asked from where he was bouncing Jamie up and down on his knee. Sergi was trying to dislodge Clara's clutching fingers from his own hair. He kept it pretty short, but it was so curly that it made a great handhold for a baby's tiny fingers.

He'd offer Sergi to shave it off for him, Josh thought, even as his own fingers twitched to bury themselves in Ray's hair again.

If he wanted it shorter, Ray could ask, he decided.

"I want Ray to do a portrait for my mum," he explained.

Sergi's eyes widened, his severe mouth curving slightly. "You should. You are so good at capturing people's... dunno, personality?" he tried, looking a little shy.

Josh didn't know anything about art but he could tell Ray was good anyway. Sergi had actually gone to the trouble of tracking Ray down because of the paintings the school had displayed on their walls. He didn't think Sergi painted or drew himself, but he clearly knew enough to be impressed. "See?" he insisted. "The expert has spoken."

"It's not like it'd take you long," Iesu pointed out. "We could do it now, right?"

Ray shook his head. "It's too late... The light..."

"Lamps," Iesu said at once. "Here," he told Josh, handing Jamie over. "I'll get an extension cord and we will have this brighter than Christmas."

They heard him rushing down the corridor. Josh caught Sergi smiling after him, and across the room from where he'd gone to keep Sasha from sharpening her teeth on a table leg, Ray met his eyes with a smile of his own—amused and fond. It wasn't the irrepressible grin of the boy he'd known, but it wasn't little. And maybe he didn't have so much to envy Sergi and Iesu as he'd thought.

Iesu had the whole thing set up before any of them could say much; or maybe Ray intentionally waited until Iesu directed them to put all five pups on the sofa—Mikey had changed into his wolf form and was snuggled against his brother's side—before he bothered to say, "I don't know if I have any canvases."

"Ray!" Iesu exclaimed, indignant.

"I could go buy..." Sergi started to say. But Ray couldn't keep a straight face anymore. He snorted, almost a real laugh.

"Are you messing with me?" Iesu asked, staring at him.

Ray shrugged. "Serves you right, when did I say I would do it?"

"You don't want to?" Sergi asked, sounding crestfallen. "But you love to draw..."

Ray shook his head, then sighed. "Okay, yes, I do. But that doesn't mean it's good enough to be a present."

"We can just hang it in the living room," Josh offered, putting a hand out to keep Clara from decamping.

Ray shot him a look, then pointed at the babies. "There's no way they'll stay still for long if they are awake. Josh, go get the iPad so we can take a picture."

Ray had spent a few minutes trying to get Mikey to change back before Iesu had brought out the chocolate. It tasted terrible to wolves and the babies, young as they were, had learned that lesson well, so his son had conceded.

Between wiping the chocolate off everyone's faces and hands and getting Mikey into nappies again, the photos hadn't started happening until about half an hour later. Marisa showed up well before they had got any shots in which most of their children looked decent—Ray didn't trust himself to combine them in his portrait—but she'd agreed to wait for them to be done even if it delayed bath time.

Josh had let Gabriel have a bit of food and a long nap once he'd returned home in the early hours of the morning, but he still looked pretty beat after working through the night. Maybe that was why he seemed so confused when Josh cornered him in the kitchen as he put a sandwich together. It was around five in the afternoon and even though it was Iesu's day off and he had kept Josh busy stuccoing the inner walls, he'd managed to sneak off to catch Gabriel right on time.

"You want to ask Ray to help with building?" Gabriel echoed.

He shrugged. "Yes, why not? We are behind schedule and he's an artist, he'll be good at it."

"This is hardly drawing..." Gabriel started, then stopped himself and put the knife he was using to spread butter on his bread down. "I mean, if you think it'll help him to keep busy, sure."

"It'll help him to be *useful*," Josh clarified a little testily. He pressed the fridge door closed, only to find it was already as closed as it'd get. Maybe he'd needed Ray's mum to tell him the exact same thing, but he still couldn't keep from being pissed at Gabriel for not getting it. "He's not a child we are humouring."

"Of course not," Gabriel replied, but he sounded sad, not angry. He pushed away from the counter altogether and turned to face Josh fully. *What had happened to the egotistical bastard that had insisted Ray stay home while they build their house?*

"I didn't mean it like that. You are all always... I'm *trying*, okay?" He met Josh's eyes. His eyelids were drooping a little over the pretty blue eyes that turned everyone's heads. "I know I fucked up, I don't need anybody to tell me. And I want to do better. So if this is what doing better looks like, then I'm game."

"Okay," Josh said slowly. It was hard to stay angry with a guy who was practically showing you his belly. "I think it'd be good for him to let the babies out of his sight for a minute and he will be close enough to go to them if he needs to... This is what *I* think it looks like. I'll ask him if he wants to do it. That's the most important thing," he added.

Gabriel huffed, pushing his fingers into his eye like he had a headache. Only, of course, werewolves didn't get headaches. But for Gabriel to show this much emotion, to falter in front of another alpha... That was just as telling. "I got five hundred quid for the night work, should we buy the sensors instead of paying for the plumbing?"

"No." Josh shook his head. "We are safe. Just because we are scared it doesn't mean we have to run from shadows." He stepped up and started putting together the sandwich Gabriel seemed to have forgotten. The last thing they needed was for their head builder to cut off half a finger. "But let's have a meeting, maybe the others will agree with you."

Gabriel nodded, and Josh thought he looked a little sheepish. He mumbled a thanks as he took half of the sandwich, but he didn't step away. It was like he didn't remember that Josh was an alpha, or like being close to him didn't make his wolf feel threatened. "Yes, sure... Guess I'll go get Marisa and ask about the calendar. If Ray agrees, you can just get her to put herself on babysitting duty. You should tell her that was my idea because she hates it with a passion."

As he watched him speak, Josh realised that his own wolf didn't mind the close proximity either. Maybe it was because Gabriel was pack. He waved away Gabriel's thanks and stepped away, "Does she?"

"Have you met her? She hates to be dirty. You could eat off the floor after she's done with it!" Gabriel sounded fond but exasperated. He was probably indifferent to dusty lunches after years of working construction—it wasn't like their immune systems couldn't handle it.

"Pretty sure most of our kids have," Josh commented. He was just beginning to remember the guy he'd liked, who'd talk to kids like they were people and listened like their small squabbles were serious issues. "Just—" he started, but then cut himself off. "Gonna go talk to him now."

Chapter three

Josh found Ray bent over his drawing pad, bedroom door mostly open and so lost in the work that he didn't notice Josh walking in. And then he saw Mikey on the bed, curled up and deeply asleep. Maybe Ray wasn't the only one distracted.

"He was the only one we could get to take a nap," Ray explained without looking up. "Marisa's got the other four with her."

"Oh," Josh said. "I didn't think you knew I was here..."

That made Ray look up, blue eyes serious. "I know where every one of you is every second of every day."

Josh swallowed, trying not to give away his alarm. It was probably pointless, even if Ray wasn't using his hearing and keen nose to keep track of them and somehow knew by some other omega ability, he still couldn't miss Josh's heart racing when Josh was standing in front of him. "Even outside pack territory?"

"No," Ray said curtly, turning away again. He clearly resented the limitation.

Josh's heart contracted. And then he realised he was feeling sorry for Ray instead of doing something to help him. Again. He'd been thinking of simply offering the work and hoping Ray accepted, but why the pretence? Ray hadn't lost his mind when he'd acquired the ability to tell where everyone in his territory was, or even when he'd been assaulted in that same territory and forced— He was hurt, and he wanted to heal just as much as Josh wanted him to. He didn't need to be deceived like a child refusing medicine.

"About that... I have an idea." Ray didn't look up, but Josh saw him pause in his shading. It wasn't the portrait, just a study of Clara's face in profile—probably in preparation for the bigger piece but already a beauty in its own right. "What if you helped with the building?"

Ray looked up, bemused. "The beta wing?"

"Yeah, the main rooms are done, but Gabriel says we better prepare for more betas now and we can't do the plumbing without a specialist, so..."

"Just putting bricks one on top of the other?" Ray checked. He sounded dubious, but he tended to be a little negative.

"It's a little more complicated than that," Josh argued. Of course, if you didn't need to be told the bricks had to be perfectly aligned in an alternating pattern because you had an eye for design... "And you'd be close, but... you wouldn't be with them all day, every day."

"You are really selling this," Ray said tersely. Josh didn't reply. Ray wasn't really objecting; he knew what had to be done, he just didn't want to do it. "Who... I mean, someone else will take over for me, right?"

"Gabriel said Marisa would want to. She doesn't like the work, the—"

"Dirt," Ray finished, wryly amused. "Of course she's freaking out." Ray paused. Josh bit his lip and let the silence stand. He wasn't blind; Ray had avoided leaving the babies with Marisa since he'd been taken. He loved her, but he didn't trust her—or his wolf didn't. "I don't know—"

"I'll come with," Josh interrupted. Ray stared at him, which was fair enough because it obviously had nothing to do with Ray's reluctance. "I'll be with you if you need me for anything," Josh offered lamely.

"You are right, I'm just..." He shrugged, twisting his pencil in his hands fast enough it blurred. It clearly required all his concentration to keep it from flying away—that explained why he wouldn't look up and meet Josh's eyes.

"You need time," Josh said softly. "But the sooner you start..."

"Yeah," Ray agreed. "Come here," he demanded, and Josh was by his side at once, looking down at the sketch. "Is her nose weird? No," he added when Josh pulled a face, "not her real nose, did I get it wrong?"

"Mmm..." He concentrated on the photo reference, trying to imprint the image of his daughter's face in his mind, then looked at the drawing. He'd learned to do this for Ray years ago. It had been too long since he'd been asked to. Had Ray asked Sergi when he'd taken it up again after presenting? He knew he hadn't been drawing lately, but...

"Josh?"

"Ah, yeah, sorry. I think it's a little too high." He pointed. "It's only a little but it's too close to the eyes, so..."

Ray was already humming his agreement. "Okay, I can..." He leaned in, not seeming to notice that his shoulder was resting against Josh's arm.

Josh stayed very still, not wanting to mess up his work, and just watched as Ray erased, then blew away the remains and marked the vague outline before straightening to have a look at the photograph again. "Yeah?" he asked Josh.

"Better," Josh said. His voice came out too rough. He thought Ray tensed up, but he went back to drawing too quickly to be sure.

As if he truly was an angel sent to look over his parents, Mikey grumbled on the bed, clearly waking up. Ray glanced up, but Josh waved him away. "You have a deadline," he joked and went to pick up his son.

At least Alec had talked Ray into weaning the babies off his milk. It made a new pregnancy more likely, but it wasn't like that was a concern at the moment anyway. After seeing him injured and covered in a strange alpha's scent, Josh's wolf was insisting on never letting him out of its sight again, but it had no interest in anything besides rubbing its side against its mate. It was the same for the others, Alec had said.

Alec wanted to find out why, Josh... Josh just wanted it to last. He didn't need to ever touch Ray again in anything but friendship; he'd give up every kiss, maybe even every touch like in some outlandish science fiction plot in which one lover's skin became poison to the other... He'd do anything in his power to keep Ray safe.

He still wanted him. He'd wanted him since he was thirteen years old— maybe the first person who'd made him stop and wonder what kissing felt like.

But he'd loved him even longer.

Gabriel took them over to the site the very next day; twenty metres away from the main house and facing east instead of west—both for defensibility and a modicum of privacy.

"Oh," Ray said. "I didn't realise it was going to be this large. "And you are making it bigger? Won't that make it larger than the main house?"

"Well, it's not just for the betas. I figured we are better off setting up the children's rooms now even if they are just brick and cement for the next three years." He'd said it easily, a professional confident in his work, but he stopped at once, catching Ray's alarm. He didn't open his mouth fast enough, though.

"You want to set up the children's all the way over here?" Ray demanded between gritted teeth.

"It's traditional, the betas—" Gabriel started.

Maybe he was sorry for how he'd acted during... the incident. Maybe Ray's fury just intimidated him. "*Traditional?*" Ray echoed with pure, unrestrained disdain. "You know what else is traditional? This whole plan where you throw an omega at multiple mates and let them figure it out on their own! How's that been working out for you?"

"Ray..." Gabriel sounded pained. Ray was staring him down and the alpha wolf didn't react in any of the ways an alpha should have. *Did he not feel the challenge? Or was he just keeping it down for Ray?*

"If you think any of my children are going to have more than one mate..." Ray said in a low menacing voice.

"Stop," Josh asked. He made sure it was just a word, none of the wolf's authority in his voice. Ray turned to him, eyes blazing. "Of course we wouldn't want that, Ray, you know we can see you..." He looked down at the soil they'd given up so much for. "You aren't happy. We aren't blind."

"They will all get a choice," Gabriel added. He took a step closer to Ray, hand slightly raised but thought better of it—perhaps he wanted to keep the hand—and just crossed his massive arms across his own chest. He should have looked intimidating but it was clear he was simply holding himself back. "I swear to you," he said, heartbeat too fast, and meeting Ray's eyes like a man looking at his executioner. "They will get a choice. Anything that's possible. Anything we can... We will find ways."

He was honest, Josh thought it'd have been obvious by the rawness of his voice even if they couldn't hear his accelerated but steady pulse. Ray turned his back on them. "Show me the rest," he told Gabriel quietly.

Ray didn't speak again until the tour was over. "I thought so," he said with a sigh. "You haven't planned for any storage, have you?"

"Storage? We'll have closets..."

Ray shook his head. Josh could see him hesitate for a second longer, maybe biting back a cutting remark. Ray was, at heart, a kind soul, but he had a mouth on him and not much patience for mistakes that seemed obvious to him. "Are you going to put the vacuum cleaner in the closet with your shoes?" he asked patiently. His body gave away the irritation he'd mainly managed to keep out of his voice, but Gabriel and Josh politely didn't mention it.

Josh nodded his support. "Ugh, yes, and brooms and all that. Spare blankets..."

"Exactly," Ray said. "So can I have a look at the blueprints?"

Gabriel had acceded to it, even though he was a decade older than them and had spent all of the last ten years of his life knee-deep in the business. He wasn't an architect, of course, but Josh heard him drop terminology like he didn't even notice it wasn't common parlance. He objected to Ray's first choice for the bathroom—after he'd decided the original one had to be a storage room instead—but he gave him two other choices. Ray ended up agreeing to split one of the bigger rooms with a false wall they'd soundproof once they had some cash. The bathroom could be on one side, the smaller bedroom could be available to someone who needed the solitude. Ray had looked at Gabriel approvingly as he said it and Gabriel had given a tight nod at once. Josh wondered if they were thinking of someone in particular—it wasn't unusual for betas to share bedrooms, after all. All five of the betas who'd agreed to join their pack knew about the tight quarters, too. But it seemed oddly specific still.

He'd grown up with both of them, but that didn't mean he couldn't have missed a smaller, more private family reunion or two. His parents did take the holidays off and often dragged Josh away from pack territory—mostly to visit cousins in other packs, but they'd made it as far as France once when his mother was feeling particularly cosmopolitan. He bit his lip to keep from asking.

"So you are happy with it?" Gabriel asked after about an hour's debate. He sounded so much like the man who'd sat on the floor and listened to them babble about their private games that Josh had to look at him to check. But, of course, he looked the same, werewolves didn't age that much and it had only been about ten years anyway— even a human would not show much sign of ageing.

Ray, on the other side of the makeshift table they were using to keep the blueprint tacked to, was already watching Gabriel too closely. Gabriel's index finger twitched, as if he wanted to move, but he stayed still and withstood the scrutiny anyway.

"I'm happy with it," Ray echoed. "I'm sorry, I should have looked at the blueprints earlier. I know it'll be a lot of work to change it now..."

"Nah," Gabriel said, smiling easily for the first time in... Josh didn't quite remember. He'd thought Gabriel liked the responsibility, but maybe he'd imagined things would go more smoothly for their nascent pack. Maybe he wasn't enjoying the ride so much when the road was pretty much one big pothole. "It's good you told me now, we only need to change where we put the plumbing, really."

Ray frowned, thoughtfully. "I haven't looked at the numbers this week, but I thought you did that overnight thing? And Alec should have got paid for the extra hours he put in last month, right? You said three thousand, right? We should have enough." He glanced at Josh, even though Josh didn't have a head for numbers and Ray and Gabriel had been dealing with it and telling them about it at meetings. "Anything extra?"

Josh shook his head. "No, Marisa spent a little more buying in bulk but she used her savings. She said we can pay her back when we are a little more stable."

"Did she write it down anywhere?" Gabriel asked.

"Well, it's Marisa so..." Josh assumed she had either a ledger or a spreadsheet she considered them too disorganized to look at.

"Yeah, but if we don't know we owe her money," Ray explained. "Then we can't take the expense into account."

"Oh, sorry," Josh said, feeling like an idiot. "She just mentioned it because I said we really had to stick to the budget. I think she didn't want to bother you with it. I don't think it was a lot, maybe a hundred quid?"

"It's fine," Gabriel assured him, turning back to Ray already. Josh felt a bit stupid; he was an adult and maybe he wasn't good at numbers but he certainly could keep track of household expenses. But he'd never lived on his own before they'd formed the pack and his parents had never involved him in such matters. Gabriel and Ray had a spreadsheet and a notebook they took to pack meetings. Josh could at least try to read it so he knew what his mate was talking about. Ray had grown up dealing with the small annoyances of running a household; he didn't deserve to be left to it by default, though. He probably didn't like it much either. Who would?

"...maybe this weekend," Gabriel was saying when he tuned in again.

"Weren't we going to have a meeting?" he cut in.

Gabriel stopped talking, but Ray shot him a confused look. "A meeting? What for? We have been saving for this. We need to finish it so the other betas can come over."

"What about the sensors, though?" Josh asked.

"The sensors," Ray said, like the words were foreign in his tongue.

"We were going to have a meeting about it," Josh explained, more to fill the heavy silence than because he supposed Ray hadn't heard him the first time around. "I thought it was important to you...?"

"Yes," Ray said at once, sounding more certain.

"We should have a meeting anyway." Josh turned at Gabriel's unexpected support. "It's the right way to do things, isn't it?"

Ray nodded, blinking a little too much, then shrugged. "I guess."

Josh put his hand on his elbow. Ray jerked. Not away, just in surprise. He shot Josh a contrite look, lips parted, but didn't explain himself.

Josh shook his head, dismissing it at once. He'd promised himself not to coddle Ray when it wasn't necessary, but he couldn't be expected to do anything but give him a break—not as an alpha, as a friend—when he looked like he was so out of it.

He crossed his arms and turned to Gabriel. "I can show Ray how it goes tomorrow morning, but if we want to get the others together tonight we should head back. Alec was making dinner, right?"

Gabriel took the change in topic and ran with it, raising his eyebrows at him. "Sure, you want to have a meeting, not like you can smell that we are having roast lamb, is it?"

"Hey," Josh said, smiling. "You can't blame a wolf for having a nose!"

Chapter four

"Hey guys, you busy?"

Josh looked up to see Sergi leaning in the doorway of Ray's bedroom. This time they'd got all the pups down for a nap—they'd earned their break and more.

It was stupid to feel annoyed at being interrupted; hadn't they left Ray's door open? It wasn't for the light, the window of Ray's bedroom faced exactly the right way to get the best afternoon light and the corridor didn't have any windows anyway.

Sergi, normally so circumspect, walked into the room already smiling. About as subtle as a tornado and not giving a reason for his presence at all.

"You can look," Ray said, long-suffering. But Josh could tell his friend was pleased with the attention.

Maybe it was only natural; the only attention Ray had got in the last year was for something he had no choice about, and here was Sergi expressing an interest in what basically amounted to the contents of Ray's soul. Since he was starting to sketch group portraits of their children, maybe even literally so.

Josh clenched his fist under the table next to Ray and turned his face back to the drawing as Sergi leaned closer and whistled. "Not to brag but... we make some pretty kids," he whispered, close enough to Ray's ear he could probably feel his breath.

Ray laughed, too loud in Josh's ears. It was ridiculous, absolutely stupid. He'd watched Sergi *fuck* Ray, why was it so unbearable to hear him make Ray laugh? But it was different, somehow. Maybe because for all that Josh wanted to sleep with Ray, he didn't need it. Ray's attention, though... That he did. And he'd had it. For a long time, it had just been Ray and him; everyone else just an occasional plus one to their adventures. They lived in a pack and they hung out with other kids their age, of course, but Josh had never had any competition for Ray's friendship. People had been interested, of course, Ray was tough but charming and beautiful to boot. Josh hadn't stood in his way when girls had shown an interest—but girlfriends couldn't take his place.

Even if he wanted to take theirs.

It was different now. Alec had confirmed that it wasn't the bond calling the alphas to pay Ray attention. And it was Josh's own fault. The only reason Josh had not only listened to Sergi's request to be considered as a potential mate for Ray but actually agreed to it was that the man had confessed he'd been crushing on Ray since before their ridiculous enmity began. He'd seemed so vulnerable as he admitted that he'd never dared tell Ray what he felt after he'd botched his attempt at friendship so badly. And Josh had seen the truth of it: that Sergi hadn't given up on his feelings—maybe he hadn't been able to, maybe he was too smart to let go of someone of Ray's calibre—despite how much it hurt to be ignored.

And Josh had seen it because he saw it all the time. He felt it all the time—maybe all the more because of how very close Ray let him get.

But in that moment of empathy, he somehow had neglected to think of the fact that Sergi's crush could only become more once Ray accepted him as his mate. Now that he'd had Ray in body, now that Ray wore his mark and had given him Sasha... Who could blame him for wanting more?

He startled as Sergi moved to take a picture. Ray was watching him do it with a sceptical twist to his mouth. He caught Josh looking and rolled his eyes, but his own were shining. "He wants to document 'the process' or something."

"Oh, shut up," Sergi said from behind his phone. "I'm just making sure you don't forget to give me a copy because it's an exclusive work of art."

"We could scan them," Josh suggested.

"Nah, phones are better now, nobody's updating the quality of scanners anymore," Ray explained.

"Oh," he said and closed his mouth. He obviously didn't know enough about art to be any help. He'd always thought he was helping Ray by being a second pair of eyes, but it was hard to miss the way Sergi was asking questions about the type of pencil and shading Ray had used and planned to add.

He stepped back, turning towards the bed to check on the babies. He almost sagged with relief when he saw Sasha was awake and tugging on Jamie's floppy hair. He sat on the bed and picked her up, getting a delighted gurgle in response as she turned to play with his hair instead. Sergi was right; she was pretty as a picture, dark eyes on chocolate skin—a little lighter than Sergi's own, although that could have just been the amount of time Sergi had been spending in the sun working construction both at home and at Gabriel's site.

Sergi was the perfect picture of an alpha: broad across the shoulders, devoted but strong. He was beautiful too, like a man was beautiful, his long dark lashes off-set by the stubble on his cheeks. Josh had tried to grow facial hair when he was younger—he had to be the only werewolf in the history of the world to fail.

And Ray was turned towards him, heads bent close together, unbothered when their sides brushed as they turned the pages and tried different angles.

And if it was what Ray wanted... If it would make Ray light up with excitement and actually laugh? Josh should be happy for him. But he wasn't, he couldn't be. Ray had said he had feelings for Josh—not what feelings, but more than enough to give Josh hope—and now... Well, of course Ray didn't want anything like that. Josh's stomach still turned when he thought about how Ray sometimes recoiled when he was touched. Whatever Ray had felt before presenting omega, whatever had remained... It couldn't compete with that kind of trauma. And Josh couldn't tell Ray he simply wanted to know if he felt those things still, not a single brush of his fingers required. Not now and not ever.

It was a cruel promise to make when they all knew Ray would go into heat sooner rather than later.

It didn't mean a thing that Josh was willing to give up all physical contact if his best friend would just smile at him. Not when he couldn't follow through.

Marisa knocked on the open door and Josh looked away from Ray to meet her eyes. He had known her since before she could speak—her apprehension was obvious at a glance. He had missed something between Ray and her but he couldn't bring himself to ask either of them for details. Ray was clearly reluctant to leave her with the kids after she had missed him being taken through the kitchen door while she entertained the rest of Nicholas's alphas in the sitting room. Josh didn't think Ray truly blamed her for it; she was a smart girl but she was a seventeen-year-old beta who'd been left in charge of five babies in a room with five grown alphas. Even if she had noticed something was amiss, there had been nothing she could have done without putting her charges at risk.

Ray's voice cut off abruptly, but he didn't speak to her. Josh could almost feel her cringe.

"Is nap time over?" Josh asked, maybe with excessive cheer.

"Well... I guess. I mean, if you want to sleep tonight," Marisa said, regaining confidence as if she was remembering that she had three younger siblings she'd helped raise.

Josh had completely forgotten it was his turn to get up if the babies cried during the night but if Marisa said it was, he believed her—she both wrote their schedules and was in charge of changing them if something came up. The kids rarely woke now that they weren't being breastfed anymore but still, it was better if only one of them was sleep-deprived at a time. Josh could always take a nap when Irina took over the next morning.

He got up with Sasha and gestured at the bed. "Take your pick!" he offered grandly.

That got Marisa to smile—looking a little like she also wanted to roll her eyes at him, but Josh wasn't picky.

"We could just get them leashes," she suggested picking up Maria. The girl woke, groggy and moody at once and then she noticed who was holding her and snuggled into the warm space of Marisa's neck. Josh passed Sasha to her so she wouldn't have to bend over again, then turned and tickled Mikey until he blinked his pretty hazel eyes open. Both Mikey and Sasha had proved strong enough to sit on Josh's shoulders and cling to his neck so he sat his son on his shoulders and checked his grip was firm before he reached for Clara, who was ready to roll right off the bed.

"Josh!" came Ray's tense voice. Mikey was settled so Josh slowly turned to Ray.

Ray stood staring at him. Was he... afraid? Josh frowned. "Are you okay?"

"What are you *doing*?" Ray asked, looking over Josh's head. "He's not even six months old!"

"He's fine, he's holding on to me," Josh said. "Look, come here and stand behind me and I'll let go—"

"Just... Just don't," Ray gritted out, looking even more agitated. He took a step closer to them, then stopped. His heart was beating fast enough to be worrying. He wasn't concerned, he was *terrified*.

"Okay," Josh said at once. "I didn't... It's fine, I'll..." He reached for Mikey, who clung for a moment longer before allowing himself to be pulled over his right shoulder and into his arms again. Josh looked back at Ray, who was looking at Michael, arms so tense Josh could see his muscles twitching. He stepped forward and crossed the space between them, certain of his welcome for once, and put Michael against his other father's chest, pressing himself close to Ray for a long moment before Ray reacted and took the baby.

It was long enough to tell Ray was trembling. He tucked his face into their son's neck, holding him carefully, breathing gone ragged. Josh had to look away.

He didn't know how to fix this. He couldn't... He turned his back to Ray, giving his proud omega at least the illusion of privacy even if both he and Sergi could hear the effect terror had on his body.

Sergi was on the bed—for all the world like he hadn't noticed the altercation—trying to convince Clara to turn back into a girl and to keep Jamie from wandering off now that he was fully awake. He looked up at Josh when he approached. "Oh, can you...?" he asked, offering him the twisting pup.

The babies could understand some of what they said already—Alec said their development was accelerated compared to humans—but that didn't mean they had to listen. For some reason, Josh had luck more often than anybody except Ray and Marisa. He took Clara and rubbed behind her ears, cradling her close and keeping her from trying to run in the air. She wouldn't listen to a thing he said unless she calmed down a little first.

He was so focused on his task that it wasn't until he looked up from Clara's very human nose trying to smell his shirt that he saw Ray had walked away from his desk and was standing by his side.

Sergi had taken Jamie to Marisa, so they were alone except for the baby each of them held. Josh swallowed, ready to apologize again, but Ray beat him to it. "I'm sorry, I know he's safe with you. I just... I don't know. I saw him there and all I could think was that he'd fall and—"

"Ray," Josh cut him off. "I get it, I'm not offended. You have reasons to be... It's normal to worry, they are so small still, even if they are tough." He reached out and cupped Mikey's shoulder, rubbing his thumb against the soft skin of his neck. Ray's eyes followed the movement with... Josh didn't know. Was Ray trying to make sure Josh didn't touch him? Or the opposite? Did he want a hug?

Clara shifted in his arms, always impatient to be on the move and Josh discarded the idea.

"Here," Ray said, and glanced at Josh so briefly he couldn't read his expression before he stepped forward and pushed Mikey against Josh's free side, letting his own body lean close for a moment... too long? Josh couldn't tell; to him, it just felt like not long enough.

"Get back to work then," Josh tried to tease, but it sounded flat after everything. "I want to see the final product."

"Yeah," Ray agreed, already pulling away. "Me too."

I t turned out Martha had been right about Ray liking the hard work—but perhaps she'd forgotten how much of a perfectionist he was. Gabriel had set them up with the simple task of building yet another wall—thanks to Ray's contribution, they had three rooms left to go instead of the two they had originally planned. They had a level to make sure they were building evenly—although Josh would have guessed it was hard to fuck that up with factory made bricks of identical size—and Ray was still being a little too methodical when it came to spreading the cement.

Josh was happy to watch him frown at the grey mixture while he waited for his turn to put the next set of bricks in place—it made a nice change from watching him out of the corner of his eye to make sure he wasn't about to break down crying or abruptly leave the room without an explanation.

"Stare much?" Ray asked, not looking up.

Josh swallowed, but it was clearly a joke. "Best thing in my view."

Ray's mouth twisted and Josh thought he would have rolled his eyes at him if he hadn't convinced himself he needed to keep his attention on his work. "I like this."

Josh laughed. "You don't say! You have been staring at that for ten minutes."

Ray spared him an unimpressed look. "This is our children's home. Forgive me if I don't want the walls to fall on them."

"I promise you that Gabriel didn't check the cement was perfectly even and we have lived in the main house for six months without any walls falling on us, haven't we?"

Ray huffed. "Gabriel knows what he's doing. He can wing it."

"Okay," Josh agreed. Ray seemed to have forgotten that he'd argued with Gabriel about the house's design only the day before and been right for all of his cousin's experience.

Josh didn't mention it—he liked seeing Ray that confident, even if only about something as insignificant as storage.

He'd have liked it even more if Ray could have been that sure of himself when it came to everything else.

But for that... He hesitated. Ray seemed relaxed for the first time in ages. The only time, except when he was drawing, that Josh didn't suspect darker thoughts lurked beneath his brave smiles. But it wasn't like Josh could bring it up when Ray looked sad, and if they never talked about it, nothing would ever change. "Ray..."

His friend looked up, clearly sensing Josh's distress. "What is it?"

"I don't want..." He exhaled, struggling against the tightness in his chest. "I can't keep pretending everything is fine. I just... I don't think it's good for you."

Ray's eyes were stuck to the ground between them, mouth a sour line. "And you know what's good for me better than I do?"

"What? No!" Josh said at once. "I'm just... it's my opinion. I can have an opinion even if I'm your alpha, can't I?" he demanded with a little more anger than he'd meant to show.

Ray shot him a surprised look, maybe because Josh had been so gentle lately. He'd thought he needed to be, but being gentle had only got Ray to retreat further and further from him. "You can have an opinion, doesn't mean I have to agree," Ray bit off, his own resentment clear in his voice.

"No, it doesn't," Josh agreed reasonably. "But you can listen."

"I'm listening," his friend said, gaze lost somewhere in the distance.

"You know we need to talk about what happened, don't you?" he asked Ray softly. Ray didn't respond, maybe he was just planning on listening. That was fine with Josh; he didn't need Ray to agree now, just to start getting used to the idea. It'd be hard, and it'd hurt them both. But if they didn't do it... If he let Ray bury his fear and his pain... he might never be able to let them go.

"And you want to be my shrink?" Ray asked, voice flat and posture rigid.

Josh bit back an imprecation, clutching at the brick he'd been fiddling with hard enough to hurt his hand. "I want to be your *friend*."

"Then *be* my friend. This..." He waved around them both. "This is good. I'm *trying*, Josh. I have left them inside, even if they are the only thing I can think of. I can still feel them or I don't know what I'd do..."

Josh's feet propelled him forward before he thought about it, dropping the brick without looking where it fell. "I know," he said honestly. He barely kept himself from touching Ray. "I don't... I don't mean now. Just... think about it?"

Ray huffed wearily. "Okay, I will think about it."

He was telling the truth and that was all Josh could ask for now. Ray stepped toward him and for a second Josh thought— Ray picked up the brick he'd dropped and offered it to him. "Let's get back to work," he said decisively. "I know we have an in with the boss but I don't want to take advantage."

Josh offered him a smile, weak but real, his mind still half lost in words that hadn't yet been pronounced, words that had to be stuck in Ray's brain where he could do nothing to help.

But he could only offer; it wasn't his choice to make.

Maybe Ray needed more time. Time and work. Gabriel wouldn't even let them do anything complicated. The moment the bricklaying was done, he'd take his overdue holidays from his day job and start on the more complex work himself. Josh had been meant to help him but he'd stepped back and offered Ray the chance instead. Ray had seen right through him—not that Josh had pretended he was keen to take more shifts at the gas station—but he'd accepted.

He thought Ray might have been a little offended anyway, but he wasn't sure. He couldn't get over how wrong that was: that he couldn't assume Ray would want and like certain things based on what Josh knew of him, that he couldn't trust Ray would disabuse him of any misconceptions he happened to harbour loudly and unequivocally.

It hurt, but he didn't know Ray that well anymore. He wasn't sure Ray knew himself that well, either, not when he'd gone through so much so fast. He was still the man Josh loved, but he didn't want the same things. He wasn't *allowed* to. And even if he'd started to accept that he was an omega and his life was here with his new pack... That had been before Nicholas.

But the work helped, and drawing definitely helped. Even if Josh couldn't tell Ray's pens apart, much less the types of shadowing, Ray seemed happy enough to have him sit in the room with his laptop or playing with the babies on the bed.

And maybe it helped Josh a little, to be there, to know they were all safe and he'd be in the right place if... But it was crazy, of course. Except that he still found himself arguing for the sensors at the pack meeting when they finally managed to sit down and make it happen. Marisa and Irina had bowed out, claiming it would be a conflict of interest since the beta wing was meant to be theirs. Or maybe they'd decided the only way the six of them would be able to have a serious conversation was if they teamed up to get the babies to bed the one time none of the alphas was working late.

It had been so easy to dismiss Gabriel's reluctance as paranoia when Josh had been home all day, right next to Ray, who'd know at once if anybody in the pack as much as got a splinter. But now that he was out for hours at a time...

"I'm just saying we shouldn't dismiss the idea without—" Josh explained.

"We aren't," Ray cut him off, the strain in his voice very audible to all of them. But he didn't seem to care about the discomfort it brought him to break protocol and defy his alphas. Knowing Ray, he was doing it *because* it was uncomfortable and because he still could. "But having more adults around will be a lot safer than having an alarm go off if someone trespasses. And we can't even be sure we can adjust it so it'll only react with people."

"I..." Josh faltered. "I just don't want that responsibility to be just yours. It isn't fair."

Ray looked away, pulse speeding and body tensing up where he was sat on the couch. "You all got eyes and ears," he said after a long moment. "And the more of those we have..."

He was so intensely uncomfortable—scent sour and acrid—that Josh couldn't even process his words for a moment, and then he realised what he'd implied: that Ray should choose a First Alpha. Because an alpha who had a mutual bond with a First Omega would share his powers of knowing who was where in their territory.

"We should vote," Iesu said before Josh could apologize.

It was for the best, really, and the plumber won by a landslide. At the last minute, Josh raised his own hand—as much of an apology as he could make in public.

"Okay, I'll get it booked," Gabriel declared, standing up. "If we're doing that first, we can delay the roof but we'll need to put up the central pillars to keep everything steady for them."

"Can I help with that?" Ray asked at once.

Gabriel smiled at him, looking oddly proud. "Yes, of course. You like this, don't you?" he commented. "I thought you'd get bored."

Ray shrugged, but Josh noticed his posture had relaxed. "I like making things."

"Oh, did you finish the portrait?" Sergi asked. He sounded excited, which only the children and Ray's art seemed to inspire in him as far Josh could tell.

"Well, I think so?" Ray said. "I don't know if I got the depth quite right..."

To Josh's surprise, Sergi turned to him next. "You saw it already, right?"

"Ah, no," he admitted, trying to pretend like it'd been accidental and not Ray deliberately not asking him to look the previous evening.

"I can't show it to you," Ray explained, probably seeing something on his face. "I'm making it *for* you."

Josh blinked at him, then frowned. "But I have seen it..."

"That was before it was ready," Ray replied. "I want a second opinion, and then you can have it and you have to say it's amazing anyway."

Josh couldn't keep a small smile from escaping. He'd thought Ray didn't trust his opinion, but this... "Well, I will lie," he promised, meeting his friend's eyes. His heart skipped a beat, but he couldn't have said if it was the lie or the emotion.

"We are done here, right?" Iesu checked. "Alec is going to teach me to cook and it's almost six."

Out of the corner of his eye, Josh caught Sergi shooting his lover a look. Whatever it was, Sergi turned to Ray. "I could have a look now if you want."

Ray looked away from Josh. "Ah, yeah, if..." he stopped, unsure. "You and Iesu usually..." He looked around at them all as if expecting confirmation. It was true, of course, Marisa assigned Iesu and Sergi to work together if they were in the house at the same time.

Surprisingly, it was Alec who spoke up, "They do, but resilient as we are, I would still like something edible for dinner, so I offered to teach them."

It was a lie and unlike Iesu, who had phrased it ambiguously to avoid detection, Alec had simply said it. He shrugged when Ray met his eyes and for a moment Josh feared Ray would get angry. But maybe he didn't see it as a real attempt at deception, or maybe he was starting to understand that the little kindnesses they offered him weren't pity, but love. They were his alphas and they wanted to protect him, but they also wanted him to be happy.

Sergi had found a way—and all of them would support it.

"Okay, thanks," Ray said to Alec, but too seriously for it to be for the cooking class.

He and Sergi headed down the corridor together, already talking about the possibility of putting the portrait through some Instagram filter. Josh turned and smiled at Alec.

The other alpha gave him a startled smile back. He seemed to be coming out of his shell lately, maybe because his research into the babies' growth was going well—Gabriel had found him a lot of people in their old pack willing to help.

"Do you want some help peeling or something?" he offered. He felt a little responsible—after all, he'd asked Ray to do the portrait.

"You can dice the peppers," Alec offered. "Iesu's doing the onions!"

"Hey!" Iesu complained. "Why me?"

"Because you stole Irina's brownies and she's still pissed off about it," Alec said simply.

"Proof!" Iesu said at once.

Alec shrugged. "You also left the Tupperware unwashed in the sink. Marisa picked up your scent on it."

"Dammit," Iesu complained. He sounded more amused than rueful. "I guess I'll pay for my crimes."

Josh thought about telling him he could wear the swimming goggles they kept next to the sink, but he guessed that was up to Alec.

He followed them to the kitchen; he could use the distraction from wondering what Ray and Sergi were up to besides art.

Chapter five

"Sergi got me a frame for it," Ray said, walking into his room ahead of Josh. "Untreated wood, very... tasteful? It looks like the ones at your... your parents' place."

"She won't care about the frame," Josh said, then realised he was lying and clarified, "Well, no, she will, but she can buy a new one if it doesn't match her carpet or something. No point in trying to guess what's the latest."

"Um," Ray said, "I—" He cut himself off and opened his wardrobe drawer so fast he had to catch it when it came off its rails. Josh stepped forwards to help him and they ended up cupping it between their hands. "Fuck," Ray exhaled.

"Ray, why are you freaking out?" he asked incredulously. "I saw most of it and it's amazing. You know I think you are really talented."

Ray raised his eyes to his. "Do you? Or are you just... I don't know, phrasing it in the right way?"

Lying outright wasn't possible—not unless you believed the lie to be true, of course—because there were too many physiological markers for other werewolves to miss if they were paying any attention. But you could say things in ways that were not untrue while leading to the wrong assumptions.

Josh's fingers itched to let go of the drawer and touch Ray instead. But would that comfort Ray or freak him out? "Let me put this back," he asked, and Ray let go, taking the frame—face down—from between his jumpers and backing away.

Josh slotted the drawer into place, giving himself a few seconds to think. Ray was watching him when he looked up, as steady as his pulse was not.

He could have offered reassurances, but Ray didn't want to be comforted, he wanted the truth. It was a lesson Josh could never quite get the hang of instinctively, but he could remember, at least. "Show me."

He heard Ray gulp, but he turned the frame around. He understood why Ray had kept it in the dresser; it was too long to fit in the desk drawers with the new frame. Josh could recognize the piece he'd seen come together day in and day out, but it was like he'd been looking at it in low light and now—in the falling afternoon light—it'd come into sudden focus. The details Ray had suggested with a few lines had acquired the depth of reality.

It wasn't a photograph; it was too wistful, too full of emotion despite the simple facts of their children's faces and bodies, to be anything but the work of someone's hand. But it was true in a way photos didn't always manage: each of them looked bright inside, full of that indefinable quality that both wolf and man recognized. Mikey, to whom Josh's eyes were drawn at once, was leaning close to Maria, cuddling up to her like he was an actual puppy. Maria herself was smiling with parted lips—she'd spoken for the first time only the other day, so it might have been an artistic liberty on Ray's part. Clara was playing with her sister's blond curls, ignoring the camera but with her face in full view. On her other side, Jamie sat nearly a head taller than her—even without colour, Ray had captured the unearthly quality of Alec's eyes on his chubby baby face. Sasha was on Mikey's left, pouting a little—probably because she'd tried to escape the confines of the sofa five times in the twenty minutes it'd taken to get some decent pictures of them all. She wouldn't be six months for another two weeks, but she didn't look like a baby about to cry. Instead her expression was like a small version of Sergi's own disapproving look.

Josh laughed loud and looked at Ray. "I can't believe you were worried. This is beyond amazing. It's not just gorgeous, it's cute and *funny.*" Ray's smile was still too tentative. "And I will tell it to you in any way you like. It's beautiful, Ray, and I don't know anything about, like, traces and pencils and shadows like Sergi does but I have perfect vision and I can... I can *feel* you in this. You and them, what you... How much you love them."

"I..." Ray offered the frame to him. He shivered when their fingers brushed but waited until Josh's hold was secure before letting go. Josh looked down at it, aware that Ray needed a moment to compose himself. But he ended up caught in the details of Sasha's dress—a present from his own mother, who of course hadn't thought of something more practical than fancy clothing for babies that would outgrow them in a matter of weeks. Ray had captured the way only part of the print showed through the natural folds of the cloth against Sasha's body. "I didn't want them," Ray finished, like he couldn't hold it back. Like he'd been holding it back and he couldn't anymore.

Josh jerked so hard it was pure luck his fingers tightened on the picture instead of letting go. He stared at Ray, who couldn't quite hide that his eyes were wet no matter how much he blinked and lowered his chin. Josh put the picture down on the desk, then allowed himself a single step closer to his omega. Ray was visibly shaking, heartbeat more like a buzz and body held so tight Josh thought he'd either bolt or collapse.

Ray did neither. Instead, he met Josh halfway, throwing his arms around Josh's neck and clinging hard. "I'm *sorry*," he said. No, he begged. "I don't... I'm sorry. I didn't know. I didn't..." He choked on the next words and Josh finally got his own arms around him, clutching at him as hard as he could.

"Shhh..." he whispered in Ray's ear. "Don't. Don't be sorry. You didn't do anything wrong."

"But I—" Ray started, clinging to him, fingers digging into Josh, his chest pressing hard enough against Josh's collarbone that it had to hurt.

"No," Josh interrupted firmly. He'd been trying not to do it now that Ray was an omega, but he wasn't going to stand back and let him go down this road. Ray had the right to make choices, but it was Josh's job to tell him when he was being an idiot and that wasn't going to change now. "Of course you didn't want to have kids yet, who would? We just finished *school*." He rubbed Ray's lower back, then his hip. At least he wasn't as skinny as he'd been right after spending two weeks as a wolf eating mainly protein. "You didn't expect them. And you didn't expect to love them, but you do."

He tried to pull back to look at him, but Ray refused to let go of him. Josh stopped, taking Ray's weight and hoping he could take some of his pain too. Ray's breathing was ragged still, and he was sniffling a little, but the shaking was subsiding.

"Do I have to give my mum the original?" Josh asked, only half joking. "Like, wouldn't she like one of those Instagram filter versions more?"

Ray snorted, a little weakly, but his hold was weakening too. He pulled back slowly, keeping his arms around Josh's neck. Josh loosened his own hold—heart half in his throat, because now they weren't just close enough to embrace, but also to kiss. Ray's eyes were still wet, but he was smiling a little at Josh's question, and his lips were...

He wanted it too much, and it was... It wasn't right. Ray couldn't... He lowered his eyes and tried for a joke. "She likes colour, red especially, is there a red filter?"

Ray's hands slid down his shoulders as he let go of his neck. Josh barely reacted in time to let go of Ray's waist. "I will do another one for you if you want," he offered.

He sounded unsure again, so Josh made an effort to smile and looked up as Ray opened up the space between their bodies again. He didn't know how to express both that he loved to see Ray's open adoration for their kids and that he couldn't quite repress his longing for Ray himself. How could he be both happy and sad in such a short span of time?

"But won't it take you ages? I mean, I would love to. You could do it on my wall, really, because I would probably not want to look at anything else ever again."

Ray laughed. It was shaky but sincere; he could tell Josh meant it.

"But you have your projects. Like, you don't usually do portraits, so I don't want to take up all the time you have for your painting—"

"Josh," Ray said patiently. "I like doing portraits, I had just never done any of someone I knew personally. It's different. And, anyway, I have done all the studies already and I had some ideas I didn't get to use, so..." He shrugged. He wasn't smiling but he was relaxed, he was... eager, excited. Maybe even happy.

"Okay," Josh agreed, caught on the clarity of purpose on his friend's face. It took him a moment to realise he was staring, and he turned his face away. It was merely a coincidence he looked towards the picture, but he took the opportunity to pick it up again—a barrier between them to keep himself from crossing a line he knew he couldn't even smudge. "Thank you for this. I... Well, I'm kinda broke," he repeated, daring to glance at Ray so he could take the edge off the statement with a smile. "Got these kids who go through food like they got a black hole in their stomachs. But you could ask me for something? Like, I mean, you can always ask me, obviously. But if there's..." He stopped himself.

"You are welcome," Ray said into his silence. He sounded pleased but also a little strange.

Josh wondered if offering something in exchange had been a mistake. He hadn't meant to give offence; it was just that Ray had spent so much time on the portrait... "Okay, well, if... you know where to find me," he added insanely.

Ray kindly didn't laugh at him.

As soon as he saw them together, Josh stopped. He was maybe a step away from the doorway connecting the corridor and the living room, but they were directly in his line of sight. Marisa had her back to him. Past her, he could see Ray's profile, but what surprised him into immobility was how close together they were. The last time he had seen them interact with each other, Ray had barely been able to look in his sister's direction and yet here they were; kneeling on the floor and struggling with a pile of multi-coloured plastic pieces Josh recognized as the jungle gym Sergi's father had bought them now that he was back from his yearly visit to Nigeria to see his own parents.

He'd been trying to find Marisa to ask her to change his schedule for babysitting so he could do another shift at work—Gabriel was working full time on the house with Ray now and Josh was trying to do as many shifts as possible to make up for the dent it was making in their finances. But if they had really made up...

"Couldn't he have just offered to babysit sometimes?" Marisa asked Ray as another of the poles refused to fit together with the base.

"He did offer, though. He's my favourite father-in-law at the moment," Ray declared, then put his hand on hers to stop her trying something else. "Just let me read the instructions; stop fiddling with random pieces."

"How hard can it be?" she asked but desisted, leaning over to tug on Jamie's shirt to keep him from climbing up the couch—he'd taken to jumping off it. They were unusually resilient babies, but everybody preferred if he didn't actively try to break his neck.

Hopefully, the jungle gym would help them all burn some energy, even if it took up half their living room and required several hours to put together.

"Ah!" came Ray's triumphant exclamation. "It's the *long* one," he told his sister. Then, without looking up, called, "Clara! Quit that."

Josh glanced around and saw Clara had her hands in Maria's hair. With both Ray and Gabriel to take after, Maria's hair was almost white—an irresistible beacon to her siblings. Maria rolled away as soon as Ray's words made her sister let go. Nobody else could get them to react with just words—as pups, a growl from any adult would stop them in their tracks but their sense of hierarchy in human form wasn't developed enough. Or maybe it was just the lack of sharp teeth in adults' mouths.

"Josh," Ray called next and Josh startled so badly he nearly tripped over his own two feet. "If you don't have anything better to do, you could come help me. You know building things is not Marisa's forte."

Marisa rolled her eyes, then jumped to her feet and headed towards Clara, asking her brother over her shoulder. "You want to eat broccoli all week?"

"Ugh, don't even joke!"

Josh walked into the room, glad for the cover of their banter. He was sure he was very red. "What do you need?"

He knelt by Ray's side and tried having a look at the instructions his friend had already discarded.

"Help me find all the bits of the base. I think the screws were all in a little bag..."

It was only when Ray crowed his success at having finished the gym that he noticed Marisa had left the room and he'd never mentioned his work rota. It was hard to care watching the satisfaction bloom on Ray's face, though. At least until Ray pointed at the castle. "Okay, get inside, we gotta test it's safe."

"What?"

"Well, I'm not going to let them test it! Their skulls aren't even completely closed yet."

Josh remembered his terror when he'd tried to give Mikey a piggyback ride and decided not to argue. "Well, it still doesn't mean it can take an adult's weight."

"You must weigh about the same as all of them together," Ray pointed out.

"Ray, Jamie's not that big. I'm way heavier than them."

"You don't have to jump in it, it'll be about the same pressure," Ray insisted. Josh loved the guy but he could be persistent as hell.

"Why me?" Josh asked, out of logical arguments. "You do it."

"Do what?" Marisa had just walked back in. "Because if you two are done playing builders, Irina and I can use some help with dinner."

Josh almost laughed when he saw the way Ray's eyes lit up. "That's great! You're small, you should try it."

Marisa didn't bother to do more than raise her eyebrows. "The jungle gym," Ray explained, his expression softening. "Please?"

"Ray, it's for children," Marisa explained patiently. "I know you forget, but I'm not a child anymore."

"Oh, yeah," Ray joked. "I totally forget every time you tell *me* what to eat and do. But you're smaller, can't you just lie down inside for a minute and, like, wiggle?"

She sighed but Josh could tell she was giving in. "If Josh goes and peels potatoes," she said. "I don't want Irina to think I'm slacking off."

Josh nodded. "At once," he told her, and saluted.

He knew his sacrifice was worth it when he heard both Marisa and Ray laughing from the kitchen. He met Irina's eyes as he turned back to cutting the potatoes. She was smiling too, the corner of her mouth slightly turned up and dark eyes crinkling.

"Get to work," she told him, attempting to sound tough. She was good at it as a rule, so it was even funnier when she couldn't keep a straight face.

He snorted but did it anyway. It didn't sound like Ray and Marisa were going to come and help and it took a lot of potatoes to feed eight adult werewolves, not to mention decorate their clothes and the floor to their children's standards.

Chapter six

Ray got up before anyone else to take his plate to the kitchen. His half-full plate because Alec's comment about blood and Iesu's stupid story about his cousin dyeing a chair red with his own blood had put an end to his appetite. Josh hadn't been able to eat another bite after that either, blood thrumming with anger and concern. How could they be so careless? Alec had at least noticed, but he would have bet Iesu was completely unaware of close he'd come to causing his omega have a meltdown. Or a flashback.

Josh didn't know. He wasn't a shrink and if friendship had been a class, he'd have been scraping by. But he wasn't going to stop trying. He got up and followed Ray to the kitchen. Normally, he'd have left it at that. He'd be the familiar presence, the safe space where Ray could rest... But it wasn't enough. He wasn't enough.

"Let's get out of here," he said, trying for casual.

Ray's plate clinked too hard as he put it in the sink to soak. He turned to Josh, shocked and confused. "What?"

"You need a break," Josh replied. "We can get ice cream at Freggo's."

"In town?" Ray asked, clearing his throat like he about to develop a cough.

"It's Sunday. You can choose who you want to stay with them."

"They..." Ray started to say, taking Josh's plate and emptying it in the organic bin as well—Marisa insisted they have one.

"If you tell me they won't or that they have plans already, I will punch you in the face," Josh cut him off. "Anyone in this pack will do it for you *if you ask*."

"Yes!" Ray snapped, dropping the plate in dishwasher without looking. His eyes were glued to Josh's face. "I know that. I'm not *stupid*. You all feel sorry for me and want me to... to stop this. To stop feeling... to stop being scared all the goddamned time. But I—"

"Sorry?" Josh interrupted. "We don't feel sorry for you, Raymond. We feel *guilty*. Because we failed you and we failed the babies. But yes, we do want you to stop suffering, is that so bad?"

"Well, you can't fix me," Ray said softly, leaning back against the counter. He was trembling slightly. Pent-up adrenaline, Josh realised. Because Ray was *scared*.

Josh backtracked so fast he almost choked on the words. "You are not... you know I was... I would never hit you, you know that, right?"

Ray exhaled, but he didn't relax. "Yes, Josh, I remember. You can't anymore, can you?"

"And you are upset about it?" Josh asked, disbelieving. "Of all the things... Ray, I know I can't fix you. The only one who can is you. I just... I want you to try. To *keep* trying. You have been doing great: yesterday, I had to remind you to go in for lunch. You forg... You trusted them to look after the babies while you worked. That's good, really good. But it's just the first step."

"Just the *idea* is making me want to throw up," Ray admitted. He sounded it sick with dread, alright.

"Okay, not town then," Josh conceded. "Let's go for a walk, up to the river."

Ray held on for a moment longer before offering a shaky nod. "I want Alec," he said, to Josh's surprise. "Can you...?" He waved in the direction of the dining room, where the other alphas had to be pretending really hard not to hear them fight.

"Yes," Josh said. "Gimme a minute."

As soon as Josh had walked back into the kitchen, Ray nodded and headed for the front door despite the kitchen door being only a few meters away. Then Josh understood how stupid he was being; it was in the kitchen that Nicholas had cornered Ray. They'd left through that door. He wondered if Gabriel would agree to board it up. Not that he needed to agree; if Ray wanted it done, Josh would go cut the wood from the forest himself.

But, of course, he thought as Ray started speed-walking towards the river, to truly erase that poor excuse for an alpha from their lives, they'd need to change territories.

It just wouldn't work.

"Ray! Wait up!"

His friend spun around to give him a look. "Why?" he demanded and only gave Josh a few seconds to run up to him before he started up again. "I want to get it done."

Josh reached out and took hold of his wrist. Ray jerked like he'd burned him. This time he glared instead of apologizing. "You forgot your words? Don't—" He stopped. Maybe he couldn't tell his alpha not to touch him, maybe he'd realised he was freaking out over Josh holding his arm.

Josh let go. It didn't matter to him what rights being Ray's alpha gave him in the eyes of the pack or the moon; if he could stop himself when Ray asked him, he would.

"Just... slow down," he asked, intentionally keeping his voice low. "This is supposed to be a walk. If you run, it's too easy."

"Easy?" Ray sneered. He looked like he was sorely tempted to hit Josh again—not that he would, not knowing Josh couldn't hit him back. "This is not fucking easy, Josh!"

"Sorry," Josh said at once. "I just mean... You have to give yourself time to process what you are doing. You need—"

"I need you to shut up," Ray said, and Josh saw that he was shaking again. He couldn't tell if it was terror or fury, but what did it matter? He closed his mouth. Ray inhaled, turning his face away towards the water already visible in the distance. "I thought... I thought I caught his scent."

It was clear by Ray's tone that he knew he hadn't actually smelt a man long dead and buried in a completely different area. He knew it was his brain playing tricks on him. But it didn't need to be real to scare him.

"I can only smell you and me," Josh offered, for lack of anything better. "And a little bit of Iesu and Sergi because they've been doing patrols."

Ray nodded, rubbing his palms against his jeans. Then nodded again, a little jerkily. "Okay. Let's walk."

So they walked, and Josh let the sounds of the afternoon envelop them. There were two or three types of birds, but Josh could only tell apart the kingfishers because he'd always loved their bright blue coats—his fine hearing was no help in naming, the wolf just knew none of them were big enough to eat.

The water was calm, nearly inaudible because of the wind whispering with the trees growing to the east... Then he noticed Ray's pulse was too fast for a walk and risked a glance. Ray's fists were clenched and so was his jaw.

"Can you tell if they're awake?" Josh asked, hoping to distract them both.

Ray's steps faltered, then he looked over at him. "Who?"

"The babies," Josh replied. He'd have thought that was why Ray was freaking out, but maybe he was imagining scents that weren't there again.

He exhaled and nodded but kept walking, obviously hoping to get through it as fast as possible. "Yeah, I can tell... I can tell if they're awake because they feel things more strongly. And sometimes, if they have a bad night, I can hear that."

"You can... feel what they feel?" he asked, half in wonder and half in terror. It wasn't like he'd been trying to hide his own feelings from Ray, but still, to have no control at all over what got out...

Ray saw right through him and shook his head. "They are babies, they need it. And I have to concentrate. I can't do it with you. I know where you are and I think... maybe I'd know if you were in danger as long as we were both..." He turned away, avoiding Josh's eyes. "Here."

"You couldn't feel us at all?" he dared to ask. "When... when you weren't here?"

Ray shook his head. "No, but... I was... Maybe I could have, if I had been able to focus. But once we crossed the border it was like I couldn't hear you anymore."

Josh inhaled, unable to find any words that would help. Ray didn't have to say it; his voice revealed how painful the experience must have been well enough. Every part of Josh: man and wolf, friend and lover, wanted to obliterate that pain.

But there was nothing he could do. He'd been too late. He exhaled and noticed they were by the river already. It was a quiet section, the current more of a tickle than a rush, but deep enough. He turned to Ray and felt an attempt at a smile break on his lips. He pushed the words out anyway. "Race you to the other side and back."

It wasn't a question and it wasn't confident enough to be a dare, but Ray only hesitated a moment before shoving his shoes off his feet. Josh hurried to follow, swearing when he saw he was the only one wearing laces. Ray waited anyway, even if only until Josh got back upright.

They dived in together, fully clothed, and that was the last Josh saw of him until he pushed himself up to breathe in before swimming back. Ray was ahead, nearly a third of the way back and Josh didn't even have time to swear at him and call him a cheat. He submerged again, shoving hard against one of the big rocks on the side, and swam like he was drowning, like every stroke could decide his fate, like one more push could bring him to the surface.

He didn't drown but when he came back out, Ray was already rolling onto the grass, soaked and panting. And laughing a little. He pushed himself out of the water, shivering against the rapidly cooling air and followed his friend's example, rolling on the ground, hoping to squeeze some of the water out of his clothes.

It was pointless, of course. He wasn't going to get dry again, so after a few moments he gave up the pretence and took his shirt off, then started on his belt. He didn't know what made him look up as he finally managed to make the mechanism disengage, but when he did, he found Ray was watching him, on his side and so still he had to be freezing.

"You okay?" he asked, inanely. But he had to say something because he couldn't look away from the water still clinging to Ray's eyelashes, making his blue eyes shine in the falling light. "Aren't you cold?"

Ray blinked, shuddering a little, and sat up, pulling his gaze towards his own body. He took his shirt off fast enough Josh heard something rip, but he didn't start on his trousers, instead, he jumped to his feet. "That enough? Have I taken enough steps?"

He sounded a little angry, but maybe he was just cold. Except if he was; why was he still wearing his wet clothes? It wasn't like Ray to be modest about his body, much... Then Josh's mind caught up with him and he had to force back a wave of nausea. Did Ray think that if Josh saw him naked he would...?

"Let's shift," he suggested because he was too afraid to say the words. If a part of Ray, maybe the same part that flinched when touched, felt being naked in front of other men was dangerous, it wasn't something Josh had a right to resent.

"What about our clothes? I'm not carrying my shoes in my mouth," Ray said, sounding disgusted.

"Let's just leave them, they'll dry in the sun. I need my shoes, but I'll shift first and you can tie them around my neck."

Ray hesitated but then sighed. "Okay, but I'm getting extra points for this."

"Sure," Josh agreed. "You will get ice cream."

Ray shot him an annoyed look, arms crossed and still shivering a little, but apparently not intending to undress any time soon. "It'll be closed now," he replied moodily.

Josh shrugged. "Could have gone to town," he said, and undid the button of his jeans, peeling them down his legs with difficulty. "Ugh, gross," he complained. "We should have taken them off," he said but kept his gaze firmly on the ground when Ray didn't respond.

He turned towards the river to spread the wet trousers on the ground so the sun would hit them directly in the morning, eyes carefully averted in case Ray had decided to join him. He kept himself turned away as he also took off his underwear. Not that there was anything to hide; even without the cold, there was little as unappealing as the idea of Ray's fear.

He shifted still watching the river and only then did he turn to check on his mate. The wolf's eyes could see well enough in the dark but the wolf didn't care much what its mate looked like—it was scent that would distract it. And Ray just smelled like Ray; mate, home, omega, mine.

He was still wearing his trousers when he went over and tied Josh's shoes around his neck, rubbing behind his ears in the process and making it impossible not to rumble in satisfaction. No wolf would ever turn down a good head rub and getting it from someone you loved always made it better. There was a reason puppies slept in piles even in summer—they needed the physical contact. Maybe it was simply a mechanism to keep the pack members close to each other because a pack together was nearly indestructible, but whatever the reason, it felt good in a way that went beyond the physical gratification of a good scratch.

Ray snorted. "Okay, okay, that's enough."

He turned his back to Josh to undo his trousers, but Josh did him one better and turned tail and started running, ignoring his mate's shout until he was a good hundred meters away. He turned then, tail wagging and by the time he ran back to Ray, his friend was in fur. Just in time for Josh to tackle him onto the ground. Ray snapped his teeth at him in warning and off they were, tugging on ears and playfully shoving at each other until they almost ended up back in the river.

With their game, the shoes hadn't made it long attached to Josh's neck so he'd ended up dragging them with his teeth when they'd finally tired of playing. He spit on the ground as soon as he recovered his human form on the porch. He couldn't understand how in wolf form the smell of his own feet didn't turn his stomach but he felt like he needed some tequila to get the scent and taste out of his mouth now.

"Come on," he told Ray, who hadn't shifted back, and opened the door to let him through. Ray immediately scurried through without looking back. Josh went to the kitchen and got a finger of the liquor their old pack produced for themselves, swashing it in his mouth before swallowing.

"What's the occasion?" Gabriel asked, appearing silently enough Josh jumped.

"Goddess! Warn a guy!" He put down the glass and turned to Gabriel. "Just carried my shoes in my mouth, needed to get the taste out."

Gabriel snorted. "You should have left them."

"Well, Sasha ate my other pair, so..."

"Well, you should have put those away," Gabriel said reasonably.

Josh glared at him. "Thanks, dad," he said icily. "Any other useless advice?"

Gabriel raised his hands, palms forward, shaking his head. "Did it go alright?"

Josh wanted to refuse to answer, but it'd have been petty. Gabriel was honestly worried about Ray. "Yeah, we walked there, swam for a bit. It was nice."

Gabriel nodded, smiling, but Ray spoke before he could ask anything else. "You can ask me, you know."

They eyed him warily, neither of them had heard him approach and this was new. He looked rumpled, hair only towel-dry and skin a little flushed from the run and the warmth of the house. But the strangest thing was what he'd said: he'd spent the last year telling them that he needed to ignore everything that was happening between them to be able to live with it.

"We can?" Josh asked when Gabriel couldn't seem to find words.

His friend nodded, then shrugged. "I reserve the right not to answer."

"So do you like the work? In the beta wing?" Gabriel asked.

Ray nodded, going to the fridge and retrieving some pickles. The pregnancy seemed to have sent his diet into a tailspin from which it'd never quite recovered, pickles on bread was pretty tame, really. "Yeah, more than I thought I would. And I like being close to the house, but not *in* it. I was staring at the walls so much, I was starting to think about decorating. Marisa would never forgive me."

Gabriel dutifully chuckled at that. Josh silently lifted the cheese he was cutting in offer and the other alpha nodded, but Ray shook his head, taking another bite of his pickle. "Well, any time you change your mind..."

"And do what instead?" Ray asked, voice even. No, not even, *flat*.

"Whatever you want," Gabriel said.

"I can't really do much more here." Ray gestured to the house and Gabriel shot Josh a pleading look.

He would have liked to promise Ray that he could go back to college, or even get a job with Gabriel at the site if he fancied. But it wasn't the time, and he didn't think Ray would believe it. "Well, I guess you're not getting that ice cream from Freggo's then," he said instead.

"Hey," Ray shot back. "That was a deal, you can't take it back!"

Chapter seven

J osh had got his parents to visit so Ray could see their reaction to the present. Neither of them had mentioned Ray's self-imposed house-arrest to Josh, other than to ask how his mate was doing, but the members of their old pack knew about the babies being taken hostage, at least. Any parent would have sympathized with Ray's refusal to go any farther from his children than he needed to.

It had been Ray's idea to invite his own mother too—although Josh would have bet good money Marisa had something to do with it—and she'd brought his other siblings along so they'd ended up setting up some tables outside so they could all eat lunch together. October was already chilly but still sunny enough to enjoy the fresh air, especially if that air smelled like barbecued meat that was going to make its way to your plate shortly.

By the time Josh got Ray to fetch the portrait, they were all pleasantly full. Even Ray's little brother, Glen, and Clara had had enough to lay them flat. Glen had been proud as a peacock when Ray had asked him to look after the pups—they never stayed in human shape long once they were outside—and he'd been leading them on wild goose chases around the lawn all morning. Harry and Anne had sat with the adults and eaten with cutlery, but Josh had caught both of them eyeing the puppy pile wistfully a couple of times—not that he could blame them.

He forgot about napping when Ray handed him the wrapped frame, looking tense and uncertain. Josh took it from him and elbowed him gently. "Seriously, man, cut it out," he told him.

Ray just shrugged and waved him away. Josh gave him a last look, but if Ray hadn't believed him the two hundred times he'd told him already, it seemed unlikely he could sell it now. In any case, his mother was a much harsher judge and her approval would have more weight.

"Mum," he called out and she turned to the sound of his voice from all the way across the lawn, alert. Once their eyes met, she stepped away from the group of adults—mostly parents of the other alphas of the pack—and waited for him to approach. "This is for you," he said simply and passed it over.

She took it too gently, then readjusted when she realised its weight. "Oh, a picture?" She looked around before heading for one of the tables. "Make me some room," she demanded as Josh followed. He did, placing some plates on chairs and hoping Marisa wouldn't complain—or worse, that Alec wouldn't give him that disappointed frown he had.

"Oh," his mother said, sounding a little shocked. "The... This is incredible," she said slowly. "Did...?" She twisted her neck, looking around, then glanced back down as if she needed to check the picture again. "Did Ray do this?" she asked Josh, meeting his eyes.

He nodded and smiled. He didn't need her to say more, he could hear the wonder in her voice.

His mother looked down again. "I didn't realise he was this talented," she admitted. "Is he...?" This time she kept looking around until she located Ray. "Go get him for me, I have to tell him how amazing this is."

"You could tell me, too," Josh offered, a little miffed. "It's my present."

She snorted, then let go of the picture and took his face in her hands, kissing both his cheeks. "You are my favourite, and this is a very thoughtful present," she told him easily. She wasn't shy; it simply didn't seem to occur to her that he needed to be told such things. "Now, can I tell your mate how wonderfully talented he is? It must have taken such a long time to get this much detail in! I think I could paint their fingernails!"

"I'll get him," Josh conceded, leaning in to kiss her cheek. "Happy birthday."

Ray was standing near Sergi and his parents, but it was clear his attention was divided between the sleeping pups on the grass and Josh himself because he looked up as soon as Josh was close enough to look him in the face. "She loves it," Josh said pre-emptively. "She wants to tell you, actually. You can check *she* isn't lying, too."

Ray rolled his eyes at him. "I don't think you're lying, it's just... You are biased."

"Well, yeah, they are my kids," Josh agreed, deliberately misunderstanding.

Ray huffed but before he could object again or dismiss his own talent somehow, Sergi interrupted them. "Wait, you showed her the picture?" he asked, leaving his own mother hanging. Josh saw her surprised expression when he turned to look at his fellow alpha.

"Yeah." He signalled towards the table with his head.

Sergi turned to Ray. "Can I show them?" he checked, sounding a little anxious.

Ray gaped at him, then offered a tentative nod. "Yeah, I mean, if you want..."

Sergi didn't wait around to cater to Ray's insecurity, taking his mother by the elbow and dragging her along towards the table. She didn't appear that pleased to be hurried along, but she went and with her went Sergi's father—a powerfully built beta with arms like cannons who had just got back from a trip.

"So... are we going?" Josh prompted.

Ray hesitated a moment longer before giving a little nod and heading towards the others, lips pressed together and expression closed off. One look at the group revealed that Ray had more to worry about than his multiple parents-in-law—Ray's mother had somehow made her way to see her son's latest creation and TJ had joined her. Josh had no doubt Martha would approve of her son's creation, but Ray's younger brother was another story.

Ray was only a step or two in front of Josh, but by the time Josh got to them, he was already being hugged. First by Josh's mum and then by his own, who held on for a long minute while she whispered in her son's ear and left Ray looking a little shakier with whatever she'd told him. Then Sergi's mother spoke up to ask if she could take a picture and her son started to explain they had done good ones already without the glass in the way and, if Josh's mum agreed, they could share them.

"Of course," Juliet said, waving her hand. "None of them will be the original."

Josh suppressed a groan, but Martha laughed at her—not meanly, but with the warmth of knowing someone well enough to be delighted even by their flaws. They had followed completely different paths in life, but they'd shared a lot too thanks to Josh's and Ray's friendship. Josh remembered his mother, who was one of the few people he knew who actually enjoyed working late, taking a week off when Ray's dad had died so she could support Ray's family. She'd told her boss her sister's husband had died and at least in the retelling, it had sounded like she believed it.

Ray accepted the congratulations and pats on the back with a smile but started edging away from the group not long afterwards. He smelled sunny and his lips kept curving up as if he couldn't help himself, but maybe the whole thing was a bit too much after months of isolation.

Josh sidestepped his father and went to stand next to him. "Told you," he hissed, keeping his eyes front.

"Whatever," his omega replied, a smile still in his voice.

Josh darted a glance at him, unable to resist, and then almost regretted it when he found Ray already looking at him. Ray shrugged and looked away.

"**A**re you serious?" Sergi was asking, sounding more excited than Josh could ever remember hearing him. He was in the process of changing Mikey's diaper and Ray was forcing Clara into clothes—none of the babies were fond of them, but they'd realised they'd never be able to take them anywhere if they didn't get them used to it. Maybe they couldn't get sick, but there was no way to go out with a baby in diapers in northern England and not freak people out, not even if you drove.

"Well, they *said* they were," Ray replied. "I don't know, I mean, I guess it's a cheap present and, like, original?"

"What is?" Josh asked, and Ray jumped a little. Josh frowned at him; hadn't he said he always knew where they all were?

"You know Yamila Cohen? She called me up about a portrait," Ray explained. "I didn't even know she and your mum spoke to each other but apparently they have a book club."

"Wait. Cheap?" Josh asked, suddenly understanding. "Why would it be cheap for you to do a portrait for her?"

"Wh—I don't even, I told her I would think about it!" Ray said, sounding shocked.

"Okay," Sergi interrupted calmly. "Do you want to do it? Would you like to try it, at least?"

Ray glanced at him, visibly hesitant. "I... I liked doing it, but it'd be different with strangers. I haven't even met her kids."

"They must be around six or seven," Josh told him, picking up Sasha and swinging her around to distract her from picking at her clothes. "They were technically your pack less than a year ago." He reached for Clara, too, who Ray had put down so he could attend to Jamie's clothes. "Shouldn't Irina be here?"

"She's got something to do. I told her we'd manage," Sergi explained absently. "I mean, I figure if we pop them into the jungle gym, they'll forget about the clothes."

It was an idea, at least, so Josh helped them transport the babies from Ray's bedroom into the living room where the jungle gym had a place of honour as far from the windows as possible. It left the sofa most of them used to watch TV at an awkward angle, but nobody had argued with Ray about it.

Ray sat down on said sofa with Jamie on his lap—Josh thought it was Jamie who was clinging to Ray, but it was hard to say for sure. "I know you guys are trying to be supportive, but I don't need more work. There's a lot to do here and there's always going to be more. Even if the betas come—"

"What do you mean by 'even'?" Josh cut him off. "Of course they are coming, you talked to them. Marisa and Irina are already here!"

"Well, yeah, but that was a month and a half ago and we still don't have the beta wing."

"It'll get done," Sergi told him. "Gabriel said the guys will be here next weekend and you got the pillars up like he said you needed too, right?"

"Yeah, we're done with them. We could insulate them but he said it's better to get the plumbing done first, just in case we need to cover any holes..."

"See?" Josh prompted. "You're ahead of schedule. Also, even if you weren't, you are allowed to have time to yourself and do what you want."

"And Yamila's mate is a lawyer," Sergi added. "She'll pay you whatever you ask just so she can show off your original masterpiece."

Ray shifted in place, resettling his son in his lap, eyes fixed somewhere in the distance. "What if I can't do it? I mean, I look at Clara every day and I couldn't get her nose right."

"Then you tell us," Sergi said at once, "and we'll tell you what you'are missing. I... I liked doing that for you." He shot Josh a wary look. "It's nice to do something together, don't you think?"

Ray seemed startled by the statement, but he nodded. "Yeah, I... Yeah, it was nice. You really helped me." He smiled and looked at Josh to include him. "Clara's nose would be a mess and Mikey's foot would have four toes."

"What?" Josh asked with a laugh. "You forgot a *toe*?"

"Well, they were all squished up!" Ray complained. Jamie chose that moment to shift in his lap and promptly got tangled in his shirt and trousers. "Oh, *Jamie*, don't do that!"

"Give him here," Sergi offered and Ray let him take the squirming pup. The trousers and nappies fell right off and when both Ray and Josh leaned down to pick them up—their heads knocked together.

Sergi laughed at them. "Supernatural reflexes much?"

"Oh, shush," Ray shot back. "Try and make him change back."

Sergi froze, then cleared his throat and frowned down at the puppy in his arms. "Jamie, change," he said, infusing his voice with the will of an alpha.

Jamie licked his face. Josh burst out laughing and Ray soon joined him. All in all, it took them about twenty more minutes to stop laughing long enough to talk Jamie into changing back—Josh failed miserably and then Ray did as well because he couldn't keep a straight face—and get Jamie back into his clothes. At that point, it was lunch time anyway and it was a given the clothes would end up in the wash because Jamie was, as Alec liked to put it, a 'creative eater.'"

Ray didn't say whether he'd do Yamila's portrait or not, but there was no rush, really, and there was supportive and there was demanding, and Josh preferred to stay as far away as possible from that line.

Chapter eight

Ray looked up as soon as Josh walked through his open door. He was alone so there was no reason to leave it open unless he wanted company. But maybe he had forgotten it was Iesu's and Sergi's turns to babysit.

"You busy?" Josh checked, stopping himself.

"Ah, no," Ray said, looking away. He wasn't drawing for once but looking at a spreadsheet on his old laptop.

"Is that the bills? I can help if you want."

Ray looked up, clearly surprised. "You don't need to do that. Gabriel and I got it covered, and Marisa's taken over buying the household supplies. She's insisting everything needs to be bought in bulk, so I have to figure out how much of each thing we use."

"That's why you need more storage space, isn't it?" Josh joked, taking a seat on the extra chair Ray kept in a corner of his room—it was a huge room, to be fair.

"Well, it doesn't help," Ray admitted, smiling a little.

"I..." He hesitated and Ray's expression turned serious. "I wanted to ask you something."

Ray nodded for him to continue. He had to know what it was about, but it was still hard to bring himself to speak of it. "Well, I owe you that ice cream," he said in the end, trying to keep it light.

"Oh, now?" Ray's heartbeat sped up a little and Josh was tempted to put a hand on his arm. Luckily, he'd sat down too far to reach out.

He clenched his fist instead and nodded. "Weather isn't going to get any warmer. You can get hot chocolate instead—"

Ray shook his head. "No. It's... Ice cream, you promised me ice cream."

Josh waited, uncertain if this was agreement or just very awkward banter.

Ray got to his feet and turned away. For a moment Josh thought he was meant to leave, then he saw that his friend was getting a pair of socks from his chest of drawers. "I need to talk to Iesu and Sergi." He picked up his mobile from his desk and Josh suddenly realised he'd been keeping it close lately when before he'd barely remembered to charge it.

Ray hadn't allowed himself to linger and the other alphas had pretended not to notice he was shaking a little when he asked them to call him to check all their phones were working. Josh stayed quiet, keeping Mikey and Maria entertained while their caretakers were busy checking their phones did what they were supposed to, and then followed Ray to the door without a word.

R ay headed for the passenger seat unthinkingly, but Josh spoke up, "You should drive."

Ray stopped cold and frowned at him. He'd learned to drive in Josh's Jeep, in fact, Josh had more or less taught him after Josh's grandfather had decided Ray had got the hang of the basics. "What?"

"You have to practice, you might need to at some point."

His friend looked doubtful, but he took the keys. He didn't hesitate getting out of the driveway—a patch of ground they had flattened and cleaned, but that was already growing weeds—and if he was gripping the steering wheel a little harder than was strictly necessary, Josh didn't mention it.

Josh put on some music—something bland and poppy to fill the silence—and looked out the window, trying to give Ray some space.

He couldn't stop listening for any signs of distress, but other than a bit of an accelerated heart rate that could have been due to the excitement of driving again, his friend remained steady throughout the journey. Josh turned to face him only when they approached the ice cream parlour, but there was nowhere to park around the row of restaurants and clothing stores this late in the afternoon, so Ray kept going.

"Do you want to call them?" Josh asked when Ray stopped the engine but didn't get out for a long minute.

Ray shook his head—now he was breathing heavily. "I... I have to do this."

"You *are*," Josh insisted. "But you don't need to suffer through it."

"I... Maybe when we get to Freggo's," Ray decided and shoved the door open hard enough to make Josh wince.

He kept his complaint back—much as he loved the Jeep his grandfather had given him when he'd presented, he couldn't ask Ray for more.

The place didn't look like much, but their product was well worth the trip. Despite being best friends all their lives, Ray and he weren't particularly similar in their tastes, but they were both in agreement over their appreciation for sweet, creamy goods. They'd spent many a day after school sitting in a corner—Josh often going for hot chocolate while Ray insisted on ice cream, even in December. Watching him eat it was almost as much of a treat as his own dessert—even if he had to be careful not to get too lost in the view for fear of giving away his enjoyment.

Of course, that had turned out to be the stupidest thing he could have done. If he had just told Ray... or even been obvious enough for Ray to tell him... But that chance was gone. What mattered now was that Josh got Ray past this. If he didn't and Ray went into heat... Technically, Josh knew what had happened to Ray wasn't his fault, but technically wouldn't cut it for his wolf or for his guilt—every cell in his body knew he was meant to protect his mate. He'd known long before Ray had *been* his mate. Even when the hand fate dealt Ray had nothing to do with Josh at all—like his father's unexpected death—it had always felt like it was Josh's place to be there when things got tough.

Ray hadn't chosen Josh for it, maybe, but he'd held on when Josh had opened his arms. He'd stayed by Josh's side when he'd got his own shitty cards. He had told Josh he had feelings for him.

Not that Josh expected that to come up again.

He'd been wrong to doubt Ray's feelings, apparently, but not about the results. He could have Ray in his bed, but he couldn't keep him there. Even if Ray had feelings for him—vague as that declaration was—he'd made it clear he was only confessing so he could move on.

Josh couldn't blame him. Josh hadn't lied; he'd been trying to protect Ray most of all. But Ray hadn't been wrong either; he'd wanted to be with Ray too badly to walk away.

He couldn't help his feelings or his attraction, but he could have helped his silence. Ray had never asked to be protected or cared for; he'd just expected Josh to be his friend.

And being Ray's alpha wasn't that different from being his friend. He could do both: he would be there to show Ray the options he had and make more if he could.

He just had to hope that it would be enough and that Ray believed him when he said he could ask for anything if Josh couldn't think of it first.

Ray had got a cup instead of a cone like he normally did and now he was eating it half-heartedly in a way that broke Josh's heart. He'd hoped the outing would be a treat, at least, stressful as it was bound to be.

"I'm calling now," he decided and whipped out his mobile before Ray could object.

Iesu picked up on the second ring and Josh could hear both Sergi and the pups in the background even as he reassured Josh that everyone was fine and they'd only let Clara chew on a table leg a little bit.

Ray heard and let out a shaky exhale. Josh tried to meet his eyes as he thanked Iesu, but his friend kept his gaze on the table top. "Okay, yeah, I'll talk to you later. Text me if there's anything we need to get."

His omega didn't thank him or even speak, but he picked up his spoon and ate some more of his dessert. Josh sipped at his drink, trying to focus on the flavour. This was their place: a safe space where they could relax and just chill. He thought about making a joke or reminding Ray of the time someone had bumped him and he'd ended up with a faceful of ice cream.

But before he could, Ray spoke, "I want you to take leadership of the pack."

The words were so unexpected that it took Josh a moment to even understand them. "What?"

Ray still didn't look up at him. "I want you to be First Alpha," he gritted out.

Josh barely held back a gasp. "You... you don't have to do that. We... The other day, when I said it shouldn't be only your responsibility, that's not what I meant. I meant—"

"I know that," Ray stopped him. "But you are the right choice."

"Ray..." Josh said quietly. He didn't want to hurt Ray, as much as Ray was hurting him. Offering him what he'd always wanted because it was *practical* when all Josh had ever wanted was for Ray to choose him because...

"You made the right call," Ray explained patiently. Josh could barely hold back a scream—why was he being reasonable now? About this? Josh could accept that his mistakes were too big for Ray to ever forgive him, but Ray had to know that he was stomping all over Josh's heart. "I wasn't around and you took care of them for me. So, I want you to."

"What about Gabriel...?" Josh objected weakly. It only crossed his mind because they had all half-expected Ray to give in and ask Gabriel at some point.

"Gabriel?" Ray spat and for once he didn't need to push down what he really felt. "Gabriel left the pups when they were under attack!"

Josh could hardly disagree with that, but it was the first time Ray mentioned what had happened of his own volition. It wasn't fair of Josh to insist that he talk about what had been done to him, but maybe if he could talk about Gabriel, about how all his alphas had failed him... "You were in danger, too," Josh said. "And we stayed, so..."

"So why didn't you leave them?" Ray challenged.

Josh felt like he'd been kicked in the face. "He came out after me, just when Marisa told us Ni—*he*," Josh amended with a wince, "had gone to the kitchen after you. I think Gabriel just... reacted."

"And you didn't."

"Clara got away from them, so I was holding her, I couldn't really..." He shrugged, swallowing hard at the memory. He didn't know why *he* was falling apart, when it'd been Ray who'd gone through the worst of it, but he could still feel Clara's weight in his arms and hear Marisa's terrified words.

"Josh," Ray said softly. "I can't make you tell me the truth, but I've known you too long to buy that."

Josh sighed, then met his eyes. "You're not wrong, I'm not... Okay, Gabriel fucked up. He knows that; he's told me. But he meant well and he acted to protect you, I don't think... I am angry with him, too, but..." He looked down. "You have to let it go, or it'll..."

"Forget Gabriel," Ray asked him softly. "You stayed, even when you knew I was in danger, even when the moon rose. You stayed and you looked after them for me. You overcame every instinct, or maybe you listened to the right ones. I don't care, because I know my children are safe with you. Can I fucking value you for that?"

Josh exhaled shakily, then swallowed thickly. His eyes were bright when he met Ray's. "Ray, I left you to... I—"

"*No,*" Ray growled. He was tense as a bow, bent over the table as he gripped his own legs. "This was a mistake."

"I'm sorry..." Josh started, then found he had no more to offer. He'd promised himself he'd give Ray time, take it one step at a time, and now he'd pushed him too far.

"Let's go home," he asked Josh very quietly.

Josh got up and followed him outside, letting him lead the way to the car. Ray shoved his keys back at him and they sat in the Jeep for a long minute because Josh felt like he could barely breathe right, let alone drive.

"Josh?"

"I'm sorry, I just— Just give me a minute," he asked, swallowing hard.

"Have you... Have you talked about this with anyone?" Ray asked him softly. Josh exhaled, shaky and so tense it hurt. He was half afraid of breaking the steering wheel. And then Ray placed a tentative hand on his shoulder and he let go so he could move away.

Ray took his hand away like he'd been burnt, already half mumbling an apology.

"No, don't..." Josh asked. "I just... I know I have no right. I mean, I was scared and I... I'm glad I stayed but I..."

"You are not making sense, no right to what?"

"To *this*," Josh tried to explain, gesturing at the car and his own body, his wet eyes and trembling hands. "It didn't happen to me, I don't know why I'm so freaked out. Maybe it's the instincts because I didn't protect you..."

The words rang hollow between them and after a moment Ray confirmed it. "Don't even. If I don't get to talk about instinct bullshit, then you don't either. And what the fuck is that? Of course you have a right to be upset! Are alphas not supposed to have feelings and nobody told me?"

"No," Josh said at once. "But—"

"Josh," Ray cut in. "I appreciate everything you are doing for me, but if you need me, you got me. I can be here for you."

Josh looked up, shaking his head already. "That's not fair. I can't ask you—"

"You *can*. Maybe I'll need to say no, but you can ask," Ray insisted, eyes averted but utterly sincere.

"I don't... I can't do this if you don't talk to me," Josh said very quietly. He felt shitty saying it, but it was the truth. Ray deserved the truth. "I mean, you don't have to... I—Fuck, I'm not trying to make it about me. I just—I don't know how to help you." He wanted to take the words back as soon as they were out, but it was too late. And the way his eyes were burning, he thought if he didn't let himself speak, he might simply break down and cry.

Ray looked right past him. "It wasn't your fault."

"I should have done something," Josh insisted.

"You *did*." Now Ray was more frustrated than angry. "You did exactly what I wanted you to do, in my head, in my heart of hearts."

Josh shook his head. "But I should have done something for you. I should have checked on you sooner, and I should have tracked you down, gone after you once we rounded them up."

"But if Gabriel came straight for me, and you stayed to round his friends up..." Ray narrated. "You didn't have time."

"I—" Josh cut himself off, unable to find the words. "I don't know. I didn't do enough."

"I invited them to join the pack," Ray said quietly. "And I changed my mind, that's what freaked him out so badly. And then I asked him in *for fucking tea* and didn't tell anyone."

Josh had to fist his hands to keep himself from breaking something. He couldn't afford to replace the steering wheel or the window. "You shouldn't have to tell anyone! Why would you need to tell someone that you're having someone over for tea—"

"I knew what he wanted from me, he *told me*, and I—"

And suddenly Josh was gripping his wrist, hard and implacable, and Ray raised his head to meet his eyes. "No," he said. "Please don't, don't tell me you believe that. You can't believe that... that it was your fault." Ray looked away, curling into himself. "Okay, I get it. I know where you are coming from. I feel that way too, like there must have been something. Like I could have stopped it, because... Because I need you to be safe, and I can't spend every second of every day with you. So, if somehow you were responsible—"

"But you could," Ray said after a moment. "If you... if you were my First Alpha. You'd know where I am."

"*Ray,*" Josh said, feeling like Ray had just ripped his heart right out of his chest. Ray shook in his grip, flinching a little when Josh added, "I *can't.*" Ray kept his mouth shut and turned his face away to look out the passenger side window. "If you... if you were okay," Josh offered tentatively.

Ray didn't look back at him. He didn't pull his hand back, but Josh let go anyway. "I'll take you home," he said when Ray didn't answer.

Ray let him.

Chapter nine

"Coffee?" Josh offered when he caught sight of Ray at the kitchen table with his laptop.

"Yeah, thanks," Ray said. No smiles, not even a glance.

He gave it to him, black with too much sugar just like he liked it, the spoon propped on top so he could mix it to his satisfaction. He might have paused a moment too long before turning back to the counter to his own drink, but Ray didn't react.

He concentrated on letting the tea brew for exactly a minute and a half and tried to keep his body from giving away his distress.

After their failed visit to Freggo's—Ray hadn't even finished his ice cream—Ray had closed right up.

It was stupid because he'd spent the last two months wondering if Ray had meant his confession the way Josh had meant his and if those feelings could survive everything they'd been through. And now he knew: they had. He knew because he could feel their absence now. Like a hole right in the middle of his chest, a combination of nausea, fear and crushing guilt.

He dropped the tea bag in the sink, knowing it'd piss someone off but unable to spare the time to open the cupboard under the sink to get to the organic bin before he walked out.

Josh knew he was doing the right thing, that Ray was okay. Or getting there, at least. He was not only talking to his mother and Marisa regularly, but seemed to have decided to give Gabriel a chance to make it up to him—and his cousin had dived into it with his usual dedication. Ray had also welcomed Sergi's interest in his art now that Josh had stopped trying to wedge his way in.

Josh closed his bedroom door behind himself and allowed himself a moment to lean back against it and just breathe. It might have been right, but it didn't make it stop hurting.

Maybe it was stupid to expect the right thing to be easy, but it had always been easy before. He'd had Ray's attention for so long, and not just his attention, really. Because Ray had needed him. And it wasn't the same as Ray wanting him or choosing him. But it felt pretty close. Ray had trusted him and relied on him, and it'd been...

Only he wasn't doing it for Ray. Ray had made a choice and Josh had made his own. For *himself.*

It was not just Ray who had needed Josh; Josh had needed Ray. Not to help with homework that was late because Ray had been washing the dishes or helping out with something else at home his mum couldn't cope with. Not with a place to crash when he couldn't put up with more screaming children running around. No, strangely Josh had needed some of the very things Ray needed less of. He'd needed the warmth of a puppy pile, and the TV too loud because somebody was always talking over it, and delicious food served on mismatched plates that often came with hilarious stories. And he'd needed to be Ray's comfort, his safe place, his secret keeper.

He had needed Ray to love him, and he'd settled for Ray needing him.

It had worked out okay for them both until Josh had confused the needs of Ray's wolf with Ray's own. He'd given Ray what he thought he needed because he always had, and he hadn't even thought to ask if he was right.

He'd always known before—it was part of his constant watching, his hopeless admiring from afar.

But he'd been wrong. Ray hadn't needed to be bonded and bred as soon as he presented, he'd needed time to think about his options—even as little time as a few hours. He'd needed Josh to be the shield against the chaos his life had fallen into. And Josh had failed him.

But he wouldn't fail him again. And he wouldn't fail himself.

He wasn't hiding how he felt anymore, and he wouldn't let Ray pretend it wasn't real. Ray had a right to think that giving into what he felt for Josh was a mistake, but he could not ask Josh to be his First Alpha like it had no effect on him.

Or like it would have no effect on Ray.

Even if Ray had felt nothing for Josh—and Josh was sure that wasn't true—it would have still required them to have sex. Sex Ray was most definitely not ready to have after being raped not even a month earlier. Sex *Josh* wasn't ready to have before Ray could talk about what had happened and how he felt.

Josh would have done almost anything else for him, but he couldn't let him make a permanent decision like that when he was still in shock from what had happened. It wouldn't have been fair. It wouldn't have been right. If you loved someone, you were supposed to free them and hope they returned to you.

Josh couldn't undo the mark he'd left on Ray's neck, but he could keep them both from making the same mistake again. He didn't know why they'd gotten a reprieve from Ray's heats—another full moon had gone by and Ray had stayed inside with the babies, trusting the betas to keep his alphas in check—but he was not going to hasten the inevitable.

Maybe he was just being selfish. It wasn't about what Ray needed, but about what *Josh* needed. He needed to understand what had happened, not just the facts but *to* Ray, in his head, in his body and heart. He needed to know Ray was okay, that Ray could welcome his touch, that, somehow, he could fix what that bastard had broken. Or maybe what they had all broken when they'd gone from first meeting to mating in a single night.

And maybe it was too much to ask, but he was done pretending he didn't have needs of his own.

He gave Ray a little space, but by the end of the week, he'd had enough of both the cold shoulder and not talking to his best friend.

It so happened they were scheduled to babysit and cook dinner together because everyone else was out. They'd lucked out and the kids had fallen prey to the well-earned nap that was the natural consequence of their first excursion into the wild that morning—Sergi and Iesu had convinced Ray to let them go hunt rabbits in the area surrounding the house. They had just caught a squirrel, but Josh thought it was time well spent if it meant Ray loosened the reins a little and the pups got some exercise that didn't involve destroying furniture.

"Ray," he said softly. Something in his tone must have alerted his friend that he was serious because he looked up from rummaging through the fridge and actually met Josh's eyes. "I'm sorry, okay?" Ray started to shake his head, but Josh raised a hand. "I know I hurt your feelings, and that you are afraid. It's not... It's not that I don't *want* to, you know that, right?"

"No, you just think it's your decision," Ray said curtly. He slammed the lettuce a little too hard against the counter. "As usual."

"Whether *I* become your First Alpha?" Josh asked incredulously. "Hell, yeah, of course it's my decision!"

"That's not what you have a problem with and we both know it," Ray shot back. "You coordinated this whole thing and now you think you can manage my recovery or some shit."

"I'm not—"

"I don't need you to babysit *me*," Ray interrupted. He winced a little, his wolf unhappy with the open defiance to his alpha, probably. It made Josh's stomach twist—if he could have turned off all those fucking instincts and...

But, of course, they wouldn't have a problem if it wasn't for their instincts. They never had before, Ray and he. And deep down, under all the bullshit, they still didn't. They both made some mistakes, but if Ray could just see...

He exhaled. "I'm not trying to babysit you, or control you, or whatever it is you think. I am trying to not screw up. Not screw you up and not screw myself up by doing something I will regret when I see how much it's hurt you."

"You're not trying to control me, sure," Ray replied. He was holding a knife, which was fortunate because the metallic handle could probably withstand the tightness of his grip better than most kitchen utensils. "You just get to decide what will hurt me and forbid me from doing it."

"Forbid?" Josh echoed. "What—? I didn't tell you what you could do or not, just that I—" He stopped himself because it was quite obvious what he was implying. Josh didn't want to sleep with Ray, but Ray could sleep with someone else.

It was too late; Ray's expression had shuttered. He gave a tiny nod, more to himself than to Josh, then spoke, "I had sex."

Josh stared at him, his brain not quite able to comprehend the words. Ray was still uncomfortable with casual touch sometimes—particularly if he wasn't expecting it—and he'd... "You— But..."

"It was fine. I'm fine," Ray said, but his heart was beating too fast already for Josh to tell if it'd skipped a beat. "I can... I can do it if I want to."

"Sergi," Josh said softly, realisation feeling like lead in his stomach.

Ray shrugged, not denying it but clearly unwilling to discuss it. "You get it now?" he demanded.

Josh swallowed, looking away. He shouldn't have felt this bad. He'd known Ray was free to sleep with any of his mates. And they were all his mates equally; what right did Josh have to resent Sergi for doing this for Ray when Josh himself had refused?

"I'm glad you are okay," he managed after a minute.

Ray growled in frustration. "Do *not* get all polite with me."

Josh looked up in surprise. "Polite? What else do you want me to say? That I think getting back into it too early might end up making it worse? That I'm afraid for you?"

"You could try the truth," Ray suggested, teeth bared, words over-enunciated like he was having trouble keeping his voice even. "Tell me you don't want a mutual bond with me because it'd mean having to deal with how fucked up I am."

"I don't care!" Josh said, too loudly. He looked towards the living room, but the goddess either loved or hated him because none of the babies reacted. He turned back to Ray and made himself speak slowly. "Listen to my heart very carefully. I *never* want to hear you use me as a reason to call yourself names. I love you. As a friend, as a lover too, and no matter what you feel for me, I want to be with you forever. That includes a mutual bond and... and a mutual relationship, if..." He put down the half-peeled potato, struggling to find the right words. "You have been... You have been my best friend for as long as I can remember, and I always thought I knew you pretty well. But I was wrong about bonding so fast, and I still— I still need to work on forgiving myself for that. And I think you need that too, even though you have been acting like you're over it." He met Ray's eyes for as long as he could bear. "You should have that time, that's all I wanted. To give you time to process all the crazy things that have happened in the last year. And if I was wrong about sex, I'm sorry about that too. It's not because I'm trying to control you, it's not... I don't think I could bear it if I scared you or made you feel... I would rather *die*, Ray, than to ever hurt you that badly again."

"You won't," Ray insisted quietly.

"You don't know that, and the least I owe both of us is to be as careful as I can." Ray didn't say anything, and Josh realised he hadn't addressed the point. "I'm... I'm glad Sergi was there to help you," he said, and he thought it was the truth but his heart was beating too hard for him to tell. "I'm glad you have other people who love you."

"I thought... you would be angry." Ray said, and Josh heard the knife clatter on the counter.

Josh shook his head, not looking at him. He didn't think he could hear this if he had to see Ray's face. "I wasn't what you wanted, I get it."

"What?" Ray snapped. "I asked *you* first."

Josh exhaled. "You asked me to become your First Alpha, to perform a duty to our pack. It has nothing to do with asking Sergi to have sex with you to..." He hesitated, not wanting to offend, but everything was a landmine. "Because you wanted to," he decided in the end.

Ray gaped at him. "Yes, but—"

Josh interrupted him, it was either speak or scream. "Just imagine someone you have confessed your feelings to coming over and asking you to have sex with them to magically create better surveillance." His omega was most definitely getting a faceful of his emotions because Josh was too worked up to keep them back, but maybe the half-bond could be of some use for once. Maybe Ray needed to see what he'd done first hand to believe it. "And then you are smart enough to say no because it'd be pretty messed up during *and* after, and they get *angry at you*."

"It wasn't like that," Ray protested as soon as Josh stopped. "It wasn't in... in a vacuum! There was context, we talked about how we felt about each other. I mean, I didn't ask Sergi for that, did I?"

"Ray, we talked about it before you were kidnapped... And, anyway, you made it pretty clear you didn't want to create tension in the pack by being with me like that," Josh reminded him. "And the other day in Freggo's, you didn't say anything about feelings, it was all about how much easier it'd be to protect the pack if we both knew where everyone was."

He turned his back to Ray, afraid of what his face might reveal. "You know what? You keep complaining that I treat you like an omega and want to make choices for you. Well, you treat me like an *alpha*. Like I'm... I'm only important because I can help you through heat, and protect you, and provide what you need." He barely bit off the words that came next; *Like this is my fault*. "And you never even *ask* what I need, what I *want*. And it doesn't matter if you can return my feelings or not, you should still be my friend. And that isn't how you treat a friend."

"Josh—"

"Don't," he said quickly, and cleared his throat, suddenly noticing his face was wet. "I can't. I can't be strong and have no feelings, and I can't just bury everything I feel all the time. I need— Space. Time. I don't know. Something. Until you can treat me as a friend, think about what I need too..."

"Josh, I'm really sorry," Ray whispered. "I... You're right. Maybe we need time to try and remember we are friends first."

He sounded like he would say more but Maria's powerful lungs interrupted them, forcing him to rush to the living room. Josh held back just long enough to wash and dry his face—he could tell when a cry was a real emergency by now. He found Ray sitting Clara down on the sofa and growling a soft order to stay. Staying still was definitely an appropriate punishment for their little adventurer.

"Hair?" he asked, seeing Ray go over to Maria and pick her up.

"Maybe we should cut it off," Ray suggested as he struggled to untangle the knots the curls had acquired from too inexpert manipulation.

"But it's so pretty," Josh replied, a little hesitant.

"Who cares? She's a little young to be staring at herself in mirrors, and I'm sure it'll make her happier not to get it pulled by the others all the time."

"You think Gabriel is gonna sign off on that?" Josh asked, pushing Jamie towards the jungle gym and away from the TV—they'd mostly baby-proofed the house already, but after Clara had broken the baby gate by shaking it, it'd become evident that they couldn't rely on human machines to do the job well for superhuman babies.

Ray kissed Maria's cheek and deposited her on the sofa in view of the TV. "I got this if you—" He stopped so abruptly that Josh turned to check if he was okay.

So he was already looking his way when Ray offered him a guilty smile. "Do you want to cook or stay with them?"

It was a deliberate effort, and it was meant to look that way. Ray normally decided who did what in the house like they were extra limbs available to him to complete all the work.

Marisa's rota had helped with that a little—she'd asked them all once what they liked and hated and tried her best to fit it with their jobs and other obligations. If she messed up, you always had the chance to approach her and ask her to swap with someone else. More often than not, Marisa volunteered herself.

It was considerably more relaxed and it made everyone feel like they were truly doing their parts but not being taken advantage of. But for Ray, who had got used to running the house because he never left it, it was still pretty natural to decide who was making dinner and who was changing nappies without consulting any of the participants involved.

Josh hadn't even realised how annoying it was until now when he was offered a choice instead. It wasn't how things had been between them before; Ray was bossy by nature and being in charge of his younger siblings had only exacerbated the trait. He had told Josh what to do when they were kids, and Josh mostly hadn't felt it was worth arguing about and done it.

But this: a choice freely offered... It was what he'd asked for.

And Ray had listened.

"I'll stay with them," he said softly.

Ray nodded but didn't make him explain that he didn't want to be alone when he felt like he might start crying again. Or maybe not, he reconsidered, as his omega gave him a warm smile and a playful salute before turning back to the kitchen.

Josh parked the Jeep, already thinking of dinner, and he was so distracted that he almost missed Gabriel sitting on the porch. He wouldn't be sitting if it was an emergency, his brain rushed to reassure him, but it did little for his sudden nerves. Gabriel wasn't the type to watch the stars and he was already getting to his feet now that Josh was out of the car.

"No one's hurt," Ray's cousin said when Josh was still across the front part of the land they called the front garden, despite there being no fences or even a picnic table to earn it the name.

"Yet?" Josh asked between gritted teeth. He wasn't an idiot and too much had gone wrong already for this to be anything other than terrible.

"We have been waiting for you," Gabriel said, getting right to the point. "We have to tell him something, and he's not going to take it well."

"We?" Josh repeated. "Who's we? How... Alec." He saw it at once. He'd seen how Gabriel had taken to hanging all over Alec lately, and Alec was a doctor. Alec had *told* Josh he was going to figure out what was going on with Ray. "He knows what's wrong." He almost took it back, because nothing was *wrong* just because the alphas didn't need their omega...

But Gabriel didn't give him enough time. "Yes, he's figured it out. And you need to hear it now, and then you need to prove you are ready to become First Alpha and keep Ray from falling apart when we tell him."

"What?" Josh echoed. "I don't... I don't want to be First Alpha."

"Well, tough," Gabriel snapped. "Because he needs one and there's no one else he will ask."

Josh clenched his jaw, and gave himself a moment to exhale, then breathe in again. "How bad is it?" he asked, because he was a coward and he couldn't face it quite yet.

"Nobody is dead," Gabriel said. "Well, that piece of shit alpha is. That's all the good news I have for you."

Josh met his eyes. "Say it."

"He's pregnant."

Part II: Raymond

Chapter ten

Irina and he had been so intent on finishing the caulking before she had to go to bed that night that they'd missed the babies' feeding time. It wasn't their turn, of course, but he wasn't meant to be working so late into the night anyway. A part of Ray that couldn't help but resurface no matter how hard he was kicked had been pleased that he'd been able to concentrate on something else for a few hours. He was getting better, slowly, and with some missteps—like that awful trip to town with Josh, where he'd managed to embarrass himself on multiple counts and freak Josh out so badly his friend had barely looked at him since—but he felt calmer, more focused. The work helped, like if he could build up a wall or finish cleaning up the buckets they'd used, it'd somehow mean he was closer to being a whole person again.

He'd been in a good mood, tired but ready to push through it for the satisfaction of finishing... And then Josh had come to get him from the beta wing. He'd looked blank, which set alarms ringing in Ray's brain. Josh always had at least half a smile poised on his lips, even if he couldn't quite make it reach his eyes. "Come," he'd asked Ray, and then spared Irina a glance. "You should head back to the house now."

Irina was a beta, but she wasn't one to follow orders unquestioningly. This time she didn't argue or question it, just told Ray she'd put away the rest of the materials on her own.

Ray knew the news was bad. It didn't take a genius to come to expect tragedy after what he'd been through. And he couldn't remember seeing Gabriel and Alec together on their own before. Gabriel had vouched for their shy doctor, but he didn't seem particularly close to him. Alec himself was visibly wary of Ray's cousin—Ray assumed it was mostly a combination of Gabriel's congenial brashness and Alec's innate nervousness.

They'd chosen the living room, not the kitchen, and that was something even if they probably didn't know that Nicholas had held him close in there as he called him a liar and promised to hurt his kids if he didn't cooperate.

If Josh's expression had been concerning, Alec's would have sent anyone running. He was naturally pale, but now Ray could swear he was about to faint from how little colour he had on his face. He wasn't just in the same room as Gabriel, either, but actually sharing the settee with him. Ray had to blink to make himself believe his eyes when he noticed his cousin was gripping Alec's elbow hard enough his knuckles were white. Ray wanted to object, but for all that Alec was shy, he didn't think an alpha would let another truly hurt him.

He stood in front of them, conscious of Josh a step behind him. "Tell me," he demanded.

"We..." Alec started, but he couldn't finish.

Gabriel took over. "We know why the wolves haven't tried to mate with you," he said. He met Ray's eyes like it hurt and didn't look away.

Maybe, deep down, Ray knew even then, because he repeated, "*Tell me.*"

Alec's eyes fell closed and he flinched away. Gabriel didn't let go, and Alec got the words out like they were being torn out of him with a broken knife "You are pregnant."

The words echoed between them, like a gunshot ringing in the air as the blood spread from a gaping wound. It was like all other sound was gone from the world, and then Josh said his name from behind him, so full of need it was impossible to ignore. Ray turned to look at him because his mate was in pain and Ray could never not come to his aid. But when their eyes met, it was like reality crashed into Ray's mind; somehow, seeing the belief in Josh's eyes made it real to him.

"No," he said, muffled. "That's..." He looked down at Josh's feet, then half turned towards the other two alphas and repeated it, "No. I— I *killed him.*"

"I can check," Alec offered in a strangled voice. Ray just stared at him. Check? *After* he'd said it?

He met Alec's eyes, suddenly so furious he nearly couldn't form words, the growl that left his lips made Alec recoil. "It wasn't even the full moon yet! And I... I didn't let him. I *didn't.* I stopped it. You—" The words seemed to scrape at his throat and he <u>dry</u>-heaved hard enough that he stumbled.

Josh was at his side at once, holding him up by the elbow. "Breathe," he told Ray. His own voice was laced with pain, but he was still firm, he was still here. He wasn't... And then Alec's words seemed to crystallise in his mind and Ray yanked away from him and stepped aside. He'd have gone farther if his feet had been willing, but he only made it far enough to dig his clawed hands into the side of the armchair, tearing the cloth as he hunched over it, breathing harshly and shaking hard enough he'd have fallen if not for his grip.

He didn't notice he was crying until Alec spoke again, "I'm so sorry, Ray. I swear, I—"

"Don't you fucking *dare*!" Ray screeched, loud enough to hurt his own ears. "You *promised me*. You swore a fucking oath to get that goddamned piece of paper you call a degree and you... you promised me you'd keep me safe. You swore... You—" He choked, the next sob surging up his throat too strong to be stopped by mere willpower. He could feel the tears falling down his face, his body betraying him in yet another way as his stomach roiled with disgust and his limbs shook with terror. And then, before he knew it, the wolf shoved him over and he was falling onto half-formed paws.

By the time he leapt through the open window, he was fully transformed and so scared he just ran, no destination in mind. The wolf didn't understand much, but it knew to get away from pain.

Josh found him. Ray didn't really want to be touched, but the wolf was as terrified as Ray himself and it knew its mate. Despite everything, it believed Josh could keep them safe from anything. Ray didn't have the strength to fight himself as well as the world, so he let his mate bury a hand in the hair on his neck and his face into Ray's furred cheek and hold on like he was afraid Ray would disappear.

Ray wished he could, but Josh didn't let go.

The wolf's sense of time wasn't great and Ray didn't care. He was confused to find himself in his own bed, Josh holding onto him as he bent over his body. He was naked under the sheets—he'd probably ripped his clothes when he'd shifted—and Josh's arm around his torso sent a shock of remembrance through him. He grunted from pain that was so much worse than any injury that he could barely even comprehend it and Josh flinched and shushed him, curling up further into him even as Ray struggled in his grip. He didn't want...

"Shhhh," his friend whispered. "It's just me. I got you, you are safe. You are okay."

Ray's exhausted muscles accepted defeat and he slumped in his mate's embrace, and then, like he'd let go of everything that held him together, came the tears. He only noticed he was sobbing when Josh pulled him up so he could breathe through it, and he only realised his nails had grown when he smelled the blood he'd drawn from Josh's back. He tried to pull back, but Josh didn't let him.

"I don't care," he told Ray, and Ray wasn't sure who was shaking or if the world itself was trembling on its foundations and they were just holding on to each other to keep from falling off. "It doesn't hurt," Josh insisted, a lie so transparent it could only be offered as a sacrifice. He curled his fingers into fists—he could remember too clearly what his claws were capable off—and pressed his closed fists against his friend's back even harder. Josh gasped a little but if the open wounds stung as they closed, he ignored it.

"I can't," he gasped against Josh's neck. "I can't..."

Josh held him harder still. "You can. You have done so much already, and you can... you can do this. I'll help you. You will be okay."

Ray tried to speak, to deny it perhaps, but he found himself crying harder, gasping for breath too hard to form words, even if he'd managed to calm down enough to think of any.

Josh shushed him again and tilted their bodies until they lay on their sides. He'd got some tissue from somewhere and put it right in front of Ray, letting him take it so he could dry his face and running nose. "Listen to me: you are in shock. That's why you're cold." It was only when he heard the word that he realised he wasn't just shaking, he was shivering too. "I'm gonna get another blanket from the—" He stopped when Ray's hold on his arm tightened. At some point, he'd forgotten not to hold on. "I won't leave the room," Josh promised, touching his face with his roughened hands so softly Ray felt like he might be about to shatter into a million pieces.

He concentrated and loosened his hold; it still pulled at his fingers when Josh rolled off the bed and crossed the room with strides so long it was closer to jumping than running. He yanked the chest of drawers open and muttered an imprecation when he saw he'd got the wrong drawer. Ray must have blinked because the next thing he knew his mate was putting a heavy woollen blanket over the lighter duvet and holding him close under it. Ray shivered harder like his body knew it finally had the insulation he needed if only he could warm up the space in between. Josh helped him along, rubbing hard to create friction and whispering encouragement, and Ray felt his body start to respond.

He closed his eyes, too exhausted to think or feel. It was too late to do anything now. He'd failed. Again. Only worse. The consequences of this mistake wouldn't just be in his head.

For a few seconds, waking up warm and curled up with the man he loved, Ray forgot.

It only made remembering all the worse and he couldn't keep back a whimper. Josh woke with a start. Ray struggled against the blankets and Josh had to scramble to get off them before his thrashing sent him to the floor. And then Ray was stumbling onto the floor, already breathing hard. The room was as big as always and empty except for the two of them, but his eyes went to the window at once, looking for an escape route.

"Ray," Josh said urgently and Ray turned, the way he'd have looked towards any other sound. "Calm down."

"How..." He shook his head. "I can't," he said, wheezing as his heart struggled against his ribs. "I—" He took a step towards the door because he needed to do *something* and Josh quickly stepped out of his way.

"Ray," he repeated. "Look down at yourself a moment before you do something you will regret."

The words didn't make a lot of sense until Ray looked down and saw he was still naked from his stint as a wolf. He almost tripped over his own two feet getting back on the bed and under the blankets. Josh came over a moment later and offered him a t-shirt. He put it on under the sheets and Josh dropped underwear and a pair of shorts on the bed next to him.

"I'm going to get you some breakfast. Have a cuppa first, let you..." His steps faltered on his way to the door. "Or I can just text Alec to bring it for us?"

Ray winced at the mention of Alec, suddenly remembering what he'd said to him the previous day. He shook his head. Josh didn't move for a moment longer, maybe waiting for Ray to look at him. Ray kept his gaze on his own hands.

The door had barely clicked shut when he was dragging his underwear under the blankets and shoving his legs into them. That done, he buried his face in the bedding, wishing to drown and remembering, suddenly and vividly, a macabre conversation he'd had with Josh about what it would take to kill one of them. They'd been drunk on werewolf whisky for the first time—too young to drink anywhere but safe under the supervision of Josh's older cousin. Ray didn't know if he'd been thinking about his dad—the insane force it'd taken to break his body beyond recovery—or if he was always going to be a maudlin, depressed drunk.

He tried to push the thought away. He didn't *want* to die. He just wanted it to *stop*. Every time he thought he was okay, that things were getting better...

He didn't want to die; he just didn't want to live like this.

It wasn't worth it.

It felt better to say it, even if only inside his own head. He breathed in his own scent and Josh's, and underneath, the babies' too. He loved them all, too much to quantify, but... they didn't really need him around. They loved him, of course, but he could see the pain on Josh's face, and Alec had looked like he'd cut his own heart out and hand it to Ray on a plate if it would help. They loved him and all they could do was watch him suffer—an endless cycle of bad luck and poor decisions.

If he was... gone, it'd hurt them, of course. But it would only hurt them once, and then they'd be free. They wouldn't have an omega but that was okay too, there were other omegas who'd come to a new pack with a house and five strong, capable alphas at the helm—not to mention a beta like his sister running the whole thing. And they'd look after the babies. He could trust Josh with that, and he was sure Alec would make sure they were healthy, and Iesu would make them relax, enjoy life, and Sergi would be a steady presence, observant and attentive—not missing the little things. He even believed Gabriel had meant it when he'd promised any of their children who were omegas would choose their own mates.

They would be okay and happy. Much happier than if Ray stayed around and kept poisoning everything with a despair so all-consuming he felt he was drowning—

"Ray?" Josh called from behind the door.

Ray didn't move and after a long pause, Josh pushed the door open rather awkwardly. Even with his nose buried in the blankets, Ray could smell the hot, greasy food. The plate clinked against the bureau. "You need to eat something, it'll help you feel more... steadier. I promise, just..."

Josh sat beside him again and placed a hand on his shoulder. Ray stayed where he was. "Just have some orange juice, I don't want you to get dehydrated." He pulled slightly and Ray didn't resist. "Okay, let me make you a deal. Half a glass of orange juice and I'll leave you alone, okay?"

It wasn't a bad deal. He needed time to think and he didn't want to think with Josh around, even if he'd refused the mate bond and he couldn't tell what Ray was feeling. He exhaled and rolled over so that he was facing towards the side of the bed. Josh got the hint and brought the glass to the bed, putting it to Ray's lips and tilting it slightly to help him drink. Ray closed his eyes and drank—it was cold and sweet, and Josh was right, damn him, it was waking him up.

Except he didn't want to wake up. He turned his face away and a little juice spilled down his front before Josh could react.

"Ray!" his friend complained. "Warn a guy."

Ray rolled over into his original position, closed his eyes and pretended to go to sleep. Josh heaved a sigh and warned him that he'd have to eat lunch. But he left.

He must have fallen asleep at some point because Josh shook him awake, already announcing what they had for lunch.

Ray grunted and pushed him away. "Not hungry."

"Ray, come *onnnn*," Josh whined in the tone he'd used with Glen when he'd got really fed up. "Just eat. I get you don't want to talk, but you can't stop eating!"

"Stop," Ray asked quietly, and he was shocked when it worked.

Maybe if he had been less keen on getting back to sleep, he'd have realised it had been too easy. Instead, he got to be startled fully awake when Josh dropped a pup right on his back. It was only by some protective instinct that he didn't push Jamie off the bed altogether.

"Josh!" he shouted, suddenly angry.

But he didn't get to be angry for long because Jamie was already licking his face, whining softly in welcome and he didn't have the heart to upset him further by raising his voice.

He vaguely recalled the babies crying in the background while he shouted at Alec. They'd felt how upset he was even through closed doors. The alphas must have made sure they were as far as possible before telling Ray the news, he realised, half grateful, half ashamed he hadn't been able to control himself for their sake. Maria nudged his side with her face—probably forgetting she didn't have a snout—and Ray gathered her close too, and just like that he was at the bottom of a puppy pile.

And goddess, he *loved* them. And what if someone hurt them like he'd been hurt? What if next time his sacrifice wasn't enough?

He didn't realise he was crying until he gasped for breath and moved Sasha off his chest. He didn't want to let her go, but he couldn't—

"Ray?" Josh asked in alarm, but Ray didn't look at him. "Are you... What's wrong?"

Ray tried to speak, to put him off or calm him down. He didn't know, it didn't work anyway, it just meant he'd opened his mouth and the sob he'd been holding back spilled free.

Josh shouted Alec's name and started getting the babies off the bed. It was way too late; Sasha was wailing, and Mikey was whimpering softly, still in fur. Ray turned away and fisted the sheets, pushing his face down into them and locking his muscles as if he could keep himself from shaking so hard he felt like he was going to fall apart. It was as much protection from his pain as he could offer them.

He didn't really hear Alec come in, but he felt him, and he felt the pups being taken away—tugging at the bond nobody talked about, the one between an omega and his children.

It *hurt*, but he didn't ask them to stop. It *should* hurt. He'd hurt them, it was all he could do. What else did he have inside himself but pain?

And no matter how much he cried, how much he screamed and tore at the cloth in his hands... it didn't seem to stop. He just wanted it to stop.

"Shhhh..." Josh's voice in his ear was soft but firm. "I will make it stop. I promise I will," he insisted, fierce and desperate.

Ray wanted nothing more than to believe him. But he couldn't. He couldn't tell if Josh believed himself, but Ray knew in his heart of hearts that it wouldn't stop. Josh pressed closer and Ray jerked but didn't try to pull away. He knew

Josh couldn't protect him, but he wanted him to. He wanted to be safe.

Josh curled up against his back, murmuring words that didn't matter as much as his warmth and his presence next to Ray. And Ray gave in and let it pour out of him.

It didn't seem like it'd ever end, but even his body had limits and, slowly, he found himself panting, no more tears coming. The coverlet was a disgusting mess, but he couldn't find the energy to turn his head around.

Josh's fingers were carding through his hair and Ray could suddenly feel them and the path they'd drawn on his scalp again and again, who knew for how long.

He seemed to sense that Ray was aware of him because he spoke, "Let me get the tissues."

Ray managed enough autonomy to clean off his own snot and threw the balled-up tissue away before Josh could attempt to take it. Josh huffed, frustrated, but this was bad enough without making his friend pick up his used tissues. Josh went back to the head massage without another word.

"Are they...?" Ray tried out, trailing off when he heard the rasp that was his voice.

"Yeah, they were upset, that's all," Josh said evenly. "Don't worry about them; Alec and Gabriel are on it."

"I'm sorry," Ray said quietly.

Josh's grip on his arm tightened. "Don't be sorry, didn't you say I was allowed to cry? What makes you so special?"

"I'm a mess," Ray replied, pushing himself up into a sitting position. His hands were still trembling slightly, but his head was quiet again—probably, he'd cried himself out, maybe it was just all buried again, waiting to erupt the moment he felt *anything*.

"You're doing pretty well, I would be jumping off a cliff at this point," Josh said, lips curving up while his eyes stayed the same. Ray couldn't hide his reaction fast enough because Josh's eyes widened and he inhaled sharply. "*Ray*," he said. He sounded terrified.

Ray swallowed, feeling like he'd throw up. He didn't want Josh to...

Josh took hold of his upper arm, too hard, nails digging a little—not that Ray cared about a little more pain. "Ray, you can't—"

"I know I can't," Ray told him, and he didn't even care that much when Josh choked out a sound of pain. He didn't have any room left for any more pain—his own or anyone else's.

"What...?"

"You don't have to worry," Ray said. "I just... I just want it to stop, okay? It's a feeling, I can't—I can't help how I feel."

"Can I— is there anything I can do?" Josh asked, and he sounded like *he* would jump off that cliff if Ray asked it of him.

Ray shook his head. He knew Josh would have helped if he could—it was just that he couldn't.

Nobody could.

"Can I hold you?" Josh asked after a moment, his voice had lost all traces of certainty now. He was scared. Ray had scared him. He nodded; he didn't hold it against Josh. There wasn't anything anyone could do, after all.

He didn't know how long they'd been pressed close when the knock came. He was warm and sleepy—he'd closed his eyes at some point and had leaned his head against Josh's neck.

"What?" Josh called out.

"I need to talk to Ray," Alec said clearly from the other side of the door.

Josh tensed and leaned back to meet Ray's eyes, alarm writ clear on his face.

Ray shrugged. He felt so blank, he could hardly imagine he'd care about whatever Alec had to say.

But Josh cared. "I'm talking to him first," he decided, letting Ray go and taking a step towards the door before suggesting. "Maybe you can have a shower? I'll change the sheets."

For some reason, it was the idea of being naked again that got through the thin layer of indifference Ray's mind had helpfully provided him with. He shook his head.

Josh paused a second longer, then nodded. "Okay, I'll go talk to him outside."

The knock came again maybe five minutes, maybe five hours later. Ray's eyes were dry from not blinking and he had to swallow before he could speak and invite his alpha to come in.

Alec opened the door slowly, then slipped in and closed it quickly behind him.

Ray almost flinched, remembering the look on Alec's face when Ray had shouted at him. "I treated you like crap," he rasped out.

"Already forgotten," Alec said. He was lying, but somehow, he was holding Ray's gaze anyway. A lie that wasn't a lie because he meant it. He'd forgive Ray for it, even though Ray didn't deserve it.

"No, I'm sorry," he said. "I know it's not your fault."

Alec swallowed, turning his body slightly away. "I promised you, and I failed."

"You promised to be my doctor, not... you aren't responsible for my actions."

"Your...?" Alec started to ask. "Ray, he..." He faltered, then spoke with obvious difficulty, pulse a hum in Ray's ears. "He raped you."

He said it quietly like he was afraid of the words.

Ray looked down at his hands, remembering how he'd fought. And how he'd *stopped*. But it wasn't just that... "I let him take me away so he wouldn't hurt the babies."

"Fuck, you think that isn't rape?"

"I decided to do it," Ray confessed. He'd known, of course, but to tell someone else... "I knew he was going to... And I went with him. It was worth it," he added almost viciously. He thought about Josh's suggestion of a shower, but he'd washed it off already. He couldn't do anything to erase the sense memory of it—no amount of soap, or bleach, could do that.

As long as he lived, he'd have to carry it with him.

He saw Alec's hand twitch, but of course, Alec wasn't Josh, he wouldn't even ask to touch Ray. "Then you couldn't consent freely and it's still rape."

"Okay," Ray agreed. What did it matter what they called it? "Nicholas still won."

"He—" Alec started to say, then cut himself off. "I have something else to tell you. Something good, do you want to hear it now?"

"Something good?" Ray echoed, uncomprehending.

"It's... I don't know, a silver lining?" he offered, and when Ray didn't say more, he continued, "You can have single pregnancies from now on. You just need to take... an alpha. And stay away for the full night. The other wolves will lose interest."

Ray stared, brain rushing with too many words to process. "What?" he asked in the end because he couldn't seem to make sense of it.

"That's why we... the wolves didn't need to..." He waved a hand, probably not wanting to mention sex in the same conversation as rape.

"But I thought..." Ray met his eyes, blinking back tears.

"I have been talking to... to other omegas," Alec explained. "I don't know a lot, but that's how I figured it out..." He stopped. "I'm sorry, I should have seen it earlier, but it was a good thing and I—I was stupid, I just didn't think of it. It's so obvious, but... I'm sorry."

Ray didn't answer, struggling to get his brain to do the math. He'd assumed he'd have a litter every year at the very least. He hadn't really allowed himself to think of the numbers. He'd instinctively known that he couldn't handle it. Alec had said an omega's cycles slowed down as he aged, but he'd assumed he'd cross the dozen in less than three years.

This meant... "But then, I would... I will go into heat more often."

"I don't really think so," Alec said. "You won't while the baby is very young and then the... feeding helps too."

"It didn't help this time," Ray said quietly.

"It's not the same," Alec objected. "Your body wasn't ready, it was just close enough it could... It could conceive if it was asked to."

"Are you sure?" Ray asked in the end, meeting Alec's eyes despite how hard it was. He couldn't stand it if this was just...

"Yes," Alec said at once, then stopped and clarified, "About the single pregnancy. The rest is a good guess based on other people's experiences."

"Okay, I— thank you."

"I can—" Alec started but he stopped when Ray raised a hand.

"I... I would like to be alone."

"Ah, yes, of course," his alpha said, scrambling for the doorknob. "I... Call if you—" But he didn't finish the sentence before he closed the door a little too hard.

Ray numbly looked down at this own hands, then pushed his shirt over his head and his boxers down his legs as fast as he could and dropped himself into the wolf's wild certainty. The wolf was in pain, too—it couldn't get away from it any more than Ray could—but it was a simpler kind, easier to combat with time and comfort than the tangle of emotions Ray's human brain couldn't process or escape.

He found a space to wedge himself into between the bed and the wall, tucked his tail in and pressed his ears against his skull, trying to block out the world for a little while.

Josh found him there in the morning, and when Ray opened his eyes, his fur already smelled of his alpha. Josh rubbed the side of his face, tracing the prickly skin of his snout. Ray licked his hand. "Hey, sleepy head," his friend greeted him. "I thought you might need some fresh meat. Got you a rabbit."

Ray almost toppled him when he sprang to his feet, but Josh laughed. "Finally!" he crowed. "Come, I left it on the front porch."

He didn't even notice he was outside until he'd eaten all the soft meat and started on the bones. Josh was standing by his side, not watching him eat but a steady presence between him and the door.

"Ray?" he asked when he saw Ray watching him. He shook the water bottle in his hand. "Wanna?"

He knelt where he was, putting himself at Ray's height, and Ray moved closer to drink from his cupped palm.

Josh didn't try to touch him, which was fine because now that he was awake all Ray and his wolf agreed on was that something was wrong.

It wasn't Josh, of course. But he needed to be alert. He turned his head, sniffing at the air. To Ray, the fact that it was only members of the pack was somewhat reassuring; to the wolf, it didn't quite help. It could feel Ray's distress and it couldn't find the source. And if it didn't know where the danger was... it meant it could be anywhere.

Josh opened the door, but Ray ignored him, settling down on the porch instead. He wasn't sure why the houses of the pack all included one, but they made a great spot to keep guard and he definitely couldn't feel the cold as a wolf.

Josh hesitated in the doorway, but then he huffed and went back inside, leaving Ray there alone. He stayed there even when everyone left for work, leaving only Marisa behind to do the babysitting since she was too young to get paid a decent wage even if she did find a job willing to take her with no experience.

Ray registered their absence—the sense of impending danger getting worse with each member of his pack that left him behind—and didn't move from his post, knowing he was the last line of defence between whatever was coming and his children.

Chapter eleven

Ray was aware of Josh at once—in fact, he'd identified the particular rumblings of the Jeep's engine long before it was visible—but he didn't feel the need to acknowledge him. Ray was guarding his pack and Josh wasn't a threat.

Iesu had rubbed Ray's head on his way in, and Sergi had simply gone inside and got him some water in a soup bowl, but Josh paused for a significantly long time. Ray tilted his head in his direction, more ear than eye. It was pretty hard to tell facial expressions with a wolf's brain, but Josh did not smell happy. When Ray didn't move, his alpha huffed. "Okay, then."

He pulled his shirt over his head and dropped it on the wooden porch beside Ray. Then unhooked his tennis without untying the laces in the way Ray's mum had always complained about—Josh's own mum likely didn't much care—and unhooked the button of his jeans. Before Ray knew it, he was completely naked.

It wasn't like the wolf had any interest in the human body, but it was their *mate*. He stood up as Josh shoved his clothes into a corner and turned around only to fall on four already formed paws. He darted closer and bit Ray's ear—not hard enough to break skin but painful anyway. Then he took off.

Ray didn't think, he just reacted to the challenge and followed. Josh had the head start but Ray was faster so it wasn't long before he could shove his whole body against his mate's and make him stumble. Josh turned around and tangled their legs together, sending Ray crashing to the ground with him and nipping playfully until he managed to get on top of him. Ray snapped right back—a wolf's kind of submission more than allowed for play fighting with his alpha, it encouraged it. An alpha wolf was meant to assert his power over omegas and betas, and this kind of struggle was both the precursor to real fights and what ensured they didn't take place.

Ray pretended to go limp under Josh and used his surprise as a decoy to shove him off and ran away, this time with Josh following instead.

He didn't know for how long they chased each other like pups, but it was pretty dark by the time they made it to the river and stopped to drink. And then they had to catch something to eat, of course.

It was lucky their birth pack had let loose a fair number of rabbits and took care to keep the population down even when they could have simply bought tastier meat. It wasn't as plentiful as deer—which they purchased alive from a slaughterhouse—but it worked better for small groups. Hunting a deer with only one other wolf would have been like asking for a swift kick to the head and, accelerated healing or not, Ray knew from personal experience that concussions still fucking hurt.

He nearly didn't notice Josh was leading him towards the body of trees they called a forest for lack of a better descriptor, but he stopped between two big oaks and whined and his mate gave up the idea. He surprised Ray by coming closer and nuzzling his neck. Ray responded in kind; he was well-fed and happy, and he knew his other mates were home with their pups. He wanted— Josh stepped back and shifted. He ended up sitting buck naked on the grass, blinking fast to try and regain some of the clarity of night vision his wolf eyes had provided. Ray thought he was going to be asked to shift back too, but Josh just crawled over to the nearest trunk and leaned against it before opening his arms in invitation, so Ray went and allowed himself to be coaxed into his lap. "Mmm..." Josh sighed. "You are so warm."

Ray licked his ear, startling him into something very close to a giggle. Josh's grip tightened around him—strong and solid—and Ray settled, happy to give into the soft pleasure of Josh's fingers behind his ears.

He was nearly asleep when his friend spoke again. "I have to tell you something," he said softly—his mouth was so close to Ray's ear that he could have probably heard his thoughts with a little effort—and Ray tensed. "Shhhh..." Josh said, almost in admonishment. "It's okay. You have a choice to make, but whatever you choose, it's okay."

He let the silence stand, rubbing Ray's side with his other hand and giving his heart time to slow down again. "Alec can end the pregnancy," Josh said, a little too fast. He held on fast when Ray tried to move, but only for a short moment, then let him spring away.

Ray didn't go far though, because he suddenly was tangled up in his own clumsy legs. He hadn't shifted unintentionally in a long time, and now he'd nearly not noticed. He turned to stare at Josh, still kneeling on the ground. "What?"

"He can..." Josh stopped. "If you want, he can do it. While you are shifted."

The reasoning was quite obvious: when Ray was shifted into a wolf now, Alec would be able to access... "Because I'm a bitch." He was used to it now, he realised. Somehow, in the months since he'd given birth—had it really been *months*?—he'd forgotten the feel of his own genitals in wolf form.

Josh nodded tightly, his whole expression shuttered. Not that it did much to hide his unhappiness from Ray.

He had been doing his best not to think about the baby growing inside him—*Nicholas's* baby—and now he truly had no choice. He could... He could forget it had ever happened, he could erase all evidence.

Except if he could forget it—the blood spilling freely down Nicholas's neck when the alpha was still buried inside him, the absolute helplessness of having someone else's will push aside his own, the way no amount of washing could ever be enough... If he could have forgotten that, even half of it, a child would not have been such a burden.

And yet, the child was the only thing he had any control over. Alec was going to follow through on his promise and break his vows for real—hurt someone instead of heal them. Maybe he thought of it as healing *Ray*. But Ray knew Alec well enough to see any kind of violence, even the type performed upon an unresisting half-formed being, would cost him dearly.

He thought about having his body belong to him again, empty of all reminders. Clean of all evidence of his betrayal—to his alphas and to himself—and... he *wanted it*. He'd wanted it for as long as he'd been an omega. To be himself again, to be free. From instinct, and responsibility, and fear.

But, of course, it wasn't possible. Presentation was irreversible.

"I can't," he said even as he realised it. "I want to, but—" He met Josh's eyes, brimming with sympathy, and had to look away. "If it... If I'm no longer pregnant and there's no child, I'll go into heat," he explained.

Josh inhaled sharply. "Maybe... Maybe not. We should ask—"

He shook his head. "No," he managed. He couldn't hear any more, couldn't bear any false hopes. "I'm not... I'm not going to do it." He was breathing hard and suddenly profoundly aware that he was naked. That they were naked. He brought his knees up against his torso and tried to slow down his breathing. He was safe. Josh was safe.

"Okay," his alpha agreed softly. "It's your choice," he repeated. It was. At least in name. It was a choice, anyway. Not the choice he wanted to make, but maybe the one he'd regret less. Except... what if the baby looked like Nicholas? If it was a boy... "Ray?" Josh asked. He was holding himself very still over by the trunk. "Just tell me. I don't care what it is, tell me."

"I just... I don't know if I can do it," he admitted, clutching at his knees and trying not to be sick. "Keep it, I mean. I don't— I don't want to hurt it. It's not the baby's fault, but... What am I going to do? Who... How am I going to explain when it grows up and how—" He stopped because he couldn't breathe and suddenly he had a hundred pounds of fur pushing into his arms. He dug his fingers in and closed his eyes tight as Josh pressed close, warm and heavy, an anchor that wouldn't let Ray get lost.

He breathed in the scent of his mate, of safety and comfort, and Josh licked up his tears when they fell, whining softly in place of words he couldn't form until Ray managed to get his breathing back under control. The wolf pulled away slightly, tilting his head at an awkward angle and tugging a little to get free—nowhere near enough to actually manage it—and Ray realised he was asking for permission. He nodded and made his hands unclench.

Josh was kneeling in front of him, hands crossed modestly across his lap like he thought Ray wouldn't be able to stand seeing him naked. It was crazy because he was only half wrong. "Ray," he said, and when Ray didn't turn to look at him he stretched himself awkwardly so that his fingers could trace Ray's cheek. Ray couldn't help but look up and meet his eyes. "Any child of yours is mine, and I would be honoured if you want to tell this baby they are a little more Scottish than they are."

Ray stared at him, heart fluttering in his throat, mouth suddenly dry. He frowned a little, too shocked to really comprehend the words. "You—"

Josh nodded and rubbed his thumb over Ray's earlobe before pulling his hand back. His eyes seemed to shine in the moonlight, but that wasn't why Ray couldn't look away. This wasn't magic. It had nothing to do with instinct. An alpha's instincts were to mate and protect its children—this was entirely human. This was just Josh being Josh and protecting Ray at all costs. Giving Ray anything he might need even if it cost Josh too much. Ray turned his head away, shaking it already. "I can't ask you that."

"You didn't ask me," Josh pointed out reasonably.

"What if *I* can't do it?" Ray countered instead. "What if I look at them and all I see—" He didn't want to say Nicholas's name aloud. He never wanted to see it again—he'd even unfriended the one person from secondary school who shared it on Facebook.

Maybe Josh could feel him retreating because his hand was suddenly on Ray's, holding tight. "Then you don't have to. I'm sure your mum will take them in, or—"

"My mum?" Ray repeated. "You think she doesn't have enough with her own children?"

"Okay, so not your mum, but we can find someone else, there's—"

"You want me to do this?" Ray dared to ask. Josh was silent.

"I will support you no matter what."

"That's not what I asked."

Josh looked down, he seemed... ashamed. He exhaled. "It's... it's a baby. Your baby. I—I don't know what it's like, to be pregnant, and I... I wish you weren't. But I will love them no matter who their other father is because they are yours."

"You *will*..." Ray repeated. He didn't think the choice of tenses was intentional but maybe Josh had heard something in his voice, a certainty underneath all the questioning.

His head snapped up, eyes worried like he thought Ray was criticizing him.

He was talking about loving a child born out of the most horrifying event of Ray's life—and it couldn't rank very high in Josh's. But he wasn't talking about loving Ray. Not anymore.

He'd said he did. But that had been *before*. Now Josh was sitting naked with him in the middle of the wilderness and the only reason he seemed concerned about Ray's nakedness was because he didn't want to freak him out.

And he was right. Because sure, Ray had rubbed off against Sergi, who'd been extra careful to follow Ray's lead at all times, but that didn't mean he was ready.

It was yet another reason he couldn't accept Alec's offer. If he went into heat now, he'd have to decide which of his alphas he wanted to father a child with.

And how could they refuse him even if they didn't want to touch him after he'd been under a strange alpha? Josh had said he *loved* Ray and now he didn't even want to have sex with Ray once to seal a mutual bond. Asking him would be as close to forcing him as an omega could come to forcing an alpha.

He wasn't sure what would happen once the baby was born, but he knew with bone-chilling certainty that he couldn't ask.

Not when he wouldn't know if it would be freely given.

It was just the kind of person Josh was. And Ray loved him for it, but right now he couldn't be sure if Josh's actions were kindness or an act of love; an honest reflection of his feelings or just... pity.

He tugged at his hand in Josh's grip and Josh let go. "I will speak with Alec," he said, just to say something. He didn't want Josh to think he was angry, or disappointed, or... heartbroken.

When he shifted, Josh didn't follow, so he headed back on his own, trotting at first and then flat out running, suddenly desperate to get back home.

Ray didn't talk to Alec. But to his surprise, Alec decided to talk to him for the second time that week. Ray was in his bedroom again—it was just easier that way, if he could be alone, if he didn't need to pretend...

His alpha was clearly determined, but he was still standing stiffly by Ray's doorway—Ray would have bet he'd only closed the door for the sake of Ray's privacy.

"Josh said... He said you didn't want to do it. But I have to ask you; if I'm your doctor... I have to ask you." He must have felt Ray's expression was doubt instead of surprised because he quickly added, "It isn't that I don't trust Josh!"

"I get it," Ray said. "But he told you the truth: I don't want to get rid of it, can't, really."

"I know I'm not a vet, but I'm sure I can—"

"And then I will go into heat," Ray interrupted with a sigh. He hadn't wanted to have this conversation once—to be asked to have it twice...

Alec swallowed. "Eventually yes, but it shouldn't happen all at once. It—your body will need to get back to the beginning of the cycle first."

"Alec," Ray said gently, "I need all the time I can get."

The next pause was even longer and then he admitted, "If you are sure going through with the pregnancy won't make you feel worse, then I'm glad."

Ray didn't have the energy to feel irritated at that—he'd have loved to be sure. Hell, he'd have taken a reasonable hope that he was making the right choice. All he had was reasons not to do it. "I'm not sure of anything. But I think I will regret this less."

Alec couldn't stand that uncertainty, naturally. "Do you want... Is there anything I can do?"

And there was one thing Ray needed to know, too. "You could tell me it's a girl," he requested.

Alec's pulse jumped and he swallowed nervously. "I can try to test you, like we test human... humans."

"I would like that," Ray said quietly.

"We might have to send it to a lab," Alec said thoughtfully.

"Is that dangerous? For the pack?"

"What? No, they'll just think the sample is contaminated, if they even bother to look at what the machine tells them."

Ray licked his lips. "And it won't cost money?"

Alec thought about that for a few moments. "No," he said in the end, "I can get it done for free through the clinic."

Ray nodded.

"If you don't... Just because you have it, you don't have to keep it. Someone could take it if—"

"I know!" Ray bit out. Too sharply.

Alec didn't back down, though. He gave Ray a moment to calm down and then asked, "Can I tell you something?"

Ray glanced up at him, unsure and scared. And a little angry too, because it was almost harder to have to choose this. To have to be responsible for his own pain and discomfort and the way he wanted to crawl out of his own skin and showering had become a shameful obligation. But Alec was truly asking. He'd go away if Ray said no, and yet... He remembered telling Alec that they were too different and that he didn't really know him. He remembered tearing into him just because Alec had been forced to tell him a truth he hadn't been able to bear hearing.

He nodded again.

Alec exhaled, not looking all that relieved, but he licked his lips and started speaking anyway, measuredly, like he was choosing every word very carefully before sharing it with Ray. "I have been... I have been dealing with this all my life. I know it's not easy. I don't... I don't have anything that made me like this, and you do. I'm not saying... It's not the same, but we both need things. Help." He stopped, looking away. "I don't blame you for being depressed."

"Depressed?" Ray repeated. He wouldn't deny he was, but Alec? He didn't seem sad, just... worried.

"And angry," Alec added, clearly thinking of Ray. "You are right, it's all...wrong. It's wrong for you and wrong for us."

"You said you have been like this, like what?"

"Anxious," Alec said softly. "I am... I have chronic anxiety, and... I don't know what else. I'm okay, but I'm not normal."

Ray stared at him, then shook his head, momentarily distracted by the turmoil he saw in every line of his mate's body and face. "That's... but... I mean, aren't we supposed to be healthy?"

Alec vacillated, then he shrugged. "Maybe I'm broken, maybe it's not true."

"You can't be broken if you were born like this," Ray pointed out. "Maybe you're just different, like your eyes."

"My eyes?" Alec repeated.

Ray shrugged. "They're golden?"

Alec blinked at him, seemingly shocked by this information. "Um, I always thought they were a weird hazel."

Ray snorted. "It's weird as in it's very rare, but it's a beautiful colour."

"Oh," Alec said. "Um, thanks."

Ray nodded, then made himself ask, more for Alec's sake than his own, "How do you... How do you do it? Deal with it?"

"I guess..." Ray caught him turning away, towards the corridor, but he didn't leave. "I try not to freak out. And when I know I will anyway, I walk away, go hide in my room." He sounded oddly calm as he described it—like it was a method tried and true, not...

"I was okay before," Ray said, so frustrated he had to dig his fingers into his palms to keep his voice even. He couldn't imagine having a method. He couldn't imagine feeling this way long enough to need one.

"Then maybe... Maybe you try and do the things you did when you were okay?" Alec suggested almost timidly. "Like drawing?"

"Oh, fuck, I never got back to Yamila about the portrait," Ray realised. "I'm such an idiot!" He got off the bed and started rummaging around his desk.

"Ray," Alec called softly. "It's normal to make mistakes when you are particularly stressed."

"Well, then I'm always going to be a fuck up, aren't I?" Ray responded bitterly. He couldn't find his phone anywhere.

Until it started ringing from across the room. When Ray turned around, Alec had it in his hand. He hung up and watched Ray. "It'll be okay," he told him, and he believed it.

"I'm not— I still don't... Like, I believe you, but—"

"I always expect things to go wrong," Alec explained, looking down at the phone. "Even though they only go wrong about half the time. But for you... well, they have gone wrong a lot, haven't they? Of course your brain is going to tell you to be worried. It's what keeps you alive, being worried and careful. Too careful, but it beats the alternative."

"I don't think I can—" Ray started and then cut himself off.

Alec took a step closer, then, when Ray didn't object, another, close enough that he could slowly extend his right hand and place it on top of Ray's. He gave it a beat before squeezing, then turned his hand upwards and placed the phone in it. "Do you remember when we talked about why you were an omega and not an alpha?" Ray nodded, stiff because a part of him wanted to lean closer. He remembered

Alec holding him, too. "You have been taking care of other people all your life, Ray. You need to look after yourself. If you need to end this pregnancy to do that, you have a right to."

Ray flinched. "I can't," he said again, voice thready. "I *really*, really want to. But...It's not the baby's fault."

"Okay," Alec said softly. "I'm not trying to... I don't really want to do it, either," he admitted. "But I love you and I want to take care of you. And—I know what it's like when you can't get out of your own head, when you can't breathe because you can't stop thinking about something that makes you feel so awful you *want* to stop breathing."

Ray sniffed, turning to hide his face. "I want to be okay," he blurted out. "But I don't think I can. I can't... I don't know how I can go back and..."

Alec squeezed his hand again and took a step closer, pausing before placing his arm around Ray. Ray leaned into the embrace and Alec gathered him close, gentle at first and then fiercer. Intent. "We will figure it out," he promised.

And Ray closed his eyes and tried to believe him.

Chapter twelve

The crash from the living room made Ray's heart stutter and he saw his alarm reflected on his mother's face—the echo of so many times as he was growing up and his younger siblings scared the living hell out of them both.

It took his brain a moment to process what had happened when they made it there. Then Glen poked his head out from under the jungle gym and he saw his brother was holding up one of the walls that had become detached from the main structure.

"Glen," his mother said, half disappointed and half relieved. Ray recognized the subtle nuances—he'd learned to, so he could play bad or good cop. It was mostly bad cop when it came to an accident that only resulted in material damage—his mother was strict, but she couldn't get past the relief long enough to be angry that they no longer had a TV or a sofa because TJ or Anne had got a little too inventive with their play.

Jamie slipped past Glen's side and landed on the floor. Ray had left him wearing his onesie, now he was only in a diaper.

It was better than naked, and he could hear all the pup's heartbeats, slightly elevated but steady. He could see it was going to get harder to play bad cop now that he was a parent too.

"Glen, where are Jamie's clothes?" he asked as he pushed the cracked red plastic toy off him and got the other babies out. They were not only okay, but also seemed to have managed to stay dressed.

His brother gave him the wide-eyed look Ray had fallen for so often and he had to steel himself to look serious and wait for an answer. "He... he shifted."

"What?" Ray repeated. "We trained them. They never shift inside the castle."

Glen got to his feet, still a little chubby at six, and shrugged.

"Glen," Martha intervened. "Did you tell Jamie to shift?"

Glen looked up at their mum. "No!"

"Then?" she pressed.

Glen couldn't resist the maternal scrutiny for long. "I... I tickled him. And he kicked it! I didn't know!"

Ray almost burst out laughing, but his mum's face darkened. "And now the castle is broken," she admonished.

"Mum..." Ray started. "It's—"

"No, Raymond, it is not okay," she interrupted. She sounded really upset.

Ray put his hand on her shoulder—sometimes it was still odd that he was taller than her. She turned his way, pulse a little fast and mouth pursed. "They are all fine," he reminded her.

"Maybe I can buy a new one..."

"What?" Ray asked. "No! You didn't break it, and I'm sure Gabriel can fix it. It's made for humans, of course it's not great at coping with werewolves."

That got him a small smile, but she still didn't look convinced. "It's just that you never had nice things like these, and—"

"What are you talking about?" Ray asked, "We had..."

They hadn't had a jungle gym or floaters shaped like sharks, and Ray remembered bitterly when everyone had got into Tamagotchi. They hadn't been that expensive, but he'd known not to even ask when it'd mean buying at least five of them for his siblings.

"We had the pack," he reminded her. "And I totally smashed the trampoline Josh's parents got for him when we got everyone to jump on it at once. Happens."

She frowned. "I thought *Josh* broke it."

"Yeah, well, we didn't want you to get angry and Josh's mum just told him that if he'd broken it, he would have to use his birthday present money to get a new one."

She sighed, picking up Sasha and cradling her close in the same way Ray had seen her hold Glen when she was upset. Sasha happily snuggled into her grandma's bosom, and the others were all busy with the toys scattered across the room. "I never got them anything," his mum said almost shyly.

"Got them anything?" Ray repeated. "Why should you? There's nothing they need."

She met his eyes and almost snapped. "They are my grandchildren, Raymond. Clearly, their other grandparents thought it was appropriate," she added and tilted her head towards the jungle gym.

"Well, Sergi's dad missed them being born because he was in Nigeria. I think he felt guilty."

"I just want—"

"Mum," Ray cut her off, catching Clara as she crawled up the couch in yet another attempt to walk that would end up with her flat on her face and crying. Ray took her hands and held her up as she stumbled forward. Maybe her shoes weren't the best for this, he thought absently. "You don't need to buy them anything," he told his mum, "You are here."

"You will let me babysit more often, then?" she pressed.

"Um, yeah, I guess," Ray agreed, sidestepping to keep up with his daughter. The others would at least follow whichever adult was leading them around—Clara acted as though they were mere accessories and she was in charge of the trajectory.

"Good," his mum declared, "It's not healthy for a young man to be cooped up in the house all day."

The words hit him hard and he knelt and picked up Clara, holding her close.

His mum noticed, of course. "Ray? What is it?"

And he couldn't speak. He pushed his face against Clara's neck and breathed her in, a reminder that it would be worth it. He hadn't wanted Clara either, but he loved her more than anything. He couldn't imagine his life without her and the others.

It would be the same this time if he could only...

He didn't realise he'd been quiet for too long until he heard Marisa's voice.

"Ray?" she asked softly. "Can I have Clara? It's lunchtime."

He looked up and saw the carefully neutral looks on both his mother's and sister's faces. He passed Clara over and stepped back, feeling like he'd exposed his very thoughts by blanking like that.

"Glen, go with your sister," his mother said, then walked up to Ray and put an arm around his waist to guide him in the opposite direction, towards the bedrooms.

Ray let her and she walked him down the hall to his room. *Did she know?* he wondered. Marisa knew, of course, everyone in his pack did. It hadn't occurred to him to ask her to keep it a secret. Maybe it was better if she'd told, really, then Ray wouldn't have to.

His mum made him take a seat on the side of the bed and rubbed his shoulders. "Tell me?" she asked softly.

"I—" he started and promptly choked on the words. He was shaking a little. He wasn't afraid, he was... ashamed.

His mum touched his face softly, not making him look up but offering silent comfort. "You will feel better if you tell me," she promised.

It was a familiar promise—and it had always been true before. But this...

He closed his eyes and took her hand in his, then pressed it against his belly. She stumbled a little closer, then gasped. She didn't pull away or say anything for a long moment. When she pulled her hand away from his middle it was to sit next to him on the bed and hold him close.

Ray turned this body towards her, a part of him desperate for her scent—the same scent he'd always known meant he was safe.

He didn't cry—maybe he'd cried too much already. Maybe a part of him understood the milk was spilt and nothing could be done.

He was conscious that he hadn't told her everything, but he didn't need to ask if she'd forgive him for not being strong enough. He had all the answer he needed in the weight of her hands on his back and steady presence by his side. He was loved and there was nothing to forgive.

He had made the right choice about the baby, he realised. He couldn't destroy something like this, even if he couldn't be half the parent his mum was.

It was almost easy to whisper, "It's not... my alphas'. It's—"

His mum shushed him. "I know."

He frowned, then closed his eyes again. So Marisa had told her. That was fine. It wouldn't have been fair of Ray to ask her not to talk to her own mother about something like this.

"So... we got a little side-tracked and all, but I thought maybe we could try the cinema? New Avengers movie is out."

Ray glanced up from his drawing, body tensing at the idea of leaving the house. He'd left his door open, but now he wasn't sure why. Still, it was too late. Josh was leaning against his doorway, a hopeful smile on his lips. Ray knew he was right, that he hadn't left the house in almost two weeks. The beta wing was pretty much done except for some painting—and Alec had very softly suggested Ray might want to avoid inhaling the fumes—and he hadn't gone further than the back garden in a month.

"Alec will be back at six from work," Josh added. "I know he's your favourite babysitter."

Guilt twisted in Ray's stomach. "It's not..."

"I'm just teasing," Josh interrupted. "You know that, right?"

"It's true, though," Ray said and put his pad down. "And it's pretty shitty of me to feel better if he's with them because I know he can't stop worrying."

"Is it?" Josh asked. "It's not like he would be fine if you didn't ask him to babysit, or if you didn't feel better. At least this way his worrying has a purpose."

"Sure," Ray bit out. "I'm taking advantage of my lover's mental illness, but at least that way it isn't going to waste! Do you hear yourself?"

"Ray, Alec loves to babysit. He has wanted to be a paediatrician forever," Josh said softly, refusing to be baited.

Ray deflated. "It's just fucked up."

"Well, yeah, it can't be fun to be... I don't know what to call it, but it looks stressful." Josh stepped past the threshold. "But I do know Alec cares about you and he wants you to feel better, and for that..."

"Is this, like, therapy?" Ray asked.

"Yes," Josh said easily. "Cinema therapy, we go and stare at a lot of attractive people jump and fly around defeating evil and if you are up for it, I'll take you to dinner afterwards."

Take him to dinner? Ray licked his lips, raising his eyebrows at Josh. "That doesn't sound like therapy."

Josh shrugged. "It'll get you out of the house."

He was right, of course, even if it sounded like a date.

J osh and he had gone to town and watched movies all their lives, and sometimes they'd gone to dinner afterwards. And that was obviously why Josh thought it'd make a good distraction. Also, because there wasn't that much to do in Lanchester.

Ray had given Alec a hug when he'd shown up and taken over the babysitting, and his alpha had seemed surprised but pleased. Ray had even managed not to ask him to check if his phone was charged. Given, it was mostly because Irina, Iesu and Sergi were back and Gabriel was on his way from across the river with Hugo and Yousuf.

But still. The least he could do was trust Alec's... attention to detail.

"M&Ms or crisps?" Josh checked.

Ray was startled to realise they were already at the cinema. "But we didn't stop at Tesco's," he objected.

Josh grinned. "Ah, you of little faith. Check the backseat."

Ray twisted around and saw the supermarket bags in the footrests. "Oh."

Josh had always been able to afford the overpriced treats at the cinema stands, of course, but he'd gone shopping with

Ray and snuck their sweets under their jackets anyway. And he'd remembered now.

Ray occupied himself looking through the bags so he wouldn't have to meet his friend's eyes. Their nascent pack was nowhere near as short on cash as his family had been growing up with a single adult and a little support from the pack, but thrift wasn't a habit one unlearned. It had been a year and it still made Ray uncomfortable to overspend—not to mention Marisa was likely to shout at anyone who couldn't figure out if something was actually cheaper just because it was on sale.

"Thanks," he told Josh, shoving the M&Ms into the inside pocket of his jacket.

Josh gave him a sunny smile. "My pleasure."

They bought drinks inside so they would be hot and made their way to the middle row of seats—where neither their sight nor their hearing would be overwhelmed by the surround sound system and giant screen.

For the most part, being a werewolf gave them an edge over regular humans, so it was easy to forget the world wasn't made for people like them. Once, they had made the mistake of trying to watch a 3D movie and ended up throwing up. At least it had been in Durham and nobody else had witnessed their humiliation.

"Do you remember Durham?" Ray asked as they settled.

Josh made a disgusted noise. "I thought we didn't speak of Durham," he replied in an overly dramatic tone.

"We don't speak about Durham to *other people*."

"Because it's so fun to reminisce about getting sick in a public toilet," Josh said dryly. He passed Ray his phone and Ray saw that it was already ringing.

"What—"

"Therapy," Josh reminded him. "You get it before you need it."

Ray didn't get a chance to object because Alec picked up. He sounded breathless but after a moment it became clear it was laughter and not running for the phone. "Sorry, Ray. Everything's okay, just— Gabriel is singing."

"Is he drunk?" Ray demanded.

"Lost a bet", Alec replied. "Oh, goddess," he chortled. "Marisa told me, but..."

Josh touched his arm and glanced around meaningfully.

"You should record it," Ray told Alec. "Gotta go!"

"I predict a dry spell coming Gabriel's way," Josh said mirthfully.

Ray snorted. It was true that his singing voice was the one thing that could dispel the effect of his cousin's good looks and confidence. "Nah, Alec's too gone on him to care. I bet this bet he lost was a sex thing."

"Doubt it," Josh whispered back.

"Why?"

"Well, I want to respect their privacy and all but let's put it this way: we really need to invest in soundproofing Gabriel's bedroom before the babies get to an age where they might understand what's going on."

Ray turned to look at him. His own bedroom was on the opposite side of the corridor from Gabriel's. "What *is* going on?"

Josh swallowed, licking his lips, eyes flickering towards the screen scolding them for leaving their mobiles on with weirdly disturbing caricatures. "I don't think they need to bet on sex to keep things... interesting."

"So... they are doing kinky shit."

Josh shrugged, and Ray noticed his cheeks were flushed. "Sounds like it."

"But it's... good?" he couldn't help but ask.

Josh gave him a surprised look. "Yes, of course. I mean, the sounds are good. From both of them."

"That's..." He stopped himself. "I'm glad it works for Alec," he settled for.

Josh nodded, then pushed his elbow against Ray's until their upper arms were pressed together.

That was definitely new, but Ray didn't move, allowing himself to enjoy the warmth as the movie began.

They were mostly silent until Josh sighed. "Can Scarlett Johansson be on my celebrity cheat list?"

"Only if she can be on mine too," Ray said easily. Josh twitched next to him and he looked away from the gorgeous redhead onscreen to the gorgeous man next to him. "What?"

"*Threesome,*" Josh hissed, half wistful, half annoyed.

Ray got distracted by the image for a moment, but in truth, it didn't appeal.

Not that he wouldn't have liked to give it a go with Black Widow—or her real-life alter ego—but he didn't think he wanted to see Josh with her.

No. He wanted Josh's attention on *him*.

Maybe Josh could feel his distraction; maybe he was still thinking about the threesome because he twisted his arm until his hand was hanging over Ray's own lap in invitation.

Ray glanced down, then back at the screen—feeling as nervous as a kid on a first date.

He exhaled and put his hand on top of Josh's, squeezing a bit.

He felt Josh shiver against his shoulder, but kept staring at the screen—something was exploding and Iron Man was flying in a way that meant someone else was about to die a messy death.

Iron Man picked up Captain America and Josh extended his fingers under Ray's. Ray cautiously curled his own fingers in the gaps between, effectively entwining their hands.

His heart was hammering too fast and it took him a good few seconds to focus his gaze on the screen again.

It was ridiculous. Josh and he had... Well, they had a child together, for one thing. But that didn't matter to Ray's traitorous pulse.

Maybe it was a part of therapy—Josh desensitizing Ray to touch the way he was trying to get him used to being away from their territory. As if he could read Ray's mind, Josh's thumb curved upwards to caress the side of Ray's hand.

Ray startled a little and lost track of who'd shot whom, but he managed not to look down at their hands. If this was just a technique or whatever, he didn't want to seem... He squeezed Josh's hand. Easy. No big deal.

They held hands the rest of the movie and Josh caught Ray by surprise when he didn't let go even when the lights came on, meeting his eyes while they were still joined. He was smiling, a little nervous but pleased with himself. Maybe he...

Ray licked his lips. He didn't know what to say.

But he didn't have time to think of anything; a female voice came from his side. "Excuse me? Could you...?"

Ray yanked his hand back, scrambling to get out of the way. "Sorry," he said automatically.

Josh looked amused after the lady and her three boys made their way past them, but he offered Ray a hand up with a little bow. Ray took it. He'd take what he could get.

He was a little worried dinner would be awkward after that, but Josh clearly had planned in advance.

"Call," he told Ray as soon as they sat in the car.

Ray was fine, he had been too distracted by the double stimulation of the movie and Josh's light... flirting? to wonder too much what was going on at home.

And he trusted Alec to have things under control, especially with the rest of his pack there.

But he could see Josh's point: if he checked before he worried, his thoughts couldn't wander away from him when he wasn't paying attention.

Still, didn't mean he had to waste the call. He dialled his cousin's number.

"Heard you were putting on a show," he said, not bothering with a greeting.

Gabriel groaned. "He told you?"

"It was more like he couldn't stop laughing long enough to answer the phone," Ray answered with perhaps a little too much glee.

"I do think the punishment is a little disproportionate to my crime," Gabriel groused. "I had no idea Marisa had snitched."

"Well, you shouldn't bet if you don't want to pay up," Ray said, hoping for a hint of what had been at stake.

Gabriel laughed, clearly seeing right through him. "You want to know what the bet was, don't you?"

"Duh." Ray shifted in place, retrieving the almost empty M&M package from his pocket and stopping when Josh put a hand on top of his and mouthed at him. 'Dinner.'

He rolled his eyes at his friend and nearly missed Gabriel's next words. "Milk."

"What?"

"I forgot the milk. He called me this morning and asked me to pick up some because the one we had was spoiled. He told me to write it down, and I said I didn't need to. Alec said if I did, I'd owe him one."

Ray laughed. "Milk?!" he repeated incredulously.

"He's a smart guy."

"And he's got your number," Ray said, laughing a little. His cousin seemed incapable of doubting himself, even when it would have been sensible to do so.

"Yeah," Gabriel admitted. He sounded anything but put off by the idea.

"He promised me a recording," Ray added and hung up before Gabriel could recover from the shock.

He didn't ask if everything was okay.

He was still smiling when Josh found a parking space near the plaza where most local restaurants were.

They hadn't done this as often—when you could hunt your own food and were used to cooking for six people to save up... Well, it seemed stupid to pay ten quid for a pizza for each person.

"So what do you want?" Josh asked, undoing his seatbelt and raising his eyebrows at Ray. The Jeep was old enough that it wouldn't beep if you didn't use them, but neither Ray nor Josh needed to be taught the lesson twice.

"Pizza?" Ray asked.

"You could sound a little less interested," Josh pointed out. "I'm paying, in case it wasn't obvious."

He'd paid for the tickets and the drinks, but Ray had assumed he was using the house funds. They had all decided early on that everyone would keep their own bank accounts and transfer a percentage to the household fund that was under Ray's name. Ray had worked part-time growing up, but he'd had less than 50£ under his name when he'd got... When they'd started the pack. Since then, the account had never come even close to overdraft and Gabriel had switched him to a higher interest rate for people who had regular income they didn't immediately spend.

But it was hard to feel it was his money—even when he was happy to tell Marisa that of course, she could buy period pads and any necessities with the household funds, it didn't feel right to go out and spend the money they could use for sensors, or paint, or...

"You can stop worrying about it so much," Josh reminded him.

"I don't work," Ray pointed out.

Josh frowned. "What are you talking about?"

"I mean, obviously I do things for the pack and I know it's... equivalent or whatever, but it's not like I can say: well, I'm going to dinner and I'll make the money back in one afternoon or something."

"Oh," Josh said. "Okay, I guess that makes sense. You could think whether I will make it back?" he offered. "Like, if it takes *Alec* to make back enough to pay for it, then you are definitely overspending."

Ray snorted. "You can pay," he decided. "Let's have sushi."

"Of course I'm paying," Josh bantered, and opened the door. "It's a date."

Ray scrambled after him.

It took a lot of sushi to satisfy a werewolf, so they went a little crazy and ordered a bit of everything. The starter arrived pretty quickly, but even making a show of tasting every morsel, it was over way too soon. And underneath all the joking, Ray hadn't quite forgotten Josh's throwaway comment.

"You want to call again?" Josh asked him, clearly picking up on his unease.

"No." He placed the sticks on the mat. "I... a date?" he asked.

"Oh." Josh sounded surprised. "Um, if you want?"

Ray met his eyes. "You said... I thought *you* didn't. I mean, after..." He swallowed. He'd thought what Josh had told him before he'd been... taken didn't count anymore. He'd tried his hardest to be okay with that, to concentrate on getting better—getting out of the house, doing the work that needed doing. If before, his feelings had been inconvenient and dangerous to the pack's stability...

"After what?" Josh asked.

"Finding out. I—" He cut himself off, shrugging.

Josh was silent for a long moment, but Ray still didn't look up. It was one thing guessing that Josh might not... might not want to touch him anymore, and quite another to see it on his face. "I want to," Josh finally said. "I never stopped wanting to."

Ray swallowed. He couldn't quite process the seriousness in Josh's tone. Or maybe it was just hard to reconcile it with the facts: Josh wanted to date Ray when he was pregnant with another alpha's child? What did that even...?

"What about you?" Josh asked him, very softly, like he was afraid to push.

Ray glanced at him, frowning. "I... I told you. Yes. I have... I have wanted to for a long time. To..." He waved between them.

"What about it interfering with the pack?"

Ray snorted. "If they can get over this..." he started, glancing down at his middle with a grimace. Josh's hand shot out and grabbed his on the table, squeezing hard enough to get his attention.

"They can, and so can you," he told Ray, his tone allowing no objections.

Ray stared at him, hope and longing warring inside him. "Okay."

Josh's answering smile was like a fire in winter, slowly warming him up from the tip of his fingers to the top of his head. "Good, date it is. Means I get a kiss," he added with a little smirk.

Ray's heart jumped, but before he could respond in any way, the waiter came over and Josh had to let go of his hand to make room on the table for the food.

It turned out there was a way to eat too much sushi even if you were a werewolf with a superfast metabolism. Ray groaned. "Oh, moon, why did I have that tray of California rolls?"

Josh shrugged, manoeuvring out of the parking lot. "Not sure, it's not even real sushi."

"I know, I think there's mayo in them," Ray said, half wistful, half pained. It wasn't often that he managed to push his body past its limits.

"I take it you don't want ice cream."

Ray shot him a look. "What? You want to reach Alec levels of spending?"

Josh snorted. "Nah, just want to look good for free," he claimed with a mischievous look. "You look like you couldn't eat one more bite if I offered *to pay you*." He must have seen Ray's mulish look. "And that is *not* a dare. I don't want any more memories of you throwing up, thanks."

Ray felt full and happy, and a little sleepy too but it was like his skin was buzzing. He didn't think he could actually fall asleep. The question just slipped out, "Are you still angry with me? For asking you to…"

Josh didn't seem angry, he was warm and attentive and even flirting with Ray. Ray wasn't so sure *he* was living up to his best friend's expectations, though. He'd already fucked up once by not asking, he wasn't taking the chance again.

Josh shot him a look as he took the road towards their territory, but he was looking forward again as he responded, "Not right now. I—This is what I wanted." He glanced at Ray again. "I had a good time."

"Me too," Ray said softly. He wanted to ask more. For more. But it wasn't fair to expect Josh to forget the way Ray had asked him to be his First Alpha without even considering Josh's feelings. It felt like poison in Ray's stomach, the guilt like a weight he couldn't shake. But Josh was happy now. Ray was making him happy. "Best date ever," he added in a high-pitched voice.

Josh snorted a laugh, just like he'd expected. "You think you can fake it? I know about all your dates, remember? I know you're telling the truth."

Not that he needed to know Ray's history to figure that out, even though Ray's heart was suddenly going so fast he thought Josh might miss it if it skipped a beat.

Josh stopped the Jeep a little lopsidedly near the house—not like anybody cared where they parked—and turned to meet his eyes. Ray watched him back, heart in his throat, and Josh leaned forwards a little. A question, he thought.

And Ray knew the answer. For Josh, the answer was always going to be yes. He clutched at the side of Josh's seat and pressed his lips against the corner of Josh's mouth, a little to the left of where he'd meant to place them. But Josh didn't move, staying where he was and letting Ray correct his course on his own. And then he let Ray part his lips with his tongue and Ray found that he had his hand on Josh's biceps and his tongue in Josh's mouth, and the stick was poking him painfully in the hip.

He pulled back and looked down. "Manual transmission is protecting your virtue."

Josh laughed. "I'm pretty sure I heard a story about a girl using it as a dildo," he said. He was flushed, happy and... Ray swallowed.

He wanted more, but at the same time, he liked this. Maybe they'd done a lot with each others' bodies already, but they hadn't done this silly dance of courtship. They hadn't taken the time to discover how to be around each other when the idea of touching each other was equally appealing and terrifying.

Maybe their reasons for being wary were different than most people's, but it still felt like there was a tension building between them that would go off in technicolour once they were done resisting it.

Ray wanted to resist it a little longer and when Josh got out of the car, it felt like they were finally on the same page. Their eyes met once more with the Jeep between them and they could have gone around, or hell, jumped over it, but instead, Ray smirked. "Last one to the house is a loser!"

He set off and heard Josh laughing in his wake.

Chapter thirteen

"Um, Ray?" Alec asked softly.

Ray looked up from the computer where he was checking the spreadsheet he kept of the household expenses. He'd known Alec was there, of course, but that didn't necessarily mean Alec wanted his attention. "Yeah?"

"Would you mind if I cut Maria's hair?"

Ray blinked at him. "No, I was thinking about it, but I thought maybe Gabriel wouldn't want to..."

Alec smiled. "He is a little vain about his hair," he admitted fondly. He took a seat on the armchair without asking—which Ray counted as a win. "But he's tired of her crying, and I promised it'd grow stronger if we cut her baby hair."

"Huh," Ray said, intrigued. Was this what had made Alec open up lately? "Did you... I mean, when did this happen?"

Alec's face turned serious and he straightened from his easy posture. "Me and...?"

Ray hesitated, but then forged ahead. He didn't want to make him uncomfortable, but they couldn't have a relationship if he did that by never talking to the guy. "Yeah. I mean, he said he trusted you when... when we started this pack. But you guys never used to talk. I thought you were afraid of him, really."

Alec scoffed. "More like ashamed," he said quietly. "He...
I met him in a club in Durham when I was at uni; he didn't
even realize we were from the same pack, but it was almost
the full moon, so..."

"Wait, are you saying...?" Ray stared at him. "There's no
way you guys have been together all this time!"

"What? No, that's not... we haven't. We were for a while,
sort of, except... I presented."

"Oh, fuck," Ray exhaled. For all that Sergi and Iesu had
pretended otherwise, alphas weren't really meant to do
anything with each other except get each other off when
they were moon-high and there were no omegas or betas
available. "Did he...? Was he a dick about it?"

Gabriel was doing much better lately—likely due to
Alec's influence—but kind as he could be, he was too set in
doing to really consider other people's feelings first.

But Alec shook his head and sighed. "No, actually, I
was."

"You?" Ray asked, and maybe it was a little offensive to
assume that Alec *couldn't* be a dick. It wasn't even true; he'd
been so worried about Ray that he'd often not been able to
hear what Ray had told him he needed.

The alpha shrugged. "Thanks, I guess, but I think most
people are dicks because they're scared, so I'm pretty good
at it. I thought he wouldn't want to... keep going, so I just
stopped answering his calls."

Ray thought back to his own presentation. He'd have
definitely stopped answering calls if it had been an option.
"Can't blame you. So when did it start again?"

Alec didn't answer for a long moment, but then he seemed to think of something because his face cleared. "He came to me to find out why we didn't need you," he said very carefully. He couldn't keep his gaze on Ray but kept glancing at him for a reaction.

"That's... nice of him, I guess."

"He cares about you," Alec said, sounding reproachful.

"I know, I know, it's just... I'm still a little angry about him leaving the babies. Can you get that?" Alec nodded. "So anyway, you didn't know why, so what happened?"

"We... Well, I needed to talk to other omegas, get an idea of how it really worked, so he got them to talk to me. And then he also asked if I could measure babies."

"So it's been like... a month?" Ray guessed.

Alec glanced at him, vacillating, but finally, he said, "A month since we kissed, about two months since we started investigating."

"Oh, so..." Ray licked his lips, looking at the screen in front of him and noticing it had gone black to save energy. "You figured it out pretty fast."

"Not fast enough," Alec said at once.

Ray looked up and put the laptop on the low table. He wanted to comfort Alec, but he wasn't very sure he wanted to touch him. "You had no way to do it faster," he reminded him firmly. "And I'm grateful you figured it out when you did, that you... that you gave me a choice about it."

Alec didn't look up from his own hands clenched between his knees and Ray couldn't resist any longer, he leaned forwards and squeezed them. Alec startled and nearly pulled away. But he exhaled and stayed put—not looking at Ray but allowing him into his space.

"Dammit," Ray muttered. "I didn't want to freak you out. I was just trying to gossip."

Alec let out a half-muffled laugh. "Gossip? Really?"

Ray raised an eyebrow at him. "Oh, do you call it 'gathering data', doctor?"

Alec gaped at him, eyes bright. "You—"

"I just can't imagine how you get on with him, he's so..."

Alec's face fell. "Ray, he's really trying. He only—"

"No!" Ray said at once. "I mean *in bed*, he's very... well, alpha about it. And you are an alpha too, so..."

That seemed to shut Alec up. He crossed his arms over his chest, pulling his hands away from Ray's touch. "I'm not. In bed."

It took Ray a moment to put that together in a sentence that made sense. "You are not very alpha in bed?" he asked quietly. He'd suddenly remembered Josh's comments about soundproofing Gabriel's bedroom... And that they were in the living room. He concentrated on the sounds coming from the house, but there was no one moving around. It was just after lunch on a Tuesday, so the babies were napping, and Marisa was probably watching Shameless with her headphones on while she kept an eye on them.

He heard Alec swallow, but he nearly missed it when he spoke, "No."

"Um, okay. That's... good," he tried. "If you guys..."

Alec shot him a look, exasperated. "I always thought I would be an omega."

Was he jealous of Ray? The idea nearly made him laugh. Nobody who had been watching his life could imagine it was a better one than that of an alpha. "Well," he replied. "You dodged that bullet."

His mate looked away again, seemingly at a loss for words. "I know I hurt you when I... I know you didn't want to... to submit." Ray didn't confirm it. He thought it had become obvious to all of them by now. "But I... I didn't want to dominate you."

"Oh," Ray exhaled. He remembered that Alec, who was second oldest, had been the last one to... "Did you... did the wolf...?"

Alec shrugged. "Mostly, yeah. I mean, you are... You are beautiful, of course I'm attracted to you."

"But you didn't want to fuck me," Ray said evenly. The idea didn't upset him, but it did confuse him. Maybe it was stupid. *He* hadn't wanted to get fucked. "But then why did you join the pack?"

"I told you; I'm gay. I wanted..." He met Ray's eyes for a moment but couldn't hold his gaze. "I wanted a family and I wanted a partner and the chance of another male omega presenting in my lifetime..."

Ray swallowed. "Do you regret it?"

"What?" Alec seemed perfectly shocked. "No! I—"

"I guess you have Gabriel now," Ray allowed.

Alec's hand closed over his forearm and he looked up in surprise. Alec's jaw was tense with the effort of facing him, but he didn't look away as he spoke, "I do not regret becoming your mate."

It was true. It just didn't make a lot of sense. "But if you don't..."

"Ray," Alec said quietly. He didn't speak until Ray stopped trying to. "I love you, okay? And I want to take care of you. And if you wanted to, I'd enjoy making you feel good."

Ray swallowed, not quite able to look away from Alec's golden eyes. "I'm trying to get better," he admitted suddenly. "Before..." He glanced down at himself.

Alec nodded. "That's good. Do you..."

Ray shrugged, thinking of kissing Josh. And of Sergi letting him take the lead. It'd felt good, to know he could, and to be able to be in his body instead of constantly flinching from it.

Of course, he hadn't known *just how* fucked he was back then.

Alec's grip turned into a caress, thumb rubbing against the delicate skin of Ray's inner arm. Ray let him, drawing comfort from this single point of contact, this very controlled experiment. "Had you ever... been with a guy?"

Ray shook his head.

"Wanted to?" Alec asked next, failing to hide his apprehension.

Ray nodded, shrugging a little, not enough to dislodge Alec's hand. "I'm... bi, I guess."

It was weird to say it. He'd thought it before, he still remembered learning the word and making sense of it, making sense of how close he felt to Gabriel and Josh, and how his eyes wandered to the back of girls' necks, the dip of their blouses... "I just figured... it was too much trouble. Guys."

It hadn't been guys, really, it had been *a* guy. Not like he hadn't checked out kids at school or considered going a little crazy during the full moon run, but... He'd thought, if he was going to go there, it wasn't going to be for a random grope.

"So, do you... do you know what you like?" Alec asked.

Ray's head snapped up at the question. He hadn't expected...

Alec was blushing a little. "I mean, it's okay if you don't want to—"

"No," Ray cut in, it seemed easier to interrupt Alec than his other alphas. Maybe the wolf could tell Alec didn't care? "I mean, I don't really..."

"Do you want to be in charge?" Alec offered, keeping his eyes lowered. He had a lot of mannerisms improper for an alpha, which Ray had known, of course, but he wondered...

"I don't know," Ray admitted. "I mean, girls always... they kinda expect you to be in charge, I guess. And it's fun, to lift them up and play the strong man and everything. But I didn't... I didn't like it that much if they just lay there or whatever. I wanted them to... to be into it, like, touch me back..."

"What do you want to do now?" Alec asked, redirecting his thoughts.

"Does it matter?"

"Of course it matters," Alec sounded upset, but Ray couldn't look at him to check. "I mean, you don't have to tell me," he hurried to assure him. "Just... maybe it's something to think about. On your own, without any pressure from pheromones."

"But I'm still an omega," Ray pointed out.

"Yeah, but it's not like the Moon is going to meddle in your thoughts, what would be the evolutionary purpose of that? You get turned on for alphas so you can have sex with them and conceive, and then so they will stay around and protect you. The rest of the time... you are just you."

He said it so simply, like he had no idea that Ray had been wondering for over a year. "How do you know?"

Alec met his eyes, unsure, as if he understood how important the question was to Ray. "I was like this before, with... with Gabriel. And I was... I'm still like that. And I'm still... I still worry a lot, but the wolf doesn't care. It wants to hunt and to run and to..." He lowered his eyes.

"I get it," Ray said, putting him out of his misery. "But how do you know it's not making you, I don't know, care about me?"

Alec glanced up, frowning a little. "Right now, it doesn't even want to mate with you, Ray. If you wanted the perfect way to check if my feelings for you are my own, this is it. You have my bite and you are pack, but anything else... It's not the wolf."

He sounded oddly calm, nothing like he'd sounded a few minutes ago explaining he didn't really want to push Ray down and fuck him. And if he knew that... if he could tell the difference between his wolf's instincts and his own desires... Maybe he was right; maybe *Ray* could tell.

"You can..." Alec started, then stopped until Ray gave him a curious look. "You can talk to me about... about Josh. Or boys. We can gossip all you want," he joked.

"And kiss?" Ray asked on impulse. He wasn't sure he wanted to, but he definitely liked the way Alec blushed, and it was fine anyway, Alec could hardly hold his hand without asking for permission. "Will... Gabriel mind?" he asked when the alpha didn't respond right away.

Alec took his hand away so he could rub at his own knees. "I don't think so," he said distractedly, but he was frowning.

"It's cool, I was just—"

"No, I want to, but..."

Ray leaned in close and pressed a peck to his cheek. "It's fine, really, I was just trying to flirt. I'm not very good at it."

This made Alec snort. "You or me?"

Ray shrugged, smiling easily now. "I guess we can both be bad at it. It would explain a lot, right?"

Chapter fourteen

He had honestly believed presenting had been the end of his sexuality as it was. It'd been so sudden and so absolute, he hadn't even been sure what to mourn. Women? Choice? Being the one doing the fucking? He'd had sex for the first time at sixteen with a classmate he'd been calling his girlfriend for a couple months, and after that hadn't worked out, he'd done things with a few other girls. Well, two other girls.

And that was it. Then it had become all about what his omega wolf wanted, and what Ray felt...

It hadn't mattered, but it'd never stopped existing, he realised. But what Alec had said made sense: outside of heat and away from an alpha, the wolf didn't crave sex.

And Ray did.

It was just the inside of his own head and the touch of his own hand, but it felt like being offered a banquet of limitless dishes to try. He could fantasize about whatever he wanted, and he didn't even have to stop any thoughts about Josh for fear of giving himself away later.

He started with women anyway, because it was safe and familiar and because he thought he'd lost it forever. Also because Scarlett Johansson was on his celebrity exceptions list and she was smoking hot—it was a fantasy, but technically it could happen. He didn't think alphas would care much if their omega slept with a human. He stroked himself slowly, making it last, letting it build until he was trembling a little and only then tightening his grip.

He arched off the bed and made a mess, which anyone with a nose would be able to smell right away, but he closed his eyes and let himself enjoy the afterglow for a few minutes longer before he got up to shove his sheets into the washing machine.

And because reliving his preteen years at nineteen wasn't embarrassing enough, Irina was in the laundry room making piles of clean clothes to go to each bedroom. She definitely had a nose and she barely kept back her smirk. Ray didn't know enough about her to tease her, so all he could do was set the machine on and walk out with a flaming face. He should ask Iesu for some dirt on his cousin—there had to be more to Irina than a tough, efficient woman who loved kids and football and was particularly bad at putting up with alphas' bullshit.

The next day, he used the bathroom instead. Naptime was really ideal to spend a little solo time—his sister was like a clock with her show and because she wanted the quiet time, she made sure all the babies were asleep. He didn't want to have any other awkward encounters so he checked the timetables on the fridge door. Soon they'd need to buy a bigger fridge to fit them all, even if the betas had another one in their kitchenette. Hugo was off work, but, of course, the betas had a bathroom in their wing now so there was little chance of his newest beta deciding he needed the one next to Ray's bedroom.

He'd been saving this fantasy since the night before when he'd barely been able to get to sleep after a quick jerk in the shower after dinner—he couldn't be selfish when the five of them were sharing two bathrooms and everyone else had an early morning ahead of them. It wasn't anything fancy, just a man kneeling at his feet and letting him fuck his mouth. Well, not a man, Gabriel. It was a little... humiliating, he could admit that. And it was a lot about how Gabriel had made *him* feel when he'd... It wasn't something he wanted to happen. He didn't want to make anyone feel like that. No matter how badly they'd fucked up—he didn't want to touch anyone real with that in his head. But it didn't hurt anyone to get some of the anger out this way, and it was *hot*. He pictured pulling on Gabriel's long blond hair, twisting his left hand to keep his neck stretched so Ray could shove his cock down his throat. Gabriel's blue eyes wide and tearing a little as Ray pushed in too fast for him to quite draw breath.

He didn't last long after that. He leaned back against the wall of the shower and his elbow bumped against his belly. It was hard already and the sensation made him jolt upright with a vicious swear. He couldn't— He turned off the shower and went out without even trying to shake off some of the water.

Didn't matter, he needed to clean the toilet anyway.

He was halfway through scrubbing the sink when there was a knock.

"Ray?" came Marisa's voice. "You okay? You have been in there for ages."

"I'm fine. Cleaning!" he called out too loudly. Marisa obviously could hear him perfectly well through the closed door when standing on the other side of it.

"Okay," she said easily. "I'm making some tea, want some?"

"No," Ray said, then remembered to add, "thanks, I'm good."

Her silence went on too long for her to have been fooled, but she did go so he'd count it as a win. They were okay now, his sister and he, and they would be okay as long as she gave him space—it was good she got that.

They hadn't had any visitors except Ray's mother and siblings since... It would have been fair to say Ray was hardly in the mood for the Gosdens. Ray had never really liked his aunt Serene. She wasn't really his aunt, not by blood and not by marriage, but of course, that didn't matter much when someone was pack. Werewolves were old hats at adoption and although a parent-child bond was still strongest, Ray had grown up indifferent and mostly unaware of how much blood he shared with other members of his family.

He'd called Gabriel his cousin without really knowing what it meant and hadn't bothered thinking how true it was until he'd started looking at him a little too closely. Fortunately for him, their connection was thin: their grandparents were siblings.

So it was definitely not about the fact that Serene had been born in another pack and Nathan Gosden had swept her off her feet and brought her over thirty odd years ago. Ray liked Nathan even less—where Gabriel was charming and good-natured in his extroversion, his father was... too much. Ray wasn't sure if he tried too hard to impress others or if he didn't try hard enough to tone it down.

Nathan probably didn't even know he needed to tone it down, he thought as he saw the man shake Alec's hand too hard. It was an alpha technique to establish seniority and superiority over other alphas and Ray had seen it all around him growing up—but he couldn't help but resent someone making his mate uncomfortable in their own territory.

Alec might not have wanted it, but by being a member of Ray's pack, he had seniority while in their land and being older didn't mean Gabriel's dad got to waltz in and challenge that. Ray saw Gabriel easily place himself between his father and his lover. It wasn't an outright challenge but couldn't possibly be read as anything but a warning to back off.

Nathan chuckled and backed a step, powerful shoulders shrugging off the unspoken reprimand. "And where's this omega of yours?"

"*Ray*," Gabriel corrected. "Not like you haven't met him."

"Sure," his father agreed, completely missing the point. "But I haven't seen him in a long while. What's the problem with asking?"

Ray had been hanging back, but he stepped forwards now. It didn't matter that Nathan was an alpha, this was *Ray's* territory and *he* wasn't planning on letting the man forget. "Hey, Uncle Nathan."

Gabriel's father grinned. "There he is." He gave Ray a once over and even though he'd dressed in a loose hoodie to hide his condition, Ray couldn't keep from shivering. "Heard congratulations are in order," he added.

Ray's heart skipped a beat. Nathan couldn't know, nobody outside his own pack knew—except his mum. And nobody would tell a stranger... And that was what Nathan Gosden was now.

What he'd always be, if he thought presenting omega was something to congratulate him for.

Ray didn't know what he might have said if Irina hadn't stepped in with a big, cheesy smile. "Here's the little princess," she announced in a voice so syrupy it made Ray turn to check it was actually her. Nathan took a step away from the baby and caught his wife's elbow. Suddenly, it occurred to Ray that his uncle might have been speaking about his daughter, not his condition.

It didn't make Ray feel much better—Maria's existence hadn't been his decision—but it probably meant the man hadn't meant any offence by it.

Serene spoke up for the first time. "Oh, dear, look at her, she's a *darling*," she said sweetly. She was sincere in her admiration as far as Ray could tell. A moment later it was confirmed when she frowned and added, "But who cut her hair off? I remember my boys' curls when they were this age, they looked like little angels."

"They looked like girls," her husband grumbled, and Ray forgot all about his possible good intentions. Serene didn't seem to hear—which must have been an essential skill around her husband—and extended her arms for Maria.

Irina's reluctance to pass her over endeared her to Ray even more than the timely interruption. When the beta warned Maria's grandma that she sometimes became a wolf unexpectedly, he could barely hold back his laughter.

Serene seemed quite shocked, even though Ray remembered Anne had done it too. Had she somehow trained Gabriel and his three younger brothers out of shifting even when they were toddlers?

He looked for Gabriel and found he was talking to his father a little way off—with Alec next to him, way too close for alpha protocol. Hell, he was actually leaning his side against Alec's. Alec seemed acutely aware of it, and Gabriel totally oblivious. Except, of course, even *Ray* knew it, there was no way in hell both Gabriel and his alpha father didn't know it too. *What was Gabriel doing?*

He wondered if this was some sort of game the two of them were playing, but if it was, shouldn't Alec have looked okay with it? There was liking submission and there was looking like you wanted to bolt. Ray glanced at Serene and Maria; the older woman was gurgling at the baby, making her smile. Ray had always found the way she was silent unless spoken to and the way she only seemed to have an opinion on domestic matters off-putting, but he hardly imagined she was planning to run off his with his daughter.

Irina met his eyes. "Should we get the others and give them a chance to run around for a bit?" she asked Ray. Because Gabriel's parents had only asked to meet Maria—and only six months after she'd been born, at that—the other babies were still inside.

He thought about it. "You will stay outside with them?"

"Sure, and Marisa will come along. Only approved babysitters," she teased him lightly.

He nodded. "Thank you."

Ray really needed to do something for the betas to show them how much he appreciated their help—he certainly had way too much to do to also care for his children on his own. He turned towards Gabriel. He'd hooked a finger in one of the loops of Alec's trousers. Alec, of course, was about to vibrate out of his own skin.

Ray didn't interrupt the conversation between Gabriel and his father, just sidled up to Alec. "Hey, need your help with something."

Alec should have felt him approach but he still jumped a little. "Yeah," he said at once, trying to cover it up. Ray stepped away and he followed, forcing Gabriel to pull his hand away rather awkwardly. Alec didn't seem to notice he'd done it and Ray used the excuse of lowering his gaze in an appropriately submissive manner to avoid Gabriel's startled look.

They didn't speak as they went up to the house. Once there, Ray gave Alec a moment to decide which way to head and the alpha went for his own room. Ray followed him in there and closed the door.

Alec was sitting on his bed, his fingers pressing against the skin of his forehead, back bent forwards and breathing a little ragged.

"Do you want me to leave you alone?" Ray checked, and Alec raised a hand and waved a clumsy denial. So Ray took Alec's ergonomic desk chair, leaning indulgently into the cushiness of it. He should get one himself, he thought idly.

"Thank you," Alec said. His hands were on his lap, but he still wasn't looking at Ray.

"What are mates for?" Ray asked, earning himself a little look. But Alec couldn't seem to think of a response. He was just fidgeting in place, so Ray got up and went to sit by his side, pressing them together from shoulder to thighs, but keeping his hands front and centre. "I take it he didn't ask you if he could do that."

Alec shook his head. Ray huffed. "That's shitty."

"I... I said it was okay with me if you guys knew," Alec explained. "I think— maybe I said pack? Maybe he thought..."

"Oh, come on." Ray turned to look at him, and slowly placed a hand on his forearm. Alec leaned into the touch. "Don't do that. He was clearly trying to—I don't know, one-up his father."

Alec snorted. "You think his father would think being with me..."

"Well, maybe not, but maybe Gabriel does. Maybe he thinks if he is with you, then he's won because he did whatever he wanted, not what his father told him to."

"That doesn't sound bad," Alec pointed out, meeting his eyes. "That sounds like he... like he chose me."

Ray thought about it, about Gabriel defying all expectations and moving out of his parents' house before finding a mate, about him finding a mate so late in life and inviting his alpha ex to join him... Was he doing all that because he wanted to show his father he couldn't be controlled or because he simply wanted all those things even though he shouldn't have? But that wasn't the point, anyway. The point was that he'd made Alec feel tense and scared; he'd forgotten to think about his feelings and needs.

That wasn't what an alpha did. And it definitely wasn't what a lover did.

"He should have asked you what you wanted," he told Alec firmly.

Alec exhaled a little shakily, then surprised Ray by turning his torso towards him and sliding his free hand around Ray's shoulder in a loose hug. "Thank you for rescuing me," he said and shocked him even further by placing a soft kiss on Ray's cheek before pulling back.

Ray stared at him. "What are you going to do?" he asked. It was an easier question and he did want to know.

Alec's heartbeat had evened out. "Tell him that," he said simply.

There was a knock at the door and Ray listened. It had to be Gabriel...

"It's not him," Alec mouthed at him. "Gabriel won't leave Maria alone with strangers."

Ray shot him a look as they got up. "Strangers?" he repeated. "They're his parents."

Alec shook his head. "They aren't pack and—" He stopped himself.

"It doesn't matter, I'm going to go get them inside," Ray said and opened the door. He gave Irina a smile and she responded with a long-suffering look.

"Marisa and Gabriel are there," she informed him at once, so matter-of-factly he didn't even feel embarrassed by the rush of relief. "But they aren't very happy about it."

Ray risked touching her arm lightly. "Thanks for the rescue," he told her, echoing Alec.

She seemed surprised but nodded. "No problem, Ray."

"Hey," Ray said when Iesu told him to come in.

Iesu was laying half on top of Sergi, using his phone with his left hand and shirtless. Ray wasn't sure if he was really that hot all the time or he just liked showing off his considerable assets in the arms department.

He smiled when he saw Ray. "Come in, and sit down, you're giving me a neck ache."

Ray glanced around but with the big dresser the alphas shared there was no room for chairs or desks so he went for the bureau and hoisted himself up. He was still pretty high up, but Iesu didn't complain, blinking sleepily at him. "What's up?"

"Well, remember how you told the betas there would be football?" he asked. "I think it's time we deliver. I was thinking this Sunday we could have a match."

"Oh," Iesu sprang up. "Ray, you're a genius!"

"It was your idea," Ray pointed out, sharing an amused look with Sergi, still flat on the bed and seemingly disinclined to move or talk.

"Whatever, I'm a genius, but you reminded me of my genius so you can be a genius too," Iesu decided. "So, we need at least ten players. Will your sister play?" he checked.

"Marisa? No, Anne likes to but she's not big enough. There's TJ, if you need an extra body, I'm sure he'd come for football and meat."

"Meat? Oh, you want to have a barbecue, too?"

"Well." Ray shrugged. "We *are* werewolves, I figured food couldn't hurt..."

Iesu gave him a toothy grin for that. "See? Told you that you were a genius."

Ray rolled his eyes at him. "Anyway, who else?" He tilted his head. "Sergi?"

"I'll play."

"Okay, so Sergi, Irina, you, Gabriel and Josh. That's one team's worth."

"You're not playing?" Iesu asked softly, his face oddly blank.

Ray sighed. "I—I don't know. Maybe I shouldn't?"

"We could ask Alec," Sergi offered. "Do you want to?"

Ray vacillated, not because he didn't know the answer. He wanted to play, of course, but even worse than not being allowed to would be not being allowed to and having the alphas feel sorry for him. "I'll ask," he said instead.

"Okay, so TJ, Hugo, Yousuf. Will Kaylee play?" Iesu asked with a doubtful look. It was understandable. Kaylee, the last beta to join them, was a little older than Marisa but so quiet the pack often forgot she was in the room. Ray had known her all her life and she'd always kept to herself, never much joined in when the pack's children played together.

"Don't think so, but I'll ask her," Ray decided. "Maybe there's something else she'd like to do. I want the betas to know how important they are to us."

"You are good at this," Iesu commented admiringly.

Ray huffed. "Good? I'm making it up as I go. Irina was nice enough to rescue me from Gabriel's dad, least I can do is pay up with a football match."

"Well... I could ask my sister and brother," Iesu suggested. He must have seen on his face that Ray hadn't known of their existence, and he waved it away at once. "Please don't. What are you meant to do? Create a pack, corral five pups, organize a household *and* learn all of our family trees? It's fine. They're older than me. Sorina is twenty-eight and Codrin is twenty-six. We all played football together, Irina, me, and Irina's two brothers."

Ray did the math. "So your sister was an adult when you guys came over?"

Iesu smiled. "Yeah, and thank god for that. My parents... I mean, they had the pack and everything, but they needed to speak English to talk to humans and it turns out they are not that good at learning languages that aren't Russian."

"Russi—" Ray started to ask, then stopped himself with a frown. "Wait, Soviet Union, right?"

"Yeah," Iesu smiled, sounding pleased. "Someone was paying attention in history class!"

Sergi kneed him in the side. "Stop teasing Ray and get some paper, you'll forget half of your brilliant ideas the moment he walks out of the room."

Iesu turned to shoot him a look but did as he was told, rolling off the bed with effortless grace and getting a notebook out of the first drawer with a little tap to request Ray's permission to raise his leg high enough to reach. He set it down next to Ray's hip and started writing, silent for the first time since Ray had walked in.

"So, we have a team," he said after a moment. "And we're inviting your mother and siblings, of course."

"You could ask your parents, too," Ray suggested. "I haven't seen them since they came to meet the babies."

"Mmm... I'll ask," Iesu allowed. "Josh's folks?" he asked, even as he turned to the bed and raised his head to Sergi. "Yours?"

Sergi shrugged. "You can ask, they might have plans already."

"From what Irina said, Gabriel isn't keen to see his parents again anytime soon, but I think we better ask, we don't want a grumpy wolf."

"Alec's parents would probably come. They really seemed to love Jamie."

Iesu raised his head to look at Ray. "And you don't mind that?"

Ray gave him a blank look. "He is their grandchild. It's not like they were rude to anyone else."

"Okay," Iesu agreed. "I'm going to go ask Marisa about the food. It might not fit in our budget or something," he added with a sigh.

"We can just each give her an extra tenner or two from our personal accounts," Sergi suggested. "Not the betas, of course, just us. Should cover a little extra food and drink and people won't show up empty-handed anyway."

"Yes!" Iesu exclaimed. "I swear, geniuses all around," he said dramatically, then jumped on the bed and tried to tickle Sergi, startling the other alpha into a jerk that ended with him getting an elbow to the chest. He whimpered a little and Sergi leaned over him to check he was okay, which he turned out to be because he used Sergi's nearness to coax him into kissing him better. Slow and sweet and private, except Iesu had initiated it right in front of Ray.

Sergi let it continue for a few moments, seemingly unable to pull away, before he gave Iesu a half-hearted shove and rolled away. "One track mind," he complained.

Iesu followed him off the bed but turned towards the door and the chest of drawers next to it. He gave Ray a red-lipped smile and pecked him on the lips as he passed. "Gotta go. Don't do anything I wouldn't do!" he warned them cheerfully.

Ray felt himself blush and then the door was clicking shut.

It took him a moment to gather the courage to look at Sergi. The alpha was watching him intently. "You don't mind, right?"

Ray shook his head. He'd been a bit of a dick about it when Sergi had first asked, mostly because asking Sergi to make out with him to help him get over his trauma had made him feel vulnerable as hell. "Nah, it's... it's fine. I don't want to come between the two of you."

Sergi crossed his arms and leaned against the far wall. "You wouldn't. It was nice, but I know it's not... I get I'm not the one you want to do this with."

"That's not—" He stopped. "It's not like that, I do want to... to do stuff with you. And Iesu too." He shot Sergi a quick look, unsure of how he'd take that. "But Josh..."

"I get it," Sergi insisted patiently.

"Okay, so you see how I couldn't ask him for that. I couldn't... His feelings for me... I mean, I'm not saying you don't care, but Josh and I... It's too much. It would have been too much to have that when I didn't even know if I could follow through."

"I get that," Sergi repeated. "I'm fine with it."

He was telling the truth. "Good, because you are... You really helped me." Ray made himself look him in the face for that, even if it wasn't necessary for Sergi to know he was telling the truth too.

Sergi's smile was a little weak, but it was there. "Glad to be of service."

"Excellent service," Ray agreed. "Now I see why Iesu puts up with you."

That actually made Sergi laugh out loud and Ray decided it was enough confessions for the day. "Ask your parents," he said as he jumped off the bureau.

"Hey," Josh said, walking into Ray's room. "Heard you're throwing a party!"

He sounded way too pleased for a football match turned barbecue, and when Ray glanced up from his commission, he saw he was grinning widely. Ray's heart stuttered a little in his chest. He looked down at the paper, pencil hanging uselessly from his right hand. There was no reason to make a big deal out of it, and much less to get flustered by Josh's excitement—it had nothing to do with Ray and everything to do with Josh loving a good party. "Yeah, wanted to thank the betas and I think I promised them all football when I invited them to join, so..."

The door clicked shut and he nearly dropped the pencil. Josh was leaning against his desk, smelling of sunlight and a little fresh sweat, and Ray wanted to look up—except he felt flushed and he didn't want Josh to think— "It's on Sunday," he said to stop himself from thinking, "You're not working, right?"

"Nope." He stretched his neck to peek at Ray's pad.

He had agreed to a more regular timetable at the gas station and he'd promised Marisa he would stop taking extra shifts when his co-workers failed to show up. He couldn't exactly tell humans about their five kids, but Josh had always been creative, and he'd managed to explain he needed regular hours to help his family with childcare without quite explaining whose children he was looking after.

Ray nodded and started straightening his desk rather than risk ruining his work with his suddenly clumsy hands. "Are you thinking of working with Gabriel maybe?" he asked, just for something to say.

"Mmm... Yeah, but, dunno, he is a bit of a pain about the whole thing? And I want to do things well, sure, but maybe I don't care that much if it's not my own house?"

"That makes sense," Ray agreed.

"The money is a little better," Josh pointed out, bordering on shy.

That made Ray look up just so he could roll his eyes at him. "Oh, come on, 1k a year isn't going to change anyone's life. Not now."

Josh shrugged and looked around. Ray assumed he was looking for somewhere to sit, but in the end, he just stepped back and leaned against the wall next to the doorframe. He looked like something out of a photograph, lit just right so that his eyelashes shadowed his eyes and his arms were exposed in all their glory across his chest.

Ray thought he might have said something, but when he looked up, he just caught Josh's frown. "Am I... Is this not okay?"

Ray frowned in turn, confused until Josh added, "You are all... You seem..." Josh waved in his direction, swallowing thickly. "Uncomfortable."

"Uncomfortable?" Ray repeated. The idea seemed absurd, but then again, he was half-hard in his underwear just from having Josh in the same room as him. That wasn't exactly comfortable, either. "I guess, I mean—"

Josh took a startled step away. "Should I go?"

Ray gaped at him, then pushed down his fear and got to his feet. Josh didn't look away from his face, which was rapidly flushing red. It was up to Ray to break their gaze, too overwhelmed to hold it while he... exposed himself. Because he wasn't naked, not even close, but even though Josh had seen it all and more, this felt like much more of an admission.

"Ray?"

"Are you going to make me spell it out for you?"

Ray didn't look at him, but Josh must have looked at Ray. *Really* looked this time because Ray could hear his little gasp of surprise. "Oh. I—I didn't know."

"Yeah," Ray said gruffly. "So, I can't keep my mind out of the gutter. Sorry about that, but you shouldn't think... That *you* are making me uncomfortable."

Josh, to Ray's shock, let out a breathy laugh. Ray glared at him and his friend raised a hand, laughing again. "Sorry, it's not— Not laughing at you. Just... I was so worried and..." He inhaled, still grinning. "I'm happy. Because this was definitely not me. I wasn't thinking about anything like that."

"Oh," Ray said. He was too confused to keep his interest, but that reminded him of something. "Alec said something... I mean, I guess I knew but... He said the wolves don't care about me right now, not sexually, so everything... Like, what I'm feeling is what I'm feeling. And it's the same for you."

Josh smacked his own face hard enough to make Ray wince in sympathy. "Oh, fuck, that guy is smart, why didn't we think of it like that?" he asked with a grimace.

Ray shrugged, then walked up to the window to give himself a little cover. "And I have been thinking— about what I want," he added, staring at the line of the horizon outside, sun on its way down making everything hazy and surreal.

"What do you want?" Josh asked very slowly. His heart was giving Ray's a good run for its money.

Ray licked his lips. "Everything," he said. "I just... I never got to do anything with you when I was... myself, so... I don't even know what I like. I mean, I know what I *think* I like, but..."

"I get it." Josh exhaled, a burst of air Ray could feel on his skin all the way across the room. "We can... We can do that."

Ray turned his head just enough to see him out of the corner of his eye. "There's... I know you want to go slow for my sake, but I'm not sure I will be okay with doing anything when I'm..."

"Bigger?" Josh guessed and sat on Ray's lonely chair—near the window for good light but far enough Ray could walk out of the room without even brushing by him.

Ray gave a shaky nod.

Josh huffed, crossing and uncrossing his arms. "I just—What if I don't know when to stop?"

But Ray had an answer ready for that. "We will decide first, and you can stop anytime you want and check with me." Josh frowned, obviously trying to come up with an objection. Ray tried very hard to believe it wasn't lack of interest but the opposite. He needed to believe that, even if he didn't trust his own judgement, he had to trust Josh wouldn't lie to him. "You can even order me to tell you the truth."

Josh's chair legs scraped against the floor as he almost overbalanced. He stared up at Ray. "I'm not ordering you to do a thing," he hissed, body coiled tight, face pinched.

"Sorry!" Ray said quickly, turning to face him fully again. "It was just an idea."

Josh huffed. "If you can talk about it with me first... and we decide what will happen in advance, then... okay." He met Ray's eyes. "I trust you not to let me fuck up again."

Ray exhaled, heart beating too fast. "I trust you too," he told Josh.

Josh nodded as if to further confirm their words and stumbled a little as he got up because he didn't take his eyes off Ray. *Was he...?* But he didn't step closer but away, towards the door. "I have to..." He stopped. "Do you want to go out again? Friday?"

Ray's heart skipped like he was a teenager being asked to dance for the first time, but he made himself pause and think through it.

"I don't remember my schedule," he admitted after a beat. He kind of barely remembered his name, the way he felt under the weight of Josh's gaze, with the tension of holding himself back against the windowsill instead of crossing the room and touching him like he clearly wanted to be touched.

Like Ray wanted to touch him.

It seemed to take Josh a moment to understand Ray's words and when he did, he laughed. "We're like old people, aren't we? Maybe I should ask your secretary?"

Ray laughed too, mostly at Josh. "I'm pretty sure most people our age have a work schedule, mate."

"I'm pretty sure," Josh echoed coyly, "that your boss will change your day if you ask."

Ray tilted his head and gave him a thoughtful look. "Yeah, but she'll make me do another shift at a weird time."

Josh shrugged, still smiling. "Yeah, but it'll be worth it. You need to get out more."

Was this the carrot or the stick? Ray wasn't sure. He wanted to be with Josh. Hell, he wanted to go out—he didn't like being cooped up inside all the time—but he was scared of it too. He tried to ignore the fear in the back of his brain. It wouldn't be so easy to convince his wolf it was safe to leave when it was time, but the wolf didn't care about thoughts. "Will it?"

"Make me a list," Josh replied.

"What?"

"A list of things you... you might want to do," his friend explained, gaze flickering away from Ray and face growing visibly flushed even in the low light. "With me. And then..."

"You can choose one?" Ray guessed.

"Yeah," Josh agreed. "And we will... We will talk out the details. If you want."

Ray snorted, then promised, "I want."

Josh managed to give him a jerky nod before fleeing, but he didn't need to say anything, not when he was standing right in front of Ray. Ray had heard his pulse stutter all the way across the space between their bodies.

He closed his eyes and leaned back against the glass, letting the shocking cold bring him back down to earth. Alec was right: there was nothing about this the wolf cared about; all it could think of was that Ray owed it a meal—he was starting to be hungry all the time again—and all Ray could think about was the list.

Still, he was going to need time to think about it and he was a little less pissed off at his animal side than usual, might as well reward them both with a snack.

Chapter fifteen

There was no reason to be nervous. They were going bowling like two middle-aged men who mostly liked to win and couldn't quite cope with anything more exhausting—sadly, Ray probably couldn't.

He liked the give and take a competition allowed them, the teasing and the back and forth where it didn't quite matter whose quips and jokes landed because it was all about keeping the energy going between them. Keeping the connection between them. It had always been about that. If they were more similar than not, it wasn't natural inclination, but an inability to let go of that instant kinship they'd found in each other way before they knew what bonds were.

They had called it friendship for lack of a better word, but it had never compared to the casual relationships Ray shared with other members of his pack, or his schoolmates. Maybe he could have said Josh was his only real friend, but now that he had his own pack, he was slowly learning his way around a friendship of sorts with his other alphas—learning who they were and what they needed, revealing parts of himself that he'd always hid and trusting them to care for him when he was vulnerable. *That* was friendship.

But had things ever been like that with Josh? Had it ever felt less intense than it did now? He didn't think so, he didn't think it was hormones talking—either his own or the magical type that had arrived later. He hadn't always wanted to kiss Josh, but he'd always wanted *Josh*. His attention, his company, his... He'd wanted to know he was important to him. No, not just important, *special*.

So hell, maybe there were about a hundred reasons to be nervous about bowling.

"You ready?" Josh asked, startling him enough Ray fumbled his phone.

He was smiling a little smugly when Ray looked up after having caught it by dint of superhuman reflexes. He got up, choosing not to respond to that smile—he couldn't quite manage to be annoyed and he definitely didn't want to encourage him by smiling back like a dolt just because... "All set."

Josh glanced around. "Do you want to...?"

Ray shook his head. This time, he'd planned more carefully. Maybe he couldn't stop worrying about leaving the pups behind, but at least he could take care of the practical matters on his own. He was an adult and he'd been more responsible than most grown-ups by the time he'd started growing facial hair, he wasn't going to accept getting catered to like he was sick just because life had thrown him a bit of a curveball.

"I already talked to Iesu and Alec, they are staying in," he explained and started for the door.

"Iesu and Alec?" Josh asked, sounding puzzled.

Ray shrugged. It was a bit of an odd combination, but he figured the alphas had all found ways to talk to each other—maybe Alec let Iesu do all the talking and just made noises to signal he was listening—when he wasn't around. Neither of them had given him any reason not to trust them and if he didn't rely on his alphas and his betas, it wouldn't take any real threats to send him over the edge.

"Sergi is having dinner with his parents," he explained. "I think he wants to ask them to come on Sunday."

"And the rest?" Josh asked as he patted his jacket to check for his keys. Ray smiled—like he ever removed them except to turn on the Jeep.

Ray waited him out. "The betas are around, but they are free. Gabriel isn't back yet, but I figure, it being Friday..."

"Pub crawl with the crew," Josh finished sagely.

Gabriel was undeservedly famous among his co-workers for being able to hold his drink. Ray guessed it worked well with Gabriel's image as a guy who got shit done and was ready to work hard. That much was true, but it was funny because when they brought out the real booze they distilled for the pack, he was actually kind of a lightweight for someone so tall and broad.

"Yup. We are probably safe in the bowling alley," he added, allowing himself to check his phone was charged for the tenth time in the last ten minutes.

He nearly dropped it again when Josh took him by the elbow and started leading him to the door. Ray bit back a comment about the dangers of startling people with sharp claws when his friend darted a nervous look his way. *He was nervous too.* A shiver of delight ran down Ray's spine at the idea.

The whole arm-holding thing was crazy old-fashioned, but it was also nice—close enough to Josh dragging him around with an arm around his neck, but much more comfortable than the straight friend version. There was nothing sexual about linking arms, naturally, but it wasn't something guys did with each other. Guys were obviously idiots, half-strangling their friends so they wouldn't look too affectionate or something.

As they approached the car, Ray twisted his hand so he could trail his fingers down Josh's exposed forearm. Josh shivered and Ray smiled—he was enjoying this new freedom to touch maybe a little too much. Josh must not have minded either because he stayed put until Ray let go to get into the car.

It did take him long enough to get in that Ray wondered if he wanted Ray to drive again, but in the end, he didn't ask for anything, just watched Ray intently for a moment before opening the door.

"Alec said I shouldn't play on Sunday," Ray said before he lost his nerve. He wanted it done with and then he wanted to think about something else. Something he *could* do.

"Football?" Josh guessed, pulse spiking. "You mean... Fuck, I'm sorry, that sucks."

"Yeah, well..." Ray shrugged. Next time, he'd make sure to enjoy his freedom while he had it. He did have the advantage of an in-home team at his disposal, after all, and he'd get to train the babies as soon as they could walk, too.

If Clara grew up to be half as fast on two feet as she was on four...

"Maybe we can play something else?" Josh suggested, interrupting his daydreams. "I'm sure I have my table tennis table somewhere in my parents' garage."

"I'm not going to make everyone give up football because of me," Ray bit out, shoving his seatbelt a little too hard into the fastener. *Table tennis.* Irina would probably start a beta rebellion if he tried that...

"What?" Josh's eyes darted towards the noise, but he wisely didn't mention it. Maybe he knew Ray already felt bad about being rough with Josh's precious car. It was just an inconvenient reality for them all that human-built objects weren't meant to withstand the casual anger of supernatural muscles.

Josh started the engine with his eyes on the empty path leading out of the house. "We don't need to give up football, just add some other options. I bet Anne and Harry would appreciate something they can play with the rest of us, for starters."

Ray pushed down his unreasonable anger. He wasn't less angry—he loved playing football and he knew Alec was right that he was all too likely to get a fastball to the stomach—but it was a good idea. It was something. And it was true the kids couldn't have played with the adults. It was just like Josh to take care of everyone and everything.

It wasn't his fault Ray didn't want to be taken care of.

Josh reached over to take his hand and Ray let him, relaxing his shoulder and curling his fingers around Josh's. His hand was soft, softer than when he'd been helping build the house. Ray wondered what it would feel like to be touched by him now...

"Thanks," Ray made himself say. He glanced out the window, watching the green hills pass them by as they picked up speed. And at some point, he became aware that his palm was a little sweaty. Or maybe Josh's was? For some reason, it seemed to matter that it wasn't his own.

Handholding was primary school stuff. He didn't even remember the first time he'd held a girl's hand and he couldn't believe it'd set his heart racing like this. But this was Josh, in the Jeep, like a million times before. Like a million times again.

Josh wasn't a choice he could unmake or chance he could take. If this didn't work out... If Josh let go, Ray wouldn't be able to handle it. He didn't see how anyone could: they were too close, in too many ways, and letting go wasn't just hard, it was impossible. How was he supposed to live like that? He couldn't hold onto Josh forever.

He could never let him go. *Josh* could never let him go. There was no taking back a mating bite.

And it should have been more than enough. It should have been *too much*, a trap Ray wanted to escape. But instead, it wasn't enough because he didn't want Josh's promise that he'd stay and protect Ray no matter what. He wanted to know Josh *wanted* that. He wanted Josh to love him and love required the ability to stop.

But he couldn't ask for that.

Josh tugged at his hand. "What are you thinking about? I can hear your brain going in circles."

More like his heart having a panicked race, but it didn't really matter how Josh knew: Ray didn't want to talk about it, talking about it was just another way of asking Josh to promise him something Josh had no way of guaranteeing. "Kicking your arse at bowling."

Josh could tell he was lying, but he let Ray change topics anyway. "I think you are forgetting my three consecutive strikes," he replied after a moment, taking his hand away to park the car into a tight spot. Ray clenched his empty hand shut—it was still sweaty but a little cold now.

Somehow they'd made it to the bowling alley and he hadn't even noticed.

"A strike is a strike," he said, trying his best to sound normal. "Doesn't matter if you do them in order or not. Points are the same."

"My fans disagree," Josh said, getting out of the car.

Ray snorted and pushed his door open. "You mean your teenage followers?" he asked and it came out a little harsh but Josh didn't complain. "Did you ever get your Facebook back after they all decided to follow you?"

Josh shrugged as he stepped away. "Whatever, I don't like Facebook."

Ray laughed a little. He couldn't help it, Josh was such a marshmallow around kids. "Nobody does; doesn't mean it's not sad that a random group of teens made you stop using yours."

"Maybe I should start again, share baby pictures," Josh suggested, hanging back to let Ray catch up with him.

Ray gave him a reproving look. "Maybe don't flirt with anyone today and we will be okay."

He couldn't tell if the baby pictures would announce Josh was taken and off-limits, or just make him look more approachable. Possibly, the forbidden element would make him even more appealing in their eyes.

Josh shot him a look from under his lashes. "No flirting?" he asked with a pout. "On a date? Am I also not allowed to touch any balls in bowling?" he added with a little dip to his cadence that made it clear he did not mean marble ones.

Ray swallowed—not quite able to decide between laughing and blushing. He could do this, he thought. He stopped walking and shoved his hand into the pocket of his jeans, bringing out the folded list he'd spent half the week agonizing over.

He waited until Josh stopped and took a step back towards him before he offered it to him. Josh looked wary, but he took the paper. His hand was warm when his fingers brushed Ray's. His eyes were too wide, but he didn't look away from Ray's—almost like he couldn't. "Is this...?"

Ray licked his lips. "I figured... let's get it out of the way. Or, like, you can look at it when... while I'm winning," he added a little weakly.

Josh glanced down, then met Ray's eyes. "Or I look at this and forget which way to roll the ball," he suggested.

Ray shrugged and took the last three steps towards the door, holding it open until Josh recovered enough to catch up. "That works too, I guess."

His heart was beating too fast again. But at least he wasn't worried about the kids for once. Josh had asked for the list, he reminded himself. And he hadn't even...

"Catch," Josh said suddenly and Ray barely managed to take hold of the deodorant before it flew right past him.

"*Josh*," he complained. "You could have hit someone in the face!"

"Pay attention then," Josh replied with a warning look.

Of course Josh could tell he was thinking too hard.

"Hot dog and Coke?" Ray offered as they got to their lane. They hadn't needed to wait because Josh had called in advance and made a reservation, like... Well, like it was a date.

They still needed to spray their shoes if they had any chance of putting them on without doing an interpretative dance to wiggle their feet in without getting their faces anywhere near them. Ray passed the deodorant back.

Josh raised his eyebrows. "Leaving me with all the hard work?"

Ray shrugged, then surprised himself with a joke. "Fumes are bad for me, remember?"

Josh looked so shocked by the comment it was very nearly worth the niggling discomfort of talking about *it*. Then Josh rolled his eyes at him. "Whatever, get me ice."

Ray inclined his head at him and turned for the bar.

When he got back with the food, Josh was weighing the balls to find the heaviest. He had his shoes on already and he waved at Ray to put the food down. "Sit."

Ray shoved the plates onto the table and took a sip of his Coke as he raised his eyebrows questioningly.

"So... I can do it," Josh explained, waving at the second pair of shoes. "And go wash my hands, like, three times, or we can risk our hot dogs getting stolen while we go to the toilet to scrub under our fingernails together."

Ray gaped at him for possibly thirty seconds before he couldn't hold back the laughter anymore. "Okay, whatever, you wanna play the prince, go for it." He flopped down onto one of the cushioned seats and lifted a sock-clad foot, leaning back to look down his nose at Josh because it was either play imperious noble or think about the embarrassing fact that Josh was so close to his feet.

Josh took hold of his ankle and pushed the shoe on, then did the other. Ray took no offence at the way his nose was wrinkling. He looked ridiculous but cute, and even with his fingers pinched around his nose, Ray could tell the rental shoes were pretty rank.

"That makes you Cinderella," Josh pointed out once he got to his feet and could bear to open his mouth again. Maybe his hands were still too close to his face because he grimaced. "I... Don't run away."

"That's my line!" he called out as Josh did just that.

Josh hit a respectable eight pins on his first go. Ray whooped, making him turn to glare. His second ball went straight through the gap and he came back and sat heavily, muttering, "Cheating."

"Yeah, sure," Ray agreed, taking an enormous bite of his hot dog and giving him a toothy grin that had to be at least a little gross. It made Josh laugh and Ray got to his feet with a little more spring than was probably deserved before he even had a go.

He weighed a deep red ball, but went for a black one, in the end, closing himself off to the harmless noise of the people of all ages daring each other, eating, exchanging food and shoes with equal speed. He could only see the pins in front of him, and the lane, shiny brown and framed by the gutters.

He already knew his centre of gravity had started to change, but he'd learned to compensate during his first pregnancy and what could a single one compare to five? He stepped forward with his left foot and swung. The ball didn't bounce at all, the force of the swing going into the roll pushing it forward, straight for the pins...

"Strike!" Josh shouted before he had a chance, sounding as joyous as if he'd done it himself.

Ray stared at the fallen pins, already being pulled up, before turning with a grin. Josh looked ready to hug him. But suddenly that felt like a bit much. He walked around the table, avoiding his friend's path. "Can you do better?" he asked with a smirk.

Technically, nobody could do better but Josh managed a strike of his own and the view from the seats was pretty great.

"Not bad," Ray told him, eyeing him appreciatively.

"Oh, fuck off," his friend replied. Ray thought he might have managed to make him blush a little, but Josh wasn't looking at him as he asked, "Can you manage another?"

Ray didn't respond, just shrugged and cracked his knuckles. He was faking the confidence but his body didn't seem aware of it; it just fell into position and there he was with two strikes in a row.

Josh managed another as well and licked his lips, raising his eyebrows in challenge when he crossed Ray on the way back to his seat.

That was not why Ray fumbled his next go, of course, but Josh's smug expression said he thought otherwise. Ray flipped him the bird and sucked hard at his Coke, making sure to twirl his tongue around the straw as he pulled back without looking away.

"Dick," Josh muttered, and he only managed to down nine pins, which meant if Ray did, he'd win. Josh walked back and leaned over where Ray was sitting at the table. He was close enough but he didn't touch Ray. Instead, he met his eyes and whispered, "I'm going to read your list now that I'm done."

Ray felt himself flush. "You—"

He decided not to finish that and stalked to the lane before he remembered exactly what he'd written. He checked the weight of the ball and the position of his feet and by the time he realised he was overthinking it, it was too late. He still won, just because he'd started—they were even in points.

Not that he cared much once he turned around and saw Josh staring intently at the paper in his hands, climbing pulse audible even in the crowded room.

He swallowed, looking up to meet Ray's eyes when he felt him watching. "Ah... this is... long."

Ray cringed a little, taking a step closer but keeping the little table between them. "We don't have to... I just... It's only ideas. I told you: I never got to try anything. And I wanted... I wanted you to choose what you liked."

"No, I— I get that." Josh stood up, looked at the paper he still held like he didn't quite know how it'd got there, then folded it back in four and put it in his inner pocket right where he kept his keys. "Should we go get some proper food?" he asked, not looking at Ray as he picked up the empty food packages and headed for the bin.

His pulse was already slowing down by the time he returned to get his jacket so Ray nodded.

"Wait," he had to ask once they'd swapped their shoes. "Toilet."

Josh seemed confused because they'd just toed off their shoes and used napkins to put them on the counter. Their own didn't smell of roses but their own scents were pretty easy to ignore.

Ray didn't explain why his toilet breaks were starting to get too close together again. If there was a way to fit talk of his bladder into a date-appropriate conversation, he didn't know it.

He went to the toilet, washed his hands with the heavily scented soap and his face with water, slicking his too-long hair away from his eyes. He felt a little more settled when he came back. Josh had looked at the list and he didn't think Ray was... crazy, or a perv or something.

It couldn't have been more than five minutes, but he found Josh chewing again. "Are you eating another hot dog?" Ray asked with a dubious look. He liked them as much as the next guy but they'd had three each already. Josh shrugged, visibly struggling not to laugh. "Are you making a dick joke in your head now? Seriously?"

Ray snorted and took a page from Josh's book, grabbing his elbow to steer him towards the exit. It was nice, innocent but close. "It's good I like you because you have less game—"

"Hey," Josh complained, elbowing him gently with the same arm Ray was holding on to—basically just making them sway in place a little and look like they were drunk at six in the afternoon.

Ray laughed, clutching at him for balance. "Stop!" he demanded. "We look like idiots."

Josh kept walking, dragging Ray instead of the other way around. "Not you," he said seriously. "You look hot."

Ray tensed a little and Josh turned to give him a look even as he opened the door and loosened his hold so Ray could walk through first. "Can I say that?"

Ray opened his mouth to respond when someone coming in jostled him. The guy was big but he barely moved Ray half a step. Of course, he'd done it right in front of Josh and Josh had tensed like he'd punched Ray in the face. Ray had to take a step closer and tow him out of the doorway before he went in after the arsehole and taught him that not everyone shorter than him was there for him to shove out of his way.

Josh didn't insist, just muttered a series of names they were not supposed to say around the children. It was still pretty odd to see a laid-back guy like Josh get angry that fast—all their lives, that had been Ray's thing.

Ray supposed it was what being an alpha got you, and the jerk was lucky Josh's wolf didn't consider Ray his own at the moment. The idea hurt a little; even if every logical part of Ray knew he didn't want to be owned, he couldn't quite drown the parts of him that wanted to *belong*.

"Ray," Josh said after a block Ray had spent wondering if he should try and hold his hand again. It was pretty dark and he didn't think either of them were interesting enough to catch anyone's eye, but still, two guys holding hands was bound to— "You said... well, you wrote what, but not... where."

"Where?" Ray echoed, frowning. He'd figured a bed would be involved.

"Well," Josh licked his lips. "I just mean that I don't want to... If there's something you don't like, I don't want you to remember it when... when you are alone. In your room. So..."

Ray didn't really care. He could put up with an awkward moment or two and he already knew Josh would ask more than he wanted to be asked anyway. "We could go to your room," he pointed out.

But Josh shook his head and said, "Let's get some takeaway. What do you want?"

Not food, Ray thought. But he'd take it, if Josh needed some time, to think about the list or... When he shrugged, Josh led the way to their favourite Chinese restaurant—cheap and quick and guaranteed to give them portions worthy of werewolves. Ray got out a twenty to pay and Josh didn't say a word about it—maybe he was happy Ray felt he could spend the money, maybe he got how awkward it would have been if Josh had paid again for something this cheap after he'd sprang for a whole sushi dinner last time.

They talked a bit about the menu—like they hadn't spent a whole summer trying everything on it—and then about whether they could try and cook some of it. Or more likely ask Alec if he felt like experimenting in the kitchen because the rest of them were only good at a couple easy dishes each.

It felt like it could have been any night out of hundreds like it... and then Ray stumbled a bit, forgetting about the unnecessary step right outside the shop, and Josh's hand shot out to hold him steady and it didn't feel anything like a normal night anymore.

He swallowed, meeting Josh's eyes and feeling the strength of each of Josh's fingers through his shirt and jacket like they were digging hard enough to draw blood. "I'm okay," he said, instead of stepping back.

It took Josh a little longer than it should have to let go and look away. "Be careful," he admonished, pointlessly.

Ray didn't reply. "So you want to eat out here somewhere?"

It wasn't that cold for them but November was cold enough for humans that the benches outside the local pub would be deserted. Josh shook his head, though. "Let's go to the car."

Maybe the list hadn't been such a great idea. Josh was so tense... so different than the last time they'd gone out. Ray wanted to have sex, of course, but not if the cost was this high. That had been the whole reason he'd never said anything before.

"Hey," he said once they were seating in the Jeep. Josh slanted a look at him. "You get that it's just ideas, right? You can say no. I *want* you to say no if you aren't into it. This isn't all about me."

Josh shrugged, then started rubbing at the leather gearshift between them. "I don't want to say no," he said softly. "But... I need to know I can. I need to know I will stop, and I'm..." He exhaled, frustrated.

"You are not sure," Ray finished for him. "Well, *I* am. And I'm happy to show you. Just drive us somewhere we're not going to get interrupted by your fan club."

Josh snorted, glancing up with grateful eyes. "Maybe I can promise to upload some pictures if they leave us alone."

"Ugh, gross, they were like fourteen."

Josh laughed, manoeuvring the Jeep out of the tiny parking space. "We were sixteen, remember?"

"Whatever. I'm not into exhibitionism."

Josh didn't answer. Ray checked the road first, which was nearly deserted, and then Josh, who was still quiet and staring ahead as if he was certain he was going to be required to evade a stampede in the next three seconds. "What did I say?"

"We—When we..." Josh stopped and Ray realised his grip on the steering wheel was close to dangerously tight. He definitely had the strength to break it if he wasn't careful.

Ray exhaled, feeling his own heart speed up at the mention of his first time with his alphas. "Look, let's stop here, just slow down and park it down on the side."

Josh gave a shaky nod and the car slowed to a stop at the next open side of the road. He let the Jeep roll over the grass for about fifty extra meters or so—far enough from the main road to be safe.

Ray wasn't sure if Josh was ready to hear it, but he didn't want this to detour their whole evening. "I did not enjoy that," he said clearly. "But you knew that already," he reminded him. They had spoken about it, and Ray had thought...

"Yes," Josh admitted between gritted teeth. "I know, but—"

"The exhibitionism was the least of it," Ray explained. He didn't mean to be cruel, but he was done protecting the alphas' delicate sensibilities. "I didn't even feel... I didn't feel like *I* was having sex. It was the wolf and... Goddess, it *needed it*, and I wanted to stop but it was like wanting to stop drinking when you are parched, only worse. I can't even—"

"Is that how it felt with..." Josh cut himself off before saying the name and the only reason Ray could keep himself from growling at him was that he caught his flinch.

"No," he bit out, but it didn't sound quite right. "Yes, I— I had more control, and then I lost it. I wasn't in heat so it was just him trying to—to push me down. Like, in my head, not just— And then the Moon rose enough or something and he managed. I couldn't stop him but not because my wolf wanted to... to do it. It just didn't have the strength not to submit."

Josh let out a slow, wet breath. Ray didn't look at him. If he was crying... "I'm sorry," Josh said, nearly inaudible but from the bottom of his heart. Ray could feel it in his bones. And then he added, "If there was *anything*—"

"No time travel," Ray interrupted. "Just getting over it."

Josh turned his head towards him but Ray didn't, refusing to meet his eyes. He'd said too much already, and

Josh could even *hear* him panicking, he couldn't... "How can I expect you get over that?" Josh asked.

"Me?" Ray sighed. "*You* need to get over it. I know it was an accident. I know all of you; you wouldn't have gone ahead with it if you had understood. If I had known... If we hadn't all believed we had to do it right away, and we had to let our instincts guide us..." He shrugged. He didn't want to bring up his uncle now—when he'd first understood how completely the man who had been his First Alpha all his life had abandoned him to his fate, he'd been hurt. Now, he could only be grateful he wouldn't need to hide his hatred.

"So that's it? We are forgiven?" Josh asked between gritted teeth.

"*I* have forgiven you," Ray clarified, unhooking his seat belt and turning to meet his eyes. It made no difference to Josh's ability to tell if Ray was being truthful, but he wanted him to *see*. He'd lost too much already; he wasn't going to lose Josh. "It doesn't sound like you have."

Josh looked away and this time he was definitely wiping away tears. "This is not the kind of thing you can just apologize for."

"No? So what's this? Blood sacrifice level?" Ray gritted out. "Offerings under the moonlight?"

"Ray!" Josh snapped, eyes bright still. "I'm serious."

"I'm serious too," Ray told him. "If saying sorry is not enough, and me saying I'm over it is not enough; what do you need to do to feel better?"

"I..." Josh looked away, then met his eyes rather timidly. "Whatever you want. I'll do whatever you want, whatever will make you feel better."

Ray gave him a tired smile, leaned in and plucked the folded-up list from the pocket of Josh's jacket and offered it again. Josh followed the movement with his eyes. "You should choose," he said without even looking at the list.

But that was a sacrifice, not what Ray wanted. If Josh wanted to atone, he'd have to do it by helping Ray feel better, not by making himself feel worse. And no matter how badly Ray wanted an egalitarian relationship, there was no way in hell he was putting anyone through anything even close to what he'd been through. Revenge was just violence dressed up as justice, not the real thing. And there was no justice anyway; neither of them had deserved to be put in the position their bodies and their pack had put them in.

"No," he said easily. "We are not doing an eye for an eye. We are trying not to fuck up again, remember?"

Josh nodded. "Okay, sorry." He took the paper and opened it. He licked his lips, flushing a little as he went through it again. "You didn't write if you want to... give or receive."

"Oh, either," Ray said. "Well, mostly both."

He'd done some of it already, of course, but it didn't feel that way. He'd done it either during heat or under the heavy haze of an alpha's arousal.

Josh folded the list again and leaned towards the passenger side to put it carefully into the glove compartment. Ray stayed very still as their arms brushed, waiting for a decision that felt vital.

"Um, the back okay?" Josh offered.

Ray didn't bother with words, just opened the door and hoisted himself up onto the bed of the Jeep. Josh followed, holding himself up by the arms until he could climb in without touching Ray. Ray didn't comment on the fact that Josh had never had a problem rolling on top of Ray before. In a way, it made sense to be shy about touching each other when they were *planning* to do it, when it'd be more than comfort, and more dangerous too.

"Maybe we should have brought a bottle to spin," he suggested wryly when they were both kneeling, watching each other awkward and unsure like they hadn't done a lot more than kiss.

Josh laughed and it echoed oddly in the quiet of the night. "Come here," he asked, and Ray crawled closer until he could bury his face into Josh's neck and put his arms around him. He knelt, not wanting to climb into Josh's lap without asking. Josh held him, rubbing his back slowly. "Handjobs," he said into Ray's ear, trying to keep his voice even. And failing. "That okay?" Ray nodded against his shoulder. "What... what position?"

Ray froze for a moment, suddenly uncomfortable, but Sergi hadn't minded, and Josh wouldn't either. Ray knew he could trust him.

"I need to be on top," he said slowly. He couldn't quite manage to explain that it was more about the fact that he didn't want Josh to be on top of him, but it wasn't... It was obvious. If you knew what had happened. And the last thing he needed was to think about that or he wasn't going to be in the mood ever again.

"Sure." Josh carded his fingers through his hair, a slow sensual massage, until Ray tilted his head back, moaning a little. And then Josh's hand travelled lower, towards his jaw until he was cupping his face at the perfect angle to lean down for a kiss; soft, tentative, until a hint of wetness made Ray groan and push with his own tongue and everything got messy and desperate—too much teeth, and too fast, and he wanted *more*.

Josh scrambled to keep hold of him, and Ray swung his right leg over both of his lover's and used the leverage to send him tumbling down on the bed of the Jeep. He froze for an instant, but from the way he moaned and shoved back against Ray's thigh, it was clear Josh didn't mind.

He sucked on Ray's tongue, clinging like he had no higher ambition than letting Ray try to devour his mouth. "Ray," he panted and Ray pulled back just enough to let him talk. It made his eyes cross to look at him from so close but he could barely bear even that much distance. Josh's fingers clutched at his back hard enough to bruise and his face was red. "Clothes?"

For a moment Ray blinked at him, uncomprehending. He glanced around. "Being arrested doesn't sound too hot," he hedged. He couldn't quite tell how visible kneeling would make his growing belly. And even if wasn't too obvious, wouldn't Josh feel it...?

Josh half laughed, half groaned. "Can *I* see you?"

He shifted on his elbows, trying to find a way not to put too much weight on Josh. "Shirt stays on," he decided. His eyes travelled down Josh's neck to his open collar. He had the first three buttons of his dress shirt undone, exposing some of his light chest hair. Ray had seen him shirtless countless times, but he couldn't keep from picturing following the trail much further south. "I want... I want to see you."

Josh squeezed his eyes shut, shuddering under him. "You can see me all you want," he breathed out and arched his hips in a languorous thrust that made Ray whimper and shove back without thinking.

This wasn't handjobs, but if Josh was happy being a little flexible, Ray was too.

Josh had seemed shocked by how many things Ray had included in the list, but he'd said everything and he'd meant it. He'd only left out fucking for Josh's sake. He didn't know if he could ever enjoy the act after what had happened to him, but he wasn't willing to give it up without trying—especially if there was a way it would make heat feel less like an out-of-body experience.

Then Josh pulled on his right knee until he bent it further and Ray found himself kneeling over him. The reasoning became obvious when he felt the button of his jeans pop open. Josh stopped there, glancing up at him. But Ray didn't want to follow a step by step program—he didn't want Josh to be thinking about how fucked up he was while they were... This was about *them* and there was nothing fucked up about the way Josh made him feel. He pushed his cock into Josh's hand and leaned forwards to swallow the sound his lover made when he felt how hard Ray was in his jeans.

Josh unzipped him and then he was sliding his hand into Ray's underwear and taking hold of Ray's dick—already leaking a little and hard enough he couldn't hold back a sound of relief. Josh's other hand tightened on his forearm as if he could bring Ray closer somehow without smashing all their bones in the process. Ray thrust into his grip, not thinking about angles or the laws of physics, just *wanting*. He pulled his mouth away to lick at Josh's teeth, then his chin, his neck, until Josh started wanking him in earnest and all he could do was clutch at his shoulders and tremble, panting so hard he could hardly get any air into his lungs as pleasure travelled up his spine—relentless and wild.

"*Josh,*" he said, or begged, or prayed, clutching at him like he'd fall apart if he let go. He fell apart anyway, but Josh had his arms around him, steadying him.

His forehead was pressed against his mate's—probably too hard—and he blinked to try and make his eyes adjust despite being too close. Josh's eyes were open too, but Ray couldn't read his expression. It took a supernatural effort of will to push himself into a sitting position on Josh's lap. He landed flush on Josh's swollen cock.

Josh's hips twitched, grinding up once before he stopped himself by going still as stone under Ray. Ray looked down, his cock was half-hard still and he'd made a right mess of Josh's dress shirt. He could see the flush travelling all the way down from Josh's cheeks to his chest. Josh's lips parted, maybe to ask, but Ray ground down, making him choke on whatever he'd been going to say. Ray did it again, but Josh was stubborn and even though he couldn't quite manage to keep his eyes open, he asked, "Was that okay?"

"Okay?" Ray repeated. He planted his palms on Josh's pecs for leverage and ground his arse down with each word. "That. Was. Great."

Josh tossed his head back even as his hips rose to seek more contact. "Ray," he panted. He was a dishevelled mess: shirt come-stained, starting to sweat with the effort and the heat between their bodies, eyelashes fluttering as he trembled under Ray's touch. And it was for him. Ray wanted... "*Please*," Josh begged in a raw, used voice.

Before he knew it, Ray was scooting further down until his knee was lodged in the V of Josh's legs. He unzipped him and pushed the underwear out of the way. Closing his hand around Josh's silky length was nearly as much a relief for him as it seemed to be for his lover. Josh relaxed under him like his strings had been cut. He was throbbing in Ray's hand, hard and perfectly still, and then he twisted right into the movement of Ray's thumb on the head of his cock as he pushed back against Ray's knee pressing behind his still covered balls.

Ray would have liked to touch them, but there was no way he could stay upright without his left hand for support. Not with the way Josh was writhing under him, more and more desperate, never trying to take over but slowly losing control of his own body.

Just like Ray wanted him.

Josh clenched his eyes closed tight and whimpered as yet another thrust brought him closer to the end. His hands were digging down into the metal of the Jeep like was trying to keep himself from flying away— or from touching Ray himself. *Fuck it*, Ray thought and used his left hand to bring Josh's right to his waist. He almost overbalanced before Josh's eyes snapped open and his digits tightened around Ray's waist.

"*Touch me*," Ray demanded, feeling like he might break. Feeling like he couldn't break because he was too damaged already.

But he wouldn't let it. *It wasn't true.*

Josh listened, but he was still careful. He still could be careful. It was what he wanted, Ray knew, to be sure he wouldn't hurt Ray again. But... Ray squeezed his dick hard enough to get him moaning loud into the night above them, giving him that, if he couldn't give him more.

Josh's other hand came up and tangled in Ray's hair, bringing their mouths crashing together without any requests or patience—the need too great for anything else. Ray kissed him back hard, pushing his tongue into the warm, familiar flavour if Josh's mouth—smiling at the rush of success it sent right through his veins and down to his bones. He was about to twist his wrist in the way he used to finish himself when he felt Josh start to come, pulse after pulse of alpha come coating his hand and splattering his own exposed cock as Ray milked him for it, pressing hard with his thighs to keep from being unmounted and kissing and licking anywhere he could find when Josh took his mouth away to breathe.

And just like that, it was over. All Ray could smell was sex. He raised himself slightly to look Josh in the face and found him watching already, eyes wide and shocked. He shouldn't have looked like that, Ray thought, and leaned back in and pressed a soft kiss to his mouth, almost a whisper, a caress, not a demand but an offer.

Josh opened his mouth and brushed his own lips against Ray's, slow and easy, a little wet from earlier but mostly a game of tickling with their mouths. Ray forgot his hand was covered in come until he placed it against Josh's beating heart over his shirt, and even then, it was hard to care because that was Josh's *heart*. Beating hard for him, as if trying to overcome the limits of skin.

It was just a heart, of course, an organ like any other; it beating didn't have anything to do with Ray. But Josh must have felt it too because his right hand slid under Ray's shirt until it pressed to the exact spot on his back.

They kissed again, softer and then harder, shallow and then deep. Ray kept their lower halves apart, knowing Josh had to be too sensitive from coming still, but he just couldn't pull away completely. Not yet, he needed... He touched Josh's neck with his clean hand, then his face, as if he could read his features with his fingers, as if he could ever get enough of his skin.

It must have been longer than it seemed because the position started to hurt Ray's neck, which he could never remember happening before. He rolled off Josh and then onto his side, shivering a little as the cold metal of the pickup pressed against his side where his undone trousers had left his skin exposed. Josh put a hand on his shoulder and rubbed to warm him up. Ray smiled at him, at the absurdity of trying to ward off a cold November night with just your hands, at his friend's need to try anyway.

"So what's the verdict?" Josh asked, eyes bright.

"Well..." He tried to shrug and the awkward result made Josh snort. "Not bad. Could use some practice," he added, meeting Josh's eyes and licking his lips.

That made Josh laugh out loud. His breath still smelled of sausage and Ray's stomach chose that moment to loudly remind him that snacks weren't dinner.

Josh was still laughing as Ray grumbled and rolled away, tucking himself in so he could reach for the takeaway Chinese they'd left in the corner and misuse the napkins to clean himself up a little.

"Goddess, you must be about to faint," he teased, throwing his third—or was it fourth?—balled up napkin towards the back of the Jeep. "You must lose half of your body's protein every time you jerk it."

Josh snorted and when Ray turned back around to set the containers down, he was pulling his button-down off over his shoulders, leaving himself in only a basic muscle shirt that did nothing to hide his pert nipples. Ray's mouth watered. "You are going to be cold," he said inanely.

"Better than being covered in jizz," his friend said, making Ray shiver. He probably wouldn't even be that cold; wolves were acclimated to cold weather and a lot of it translated when they were in two feet. Josh crawled closer and Ray started to turn to pass him the chow mein, but his friend didn't try to get the food, just pressed himself against Ray's side, shoulders together and backs to the front seat divider.

Ray gave him a bemused look. "Leeching off your body heat," Josh explained with a too serious expression that did nothing to disguise the way his heartbeat had skipped.

Ray would have liked to figure out what that expression meant, but he was way too hungry to resist his own food. He gave Josh his own so at least he wouldn't watch him eat, but when he'd gulped down about half his rice and looked up, his friend quickly looked away. "What?"

"Nothing." Except it was clearly something, obvious enough even without the heartbeat skip.

"It was really good," Ray said seriously. "You're not worried about... I mean, you liked it, right?" he asked a little uncertainly. He was just realising that it wasn't just his own first time without the wolves running the show.

Josh shot him an incredulous look. "Something like that," he said a little cuttingly. "As in it was fucking amazing and it was just..." He waved a hand a little, sending a noodle flying.

"So what's with the face?" Ray asked as he made himself eat another mouthful and actually chew it this time.

Josh seemed to need the time because he kept eating too. It wasn't a tense silence, exactly. Ray knew things were going okay and with Josh, he knew *they* would be okay. Sure, it had taken them a while to get on the same page, but now that they were...

"It's stupid, but I'm worried about freaking out when..." He exhaled, controlled and slow. "When I see you with them."

Ray winced. He didn't know why he hadn't seen it coming. Of course the wolves didn't care about sharing their mate, but Josh, the man... And there was nothing Ray could say to that, no reassurances to offer. He just couldn't give Josh that.

"I'm sorry," he choked out, fumbling to put down the Tupperware before he dropped it.

"What?" Josh sounded startled, then Ray felt a tentative hand on his arm. "Ray, why are you apologizing?"

"I—" He shrugged. He could hardly apologize for being an omega, or any of the consequences, could he? But he still felt responsible somehow for the doubt in Josh's voice.

His mate tugged at his arm until Ray turned his body towards him. Josh's other hand came up to touch the side of his neck—he must have put his food down somewhere, Ray thought—and slowly massaged... the mark. The bite. No, the *bites*. Josh traced each of them in turn, then lingered on his own. Ray swallowed thickly, his throat muscles pushing against Josh's fingers. "I didn't mean it like that," Josh said, hushed and grave. "I'm not... I'm not asking you for anything."

"But you want— You don't want me to—"

"I don't, but I think you should."

Ray startled and Josh barely kept his grip. "*What?*"

"Not like that!" Josh said at once and pulled back his hand like he'd just remembered Ray did indeed bite. "You should do what... whatever you want, whatever comes naturally."

Ray froze for a moment, unsure if he had cause to be offended. Or if Josh was even talking about him or his wolf. Josh knew Ray had very little choice when it came to what the omega wolf needed, so he probably... "Is this about... about Sergi?"

Josh frowned, then shrugged and leaned back a little to look him in the face. Ray clenched his fingers to keep himself from reaching out. "Not really. I mean, I don't..." He swallowed. "I don't like that you went to him first, alright? I can't help it. I thought—"

"It couldn't be you."

"I know, I said I wouldn't."

"*No*," Ray insisted, shaking his head. "It couldn't be you, even if you had said yes. And you were right to say no. I was... I was a right mess; I thought I might cry, or break down. I didn't want... I didn't want to be with you like that when I—"

Josh was frowning. "Why not? You have seen me cry, what's the big deal?"

Ray exhaled, lowering his eyes to his own lap. "You."

"I'm... the big deal?" Josh asked slowly. He sounded like he expected Ray to deny it.

"Yes," he admitted. "And this is a big deal, and if... if I couldn't, if I was going to freak out, I wanted to know before I started it. I didn't want to... to promise, I guess, and then..."

He felt the heat of Josh's fingers next to his cheek, not touching until Ray raised his eyes to meet his, and then only brushing gently again his cheekbone, the contours of his face, his chin... He licked his lips, not quite sure what he was seeing on Josh's face. "I don't need you to promise me anything, especially not sex. If you never... If you *ever* want to stop this, I won't... Well, I will mind, but I will *want you to*. I swear. I don't want to touch you just because you are beautiful, I want... I want to show you what I feel. I want to know..." He inhaled sharply and pressed his fingertips behind Ray's ear, not pulling him closer, just touching as if he needed to make sure he was there beyond the shadow pull of desire. "If sex is ever not in the package, I'll take it. No questions asked, just... Fuck, Ray, you *have* to know, if the package is fuck off to Antarctica and get one letter a year, I'll take it too."

"You think I won't?" Ray asked softly. "I—I can live with less if I have to. But I... If I can, if I'm not too—" *broken*. He cut himself off mostly for Josh's sake. "I want more. I want *everything*."

Josh watched him, wide-eyed and shocked. Like he hadn't *known*. Ray couldn't stand it; he took hold of Josh's ratty white undershirt and pulled him close enough to kiss, soft but also desperate, raw with emotion and achingly needy. Josh didn't make him wait, licking into his mouth and pulling Ray along as he fell onto his back.

Ray smelled the garlic as the chow mein spilled and didn't care. It had to be somewhere underneath Josh's body but his friend didn't object either. He pushed a leg between Josh's and rolled their hips together, easier this time, with more time for the scenic route. He loved Josh under him, he thought, remembering Alec's questions.

But he didn't want that now. He rolled off him and tugged him onto his side, face to face, their matching height slotting their bodies together exactly. Josh blinked pupil-blown eyes at him, flushed and delectable. "Want to try ticking another item off the list?" Ray offered.

Josh stiffened a little, looking down between their bodies. "Rubbing off?"

"Yes," Ray confirmed and lowered his own zipper before doing Josh's, making sure to brush his knuckles against the bulge there before bringing out his erection. His friend shuddered in his grip and dropped his forehead to Ray's shoulder. "Hey, what's this?" Ray teased. "Lay back and think of England? Give me a hand."

Josh chuckled against his throat, warm puffs of breath in the cold of the night. He sneaked a hand down, nudging between their bodies to help Ray align their cocks even as he shifted his hips forwards and pushed their shirts out of the way until they were pressed together between their bellies. Ray had to stop breathing for a second when he felt Josh's fingers brush against the increasingly noticeable bump in his middle. He exhaled. Josh's hand migrated to Ray's lower back to pull him into the roll of their hips.

It felt... hot, and a little too dry but getting wetter with each slide against Josh's belly and Ray forgot about anything with his own that wasn't quite right.

He couldn't *think*: he was too lost in Josh's mouth and the heat of his precome—as copious as his semen—starting to form a delicious mess between them as Ray hooked a leg behind Josh's knee and locked them together in a battle that could only end in victory.

They lost track of kissing, and found it again, on each others' ears and necks and chins. And then they found the end of the path. Ray's body couldn't hold all the sensations any longer, and the world was too hot and too cold at once, and he was shuddering in Josh's arms as they fell apart together.

Josh's arm was too toned to make a great pillow, but Ray snuggled close anyway—after the heat they'd generated, the night air was starting to get to him and he didn't have any fur on at the moment.

"Antarctica is off, then," he decided.

"Yeah?" Josh asked sleepily.

"Yeah," Ray promised with a kiss to his throat. "The way you smell right now you'd be polar bear food for sure."

"That good?" Josh asked and Ray could only laugh. "I guess you better keep me around," he added, a whisper of his lips against Ray's hair.

Chapter sixteen

There were always going to be too many people around for Ray's taste when they invited all their families over, but as long as he wasn't the centre of attention, it wasn't that bad. He wasn't tempted to go hide inside like Alec clearly was; it was more that he was quite keen to stay close to the edges of the crowd.

He touched Alec's elbow in passing and leaned in to whisper in his ear, "There's always more food and drinks to bring out if you need a break."

Alec gave him a grateful smile. "Don't worry, Gabriel is manning the grill. He keeps sending me inside for fresh meat," he explained. Ray paused, watching his face for a clue. "I talked to him," Alec said in response to the unspoken question, a little testily but fond. "He will behave."

"Good," Ray decided. "If he doesn't..."

Alec snorted. "You can find your own reasons to shout at him if you want," he said, pushing Ray gently towards his mother and siblings in the middle of the room.

Ray's eyes were drawn to the pups, who he could feel the most clearly of all his pack and found them chasing after Alec's father as Alec's mum watched from the sidelines. They looked like such put together people: classy without being ostentatious, warm if a little too proper—but they were both betas and professionals so maybe it was something they'd picked up from the humans they spent the day with. Except... Alec's father had to be fifty if he was a day, werewolf genetics or not, and he was laughing his head off with his grandchildren.

Ray had seen them with Alec—so formal it made him itch to ask them to give their son a hug. But what did he know? Alec had such a hard time accepting hugs, maybe they just didn't know how to offer them, slow and measured, so that he could accept their affection.

Alec's mother knelt and picked up Sasha, leaning in and blowing a raspberry on her cheek with unapologetic glee. Sasha's giggles made half the crowd near the main table turn their way and Ray spotted his mother and Josh among them.

He headed over, aware that he was hosting the event and had to at least make an effort to greet everyone.

"Ray," his mum said with a radiant smile. "You look good."

Ray smiled back. "I like your blouse."

"Oh." She tilted her head towards Josh's mother. "Juliet gave it to me for my birthday. It's gorgeous, isn't it?"

"If it caught our artist's eye," Juliet said with a glint in her eye, "I suppose I did alright."

Ray rolled his eyes at her. "Nice to see you. Josh said you finally found a frame for the picture."

"It was hard to do it justice," she responded with unapologetic hauteur.

Ray glanced away because she *meant it* and even though he had accepted a new commission and he was pretty happy with how it was coming along, it was hard to accept such sincere praise to his face—especially from someone picky enough about *frames* that she'd visited several shops before finding the right one. "Thanks," he said, for lack of anything better. "I gotta..."

They waved him away, but he didn't make it far before Anne was tugging on his arm. "Josh said you got table tennis," she said, not bothering with a greeting.

Ray raised his eyebrows. "Hello, Anne, long time no see. How are you?"

She rolled her eyes at him. "Rayyyyy."

He shrugged. He had been the tough parent for way too long and he had plenty of his own teenagers to look forward to now. Plus, he had seen enough of what could happen when kids didn't get to talk to adults like they were both just people. "Say please and I will show you," he compromised, smiling at her.

Anne widened her eyes slightly and gave him her best earnest look. "Please, Ray, may I play table tennis?"

He laughed, impressed despite himself. "Yeah, okay, come on. Where's Harry?"

"Dunno, running around somewhere. There were other boys around."

"Yeah?" Ray asked, wracking his brain to try and imagine who it could be. Iesu's brother was older than him, Alec, Sergi and Josh were only children— the product of beta marriages—and Gabriel's youngest brother was only a few months younger than Ray himself.

They found Josh adjusting the net on the table as a gaggle of boys, including Harry and Glen, waited around, clutching rackets.

"You almost got another football team here," Ray said and his mate darted a smile at him before twisting the net once more and testing it.

"Stop trying to make everyone a footie fanatic, Ray," he accused good-naturedly. "There's other games in the world."

"Football is better," Ray replied. "Okay," he told the kids. "How about you all tell me your names and ages and we'll set this up?"

It took him a minute to calm them down enough and get them to tell him who they were in order. Even Harry and Glen had tried to answer, maybe not wanting to be left out, maybe just overly-excited.

"Okay," he decided. "Harry, there's a whiteboard and a pen on the fridge, go get it for me so we can keep track of points."

It turned out the two boys were Iesu's nephews by his sister Sorina. Ray did the maths while he taught them all the basics of swinging without sending the ball across the field or smacking each other in the face, and realised she had to be an omega. That explained why she'd moved countries with her parents and the fact that she'd had Andrew and George at quite a young age. Their English had none of the traces of an accent Iesu's did, so he was shocked when a soft word in Romanian stopped Andrew from tripping his brother.

He looked up to see a young woman, green-eyed and light-haired, but with features Ray saw echoed every day on Irina's and Iesu's faces. She offered him a timid smile and a hand to shake. "Sorina," she said. "Thanks for having us."

Ray took her hand and felt her relax. Of course, she was an omega in his territory. "My pleasure," he replied. "You guys speak Romanian at home?"

"Yes," she said simply, no clue as to whether the question pleased or disturbed her.

"Iesu and Irina are trying their best," Ray said. "But maybe you can try and speak to the babies and let me know how they're doing?"

She couldn't quite hide her surprise at that. "That's... admirable." Ah, there was the song Ray had come to expect under the vowels.

He shrugged. "Would be pretty stupid to pass up the chance."

"Are you learning too?" she asked, sidestepping a little in what he immediately realised gave her a better angle of the table and the kids without forcing her to look away from him.

"Me?" Ray laughed. "I couldn't even hack French. So..."

"Well," she suggested with a sly smile that reminded him of Irina. "You don't need that much to get my brother in line."

He snorted. "Should I learn to say 'heel'?" he joked.

"I think 'shut up' might come in handy more often," she replied, unmistakeable affection in her voice.

He laughed. "Okay, what's that?"

"Taci din gurâ."

One of the children laughed from behind them and Sorina gave a shrug. "Not something you tell children," she admitted. "You ready?" she asked and repeated it slowly.

Ray repeated it, feeling like his tongue wasn't quite up to the task and she made him say it again. After four tries, he thought he had it and Iesu's sister gave him a thumbs up. Ray tilted his head towards the table. "You want to play? I feel bad about beating them at it and I'm banned from football."

Her expression flickered at that and too late he realised there weren't that many reasons he could be forced not to play football. As an omega, she'd probably guess. But if she did, she didn't let it stop her long. "Sure."

They watched Harry and Anne battle it out until she beat him with a shout of triumph that made half the adults in the place jump, Ray included. Then Ray sent them all to get some food from the grill and faced his sister-in-law. "You know how to play?"

"We had a table at school," she explained, then proceeded to swiftly score twice. It wasn't reflexes; Ray had always been one of the fastest wolves in his pack and she was maybe a little above average. It was *skill*.

He was panting after a few minutes, losing badly but grinning hard. "When you said you had a table at school..."

"I kinda beat everyone there," she admitted.

He laughed. "Okay, lemme see if I can remember how this goes and make it entertaining for you."

By the time his stomach growled and he raised his racket to admit defeat, he noticed they were being watched. It was only Iesu and Irina, and then he saw Iesu's parents were standing closer to Sorina with a man who had to be her brother. He looked a lot like Iesu, dark-haired and dark eyes, a little thicker around the shoulders even though he was a beta.

Iesu took a step forward and kissed his sister. "Showing off?"

"Taci bin gurâ, Iesuvel," she replied and Ray laughed at the unexpected pleasure of understanding her.

Iesu shot him an alarmed look. "What's she been teaching you?"

Ray shrugged, suppressing his smile. "Don't forget our guests," he reminded his mate.

Iesu seemed reluctant but sighed and introduced everyone. He spoke English for the most part but when he briefly pointed at Sergi he switched to Romanian for a word or two. Ray saw Codrin stiffen and caught Sergi's startled look but Iesu's parents didn't react and Sorina just kept smiling.

He wondered if Iesu had just shoved Sergi out of the closet as unceremoniously as Gabriel had done to Alec. But Sergi, who was normally quiet, was actually adding to the conversation quite naturally, trying out the Romanian he'd picked up and seemingly impressing Iesu's family with his pronunciation.

Iesu's brother was the only one still quiet and Ray sighed and figured he'd take one for the team. He edged closer and offered him a racket. "Want to go once before the kids get back?"

Codrin looked startled, but he nodded. It was disconcerting to see someone who looked so much like Iesu look so serious.

They played for a few minutes, light and easy. The man had clearly played before but he either had had no interest or no chance to become a machine like his older sister.

Ray scored again and looked up to prepare for Codrin's serve, but his brother-in-law shook his head. "You win," he said and Ray realised he hadn't heard his voice before.

"Going easy on me?" he teased.

Codrin's lips curved but he didn't quite smile. "Just hungry."

"Oh, sorry," Ray said at once, putting down his racket. "Let's—"

"Do you know what he said?"

Ray stopped, then glanced at Iesu and his family. Sergi wasn't there anymore. He licked his lips and met Codrin's eyes. "I can guess."

"And you are not..." The man looked concerned and he'd known Ray for the space of minutes.

"Hey," Ray whispered. "It works for us," he promised. "Really. I'm happy... I'm happy for them."

Iesu's brother watched him for a moment longer. "Okay, I— sorry, it's none of my business."

Ray waved him away. "You're family now. You can be nosy," he said and waited a beat before heading for the grill.

"I'm not, though," Codrin explained. "It's just... Iesu's..." He sighed. "I love him, but he is a bit much. Sometimes."

Ray snorted. "Yeah, your sister just taught me how to say..." He hesitated but then figured the worst that could happen was that Codrin laughed. "Taci bin gurâ."

Codrin did laugh, actually looking Ray in the face as he did. "Yeah, that's perfect."

"Hey, charmer," Gabriel said as Ray approached the grill for another burger. Alec was nowhere to be seen.

"What?"

"You charmed the in-laws," Gabriel explained, flipping a couple burgers in quick succession.

"Your parents?" Ray guessed. Gabriel's parents hadn't come to the barbecue, although he'd seen his brother Nathaniel around, so maybe...

Gabriel snorted. "You don't need to charm my parents." He extended a hand for Ray's plate and placed a bun and barely-cooked burger on it. "Baked potato?"

Ray shook his head. "Because of Maria?"

Gabriel stopped and looked straight at him. "No, because my parents are judgemental jerks."

Ray held his gaze. "And yet you seem to keep trying."

His cousin sighed. "Yeah, well, they are my parents, I'm allowed a few issues."

"Sure," Ray agreed. "As long as nobody else gets caught in the cross-fire."

Gabriel took a moment to move the burgers out of the hottest part of the grill, then glanced around and waved. To Ray's surprise, Codrin came over.

"You mind?" Gabriel checked and Iesu's brother took the spatula from him like they'd arranged it in advance.

Gabriel met Ray's eyes. "Should we go swap the Coke bottles for cool ones?"

They took a couple each, although it was obviously the privacy of the kitchen they were after and not better-refrigerated beverages.

"Did Alec talk to you?" Gabriel asked as soon as they were inside.

"Yeah," Ray admitted. Maybe it wasn't his place to get between them, but he hadn't been able to keep quiet. Not when Alec was...

Gabriel didn't seem offended. He looked relieved. "Is he really okay?"

"Ah, yeah," Ray said. "He— he's fine."

"Okay, I just— I got caught up with my dad, and— You're right, it was out of line."

"I haven't said anything."

"Alec told me what you said and that he agreed."

"Oh, I didn't mean—"

Gabriel raised a hand. "Please do," he told Ray sincerely. "You can judge me all you want, and more. You— I have given you plenty of reasons, and besides... Alec's a little... I mean, he can tell me, technically, but..." He faltered. "I know it's difficult for him," he said in the end, taking bottles out of their fridge. "And it seemed to help him to know what you thought."

Ray started emptying the flat drinks in the sink, hoping Marisa didn't walk in and shout at him for being wasteful. "It's crazy how he doubts himself. I mean, he's so smart and he... Well, he knows a lot about a lot of important things, doesn't he?" Ray said, feeling like he was babbling. But Gabriel just nodded. "And then when it comes to, dunno, people? It's like he forgets his opinion is important and valid."

Gabriel slanted a soft look his way. "I'm glad you two are talking," he said almost shyly.

But Ray could see he meant it. Maybe if you grew up with parents like Gabriel's, expected to be a man by being strong all the time and telling everyone what to do, it was difficult to stop—even if you knew it wasn't right. "Well, I'm happy for you. For the two of you, I mean. He's a good influence," he added a little teasingly, and Gabriel didn't seem able to repress a little smile.

"He is."

"And he's happier, you know that, right?" Ray asked.

Gabriel nodded. "Thank you, Ray. If there's something you need, you will tell me, right?" That gave Ray pause and Gabriel must have thought he had misunderstood somehow. "Or Alec. If that's easier—"

"Stop," Ray asked. Even a single word was hard when it was Gabriel, but Gabriel listened, holding himself back so Ray could continue. "I will ask. Not sure who, but if I need something, I will ask. I know... I know you got my back."

"Good." He picked up three bottles and signalled with his head, so Ray followed him to the corridor. "I meant Iesu's family, by the way. His sister wouldn't shut up about you getting the kids to learn Romanian."

"It was hardly my idea," Ray pointed out as they came out of the house.

"Yeah, well, apparently her mate was a bit of a dick about it with her kids."

Ray shrugged. "Such high standards..."

"She also said she taught you how to tell Iesu to shut his mouth," Gabriel added with a smirk.

Ray shot him an unimpressed look. "And you think I'm teaching it to you?" he asked. "You are out of the doghouse, doesn't mean you get treats."

"Ouch," Gabriel said, widening his eyes dramatically. "What if I promise to be good?" he wheedled.

"You already have," Ray pointed out smugly.

Gabriel's laughter followed him as he walked off to put down the drinks on the nearest table. It was only when his hands were free again that he noticed his wolf hadn't objected to him brushing his alpha off.

Chapter seventeen

"It's a pity I cannot ask you to marry me," Iesu declared that night as they shared a cold supper of leftovers.

Ray snorted. "Why is that?"

"My parents would probably buy us a house or something just to make sure I didn't let you get away," his mate explained, beaming.

Ray tsked. "Too bad you haven't let me get away," he joked.

"We do have a house," Sergi mentioned from Iesu's other side.

Iesu turned to him at once and threw an arm around his neck to bring him closer and press a loud smooch to his cheek. "Oh, are you *jealous?*" he asked, sounding absolutely delighted.

Sergi pushed him away, but Ray thought Iesu might not be far off.

"They would hardly choose me over Sergi," Ray said. "I didn't realise you could actually have a conversation in Romanian."

Sergi shrugged at him. "Just, like, how are you and stuff like that."

"Well, they looked damn impressed, let me tell you."

"It's easier when you speak another language already," Sergi explained.

Ray frowned. "But I thought you didn't speak Russian."

"I don't. But, well, I understand it, so... Like, the sounds are easier."

"See?" Iesu cut in. "We are all very impressed with your gifted tongue." He leered. Sergi grimaced, obviously helplessly amused and Ray saw his chance.

"Iesu?" His mate turned his eyes to him. "Taci bin gurâ."

Iesu choked on air and Sergi started laughing, covering his mouth but unable to stop as Iesu listened to Ray—probably more out of shock than anything else.

"So that's it," Gabriel said, eyes shining in victory. Then he tried to repeat it and Iesu started flat out giggling. Even Ray could tell Gabriel's pronunciation was awful.

"Please stop before you make someone choke," Alec asked Gabriel and pushed a bowl of salad towards him across the table.

"Is this you telling me to eat more greens?" Gabriel asked even as he served himself.

"Sure," Alec agreed easily. He seemed a lot more relaxed now that it was just the six of them. The betas had gone back for a visit with the old pack and the babies were fast asleep after all the excitement of the day. "Eat all your greens," Alec said. "And I will let you have some dessert."

Ray looked away from the oddly intense look his alphas were sharing and only realised there was nothing even remotely sweet left in the house when he heard Gabriel swallow. Josh nudged him from his other side and Ray tilted his head up towards him, sharing an incredulous smile.

Maybe Alec didn't need so much handholding after all. Josh licked his lips and raised his eyebrows. "Movie date?" he mouthed at Ray.

Ray nodded, pressing his lips together to keep from grinning.

They had Netflix because Marisa said they'd actually save money if they got a family subscription instead of renting movies at random or buying DVDs. But unlike his sister, Ray didn't particularly like TV so he let Josh browse and went to make them tea.

The other four alphas had made themselves scarce after helping shove what little food was left in the fridge and filling the dishwasher up. The kitchen was a bit of a mess, but as long as there were clean cups and spoons, Ray couldn't have cared less.

He bit his lip as he heard a low whimper on his way back to the living room on the other side of the house.

"Sounds like they're having fun," he told Josh, kicking the door closed behind himself. He'd got the baby monitor from the babies' room in the beta wing just in case—he rarely felt confident enough to let them sleep there, but he felt good today, remembering that he wasn't alone. Plus, he could hear them breathe through the open radio channel, but they couldn't hear him if he laughed at the movie or something.

Josh snorted, meeting his eyes from where he was sprawled on the middle sofa. Ray set down the tray but didn't sit. His friend crooked a finger at him. "Come on, I'm sure cuddling has to be a third date thing."

So Ray crawled over him, burying his nose in Josh's hair and inhaling deeply. Josh held him close and Ray let his warmth give him strength.

He raised himself on his elbows. "Can we skip the movie?"

Josh nodded slowly, watching him closely.

Ray licked his lips. "I want..." He exhaled, feeling ridiculous. "I want to suck you off."

He felt Josh swallow. "Um, here?"

Ray hesitated, frowning a little as he concentrated on his other alphas. He had to clutch at Josh's shirt at the wave of lust and pleasure that hit him. He blinked his eyes open, feeling a bit dazed. "They are busy," he told Josh, his voice coming out a little rough, like...

Josh slowly bent his knee, pressing his thigh right against the bulge in Ray's trousers like he'd known it was there. "Is that a good thing?" he checked.

Ray forced himself to keep his hips still and think about it. He had been able to feel their arousal, which was hot as fuck, sure, but so was porn. It wasn't like... He wasn't wet. It wasn't about them wanting *him*. It was about him wanting *them*. It was strange to realise that the two could be separate things.

"Yeah, it's not..." He shifted back a little because if he didn't, he'd shift forward. "Just..."

"Hot?" Josh offered.

He glanced up at Josh's face and saw his eyes had gone even darker. He was also smiling. "Yes," he conceded.

"Good," Josh said and his eyes drifted. "What about if they get thirsty or something?"

"I—" Ray honestly didn't think they'd come out of there for a while, but he couldn't exactly guarantee it. "Do you want to go to your room?"

Josh shrugged. "I want you to be comfortable."

Ray tsked, a little annoyed, but he could hardly get angry at Josh for being accommodating. That wasn't an alpha and omega thing, it was a Josh thing. "No," he said slowly. "Do *you* want to go your room?"

Josh looked confused, but maybe the repetition made the point well enough because he nodded. "Yeah, let's."

Ray rewarded him with a smile and tugged him to his feet before kissing him. Josh kissed him back, soft and relaxed even though Ray knew he was hard as well, and he couldn't help but press their lower halves together, seeking any friction he could get. Josh opened up to it, arching his leg to give Ray something to push against and pressing his own hard-on against Ray's hip.

Ray bit Josh's lips too hard and Josh thrust against him hard enough to make him stumble and clutch at Josh's arm and shirt in a clumsy attempt to stay upright. It wasn't necessary; Josh was holding onto him, too, and he immediately stabilized them, but it made the point well enough.

It was for the best. He wanted to do this properly, on a bed. He didn't know when he'd have the chance to be with Josh again, knowing everything he felt was just him, just them—no Moon meddling with their feelings or their bodies.

"Bedroom," he demanded. And he could feel the strain in Josh's arms as his lover reigned himself in. "Come on," he said and tugged, not needing to ask if it was okay.

He'd ask about the important stuff, of course. He knew Josh needed the list as much as Ray did himself. But they could play at easy, at normal, at natural, for a little bit longer. They both pretended not to hear the sounds coming from behind the closed door of Sergi's and Iesu's room as they passed it and then gave away the pretence as they tripped over a cuddly toy and were forced to turn to each other for support.

Josh bit his lip, eyes bright and Ray could barely resist the temptation to shush him and set him off. He didn't think Sergi would appreciate the chorus, for one, and he definitely didn't want to stop and chat if they decided to come out.

He took a step back instead and Josh followed him the couple steps left to his own doorway. It was ridiculous but he hesitated to let go of his hand to reach for the door handle. Josh didn't say anything to hurry him along, just watched him like that was enough—or like it wasn't, like there was something on Ray's face he still needed to figure out.

Ray opened the door without looking away and then they were inside. Josh kicked the door closed and he realised they were alone. A part of him had liked the idea of staying in the living room. It was silly and childish and unjustified—he trusted Josh with his life and more.

Josh caught his unease with the expertise of a mind-reader. "Hey," he said, demanding Ray's mind return from darker corners. He was smiling. "You wanna do something else? It's a long list."

It was, at that. Ray hadn't just fantasized, he'd *researched*. And Josh had been meant to choose, not him. He didn't want to be indulged. Josh needed to be careful—hell, *Ray* needed to be careful—but he didn't need to do everything Ray wanted without question.

That wasn't the name of the game. He met Josh's eyes and squeezed the hand he still held. "So choose."

"I—" Josh looked alarmed, not excited, but Ray waited him out. If he just... "Ray, I just want to be with you."

Ray swallowed, the sincerity of the words almost hurt. He nodded. "Tell me how," he repeated. "I told you," he pointed out gently.

Josh exhaled, then nodded. "Okay, rubbing off."

"Okay," Ray agreed, rubbing his thumb against Josh's knuckles. "That was nice."

Josh frowned. "Do you want to... to suck me off instead?"

"Do you want to do that?" Ray echoed.

Josh huffed and yanked his hand away. "What are you playing at? I don't care what we do, if it's with you... I want to do everything with you."

Ray hesitated for just a second, but he knew Josh just as well as Josh knew him. He knew where the line was, and every button. "So if I ask you to fuck me, you will?"

Josh took a hasty step away, staring at him. "You— No."

Ray looked up, feeling a surge of triumph. "So you do care."

"Not because... I care about not hurting you," Josh explained angrily. "Why—"

"You won't hurt me," Ray repeated, meeting the alpha's eyes in open defiance. He felt his wolf's objection in the tension in his shoulders and resisted the urge to look down or away. "You made a mistake, and I forgave you," he reminded Josh. "But if you don't forgive yourself... it doesn't matter what I say, does it?"

Josh shook his head, taking another step back. "I thought... I thought you were happy taking things slow."

"I am, but this isn't taking things slow. This is you doing whatever I want."

"We said..." Josh started to say. "We agreed you would tell me first, so I knew for sure. You didn't..."

Ray swallowed, then nodded. "I thought you would freak out if I wrote down fucking."

Josh was staring at him, looking trapped. "But you want to?"

He licked his lips, shrugged. "It sounded hot. Before. And... if I'm going to do it anyway, I want to know if I actually can enjoy it when I'm not high as a kite on hormones or whatever."

Josh took another step back until the back of his knees hit the side of the bed, then plopped down heavily on it. His pushed his fingers through his blond hair, messing it up even further than Ray's hands had. "That makes sense."

"But you don't want to," Ray guessed.

"I—" Josh started to say, then stopped, flushing darkly. Ray watched him without understanding the reason behind it. Was he embarrassed? Or... ashamed? He made himself wait it out, give Josh the space he needed just like Josh did for him and, finally, his friend managed to speak. He was staring at the floor and it was lucky Ray had supernatural hearing because even a couple meters apart, his voice would have been too quiet to be heard over the sound of the wind. "I know what it did to you, how—how it made you feel, and I still... I still want to. And I don't want to, because I know if I feel bad now for doing it without knowing... If I do it again and you... If I hurt you in the same way. If it's not a mistake..." He stopped speaking, swallowing hard a couple times and Ray suddenly understood he was holding back tears.

He took a step closer and reached out, only keeping himself from touching at the last second, and then, when Josh just sat there, trembling and stiff, he put his hand on Josh's shoulder and felt him crumple forwards into his arms. Josh didn't say anything else and Ray couldn't think of what to say so he dug his fingers into Josh's back and curled his body around his own—the instinct to protect him too deep and too old in him to stop now—and waited.

Josh gradually relaxed against him and Ray started rubbing his back instead, trying to soothe even as his brain scrambled to find the words to explain. By the time Josh pulled at his shirt to ask him for a little space, he still wasn't quite sure.

It didn't matter, there was no way he'd let Josh keep believing anything like that for a second longer than he had to. He put his hands on Josh's cheeks and made him look up into Ray's eyes. "We don't have to do anything you don't want to," he said, hearing the truth ring heavy in his voice. "And *wanting* to do something in bed doesn't make you good or bad, no matter what. It isn't a choice. The choice is what we *do*. And... And we are not going to do anything right now," he said. He'd thought Josh was taking things slow for his sake and wanted to shake him, but maybe that was the only way Josh had been able to admit *he* needed time.

It worked like a charm, Josh's frame relaxing further into him and Ray climbed onto the bed and put his arm around Josh's back, holding him close and safe and his. "Sorry," Josh mumbled. "About... I mean, it's a date and—"

"Shut up," Ray demanded, too harsh. He kissed Josh's ear in apology. "Don't... We have a rule about feelings, remember?"

Josh laughed, a little wetly but still. "Okay," he agreed.

"We can take a nap," he offered, pressing himself closer to Josh.

But Josh shook his head. "No, I... I feel better. I want—I need to talk about this." He used his elbow to push Ray gently away. "Let's get under the covers, though."

Ray let go, then hesitated until Josh gave him a wan, tired smile and said, "I could get some pyjama pants?"

Ray shook his head, then laughed when he realised what he'd said. "You don't own any pyjamas," he declared with conviction.

Josh rolled his eyes at him. "Whatever, sweatpants or something."

"Forget it. Get in the bed," Ray replied and got up. "I need the toilet."

It would have made a great excuse to give Josh a minute to himself, but unfortunately, it was also true.

Josh was curled up on his side when he got back and Ray had left his own jeans in the laundry basket in the bathroom—it wasn't like boxer shorts were revealing, much less provocative, but he still hesitated.

"Come on," Josh told him, eyelids dropping a little. "I trust you with my virtue."

Ray snorted but he crawled up the bed and rolled under the blanket. He left plenty of room between their bodies—Josh had got the king sized bed that had originally been in Ray's bedroom—but Josh reached out a hand and tugged on his sleeve. "Cuddling okay? I know it's third date stuff and this date kinda sucked..."

"There wasn't even a movie," Ray agreed, but he rolled closer and let Josh gather him in his arms, fitting his chin under Josh's and sighing at the warm skin against his.

"Maybe we should go out again," Josh said, rubbing Ray's back with his left hand. His right arm was bent awkwardly between their bodies, just under Ray's own dominant hand. But neither of them moved. "That was working well..."

"We should," Ray agreed. "And... the therapy thing. I think we both need to do that. I didn't realise..." He leaned back so he could look at his mate. "I'm sorry I didn't realise how it affected you."

Josh shook his head as well as he could manage while laying down. "That's not—"

"I can feel sorry," Ray reminded him. "It's a feeling."

Josh closed his mouth, looking torn between being annoyed and chastised. "Okay. So *I* feel like it was pretty understandable of you to miss it."

"Okay," Ray echoed. "So—"

"Can we cuddle?" Josh interrupted.

Ray blinked at him and it took him a moment to realise it was the first time Josh had dared to cut him off in ages. It was something alphas did to omegas all the time, of course, because they could and that meant a lot of them felt they had the right to. But it was also a Josh thing. A Josh *and Ray* thing, because they liked to have stupid arguments that ended with them tackling each other and they had been ten-years-olds together, and fifteen too. It didn't mean they didn't listen, it was just another way to talk.

And sometimes, it was the right way to stop talking. Like when they got into a circular argument just for the sake of needling each other. Ray had asked for normal and Josh had given it to him.

He smiled a little. "Of course," he said. "We have to, it's our third date," he reminded him and curled up closer, closing his eyes.

Waking up in Josh's arms wasn't exactly a new experience—he'd held Ray close after Ray had come back. And after Alec had told him about the pregnancy.

It was different to wake in Josh's arms and be happy, though. Different enough to be hard to believe, so Ray stayed where he was and watched Josh's eyelashes in the sunlight filtering through the half-drawn curtains.

It must have been what woke Josh eventually, making him stir slightly and tighten his grip on Ray like a child with a favoured toy. Ray watched his almost absently as his eyelashes fluttered, like it was an abstract painting instead of a beloved face. Then Josh scrunched his eyes shut against the light and it was like getting punched in the gut by the strength of the tenderness it brought up in him. He froze in an effort not to squeeze Josh back too hard and in that momentary eternity, Josh recovered enough to look at him from under hooded lids.

Ray's breath stuttered in his throat like he was looking into the sun all of a sudden, and he couldn't help but glance away.

He couldn't keep from glancing back either. Even though they were too close, even though... Josh's hand was soft on his hair and Ray leaned over him to press their mouths together like the movement was a continuation of something he'd done in his dreams.

It felt unreal, too, the way Josh's mouth opened to his, soft and slick, canines sharp against his lips but tongue so eager to tangle with his it seemed absurd that he might need to pull away to breathe. He followed the pull of Josh's body and rolled on top of him, hips locking in place—dicks more awake than their owners—as if an extension of their mouths.

It was easy. It didn't require thought to push closer, to roll faster into the wave of their shared pleasure, a rhythm they didn't need to discuss—it simply was. A truth they had just needed to let surface from the depths as if they'd hid it from themselves by some trick of the light, or the darkness. Maybe just fear—the kind that lived at the heart of every great love.

But it was gone now, defeated, drowned, exiled, and it was just Ray and Josh, bodies never close enough with clothes between them but too desperate to be closer to bother removing them. Josh arched under him, whimpering like it was breaking his very soul, and Ray felt him erupting between them. And he couldn't do anything but join him, let his own mind shatter as his body reached the edge of what was known and spilled beyond understanding—tethered to the one person that could always call him back from both darkness and light.

He remembered himself when their releases started cooling between them, seeping through their boxers and mixing in what moments before would have been hot but was now turning into a sticky mess. Ray raised his head, still dazed but starting to remember he had other needs beyond touching the man in his arms.

Josh didn't seem much more awake than he'd been earlier with his eyes closed, but when Ray pushed onto his elbows to try and get up, Josh's leg behind his knee forced him to stay. Only for a second, then Josh's brain must have registered the surprise on his face because he disentangled both his leg and his arms from around Ray.

Ray *really* needed to get up, but he didn't want to leave Josh looking anything but blissed out. He essayed a smile, though he wasn't exactly happy; it was closer to the delirious otherworldly connection the full moon brought out in him than to laughter or pleasure. And for that, he didn't have words.

He got to his knees, then took Josh's hand and pulled, tilting his head in invitation.

Josh tried to follow his lead, but it was pretty impossible to get up with someone half-sitting on top of you—even with supernatural abs—so he fell back.

Ray laughed, feeling like he was breaking through a spell. Josh rolled his eyes at him, dispelling the mist a little further, then he spoke at last.

"Shower," he said, voice raspy and dry.

Ray checked the alarm clock on his bedside table. It was a little past eight, which meant Alec was probably in the kitchen already, maybe cooking breakfast. "You have work?"

His mate looked completely blank, and Ray couldn't help but laugh again. "Well, I guess if you do, you can't show up covered in jizz," he said with a smirk. "Come on."

He turned around and opened the door, not bothering to check if anyone was in the corridor before heading for the bathroom next door.

By design or luck—Ray was assuming design—Josh gave him a couple minutes to piss before he showed up to join him in the shower. Ray was grateful for a first go at the hot water—and the chance to face away from his lover while completely naked—and Josh let him move past him with a careful hold on his arm and hip, low enough there was no chance he'd touch Ray's belly.

Ray leaned into him and let Josh massage shampoo into his hair, then run his fingers through it to help him rinse out the suds. Josh let Ray massage shower gel over his shoulders and then lower, eyes closed and trusting, expression open and close to sensual ecstasy.

They had never done that before, but it was easy.

Alec had made breakfast. For Gabriel. It was quite clear by the cooling grease on the empty plates still on the table—he must have emptied the dishwasher too, Ray figured. But maybe it was even more obvious by the way he sprang to his feet as soon as he saw Ray and offered to make him some food.

"Sure," Ray agreed. "Not like I'm going to say no to some protein," he added with a wink.

Alec gaped at him, flushing darkly despite Ray's fairly tame reference. "Eggs?" he offered.

Ray was severely tempted to add something dirtier to see what reaction he could get, but he took pity and turned to his cousin instead. Ray was no prude, but Gabriel's attitude towards sex was still too casual for him. How did Alec even cope?

Gabriel was already on his feet, opening the dishwasher—empty indeed—and stacking his plate inside before turning to open the fridge and passing Alec some bacon right on cue.

Josh walked in right then—not out of any misplaced sense of modesty, he'd just needed to go back to his own room to get fresh clothes—and didn't even blink at the strange scene.

"Morning," he said. "Mmmm... Can I have some?" he asked Alec in his sweetest tones.

Alec flashed him a smile and a nod, but Gabriel gave him an unimpressed look. "We were expecting you."

"Okay..." Josh was understandably flabbergasted by that until Gabriel's eyes slid to Ray and he raised both eyebrows as he pursed his lips. Josh swallowed, glancing at Ray.

But if either of them imagined Ray was going to be shy about who he *chose* to spend his nights with, they had another thing coming. "We slept very well," he told Gabriel. Meeting his eyes was almost easy, he discovered. "And you?"

Gabriel barked out a laugh, deep and rumbling and brightening up his face enough he went from beautiful to stunning. Ray's eyes slid past him to Josh, who was already looking at him and who looked... proud? His twisted his lips and tipped an imaginary hat at Ray before pulling back a chair.

Just then, the baby monitor went off in Ray's bedroom. He shot to his feet, feeling his stomach twist with guilt, but before he could move, Gabriel had a hand on his arm. "I got it. Have some breakfast in peace and I'll go get them."

"But—" Ray started.

Gabriel shook his head. "I'll get the stroller. I'll be back in less than five minutes and you can hear them from here," he added, thumb pointing towards the bedrooms even as he walked out towards the door in the living room that connected the two houses.

Ray stood still, adrenaline still rushing through him and feeling like every whimper pulled straight at his heartstrings. He only noticed the plate of food in front of him when Gabriel's voice on the other side of the baby monitor broke him out of his terrified waiting.

He sagged a little and felt a hand on his shoulder. Josh, he saw, glancing up to meet his mate's eyes. "Sit down." Ray did and eyed the food a little blankly. "That was good," Josh added in a whisper. "You were scared but you trusted him."

"Fuck, that was awful." He exhaled and rubbed his face, mostly so he could let his expression do whatever it wanted for a moment. "Alec, can I have coffee, please?"

Alec passed Josh a second plate and made him a black coffee in silence before sitting across from him at the kitchen table. Ray had managed to eat a few mouthfuls of eggs and the hot drink helped wake him up fully. He took another bite of bacon and tasted it for the first time. "This is good," he told Alec. "Um, thanks." Alec smiled at him, a little tight, Ray noticed. "Go on, what?"

"Just—" Alec waved towards Josh. "Nothing, it was... it was good. I'm glad you did that."

"Gabriel will be over the moon," Josh said, and Ray's brain seemed to register the sounds weren't coming through the radio anymore just as Gabriel pushed the stroller into the kitchen. Jamie and Clara got the front seat, and the other three were in the back because they were less likely to spill over the sides.

They were all getting too big for the stroller, Ray noticed, and they hadn't even taken them into town yet. It had been too hard at first, when they were liable to transform without warning, and then...

Gabriel had to have heard Josh's comment, but he didn't say a thing, just met Ray's eyes from where he was twisted to look at them. Ray nodded and purposely turned back to his breakfast, leaving Gabriel to prepare some of the formula Alec had deemed nutritious enough for werewolf babies.

It was a pretty small thing to trust him with: fetching them from next door and feeding them, but it was a start. He thought Gabriel got it, too, and Alec dropped another heap of bacon onto his plate without any prompting, which Ray took as his way to express further approval without having to actually talk.

Josh stole one of his rashers and Ray aimed an elbow at him—too slow to hit but quick enough to make him work to evade it—and decided he could have a double breakfast. He was eating for two, really.

Chapter eighteen

"Hey," Irina said, offering him a pile of folded laundry. "Great party."

Ray inhaled and smiled at her. "Oh, thanks, glad you liked it. Did you win?" he asked as an afterthought, placing the pile on his bureau to sort. "I missed the match. Sorina is seriously obsessed with table tennis."

He'd been convinced his sister wouldn't let anyone else touch the laundry after Sergi had turned all the babies' pristine whites pink. But as long as she wasn't complaining, he was happy Marisa was accepting help from someone. In that regard, he was very much aware that his sister and he were cut from the same cloth.

Irina scoffed. "Of course I won. And I let Iesu play with me so..."

"Very generous of you," he said sarcastically.

"You look good," she commented. He was pretty sure that was code for 'happy'.

"I am," he agreed. "Did you have a nice time back home?"

"I had a nice time with Sorina," she said pointedly. "But it's good to be home."

Ray rolled his eyes at the correction. "Thanks for driving Marisa back all the time, by the way."

Irina gave him a weird look, straightening from where she'd been leaning against his doorframe. "You don't have to thank me for that."

"Well, she's my little sister..."

"She's not... She's not that little anymore," she said. It was the first time Ray had heard her sound unsure of herself. "And it's no problem, not like I'm not going anyway."

"Do your parents live here too?" Ray asked, concentrating on getting his fresh sheets into his drawer—he liked to keep a set in his bedroom just in case.

"No, they're back in Romania."

"Oh, that's... that's gotta be hard."

She shrugged. "They visit sometimes, and besides, I got Sorina and her family here. And you guys are alright too, I guess," she added.

Ray straightened and met her amused eyes. "We do our best," he assured her with a little bow.

"Anyway, laundry won't sort itself," she said. "Don't forget it's your turn to make lunch, Alec took that extra shift."

He saluted, mockingly, but he was grateful—he was perfectly capable of performing all the tasks he was responsible for, but if he was stressed he found it hard to keep track of them without reminders.

It'd never been a problem before he'd become responsible for his own pack, and at first, he'd resented the way his brain was failing him. But now that it was the betas—mostly Marisa and Irina—keeping track for him, it didn't feel like such a failure on his part. It was just delegation—and a good leader knew how to use the people who worked for them.

[G ot your results.]

It was so unusual for him to get a text unrelated to groceries that it took Ray a moment to process what Alec was talking about.

[And?]

[Can't promise, but it says girl.]

"Fuck," Ray said aloud, and Gabriel looked up from changing Sasha's diaper. "Sorry," he said at once. "I—"

"Ray, sit down," his alpha said at once, body tensing as he glanced down at Sasha. "Just—give me a sec."

Ray stepped back and plopped down on the armchair they kept in the corner of the babies' room. Other than the biggest crib they had been able to find and the two sets of drawers, it was still pretty empty.

It suddenly occurred to Ray that they'd need another cradle for the new baby. The girl.

It felt impossible.

He had known there was half a chance he'd get his wish but Alec was right, he'd got what he wanted so rarely since he'd presented, he'd come to expect the worst.

"Ray?" Gabriel asked after he'd returned Sasha to the floor—Ray absently noticed someone had let them set up Legos in the corner even though they'd agreed the babies should only play in the living room where someone could keep an eye on them. "What's wrong?"

Ray glanced up at him, feeling a little guilty. "Nothing," he said honestly. "I'm sorry... Alec just texted me. It's a girl. Or... well, he's pretty sure."

Gabriel took a moment to answer. "That's what you wanted?"

"He didn't tell you?"

Gabriel frowned. "No. I mean... I guess it was a private conversation, why would he tell me?"

Ray shrugged. "Well, you two..."

"We wouldn't... I'm not saying we never talk about you, but we don't—" He faltered, then crouched down in front of Ray and sought his eyes.

Ray let himself look him in the eye for the first time in what felt like forever. Gabriel's blue gaze was focused, and earnest, and kind. "You don't what?" he asked.

"I don't tell Alec everything we talk about," Gabriel said. "And he obviously doesn't either."

"But you talk to me about him," Ray pointed out. "And you want me to talk to him about you."

"Yes, I want... I want us to help each other understand, or explain, or whatever we need. But my relationship with Alec isn't more important than my relationship with you just because it's romantic. It's just different."

Ray looked at him from under his eyelashes, a little wary. "I'm not... I'm not ready to be over it. Yet. I'm not saying—"

"Ray." Gabriel nearly overbalanced, then jumped to his feet and took a couple steps back. It meant Ray had to look up at him, of course, but he could hardly expect a guy Gabriel's size to kneel at his feet for long. "I don't expect you to be. That's not what I meant—I..." He stopped himself, then waved a hand at Ray to continue, apparently noticing he'd interrupted him.

Ray was almost too surprised to speak. "What do you mean?"

Gabriel exhaled, then leaned down to catch Clara as she tried to crawl under the dresser once again—there was probably something disgusting under there that had woken her untrained nose. "I meant our relationship doesn't depend on what we do in bed. The whole point of being your alpha is supposed to be that, but... that's fucked up. It's not really meant to be like that; the bond is not about sex and if we never... If you never want me to touch you again, it won't change the promise I made to take care of you."

Ray stared at him. *If he never...* "But I will still go into heat."

Gabriel shook his head. "You can ask Josh every time."

Ray swallowed thickly and stood up; suddenly he couldn't take the height disadvantage any longer. "Have you... Have you spoken about *this* with Alec?"

Gabriel took a moment to answer. "Yes, you were there. I mean, the whole point..." He trailed off, staring at Ray with an increasingly alarmed expression. "Okay, so I fucked up again," he said slowly.

"Language," Ray said absentmindedly. Gabriel didn't even point out that Ray himself had used the same language moments earlier. Instead, he waited until Ray was ready to speak again. "Have you spoken about this with the others too?"

"Ray," Gabriel said, sounding pained. "About what?"

"About letting me choose!" Ray snapped.

"By the Moon and the fucking stars, Ray, nobody needs to have a conversation about whether you get a choice about what you do with your own body!"

"Don't you?" Ray demanded between gritted teeth. He could barely keep his voice even for the babies' sakes. This was the wrong time and the wrong place and— "Since when?"

"Since always. If... If it had been up to us—"

"It was up to you!" Ray interrupted; it felt like ripping something, but he was too angry, too hurt to care.

Gabriel stopped, closing his eyes and taking a slow breath in. "Yes," he admitted. "But we didn't know. I know it's... it's a shitty excuse. But it's true."

It was. At least as far as Gabriel was concerned. And wasn't it exactly what Ray had told Josh had happened? He couldn't really explain why he was so much angrier at Gabriel. This had nothing to do with him going after Ray and leaving the babies.

"What about when you tried to make me enjoy it when I told you I just wanted to get it over with?"

Gabriel flinched and his whole body stiffened. "Okay, stop, we can't—Let me call Yousuf to—"

Ray nodded, feeling awful. The babies couldn't understand what they were talking about, of course, but that didn't mean they couldn't hear them raise their voices. And no matter what, this was an adult conversation to be had in private.

Yousuf came trailing after Gabriel doing his best to pretend he had no idea why he's been called away to cover for both of them at once.

"Thanks," Ray told him and walked past him and right into Gabriel's room across the hall.

Gabriel followed him in, then stopped without closing the door until Ray shot him a puzzled look. There was hardly a point to seeking privacy if they were going to leave the door wide open.

"Do you want me to close the door?" his alpha asked in a tight voice and it hit Ray like a ton of bricks that Gabriel thought...

"Yes," he said, swallowing hard. "I..."

Gabriel pushed the door until it clicked shut, then moved to face out his window across the room, as far as he could possibly get from Ray standing by the door. "You think I don't care if you want to— If you want to sleep with me," he said slowly.

"You didn't... You didn't listen," Ray made himself say. It was *true*. Maybe Gabriel regretted it, but he'd done it. He'd kept pushing until Ray had...

"I care," Gabriel said, voice scraping out of his throat. Ray didn't say anything. "I was wrong. I know that. I thought... I thought you were just shocked and, I dunno, shy about how being an omega made you feel. You are... You are young. I thought... I remembered you'd wanted me before, so I figured you still did. It seemed you did, you were so..." He stopped himself before he mentioned how absolutely Ray's body had bent to his alphas' desires. "I was wrong," he repeated, hopeless and as helpless as Ray had ever seen him. He looked up from where he was bent over the windowsill and met Ray's eyes in the glass. "But I'm not going to get it wrong again. You won't let me. And Alec won't either."

"You don't want to risk it," Ray realised.

Gabriel turned around. "No," he admitted. "Of course not, what kind of arsehole do you think I am?"

Ray looked down, suddenly uncomfortable. Because it was one thing to assume Gabriel had done it not knowing, but to imagine he'd known what he was putting Ray through and had gone ahead anyway... It wasn't something he deserved. It had just seemed so easy for him to ignore every signal Ray had been able to give. "Okay," he said, and only noticed it didn't answer Gabriel's last words when his mate stiffened. "I mean, I—I get it. You didn't know. I just—I felt like you didn't care, like you just thought if I was... if my body—" He waved down at himself. "If you could, then..."

It took Gabriel long enough to respond that Ray looked up, seeking the answer on his face. "I don't expect you to forgive me," his cousin said softly, defeated. "I don't—I'm pretty sure I don't deserve you to. But I would like to... I don't think I can leave and stay away. I mean, you are... you are my mate—"

"Leave?" Ray cut him off. "You can't leave!"

"No," Gabriel agreed gently. "I can't."

"And I don't want you to, anyway." Ray huffed out a breath and stepped back until he could lean against Gabriel's bureau. He let himself take in the room—tidy and a little bare—to avoid Gabriel's face. "What would that help?"

"What do you want, Ray?" his cousin asked softly, and there was a weight to the words, a promise implied: whatever it was, if Gabriel could give it to him, he would.

Ray wanted to look up, but it seemed to be too much for his wolf when he was trembling a little already. "I want you to stay," he managed. "And I want you to be the best alpha you can. To take care of the babies, and to help out. And to... to be careful. I need you to be careful because... I don't want to be scared of you anymore."

He had to press his lips together to keep any other sound from coming out—he didn't think it'd have been words.

He heard Gabriel swallow thickly across from him. "That's the last thing I ever wanted."

It rang true between them, like a judgement. A promise. Ray thought of words, but he wasn't sure he was physically capable of producing any, and it seemed... absurd when they both knew now.

"I won't..." Gabriel started, then seemed to think better of it. "I swear I won't ever touch you sexually again without your express invitation."

Ray's head jerked up. "You can't know—"

"*I* won't," Gabriel insisted, all the power of his will behind the words. "If... if we miscalculated, if the wolves need it or something, we'll talk about it. I will tell you about it and we will find a way. But I don't want you to wonder, and I would like it to be okay to... to hug you, or just, I don't know, give you a noogie if you score on me."

Ray swallowed, suddenly flooded with the warmth of Gabriel's body. Not—not recently. Long ago, just a hug after a match time, maybe. He'd grown up being touched casually—werewolves were a particularly touchy bunch—and then he'd gained a pack and lost that intimacy.

It was crazy, but it was like Gabriel said: they were supposed to have sex and it'd seemed like sex was all they could have.

"Is that okay?" Gabriel checked, unable to stand the silence long. "You don't have to tell me now..."

"I don't know," Ray admitted, glancing up to meet his cousin's eyes. "I... I would like a hug."

Gabriel's eyes widened, blue and startled. He was stupidly beautiful, but Ray didn't really care about the regularity of his features. He wanted the tenderness on his face, the insecurity born from love—it wasn't possible to love someone and not be a little afraid they'd break. Anything and anyone you loved was always too fragile for your taste, too likely to be damaged—by the world but also by your own words and actions. He straightened, and Ray thought he might cross the space between them. Instead, he opened his arms in invitation and kept his eyes steady on Ray's face—vulnerable and open to Ray's refusal.

Ray wasn't sure this was a good idea, but he couldn't leave someone he loved exposed like that without responding.

He took a hesitant step closer, and then another, eyes on the slightly trembling corner of Gabriel's red lips. He didn't remember crossing the rest of the distance—it was all lost in the impact of their bodies connecting, the strength of muscle and sinew holding him steady, the tentative hands cupping his back as he threw his arms around his alpha's neck and forced him to lean down into the embrace.

Gabriel breathed out slowly next to his ear, still unsure, and Ray tugged at his long hair, demanding, until the arms around him tightened. Progressively, he relaxed against Ray, pressing the side of his face to Ray's forehead.

And Ray relaxed with him, wolf and man as one, and just held on in silence.

Gabriel had insisted on deboning and grilling chicken for dinner—knowing it was one of Ray's favourites—and Ray let himself be spoiled. They'd put the babies in the jungle gym, which Gabriel had fixed after its unfortunate encounter with Jamie's reflexes, and Ray had put on the TV as Gabriel went through chickens on the coffee table with quick, practised motions.

"I didn't think you knew how to cook," he admitted, watching the process as much as the program.

"I lived on my own for years," Gabriel pointed out good-naturedly. "And this is pretty much just prepping meat for grilling, doesn't take much."

It was true that preparing meat was a werewolf skill. Nice as it was to eat it fresh with sharper canines, sometimes it was necessary to hunt a little more to make up for the fact that they consumed about double the calories as a non-shifting human.

"Did you like that?" he asked, getting to his feet and going over to disentangle two of the pups who'd got a little too enthusiastic with their play fighting.

"Well, yeah. Though I guess it was a little lonely. I went back to visit a lot."

His parents, he must have meant, because he'd actively avoided Ray. Or so it had felt. "And that's when you met Alec, more or less?"

His cousin glanced up just as Ray turned back towards the sofa. "Yeah, couple months later. I didn't want to go back so much. My mum liked having me back, but my dad got a little annoying about it. I liked the guys from work and I figured there was nothing stopping me from hanging out with humans *and* getting laid."

"And then you fell for the first werewolf that crossed your path?"

Gabriel rolled his eyes, dropping another piece into the bowl. "Yeah, that's me, a walking cliché. Any other questions, mister?"

That shocked a laugh out of Ray. "You always called us that," he remembered. "You sound like Grandma Ruth."

"Hey," came a low greeting from the door and Gabriel turned his whole torso around to look at Alec. It made Ray smile even as Alec's gaze flickered between them. "You're cooking?" their doctor asked, walking into the room.

At their feet, there was a mini stampede as the pups realised another of their parents was home, and Alec knelt to receive their enthusiastic licks and get half climbed onto by Mikey. Gabriel was busy so Ray went over to rescue him.

Alec met his eyes with a tentative smile. "You are happy," he said, sounding pleased.

Ray nodded a little, rubbing Mikey behind the ears to get him to retract his claws so he could be removed from his perch on Alec's shoulder, where he'd climbed by stepping on Maria's head. Alec didn't seem particularly bothered by being practically at the bottom of a puppy pile, truth be told. He looked towards his lover and back at Ray, a question in his eyes. "We talked," Ray mouthed at him and tugged Mikey into his own arms.

His mate nodded, then scooped up Maria and Sasha, who were halfway in his arms already, and crouched before slowly getting to his feet and forcing the two puppies to relinquish their hold. There were yelps of complaint until Ray tsked at them and guided them back to the jungle gym.

To his shock, Alec stopped by the sofa on his way to put down his own charges. "Gabriel," he said and leaned right in to press a kiss to the other alpha's mouth—lingering just enough for a tease. It left Gabriel looking as stunned as Ray felt, which was an undoubtedly good look for him, and Ray kindly pretended not to notice.

D espite Gabriel's assurances that he wouldn't discuss what they spoke of in private with the other alphas, Ray knew he had to tell Josh the news as soon as possible. He owed him the courtesy at the very least.

But in a way, the news made his decision all the more difficult.

He would have had good reason to send a boy away. Whatever he'd told Josh, he didn't really have to ask his mother to know she'd agree to it and if he'd truly needed it...

But other than the knowledge of where she came from, could he really justify rejecting his own daughter for the sake of a man he'd personally ensured was beyond ever hurting him or his pack again?

Josh would be supportive either way, naturally. But Ray couldn't be sure he deserved that support. He needed to talk to someone who would tell him if he was making a mistake.

And that person was his mother.

It wasn't like she was perfect and, deep down, Ray still hadn't quite forgiven her for letting his uncle decide he should start a new pack and take five mates. But she didn't need to be perfect, she was his mum and one thing he knew, beyond a shadow of a doubt, was that she loved him.

Now that he had children of his own, he thought he might understand how hard it was to love someone that much and be forced to watch them stumble about, making mistakes, trying their best and failing. Just the idea of seeing a child of his being forced into a situation as the one he'd been in was... well, unthinkable. He breathed out, reminding himself of Gabriel's promise that they would ensure the same thing never happened to any of the pups if they presented as omegas.

First, he had to make the time to go see his mum, and for that, he needed Marisa to swap his schedule around so he could visit in the afternoon. He could have invited her over just as easily, but he didn't want to talk to her in his own territory—he needed the distance and it'd been a week since he'd left the house at all.

"When do you want to go?" Marisa asked, glancing at the timetable on the huge whiteboard they'd installed on the kitchen wall.

"Soon?" Ray said, and it came out hesitant enough she turned to look at him.

"You could go tomorrow," his sister suggested. "Irina is driving over and coming back not much later. Or one of the alphas could get you earlier if you want." Her eyes slid towards the whiteboard. "Alec's shift ends at six."

"Is someone free to cover for me?"

She shrugged. "I'll do it. You can take my place for the day, then I'll take your free afternoon on Tuesday."

She said it easily, like it was no big deal, but there was something a little off in her voice. "You sure that's okay? It's not—"

"You're going to tell her, aren't you?" she asked, meeting his eyes. She didn't say more or look anywhere but at his face.

"She already knows," he explained. "I... I need some advice."

Marisa was silent for a long, heavy moment. "Can I... Ray, I want to say something but I don't want you to take it the wrong way, or..."

He looked up at once, frowning. "Mari, you don't have to worry about upsetting me. I'm not... I'm not gonna break. I'm doing a lot better, you know that, right?"

"Yes!" she said quickly, voice going high. "Obviously, I can see that. But... You're still worried about what will happen..." She hesitated, then pushed ahead. "When the baby is born."

"Yes," Ray admitted. There was no point in beating around the bush. She knew everything there was to know about it, really.

"I don't... Why?"

Ray looked up and shot her an incredulous look. "*Why?*" he demanded.

Marisa raised her hands. "Don't get angry!" she said, sounding a little short of temper herself. "I told you I have to ask you something and I just—I want to make sure I get how you are feeling first."

"Then ask me, Marisa," Ray spat out. "I can't deal with all this talking in circles; what do you want to know?"

"Do you want to keep the baby?"

The question sent his pulse into overdrive at once and he had to look away from her earnest face. With a direct question like that... he could only answer the truth. He thought he might have been brave enough to do it if only he'd known what it was. "Yes," he tried, hoping it could be true. It rang hollow between them. He tried a denial next. "I don't want to keep it."

It was no better, his heart had skipped.

Marisa took a step closer to him. "Ray," she whispered. "I get it."

He exhaled, feeling like his throat was closing up. How could she get it? It didn't even make sense; how could both yes and no be lies? He had to want *something*. "You wanna explain it to me?"

"You didn't choose this. Not even like you chose your alphas," she clarified. "That... That fucking arsehole forced it on you. And it's not the baby's fault, of course, but... If it was me—" Her voice broke on the word and Ray heard her swallow thickly, maybe holding back tears. She was really close but still not touching him. He wasn't sure if he wanted her to stay away half as much as he wanted her to hold him. She didn't move, but her voice when she spoke next was even, calm, decided and ready. "I don't know if I could raise a child that came from such a terrible thing."

He didn't know why the words hit him so hard; it was nothing new, nothing he didn't know perfectly well to be true, and yet... He found himself bending forwards and covering his face with his hand to hide the tears springing from his eyes. He swallowed, trying to keep himself from breaking down and Marisa destroyed all his efforts by stepping into him and enveloping him in her arms. She was almost too small for it, but she was strong enough to make up for her size, holding him tightly enough he'd have needed to struggle to get away.

Strangely, it didn't frighten him. He didn't want to get away—he just needed a minute when someone else was holding him up, when he didn't need to keep going on pretending he was just fine and— "Shhh..." She hummed at him. He was crying, quietly wetting her hair and shirt. He clutched at her back, clinging to her hoodie as if he could keep himself afloat as long as he held on. And she held him back, rocking him a little and murmuring low, soothing words he couldn't quite process. At some point, he calmed down enough that some of the words started making sense and he realised Marisa was promising, again and again, that everything would be okay, that *she* was going to help him through this and so would everyone else in their pack.

It seemed too good to be true, but she believed it, and... so did Ray.

She let him pull back a little, and when she was sure he was breathing normally, stepped back and got him a glass of water from the sink. He drank it all, not waiting for her to insist.

He put it down and she nodded her approval. "I will take care of the baby for you," she told him. Ray frowned a little because she'd been doing that for months already, that was the whole reason she and the other betas had come over. She could see his confusion but she kept speaking, "There's milk pumps so you can do that and I'll feed the baby a bottle. I'll keep it with me in the beta wing, it's no big deal now that I have my own room. And Irina will help if it's very fussy."

Ray stared at her. "I—Do you want to... to adopt her?"

His sister's eyes widened. "Her? I didn't— Yes," she said. "I want to adopt her, but I don't want to take her from you. I just..." She glanced away. "I'm not... I do want children. I always have, and I know I can't have my own." She tried to say it evenly, Ray could tell, but she failed to hide her pain. It was too recent, too raw. "But I don't—"

"Stop," he asked her and she did, looking up at him as if awaiting judgement. "I'm not angry at you for offering," he reassured her. "I'm just... not sure. This would be forever and you are only seventeen; you can do anything you want with your life. Travel, get a job outside the house, or... I don't know, anything."

"Yes," she agreed. "And this is what I want. I mean, I'm happy being your beta and looking after your children. I don't... I don't need more than that, and if you think you will be okay looking after her yourself and it won't mess with your head, then please pretend I didn't say anything."

Except Ray didn't think any such thing. He couldn't. He wasn't that good at introspection but he'd barely turned down an abortion less than a month earlier. And what Marisa suggested was as close as not having to make another impossible choice on top of that one as he could get: the baby would be with the pack, but he wouldn't have to spend all his time with her. "I... I have to think about it."

Marisa gaped at him. "Ray! Of course you have to think about it! And talk to mum about it, obviously. We are not deciding her fate in a five-minute conversation." Her face softened. "How do you even know it's a girl? You're not even showing."

"Alec," he responded curtly. He knew he should have appreciated the reassurance that his condition wasn't noticeable yet but it simply reminded him that it would soon be.

She stiffened a little. "Well, um, you can go with Irina tomorrow. I'll... I'll go tell her."

He wondered if she'd talk to Irina about what they'd discussed—but he didn't have the energy to call her back and ask her not to. If he even had the right to ask.

Ray shifted in his seat, even though he knew perfectly well the plastic chair wouldn't get any comfier, no matter how much he fidgeted. "I have something to ask you... and it's about Marisa, but... I don't know, I want you to be impartial?"

His mother frowned a little, but nodded, pushing a cup of tea made just like he liked towards him.

"I'm thinking... Well, she asked if I would let her—" He curled his hands around his cup and brought it to his lips. He couldn't taste the tea, but strangely, he could feel the smooth porcelain against his lower lip.

"What did your sister ask you?"

Her voice came out rough, and Ray stared at the liquid as if he could find the answer to anything in its depths, as if there was a way to make this less painful for either of them. "She wants to raise the baby for me. To... to adopt it, I guess."

He wasn't here to ask for advice like he'd thought. Once Marisa had brought up the possibility, the relief he'd felt had been all the answer he'd needed. You were not meant to feel relieved when someone offered to take your child away from you.

He wondered if the wolf would care, once she was born.

But that didn't really matter; the child needed a parent that loved her, not an animal that'd make sure it was always fed and stayed away from predators and inconvenient crevices.

She'd never lack for food or shelter either way. It was something much more complex that Ray was afraid he couldn't give her. Something he'd had from his own parents, from his siblings, from his pack... Possibly the only reason he was still alive despite how terribly everything had gone since he'd presented: he knew he was loved.

He knew people had kids when they didn't have money or a home all the time, but those were things that luck could bring or take away. It was very different to have a child you knew you couldn't love.

"She's always wanted kids," his mum said after a pause.

"You don't—?" He glanced up, body tight with fear. "You don't think I'm... I'm wrong to want to do it?"

She jumped a little. "Wrong?" she repeated. "It's... It's your feelings, Ray. Your feelings can't be wrong, and... you have plenty of reason to feel the way you do."

"I just... maybe when I see her..." He stopped because his mum just looked patient. And in truth, Ray didn't want to convince *her*.

"Well, you don't have to make Marisa any promises yet, do you? And she will be staying with you regardless."

"But what about Marisa?" Ray demanded. "She's only seventeen, she shouldn't... she should enjoy her life, be young, do... I don't know, whatever she wants."

His mum snorted. "You think *Marisa* wants to go dancing and partying and whatever else it is young people do?" she asked incredulously.

"Well, she didn't really get to do it that much," he pointed out. "We always needed her too much."

"Yes," she agreed. "And we needed you too, but you went out with Josh and played football, went on dates... We made time for that because you wanted to do those things. And we did it for TJ too. But your sister... I don't know if you remember, but once when she was about eleven, we were visiting the Kendricks and at one point the children made a right mess of the garden and she came over to tell us about it. You know what she said?"

Ray shook his head.

"These children's parents should be ashamed of them," his mother said in a tiny, serious voice that did sound quite a bit like Marisa.

He laughed. "It does sound like her."

"It is like her," she said. "She's never wanted that kind of thing, she's always wanted a nice home, enough food, peace of mind and quiet time to herself to watch her shows. And a family around her to keep her busy and love her for who she is."

"She's got that," Ray said softly. "Do you really think she needs...?"

"No, she doesn't need a child of her own. But she would love one." She hesitated. "You know I will take any child of yours in if they need it, right?"

He swallowed but nodded. "I don't want to give you more work."

She shrugged. "Ray, children aren't something I have ever planned for. I most certainly did not plan to raise five on my own. But it was worth it, and it will always be worth any effort to make any of you happier. I would be happy to do it."

She would do it well, too. She would love this little girl like she was her own because she would be—she was Ray's child too, after all—but he didn't need her to tell him that she was tired too. It'd been a long six years since her mate—the man she was meant to be with forever—had been taken from her.

If he'd lived, she might have had more children. But he hadn't and now she could have time to take care of the ones she had instead—to spend time with Anne, Harry and Glen, and keep TJ in line until he presented, or moved out to explore the world, or whatever it was that Ray's brother decided to do with his life once he was eighteen.

She deserved that time. She'd earned it.

And Ray knew too well how hard her life had been to ask her to make yet another sacrifice for his sake. Not when Marisa actually *wanted* to do it.

"You have to settle any disputes we have," Ray warned her. "Like, I don't know, hair dyeing or boyfriends. If we cannot agree on anything, it's up to you."

His mother laughed. "Don't worry, I didn't think that would ever stop being my job!"

Chapter nineteen

"So it's our fourth date and everything," Josh said. Ray eyed the car door he was holding open for him in invitation. Josh pretended not to notice that it was a little weird. "So I figured we'd go to a restaurant, have dinner sitting down properly and everything."

"With cutlery?" Ray teased, remembering the sushi restaurant. It was amazing how someone with reflexes as fine as Josh's could mess up using chopsticks in so many different ways.

Josh closed his own door and shot him a look. "Yes," he said sarcastically. "There might even be several sets of cutlery if you play your cards right."

There were indeed multiple forks on their table at Ravello, the finest Italian dining Lanchester had to offer. Ray knew it, naturally, but it'd never crossed his mind to eat there before.

"My turn to pay," Josh reminded him, placing a hand on his lower back to guide him forward. "So I can choose."

Ray hesitated only for an instant. "Am I a kept man now? I can get used to this."

That made Josh laugh hard enough that the maître d' rushed over to get them seated before they made more of a spectacle of themselves. They were clearly underdressed for the venue and too loud for it as well but everyone was too polite to mention it—Ray guessed it was what you got when they were charging you the cost of an actual meal for a bread basket.

He wasn't sure what to order after that so he followed his mother's rule and went for the meat menu—more value for money. Plus, he *was* a werewolf.

Josh had let him order first and from the way he paused, Ray realised he'd been tempted. "Go on," he dared him with a raised eyebrow. "Live a little."

They decided to live a lot and ordered some starters: baby prawns as well as tomatoes and mozzarella in some sauce Ray couldn't quite figure out—maybe because he couldn't quite make himself slow down enough to separate the rich flavours melting in his mouth.

He caught Josh watching him eat and felt his face heat up. "What?"

"That was..." Josh started, then paused and licked lips, and a slow smile curved over his mouth. "Totally worth the eight quid," he finished with a smirk.

"Oh, shut up," Ray replied. "You try it and tell me it isn't amazing."

"Oh, it's pretty amazing," Josh agreed, not taking his eyes off Ray.

They had eaten most of their mains by the time Josh felt the need to turn the conversation to more serious matters.

"I have been thinking and... well, obviously it wasn't on your list, but you said you didn't write it because you thought it'd..." He was very carefully cutting another piece of meat, and just as clearly didn't mean to eat it. "Well, it did freak me out, I guess. But it would be easier if... If we did it the other way. Around."

It took Ray a moment to parse that, convoluted as it was. "What?" he asked when he did because he was pretty sure Josh had just suggested that Ray...

Josh's fork clattered a little as he fumbled to put it down. "We don't have to, and like, I get if you are not into it. Plenty of men aren't. Like, gay men, but... Fuck, sorry, I'm not saying you are gay," his best friend insisted. Like Ray would have taken offence after everything they'd done together. "I know you are bi, obviously," he added and Ray almost laughed. Not that he didn't enjoy talking about beautiful actresses with Josh and everything, but he didn't really feel the need to call himself anything. He felt plenty of people were already aware of his sexuality as it was.

"Josh?" he cut in, and Josh inhaled sharply and glanced up at him. "I know you are bi too, but I have no clue what you are trying to say."

Josh met his eyes and opened his mouth but the words seemed to fail him. He took a sip of his water, then looked at Ray again with obvious effort. "I would like you to top."

Ray blinked at him, brain not quite able to process, and Josh remained silent but couldn't manage to keep from fidgeting in place, twisting his serviette and rearranging the second set of cutlery. "But why?"

"Oh, it... Well, I would like to know what it feels like," Josh explained, so tentative it was nearly a question. "And it would help me feel... in control. I think."

"You want to be in control," Ray echoed, a little surprised. He wasn't sure how he felt about that. He remembered Alec asking if *he* wanted to be in control during sex and how little choice he'd always felt he had with girls, and how little choice he'd had with his alphas during heat. He still didn't know the answer.

"No, not like that," Josh said quickly. "I mean... of me. I—I want to be sure I can stop," he lowered his voice at this but kept his eyes on Ray's face. He was flushed and looked tense as a wire—ready to bolt but holding himself still and waiting for Ray's answer.

"Oh." Ray took a hasty sip of his own water. He still wasn't worried about Josh—his best friend had shown impressive control even right after... Well, when the others had seemed unable to stay away from Ray. He'd certainly lost control on occasion but that had been the wolves' fault, and Ray's had been just as... enthusiastic.

But the reasoning made enough sense to make him think about what Josh was asking and those weren't thoughts he really wanted to be having in public—even if humans were nose-blind. He cut another piece of his meat, more for something to do than from any desire to eat it, but once it was on his fork, he brought it to his mouth and chewed, buying himself precious seconds.

He cursed his teeth, better adapted to tearing meat apart than humans', and finally, he had to speak, "Is this... Is this something you want?"

"What?"

"Does the idea seem..." He licked his lips, searching for the right words. "Do you think it's hot?"

"Oh, yeah. I mean, sure, I—I've thought about it," Josh admitted. From under his eyelashes, Ray caught him going a dull red that spoke volumes regarding the context of that thinking.

"Really?" Ray asked, raising his head, and it came out too loud, too... eager. "I mean... I just didn't—"

"I have," Josh interrupted. "I thought about it before you presented. Like, I thought about both things. I figured... I wanted it to be fair, if..." He shrugged, then picked up his cutlery again and started carefully destroying his chips.

"I can't believe you were thinking about being fair and I—" He stopped. "I feel a bit like an idiot, I was so sure you wouldn't want to."

Josh raised his honey eyes to meet Ray's. "You are a bit of an idiot," he agreed. "But I like you anyway."

Ray attempted to glare but had to look away, struggling to control the blush taking over his face. "Well, that just shows you how smart *you* are," he said back.

Josh snorted a little but didn't outright laugh at that poor attempt at sass—given, it might have been more out of respect for the ambience than Ray's wit.

"I know you want to try doing it the usual way," Josh said kindly and very low. "And I want to try to give you that too, if—"

"Are you serious?" Ray interrupted. "Right now all I want is to finish this very expensive meal my boyfriend bought me and take you home so we can try this."

Josh's eyes widened and his heart skipped a beat before starting to work harder. Ray did not have to guess where all that blood was pumping. "I—I think we can get it to take away."

The road was empty—as it usually was, only the pack lived in that direction and most of them would be getting ready for bed this late at night.

"Oh, come on," Ray whined. "We'd go faster if we shifted and ran back!"

"You are free to do that," Josh replied agreeably.

Ray was seriously tempted, except he'd eaten quite a lot and there would be no point in being home without Josh anyway. "Are you freaking out about this? You know you can change your mind, right?"

Josh glanced at him, smiling. "Not that I'm not flattered, but no, I just don't want to crash before we get home."

That silenced Ray a little too effectively and Josh looked back. "Ray? I... I'm sorry, I wasn't—"

"Don't," he asked softly. "I'm not upset. You're right, we should be careful."

It wasn't entirely true; it was hard to think of his dad without a little twinge of regret, a little twist of... he wasn't sure. He'd loved his dad, of course, but it'd been long enough that sometimes he wondered if he'd known him at all. He didn't know what was worse: that he missed him fiercely, or that some days he forgot to.

Josh nodded, but he was only quiet for a few seconds before he added, "Check the glove box."

Ray clicked it open. There was a bag inside. From Boots Pharmacy, which was quite odd because it wasn't like... "Oh." He held the bottle up to read the label—not that its purpose wasn't obvious. "For..."

"Not that I was too confident," Josh explained quickly. "I figured there's always jerking off, right?" He looked Ray's way when he got no response, but Ray was finding it hard to think, let alone vocalize. "Did I break you?"

"A little?" Ray offered. He was painfully hard and he was pretty sure Josh could tell. Assuming he could focus better than Ray could at the moment, of course. "Can we... I actually have something I need to tell you."

He'd promised himself he would and if there was something guaranteed to keep his mind out of the gutter, it was this conversation. "I have decided something." He saw Josh nod out of the corner of his eye but kept his own eyes on the road ahead—he could feel his territory coming closer, the land calling to him like a beacon. "Marisa wants to adopt the baby. The girl," he remembered to add. "I spoke to my mum about it and she thinks it will be good for Marisa."

"Oh," Josh exhaled softly next to him and Ray forced himself not to squirm. His dick didn't even seem that fazed by his nerves.

"So I... I will let her do that," he added when nothing more was forthcoming. "At least, I think so, because maybe... Well, she's not taking her anywhere, so..."

Josh reached out and took hold of his hand. He didn't look Ray's way, but then again, he didn't seem to need to. "I'm glad you figured it out," he said softly. "I... I wasn't sure what to tell you."

"You wanted me to keep her," Ray pointed out but he didn't try to pull his hand away.

"No." Josh shook his head. "I wanted you to be okay with keeping her, or... or sending her away. That's all I ever want: for you to be okay."

"Well, I guess I couldn't be okay with either," he admitted, not just to Josh, but to himself. "But this works. I really think... I think Marisa will love her. And I... I want her to be loved. That's the most important thing, right?"

Josh took his hand back and, for a moment, Ray thought he'd said something wrong, but it turned out he just needed it to park—even though their so-called driveway was just flattened grass. He killed the engine and turned to face Ray, eyes clear and searching. "Yes," he agreed, smiling softly. "I think once you got that, you can pretty much call it a day."

Ray was man enough to admit he was freaking out slightly. In fact, he thought as Josh pulled off his shirt in a smooth move that left him bare from the waist up, he couldn't see how any man could face the experience of being allowed inside another person's body with anything but barely concealed terror.

It was just too much to be trusted like that. To be invited to touch someone's body in a way that could hurt them so badly and yet also bring them so much pleasure... But maybe most men weren't equipped to understand what they were being offered, or how fragile trust was when someone exposed their very soul to your hands.

Ray knew. He understood. Maybe more than he wished to.

But then again, knowledge of that kind never came cheap.

"Ray?" Josh asked. He'd toed off his shoes and stopped undressing. He waved vaguely in his direction. "You don't have to take off your shirt if you don't want to."

Ray's heart stuttered. It was kind of him to offer—just like Josh.

But Ray couldn't accept.

Because Josh, he understood now, didn't quite know what he was doing.

It was up to Ray to do right by him, to take care of him when he needed it. He thought about trying to explain, but the mere idea of words for this was laughable.

Josh was right, of course, he didn't want to expose the slight curve of his belly, noticeable even when he tried to hold it in. But he wasn't going to touch Josh like this without baring himself too, without giving as much as he was getting.

That wasn't the way to touch someone you loved.

It wouldn't be comfortable, he knew. But why should it be? Love was the act of believing another person could see who you truly were and embrace it. There was no way to take that kind of risk without being a little uncomfortable. It wouldn't have been sane to.

And without the crazy risk, it wouldn't have been love, either.

He shook his head and sat down to get his shoes off, then unbuttoned his trousers—still his own from before, but not for long—and threw them at the chair Josh kept by the window. He could have got a desk like Ray had, but he didn't really like being alone in his room. It was unsurprising coming from the boy who'd spent hours watching shitty cartoons with Ray's siblings when Ray hadn't been free to hang out, just to avoid going back to his empty house.

He let himself keep his shirt on a little longer and raised his head to check on Josh—heartbeat steadily increasing as Ray dropped layers. Josh watched him back, standing his ground like he'd been rooted there. Ray licked his lips and took a tentative step closer to the bed.

"Still think it's a good idea?" he checked.

Josh snorted and exhaled noisily, but then he smiled. Ray knew that smile; it was his 'this-is-crazy-but-I-can't-help-myself' smile. Ray had done many stupid things to get it and he was willing to admit that he wasn't too grown up to do a couple more.

"You—You will tell me if it's... too much, or weird?" he added with some consideration for Josh's pride.

Josh shook his head, lips pressed together, and rolled his eyes at Ray. "I will tell you if it's too much," he agreed. "As soon as it starts being *anything*."

His eyes were bright with the implied dare and Ray's body responded to the challenge before he quite knew what he was doing. He pulled his shirt over his head fast enough he almost didn't break eye contact and stepped into Josh's space before his friend had time to look down at him.

He finally got his hands on Josh's bare arms, bulging with muscle under Ray's too sharp nails as Josh exhaled right into his mouth and welcomed his tongue with a low, stuttered moan. He was clumsy reaching back for Ray, too eager and too shocked for much finesse.

Ray didn't give a fuck about it, he just wanted more. He wanted *all of it.* He shoved into Josh's mouth and rolled his hips against his belly, groaning as the sensitive skin got pressed against the too-rough cloth of his boxers instead of Josh's soft skin.

Josh didn't ask, just yanked Ray's boxers down and took him in hand, making him shudder from head to toe with the sensation and stumble into him. "Hey," Josh said, holding him up with a hand on his hip.

Ray leaned back enough to glare at him. "Stop..." he asked and Josh's hand froze on him like someone had taken out his batteries. "Or I'll come," he wheezed out.

"Oh," Josh said and Ray could see him swallow. He loosened his grip on Ray's cock. *Fuck*, Ray thought. He shouldn't have said it like that; he'd made Josh think... He shoved him back onto the bed like he could interrupt Josh's thoughts as well as his own.

Josh gasped as he bounced and glared up at him as soon as he got his breath back. "You are such a dick," he told Ray, and then his eyes widened a little and Ray realised he was naked. Completely bare to Josh's hungry eyes roaming his skin. He stiffened and, of course, Josh noticed and pulled his eyes back to Ray's face with a guilty twist to his mouth. "Sorry, I—"

"No," Ray interrupted. "I'm not..." He licked his lips. "I don't want to hide. Not from you." He made himself raise his gaze again but Josh was still caught on his face, eyes bright and body tense on the bed. Like...

"I'd rather feel you than look at you," Josh said patiently.

Ray dared anyone to resist an offer like that. He stepped forward and climbed into Josh's lap, taking hold of his chin to guide him into a kiss. He was tired of holding back, tired of being afraid. "I—" He couldn't find words beyond that so he bit at Josh's lip and then pushed his tongue inside as if he had a hope in the world of getting enough of him, getting deep enough, staying long enough. Josh sucked on his tongue, clutching at him greedily and Ray pressed down on him—not caring if he came, or if he didn't. He wanted it to last forever, and he couldn't wait to reach that point where Josh was all he could see, hear, smell or taste. All that existed. All Ray could think about.

It was just a moment, but he needed that moment, that purity, that clarity, that connection.

Josh tugged him down and shoved his hips up, desperate for some contact on his own cock, refusing to let go for even a moment. Ray fell too heavily, making him gasp for breath and dig his hand into Ray's back too hard.

He bent down and kissed him again. He had to, he had to lick at every molar and every ridge and taste Josh's tongue deep in his own mouth. He had to press his dick against Josh's stomach and grind down on Josh's erection under his arse. He had to have everything, every little thing, and all of it together and it could never stop. He couldn't stop. He couldn't bear to.

Eventually, Josh found the strength to push Ray away by the shoulders. Ray panted down at him, feeling like he was on a ledge and Josh the only thing keeping him from falling.

"Trousers?" Josh said. Because Ray hadn't given him time to undress and because he wanted...

Oh, moon, Josh wanted Ray *inside him*.

He rolled away and onto his back, fists clenched, heart going so fast it was closer to a murmur than a beat. He felt Josh sit up next to him and realised he couldn't... He shot to his feet, took a couple steps away, needing a little distance. He was afraid Josh would ask him if he was okay, but his friend just kept going: the sounds of him tugging his jeans off followed by the subtler shifting of his boxers hitting the floor.

"Ray?" he asked when he was done.

Ray could do nothing but turn towards him—he was an irresistible call, the one true place Ray knew to call home.

He didn't want to resist. It didn't matter if the wolf agreed, this was Ray's truth: he'd loved this boy all his life, in all the possible ways.

Josh was sitting on the bed. Completely bare. Not just naked, that would have had Ray throwing himself into his arms without thinking twice. But he was looking at Ray openly: lips parted as if he was about to speak but his thoughts were too fragile to voice, eyes dipping to Ray's shoulders and lower still but returning to his face as if searching for something there.

Ray didn't know what there was to find, but if it was in him... *Josh* had to see it. He swallowed, suddenly afraid. Because this was the only way to express what he felt, to finally reveal himself to the man he'd loved for as long as he could remember... And he already knew too well that their bodies were dangerous and prone to overwhelm their minds.

"Ray?" Josh asked again.

He exhaled, held himself still a moment longer. "You will tell me if I..." He knew he was repeating himself, being as overbearingly careful as he resented Josh for being. But he couldn't help it.

Josh just nodded. "Yeah," he promised easily, and leaned back on his elbows, exposing his torso and legs and drawing Ray's eyes inevitably to the rise of his erection.

Ray took a step closer, his knee bumped Josh's and somehow he was straddling him, no time in between—he was blanketing Josh's body with his own, the warmth of their skin becoming sweaty. They pressed against each other too hard and too fast as if deep down they could not believe that there was such an absurd limit between them as flesh.

"Josh," Ray begged quietly. He was clutching too hard at Josh's forearms and he couldn't... he couldn't stop pushing his cock against the hot skin of Josh's hip, his stomach, it wasn't enough. And he...

Josh's hand tightened on his arse, pressing their groins even closer together, a sweaty, sticky mess, and then he arched into Ray and their dicks slid together—silky and raw and perfect, and Ray couldn't *breathe*.

Josh took hold of his hair and crushed their mouths together even as he hooked their legs together and rolled his hips, dragging Ray under the irresistible tide of his need, the unbearable strength of his love. And just like that, tangled together as far as their skin would go, too soon and not ready, they went crashing over the edge.

The world was on fire, and it was glorious.

Ray shuddered on top of Josh, a little cold and beyond too sensitive. Josh's arms and legs tightened like he was afraid Ray would try to pull away—like he would care about the discomfort of his overstimulated nerves compared to the sheer agony it would be to stop touching Josh now.

"Told you," he breathed wetly into Josh's neck. It came out sounding like he'd been screaming. He hoped he hadn't, but he couldn't get past the fog of afterglow to actually worry about it.

Josh laughed a little hysterically from underneath him. "Yeah, that'll teach me." He kissed Ray's neck, nuzzling sleepily. "Don't go to sleep," he warned and Ray turned his face, pressing his nose against the warm prickly skin of Josh's cheek.

He hardly thought it was fair to ask him to stay awake when Josh was so warm and comfortable beneath him. And then Josh made it easier by rolling his hips and turning his body, dumping him onto the bed.

Ray grunted a complaint, not opening his eyes. He nearly jumped out of his own skin when Josh took hold of his right hand and guided it to Ray's own belly, to the very sticky remains of their pleasure. Ray's eyes flew open, but lying on his back, the bump wasn't very visible. It was also a little hard not to focus on the sticky mess on his fingers. He frowned at Josh, bemused, and then Josh smirked, dirty and provocative. "Maybe we don't need lube."

Ray exhaled noisily, glancing down at his hand and up again. "This isn't..."

Josh frowned a little. "Isn't what?"

"I mean, for— It's part of the ritual," he said weakly, raising himself onto his elbow. "And you haven't..." It wasn't exactly this, of course, most alphas wouldn't be caught dead *thinking* about letting their omega fuck them, but the ritual required the alpha swallowing his omega's seed to complete the cycle of planting his own seed inside him.

Ray had been looking forward to that part of it even if he was scared of freaking out for the actual fucking. It wasn't just the idea of a blowjob; there was something in him that craved this connection, having a part of himself in Josh's body...

But not if Josh didn't want him.

"Ray, I will," Josh said, curling up towards him. He put his hand on Ray's hip and looked up at Ray trustingly. "I will be your First Alpha. There was never any question of—just... timing."

Ray nodded slowly, so relieved he was trembling slightly. Josh didn't say anything, just rubbed his hip in slow, even circles as Ray breathed in and out a few times. He'd been almost sure because he knew Josh loved him and... But almost hadn't been enough. He pressed his face to Josh's cheek for a moment, inhaling the scent of his skin.

And of the mess they'd made between them. He glanced down. "So..."

"No ritual," Josh said at once. "I didn't—Just want to have you inside me." His voice was rough and not all that steady. Ray smiled at him, nervous but comforted, and Josh smiled back, all bravado. He didn't break their gaze as he leaned back and bent his own knee to his chest. That alone was enough to set Ray's heart racing and Josh didn't stop there, rolling onto his back and tugging at Ray's hand until he followed and knelt by his side. He guided Ray's hand to the trail behind his balls.

He was hot there. Burning. Ray trailed his wet fingers down until he found the puckered flesh, soft as silk and closed up. Josh shivered under his touch and Ray's body clenched sympathetically. He glanced up, waiting for Josh's little nod of encouragement. Ray pressed a little harder and it sucked the tip of his finger in, making him gasp. Josh laughed, from nerves or at his shock, Ray wasn't sure. He pulled his hand away, regretting it at once. But it was worth it when he pressed more of their mixed come against Josh's hole and rubbed—Josh made a sound like he'd choked on air and clutched hard at his own bent leg.

"Good?" Ray checked, half teasing, half serious.

"*More*," Josh replied. He was panting and Ray checked his face—cheeks flushed, wet tongue licking absently at his parted lips. He looked a little overwhelmed, but that was all. And he'd asked for more.

Ray crawled back and eased Josh's bent leg out of the way so that he could kneel between his lover's knees. The change in position opened Josh up enough that his finger sank past the first knuckle. Josh's eyes widened under him, heart skipping as Ray hooked his leg over his own elbow to give himself room to work.

Josh tensed in his grip and Ray stopped, finding his eyes and explaining, "Just need a better angle." Josh squirmed a little, eyelashes fluttering as he looked away. Ray put his clean hand on his face—hot to the touch—and turned him back.

He was shivering slightly, body coiled tight, Ray's finger barely fitting inside him. "Josh?" he checked. "Should I—?"

"No!" Josh's hand shot out to take hold of Ray's forearm. He huffed, shifting his shoulders on the bedding to get more comfortable. "I—Gimme a minute."

Ray would, of course, but he wasn't quite sure if he needed to say so, or... It didn't matter because Josh let go of his arm so he could bury his fingers in Ray's hair and tug him down for a kiss, pushing his tongue into his mouth like he was thinking of getting as deep into Ray's body as he planned to let Ray into his. Ray groaned at the image, opening his mouth for Josh and barely remembering to keep his finger still where it still lodged.

Josh's bent knee flexed and before Ray knew it, his friend was thrusting into his touch, impaling himself further and nearly upsetting Ray's fragile one-handed balance over him. Josh pulled at his hair and dug his fingers into his arm in an effort to keep him upright and Ray emerged from the kiss already laughing.

"Need a hand?" Josh asked.

In response, Ray curled his index finger inside him. Josh gasped a little, swallowing hard, but just when Ray was starting to wonder if he'd gone too far, he narrowed his eyes at Ray. "That all you got?"

Ray tried to remember the steps among the fog of lust, then slowly pulled his finger out and extended a second one. His fingers were still slick and wet, but he pushed gently at the delicate flesh between Josh's buttocks until just the tips were inside. He glanced up and Josh, tosser that he could be, smirked and raised his eyebrows at him.

Ray pushed his fingers in all the way.

Josh couldn't hold back a whimper at that, tossing his head to the side and clenching his eyes shut, body tightening around Ray's fingers like a vice. "More?" Ray asked sweetly.

His mate's eyes found his face, eyelashes fluttering too fast as if echoing the movement around Ray's fingers. It hit him suddenly that he was going to feel that around his cock and his hips snapped forward, pushing his dick against the back of Josh's thigh. Josh shuddered at the touch and yanked on Ray's arm even as he lifted his hips into it.

"Yes," he said, breathless and true.

More felt like an insane demand to make when two fingers barely fit, but Josh exhaled and actually relaxed enough to take all four. He was going to leave a permanent indent of his nails on Ray's arm but watching him fall apart under him, Ray couldn't find it in himself to care.

He wanted him *now*. He was too hard to wait and even though he'd come in the last half hour, it felt like the barest stimulation would end up with another embarrassing wet spot. "Okay," Josh decided and pulled on Ray's right arm hard enough Ray had to resist him.

"Wait!" he demanded, voice going high in alarm. "You'll hurt yourself. You can't—"

"I can't wait," Josh gritted out, and Ray could only nod. He still pulled his fingers out slowly, watching Josh's face twist with an emotion he couldn't quite decipher.

"Josh?" he checked again. He couldn't help himself—he was flying blind and if he...

"*Yes,*" his mate said, a yearning so profound it twisted inside Ray, making his own need burn bright as fire. "Yes, *do it.*"

For a moment, he held still, proving to himself that he could, and then he fell into it like it was the edge of a cliff and he could fly. He took hold of Josh's other leg and hoisted it over his shoulder He found his slick entrance even as his other hand tightened painfully around his own cock for long enough to make this possible at all. Then he was pressing the head against the soft, wet heat of Josh's body. It had only been a moment since he'd had half his hand inside so when his hard cock was pressed to the muscle, it opened up, easily sucking him in until Ray froze, muscles locked and eyes clenched shut against the all-consuming pleasure radiating from his groin.

He knew he had to look up. He had to check Josh was okay. But he couldn't. He couldn't do this when he... It was *too much*. He couldn't look Josh in the eye when he was *inside him*. There had to be some barriers; he didn't think he would survive if there weren't. He couldn't— He felt Josh's palm on his face as if through a fog.

He didn't mean to open his eyes, he was just surprised, and then Josh's bright eyes met his and he couldn't look away. They were... Ray could feel where they were joined together and they were... Josh's hand curved around his jaw and behind his neck and he slowly pulled Ray down, tightening his legs even though it bent him further in two. And like that, very slowly, Ray sank deep into him.

When their lips met, it felt like the final barrier had crumbled. Ray had been afraid, but as his heart battered against his chest and his body grew slick with sweat, he felt his mind soar instead, a joy so overwhelming he could hardly breathe through it.

Josh's nails dug deeper into him and Ray's hips snapped forward hard. Josh's tongue stabbed into Ray's mouth in sweet retribution. There was no stopping then; Ray bit at him, shoving in again and Josh arched into him, seeking more, arse clenching tight enough to keep Ray inside if not for the slickness of their semen and Ray's precome making every slide into his mate's body easier and faster. Josh let out a strangled sound, tearing his mouth away to gasp but pushing up into Ray's cock at the same time. He couldn't get enough, legs flexing hard enough on Ray's shoulders to hurt.

Ray gave him more. He gave him everything, pressing clumsy, uncoordinated kisses to Josh's cheeks, his forehead, his ear, and giving him sharp little jabs that had him shuddering and panting for breath.

"*Ray.*" Josh's voice broke on his name and Ray saw the tortured joy on his face grow frantic. "Touch me."

Ray's stomach fell and he almost lost his balance as he scrambled to get his left hand between them and around Josh's thick, hard cock. It seemed to grow in his grip and Josh let out a desperate whine, body struggling to get closer to both Ray's hand and Ray's cock despite his awkward position. Ray's body responded like it had been primed for it, pushing himself into Josh's arse once more, hard and true, as his hand tightened and jerked him off.

Josh screamed as he came, convulsing in place. Ray would have screamed too, except the feeling of Josh's body sucking him in was too much to breathe through. He thrust in again, helpless to stop the motion of his hips, and again as Josh pulled at him, licking at his lips because neither of them could manage the coordination for a kiss. He felt his orgasm start deep in him. It hurt for an endless instant as his mate's body locked tight around him and then he was free, soaring high in blind joy.

He clutched at Josh for too long afterwards—the mess cooling between them, Josh's legs still bent uncomfortably. But his mate didn't object and he barely seemed to notice when Ray shifted back until he could pull out of his body. Ray watched him for a long second until Josh opened his eyes and blinked at him—dazed and sleepy but exuding such contentment Ray couldn't keep himself from curling closer to his side.

Josh made an unhappy noise when Ray's smeared his own come against his skin—but curled an arm around Ray to ensure he didn't move, not seemingly planning to let go anytime soon.

Ray thought about checking once more. Just to be safe... But even their bodies had limits and not even Ray could manage to hold onto his fears while in the arms of the man he loved.

Chapter twenty

R ay woke first. He immediately wished he hadn't.
   Not because of the dried come everywhere, including stuck all over his genitals and belly, but because this was *it*. Josh would wake up and Ray would have to look at him and... He still remembered how he'd felt when Josh had first seen him in the hall, and how humiliated he'd felt after his first time. If Josh...

"Ray?" Josh asked in a whisper and Ray startled to see his eyes were open. "Why are you—Are you okay?"

Ray's heart was thundering in his chest and it took him a moment to filter out the sound of Josh's, steady and slow. Ray searched his face for something and Josh's mouth turned down. "Hey," he said. He didn't give Ray time to move, curling his fingers around his back to keep him in place and bringing his other hand to Ray's neck. "It's okay," he promised. "I mean..." He stopped, eyes flickering over Ray's face. "I'm okay, you—" He exhaled and slowly pulled his hand away. "You can move if you want," he offered in a small voice.

"What?" Ray said, his own arm around Josh tightening involuntarily. "I don't."

Josh glanced up, hand hovering between them and Ray couldn't handle it anymore, he leaned forward and pushed his face against Josh's neck, tightening his arm around Josh to bring their torsos back together. He didn't care about the mess, and if Josh wanted to push him away... Well, he damn well could.

Josh's arm returned, circling his back and tugging at him until he was half on top of his mate. "You were worried about me?" he asked into Ray's ear, quietly enough it must have been an effort.

Ray nodded into his shoulder. He didn't want to talk. He didn't think he could.

"You don't have to be. It was— It was really good. Crazy hot and—" Josh cut himself off and his heart jumped beneath Ray's cheek. "I love you," he whispered. He had to hear the way Ray's pulse spiked at that, but maybe he didn't understand because he kept talking. "I don't... I don't know if you are there yet, or—" He'd lowered his eyes like he couldn't bear to meet Ray's gaze "I understand if it's not—" Ray lifted his head, trying to pull away and Josh didn't resist, releasing him at once.

Ray hadn't expected it and he fell, but he finally managed to get himself disentangled and sit back on his knees. Josh pulled the arm he'd had under Ray's body back to curl against his own chest. He didn't seem relieved to get it back.

"Are you serious?" Ray asked in a hoarse voice. It came out all wrong, too harsh, too loud, and Josh flinched a little, curling up further. "No!" Ray said at once, wanting to reach out, to take hold of him and shake until he understood. But touch hadn't been enough. He'd thought if they did this, if they shared their bodies, it'd be obvious that... "I mean, I love you too. I have—I have loved you for as long as I can remember. I mean—"

But Josh didn't let him finish. He raised his eyes to Ray's, getting his elbow under himself but not trying to sit up yet. "I'm in love with you," he said, like a dare, like he expected...

"I know," Ray said. "You have to be; you are my fucking soulmate."

Josh gaped a little, eyes wide but unsure, and Ray couldn't bear it anymore, he leaned back down and sealed their mouths together. He made the kiss soft, almost too gentle for everything that was raging inside him. But he could be careful if Josh needed it, he could go slow and show him. He could prove himself, like a knight to a lady, careful and slow because he knew his path was true. Because Josh *loved him*. He'd known before, in a way, but it was different to hear it. It was crazy how it made him feel like he'd explode with it—a joy burning bright and dangerous that might as easily tear him apart as lift him up.

Josh's hand came up to him at once, pulling him closer, demanding it all. Ray groaned as Josh's tongue invaded his mouth, muscles going slack under the heat of his body. He'd only meant to be sweet but his knee bent of its own accord and fit perfectly between Josh's legs. The heat of Josh's erection burned against Ray's inner thigh, Josh's abs brushing tantalisingly against Ray's own cock, no matter how much he tried to push up into it.

But even they needed to breathe. Josh's mouth was red from kissing and it only made Ray want to kiss him some more—mark him up so that everyone would know. Then he became aware of the rest of Josh's body, no longer so pliant in his arms and shaking a little on top of him. *On top of him.* The words echoed in Ray's brain like thunder and when he shuddered, Josh lifted his lower body away from him, trying to move away.

But...

"*No.*" Ray dug his fingers into Josh's hips, inhaled and exhaled, taking stock of his body. Josh was tense as a wire on top of him, body ready to jerk away but letting Ray keep him close for now. It didn't feel anything like... like *Nicholas.* Ray wasn't on the ground, dirty and aching, he didn't fear for his family's lives, and he was most definitely willing.

Josh's body was on top of him, but the part he cared about was *Josh.* The position didn't matter.

Ray wasn't sure he could bear it, but he knew he couldn't ask for this without trying. He looked up and met his mate's eyes, letting him see his trepidation and his desire both, and then he licked his lips and asked, "Kiss me?"

"*Ray.*" Josh fell into him like a man starved, pressing short, clumsy kisses to his mouth until Ray managed to get hold of him and slow him down with long, indulgent sucks on his tongue as his hands roamed freely over Josh's back and buttocks.

They kissed for minutes, or centuries, faster and slower—their arousal fluctuating like the tide; their need for each other as steady as the sun.

They'd taken the edge off things earlier and now their bodies gave way to needs much deeper than pleasure.

But there was still something Ray wanted. If they were going to do this—being who they were and knowing what they knew about the future. "Josh?" he asked when his mate's lips were occupied on his neck.

Josh made a humming noise against his skin. After a moment he pulled himself up, letting Ray breathe easier. He was beautiful; eyes dark, lips red from all the kissing, and Ray wanted to paint the pleasure-drunk expression on his face a thousand times—even knowing he'd never fully capture it.

"What?" Josh asked.

"Will you...?" He swallowed, feeling trapped all of a sudden and forcing himself to stay still under his friend's warm weight. Josh *would* move if he asked, and it wouldn't help; it wasn't Josh's body making Ray feel flayed open. "I want..."

"Yes," Josh said when Ray couldn't make himself continue.

Ray's eyes flew to his and they stared at each other.

"But..." He pushed himself up, slowly enough that Ray could have brought him back down if he'd wanted. But Ray let him sit up instead until he was pressed to his side, leaning over Ray's prone body and carefully pushing his sweaty hair away from his forehead. "Do you really want to?"

Ray rolled the other way, away from his touch and his eyes. He didn't want to hide, exactly, but he needed a moment to pull himself back together. He still wasn't looking at Josh when he answered, "I don't know."

It was the truth, he could hear it. And even without looking, he could feel the pain it caused his mate. He sat up and made himself turn around, bending his own legs between their bodies. "I'm sorry," he said sincerely. "I shouldn't have—"

"You shouldn't have to," Josh cut him off. "But you do. You are *not* apologizing to me for something that isn't your choice at all."

"I could ask—" Ray started to offer.

"No!" Josh growled. His eyes widened as soon as the words were out. "I mean... Please don't, I— I can do it."

Ray frowned. "But you don't want to."

Josh's face fell. "Oh, Ray, don't you get it? I don't want *you* to have to go through with it. After everything... I—It's not fair."

Ray snorted. "Fair?" he echoed, crossing his arms over his middle, even though Josh was too close to look at him and wouldn't anyway. "When has anything been fair?"

"I..." Josh hunched forward. "Never," he agreed finally. "But I want to make it... As good as it can be. I want... If you let me, I want to be there for you. I want to take care of you."

"I don't need—" Ray started to say, but Josh didn't let him finish.

"I know you don't need me," he said bitterly. "But I need you. I need to know you are okay."

Ray sighed, "You are an idiot," he said softly. "Of course I need *you*." He reached out and gave him a sharp tap on the shoulder. "I *don't* need you to put yourself through this for me."

Josh glared at him. "I'm the idiot?" he asked. "You think I want you to ask one of them to—to be your first?

"It won't be my first." Ray shook his head. "This was my first." Josh's anger melted away. He licked his lips but didn't speak. "And what does it matter anyway? All the fuss about the first time is stupid. It's not the order that makes it good, is it?"

"No, but..." Josh swallowed, looking away for a moment before finding the strength to raise his eyes to Ray's. "This time is important; you are... I'm scared it won't be good and then you will think it *can't*."

"It looked like it was pretty good for you."

"It *was*," Josh said fervently. He reached out and placed his right hand on Ray's pulse point, cupping Ray's face and neck like words weren't enough. Ray started a little but Josh gave him time to relax without pulling away. "And... I want to give you that, too. What you did for me. I want to make you feel... I want to make you feel like there is no one else in the fucking world, like you are my everything."

Ray stared at him, heart battering in his chest. He had to swallow to be able to speak. "You will. But if it's... It doesn't have to be now. When—" He cut himself off.

Josh shook his head. "You can talk about it," he bit out.

"Can I?" Ray checked, frowning a little. He didn't think Josh was lying but his pulse had sped up like he was upset.

"Sergi's your mate too," Josh replied, not meeting his eyes.

"Yes, but he's not..." *My choice*, he thought. But it wasn't fair because Ray had chosen to ask Sergi to stay, even if the circumstances had been beyond fucked up. "He is not my First Alpha," he said instead. "You don't... Are you... are you jealous?" Josh dipped his chin, shrugging a little, his tanned skin shining in the soft light of the half-moon. He'd admitted as much in the Jeep already, but still, it made Ray's head spin a little. "Gabriel told me he wasn't going to... He didn't expect our relationship to be sexual anymore."

Josh's head snapped up, heart jumping as well. "What?"

"If... If I don't want to," Ray explained carefully. "And if we... If the wolves don't make us, then it's my choice. Gabriel... He said he won't even ask. He said none of them will."

"But he's your mate," Josh said, voice going high and thready. "You—"

"He's not the one I want," Ray said firmly. "You don't have to be jealous." Josh was watching him like he'd never seen him before, like he was a mirage in the desert or an apparition. "And you don't have to fuck me," he added with more courage than he knew he had.

Josh shook his head, not refusing as much as trying to communicate his confusion. "But... I don't get it."

"It's your choice, too," Ray reminded him. "If that isn't something you want, you don't have to fuck me just to— to make sure it goes okay. Or to make me..." He licked his lips, uncertain; it was harder to say the words now. "To make me love you."

His heart twisted when Josh abruptly pulled away and rolled off the bed. "But you need it!"

Ray dragged one of the pillows over his middle but stayed put. "No, I don't. Not now."

Josh turned to him, so frustrated it was almost possible to miss that he was stark naked. "What about when you do?"

"That's your choice too," Ray replied. He'd say it as many times as he needed to. He'd say it to Josh and to every one of his alphas—he wasn't going to make someone else feel the way he felt when the moon rose and the wolf's need took over. "I will ask and you can—"

"No," Josh cut him off like he couldn't even hear the words. "Don't..." He had to stop to take a breath but Ray didn't try to speak again. "I will be your First Alpha. I said so, and I *want* to. I... It's not... I'm afraid of hurting you again," he admitted at last, shoulders falling. He still met Ray's eyes straight on, his own shining with unshed tears. "But I'm not going to let that stop me."

Ray swallowed, then offered flatly, "Well, that's... hot."

Josh snorted a laugh that sounded a little wet and Ray felt his weight dip the bed as he crawled back to him. Ray took him by the shoulders, searching his face. "You can freak out, and stop. You *promised* me you would tell me, remember?"

"If you tell me," Josh replied, a little too seriously. "You got yourself a deal."

Ray nodded, letting his hands trail down Josh's biceps. "Would you...?" He glanced down. "Can you make me... ready?"

Josh tensed under his hands. "You don't want lube?"

He thought for a moment, then shook his head. "It's my body, I want to fucking enjoy it for once."

"Okay." Josh kissed his cheek and leaned back. "Lay back a little," he asked, guiding Ray down with little, flickering kisses to his face and neck. "I'm going to touch you there," he announced. Ray almost objected to the special treatment but held his tongue. Josh was scared of this too; he had a right to his own comforts—it cost Ray nothing but a little embarrassment to indulge him.

He closed his eyes, letting himself have that much, and felt Josh bend his knees. The pillow got trapped between them and his chest, and Ray clutched at it but didn't move it. And then he felt the soft touch of Josh's fingers on his balls, a caress and a warning both. He shivered and made himself place his feet flat on the bed and spread his knees.

He felt Josh's breath on his face a second before Josh's lips brushed his. More a question than a kiss. Ray opened his eyes, then closed them again and buried his right hand in Josh's hair to direct the kiss, licking up into his mouth like he was drinking him down. Josh responded at once, rubbing their tongues together, and seemed to forget what he was meant to be doing, putting his hand down between Ray's legs to support his weight and kiss him better. Ray yanked the pillow from between them and brought him closer to kiss him softly and leisurely a little longer. They had time. They could take it. They could be gentle with each other, as careful as they needed. Their cocks weren't that patient, though, and soon they were both hard and frustrated with the lack of contact—Ray risked running his hand down Josh's right arm and squeezing his forearm. A silent request.

Josh pulled away from the kiss, to breathe perhaps. Or to concentrate, because his fingers returned to Ray's balls and this time they didn't just touch but lifted his sack enough to push his fingers against his hole. Ray exhaled, throwing his head to the side as the sensation rushed through him—intense and intimate and so... Josh had frozen in place, and Ray elbowed him gently. "Move."

His friend didn't make him ask again, rubbing the tips of his fingers against the puckered flesh—a tantalising tease.

And then Ray felt it... Josh's fingers sliding easier against the wetness there. He was growing wet for his alpha.

It was like something screeching to a halt in his brain and he dug his fingers into Josh's neck too hard even as he arched into the touch. It felt so good, but he couldn't— Josh pulled his hand away like he'd been burned and Ray clenched on the emptiness, dizzy with need and...

"Ray?" Josh whispered and Ray realised his fingers were still clenched hard. He made himself loosen his hold, but Josh's voice was low and scared anyway when he asked, "Are you okay?"

Ray exhaled and opened his eyes to stare up blankly at him. Josh was still close enough that their sides were pressed together but he wasn't sure where the hand that had been fondling him had gone. "I— It feels good," he said and that much was true.

"You were scared," Josh said, not an accusation exactly but making it clear he would not let Ray get away with half-truths.

It wasn't what Ray wanted, either. He'd just been trying to give Josh something so he wouldn't freak out too. He didn't think he could handle it if both of them...

"Okay," his mate decided and gripped Ray's wrist to pull his fingers from his hair completely. "Come on, sit up." Ray let him guide him into a sitting position, still feeling dreamy and strange. It wasn't quite the lassitude of an omega surrendering to his alpha yet, but it did make him feel oddly absent-minded.

Once he was certain Ray was stable, Josh laid back himself, folding his arms under his head and exposing the length of his body to Ray's eyes. Ray might have been a little high off hormones, but he wasn't dead so his eyes travelled down to Josh's hard, red cock, shining with precome and standing at attention. "All yours if you want it," Josh told him, not moving an inch.

Ray looked up at his face. "What... *Oh*." He saw it at once: Josh wanted Ray to... to fuck himself on Josh's cock. He smiled. It was brilliant; it would let Ray control the pace and it wouldn't let him fall into that horrible state where he felt like he was watching himself have sex. Not without stopping the sex, at least.

Josh returned his smile with sincere happiness. "I know, I'm a genius." He seemed much more relaxed now. "And also, like, available. Anytime," he added, glancing down meaningfully.

Ray laughed. "Now you are impatient," he teased and made himself clench his buttocks once, feeling the wetness there, letting the thrill of it run through him to make sure it didn't overwhelm him. He nodded, then put a hand on Josh's hip and raised himself to sit over his thighs. It pressed Josh's hot skin directly against his balls and made him clench again.

"Fuck, Ray," his mate murmured, and Ray opened his eyes to find Josh didn't seem able to keep his anywhere for long. His mouth was open and he was straining his arms to lift his head enough to watch Ray, but he didn't try to move things along.

Ray looked down and took hold of Josh's cock, tightening his fingers when he felt it twitch in his hand. Josh let out a strangled cry, barely managing to abort his thrust in time not to unseat Ray. "Fuck, warn a guy?" he panted once Ray gentled his grip.

"Sure," Ray agreed. "Josh, fair warning; I'm going to sit on your cock now."

Josh groaned and had to give up his relaxed pose to grip at the bedding at his sides instead. "Not... fair."

Ray smiled, letting his eyes roam freely up the expanse of Josh's sculpted chest—the flush travelling all the way to his belly, his nipples pink and biteable—even as he lifted himself to his knees and shuffled forward. He placed his left hand on the bed next to Josh's waist and directed Josh's cock between his own legs, keeping his eyes on Josh's frantically heaving chest. The soft skin of the crown against his hole made him clench and his mate let out a desperate cry under him—and still didn't move—and then he lowered his hips, letting his own weight help the process along. The head popped right in past the ring of muscle, going in easy with the copious amount of slick he'd produced. He paused there, thighs trembling with the effort but still conscious he had to be careful. Except *why* did he need to be careful? It felt *good*, better than good, he was so wet it was almost like Josh'd already come. He took a little more of Josh's cock, the sensation of being opened up so good he couldn't keep from crying out, and after that, he just needed *more*. He sat down, his attention only on the hot, hard, silky wet sensation of his mate penetrating him fully. He shuddered, body clenching against the invasion. No, not an invasion, a gift. This was his to have. And to enjoy.

His and Josh's.

He made himself open his eyes and look at Josh. His mate's eyes were clenched shut and he was trembling under Ray—barely keeping himself in place, Ray understood.

"Josh?" he asked.

Josh's eyes fluttered open at once. "You okay?" Josh gave a tight nod. "Touch me?"

Josh's body tensed under him, then relaxed. It made his cock move a little inside Ray, sending shivers of pleasure up his spine and making him sway a little. Josh's hands moved up to Ray's hips to hold him steady. "Good?" he checked, his voice was raspy and used, like he'd forgotten to swallow for a while.

Ray nodded, panting and raising himself a little only to let himself fall again. He shuddered. "So..." He leaned forward, needing to put his other hand down for leverage. He did it again, higher this time with Josh's help. He shoved down again, getting used to the size of it. They had barely begun and he could already feel his orgasm building up inside, his body lighting up with sensation. Josh's cock. Josh's hands. Josh's scent.

It was different than being hard, although his dick was bobbing between them, precome already leaking steadily—this felt deeper somehow, a different type of build-up. He shoved down again, getting Josh's entire length into him, the head pushing right where he needed it to. And then again, despite his trembling arms and legs. "Help me," he demanded in a moment of clarity.

Josh thrust up like he'd been cut loose. And *fuck*, that was *it*. Ray pushed back and suddenly it was enough—or nearly so—because it was the two of them. This was how it was meant to be: two people dancing together, racing towards the end hand in hand, a perfectly coordinated exchanged—bodies so attuned to each other that—

Ray clenched hard as Josh's cock pressed straight onto his prostate, back arching involuntarily and mouth opening into a scream he couldn't hear as his cock suddenly spurted all over them both. Josh took over, giving him another hard thrust to prolong the impossible agony of all his nerve-endings exploding with pleasure at once.

He was overly sensitive but he didn't want to stop. It wasn't over, not until Josh... He clenched harder, squeezing his mate's cock inside him and shuddering as his body protested it was too much. But it wasn't—it wasn't enough, he needed Josh to—

Josh whimpered under him and Ray saw there were tears in his eyes and he couldn't bear it. He leaned down and took Josh's face in his hands, kissed his mouth hard and true—as if he could tell him with a kiss everything he hadn't been able to say with his body.

Josh's hands tightened on his hips and he gave one last thrust before slowing down to a slow grind as his cock slowly emptied itself into Ray's body. Even deep as he was, it leaked out of Ray's arse, making each slide of Josh's dick into him wetter and sweeter until it was all Ray could do to whimper into his mate's neck. A plead. He didn't know whether to stop or to continue...

Josh rolled them onto their sides, twisting his hips to pull out of Ray and Ray shuddered hard at the emptiness left behind, his own cock twitching as if it did not know it was spent.

He felt a hand in his hair, careful and easy. "Shhh," his mate whispered. He was shaking under Ray's hands too—like the world had tilted and dropped them both on unsteady ground—but that somehow helped a little. If he had Josh to hold onto, if he wasn't alone in this...

He burrowed closer and Josh welcomed him—uncaring of the mess of come and sweat, of their overheated bodies and oversensitive cocks—with a tired kiss on his forehead.

"I love you," he said once again. It didn't sound like a declaration this time—it was just the truth.

"Me too," Ray mumbled, then tensed when he realised that he hadn't... He made himself open his eyes and when he saw Josh had closed his, he cupped his mate's chin until he looked back at him—it only made it harder to say the words, but it was the first time and he wasn't going to short-charge Josh when it came to this. "I love you," he said and it came out a little too serious.

He was about to try again but he needn't have worried. Josh's heart jumped and his face broke into an irrepressible grin. "I know," he agreed. "I'm your fucking soulmate, remember?"

Epilogue

Yamila had forgiven Ray for not getting back to her about the commission sooner and afterwards, she'd even recommended Ray to her friends. But Ray had still agreed to do a portrait for Adele and Lara first—they were paying him, but they got a family priority for helping Alec with the study.

Of course, at this point, families with young children had gone from reluctant agreement to eager solicitations when it came to his mate's project. Alec looked slightly more tired but satisfied—maybe Ray could admit some of that was due to his cousin's attention, but he liked the idea that Alec's work was just that fulfilling.

His own, informal as the commissions still were, was making him stay up too late and wake up too early, fingers twitching for a pencil. Of course, at some point, the pack would get bored with his portraits and then... Well, he knew it wasn't a career, but that didn't seem to matter to his brain when he saw what he'd done and the endorphins hit him like a stampede of raging elephants.

So he was doing it. He was going to go back to college to ask about art courses—not A levels, he didn't want a paper saying he had learned, he just wanted to do it. He wanted people who were struggling with shading or had in the past, someone to bounce around ideas with who was excited about technique and not just beauty—he had Sergi for that—and just... a space, a room, time.

A little time to himself every week. It wasn't selfish. Or maybe *it was*. But he was allowed. He was a parent now, not a robot. He had always known the image of the omega who sacrificed it all for their pack was bullshit, but part of him had bought it anyway. Maybe the same part who'd grown up in a world where there was too little of everything and sacrifice had come to mean love.

"You ready?" Gabriel asked, leaning against the kitchen doorway.

Irina stepped closer to take Jamie from Ray's arms. Ray smiled at her, then nodded at his alpha. "Just let me get the canvas bag."

Gabriel had turned on the radio by the time Ray got to the car. It was crackly this far out from civilization but it filled the silence. It was pretty early still but Gabriel was used to waking at dawn so ten in the morning was practically afternoon for him.

"Where are you guys going for lunch?" Ray asked, idly fiddling with the strap of his bag.

Gabriel snorted. "You think that's up to me?" he asked. "Your mate is a foodie snob; last time he let me choose what to eat, we had Chinese in his room."

Ray frowned. "Really? When was that? Not like you can get anyone to deliver to us."

"*Three years ago*," Gabriel said pointedly.

Ray laughed, startled. "Wow, you're that whipped?"

His cousin shrugged. "Not like I can complain that my man can cook."

"So he's my mate when he's a snob about it but when it's time to eat his food, he's your man?"

Gabriel shot him a playful look. "Isn't that how it works?"

Ray rolled his eyes at him. "You are ridiculous."

"Yeah, well, being in love will do that to you. Fucks with your brain," Gabriel explained. He graced Ray with the least subtle eyebrow raise in history despite needing to keep his eyes on the road.

Ray felt his cheeks heat up. He wasn't embarrassed about the sex, but the whole romance angle was a little more... unsettling. "Sure," he agreed. "That or all the sex."

Gabriel snorted but didn't push it. "Sure, either, or both. Who knows," he said wryly.

With impeccable timing, Lanchester opened up from the rickety road connecting it to pack territory. "Oh, we are here, can you drop me next to the cinema?"

Gabriel stopped the car so he could get out and Ray pretended not to feel the weight of his gaze. But finally, he had no choice but to return the look. He pointed at the package he'd left on the floor of the passenger's seat. "Give this to Adele as soon as you get there, okay? I don't want you to forget and leave in the sun all day, it can bleach the colours—"

"I'm happy for you," Gabriel said, interrupting.

Ray stared at him, at a loss, then nodded tightly—a thank you and an acknowledgement. Gabriel wasn't the man making him happy, exactly, but he was his family too and he was trying as hard as he could to give Ray the space to be himself.

He wasn't the love of Ray's life, but he was a good alpha. "Me too," he said and closed the door.

He hadn't been to the Derwentside College in more than a year. Nobody had told him to stop attending, but he'd needed to stay home until he found a mate. And once he had... Well, he was certainly not going to need A levels to run his pack.

But this wasn't about the pack. It was about Ray. He didn't know if he could do this, but he wanted to, and now that they had five betas contributing with the childcare and housework... Well, maybe he could have it.

Nobody tried to talk to him as he walked up to the side table in the reception area and sat down to read the prospectus. He'd have to start in January, the holiday season was fast approaching and— He barely kept himself from crushing the shiny booklet in his hands when he realised what else would come with the new year.

He exhaled slowly, eyes fixed unseeing on the page.

He hadn't forgotten. Not exactly. But once he and Marisa had decided... He'd felt better about it. But, of course, that would be after the baby was born—it wouldn't keep him from showing before that. He got up, yanking his satchel too hard and wincing as the wooden box of supplies hit him on the side.

It wasn't his belly but maybe the baby could feel his agitation because it twisted inside him in what Ray assumed was unhappiness. He had to inhale deeply to keep down his breakfast. He shouldn't have come here. He—

"Ray?"

He looked up to see dark eyes peeking from under a bright purple headscarf. "Um, hi, Imran," he said, muscle memory possibly.

She essayed a smile. "I haven't seen you in... ages," she finished. "Are you coming back?"

"I—Not sure yet," he temporized. "I mean, I have... a family. Children, and, well..." He waved meaningfully.

"Oh." She seemed surprised but her smile was genuine. "Congratulations. But it's not like... I mean, not on your own, right?" she teased. She glanced down at her feet. "I mean, I'm still coming, and I'll take a little break when the baby is born, but after that, I'll be back."

Ray almost choked at that, eyes travelling down her body before he could think it through. He forced his gaze back to her face, already feeling his own grow heated with embarrassment. "Sorry! I—I didn't realise."

She just laughed. "You really dropped off the face of the earth, didn't you? It was quite a scandal."

"Why?" He frowned, shifting his satchel to cover his front. Imran and he had been friendly but not truly friends. She was smart, likeable, dedicated, but she was human, and Ray could never quite figure out how to relax around them. He had no right to come back after a year and interrogate her like— "I mean—"

Imran gave a little shrug, her beautiful smile dimming. "My parents weren't very happy for one. I was supposed to be in college to get my A levels so I could go to university.

And the college wasn't that pleased with Henry—professor Thomson—dating me, either. Even before..." She straightened and met Ray's eyes. "Before I got pregnant," she explained. Her lips were curved but her face was hard.

Ray watched her back for a moment, paralyzed by indecision. He wasn't even sure how old she was, except that she was a little older than him because she'd missed a year when her family had moved from Afghanistan. He'd thought there was no point talking to a human, except about classes or movies to pass boring lunch hours, and now here she was, nearly in exactly the same situation he'd been not long ago. He knew he had to offer something back, but how could he...?

"We—We didn't plan it either," he settled for, choosing his words carefully as if she could tell if he was lying.

Her own surprise was obvious to him; heart jumping and a sudden inhalation. "That's—" He glanced up as he heard the catch in her voice. Her face had gone blank except for her lips, pressed tightly together. She stood like that, firm and brave, even as her body revolted, heart speeding and stuttering, scent turning acrid as she fought with her fear.

Ray could barely keep himself from stepping away. It wasn't him that was making her feel like that, he knew that. Finally, he managed a step in the right direction and put a hand on her elbow. "Hey," he whispered, squeezing very carefully. "It's okay. It'll be okay." He could feel her trembling under his fingers even as she stubbornly forced herself to stillness. "You will love the baby, I promise," he said.

It was true, he realised. He could hear it in his own voice. At least it was true for him; he'd love the baby. Even this baby. It was such a relief to know that about himself that he had to make an effort to focus on the woman in front of him—scared and uncertain for all that she was strong enough to stand her ground where he'd been too scared to stand his own.

Imran gave him a tiny nod, swallowing. "You want... coffee?" she offered haltingly.

For the first time, he noticed she was alone—none of the friends she'd used to be surrounded with seemed to be around. Maybe it was a coincidence.

"Sure," Ray agreed. He glanced down at his hand on her arm, then hesitantly offered his elbow.

She snorted. "What? Now I should worry about propriety?" She hooked her arm in his. "Come on, no way I'm drinking that swill they sell in the cafeteria."

Josh was working, so he called Sergi to come pick him up after Imran said she needed to get home to her mum with dinner. Ray knew he couldn't tell her about the pregnancy—except the more she talked, the more he wanted to. It was stupid because there were plenty of pregnant women in his old pack he could have spoken to, but he didn't think any of them would have understood as well as this almost stranger who'd stumbled into his life at exactly the wrong moment—when he was raw and open and so scared he could hardly draw breath. And maybe... Well, he had her number. And he would be around college anyway, maybe they could have coffee again and maybe he could... He pushed the thought away, not discarding it but saving it for later.

"Hey," Sergi said, leaning over to open the passenger door for him. He had by far the showiest car in their little pack—a sleek Volkswagen Eos. He'd been speaking of swapping it for something more child-friendly, which Ray theoretically approved of, of course, but at the same time... He'd be sorry to give up the comfort of this seat and the view from the long windshield. "Long day?" his mate offered, reversing to get back on the road.

"I guess so," Ray admitted, eyes on the sky through the windshield. "I... I went to the college."

"Oh, that's— good?" Sergi didn't sound sure.

"I almost freaked out. Like..." He exhaled. "There's some courses starting in January. Illustration, and design... But..."

Sergi waited a beat before helping him out. "You think it will show?"

"I...I don't know. I can't... I mean, the first few weeks, I'll have to stay with... with her."

"Her?" Sergi repeated and Ray felt like a dick.

He hadn't told him. "Fuck, I— Sorry. I found out. Well, last week. Alec tested me, and he told me last week. I should have told you, I just—"

Sergi's hand shot out to take hold of his elbow. "Ray, *calm down*," he said. It was his alpha voice and it felt like a sudden breath of air after being too long underwater.

Ray was still trembling with the after-effects when Sergi found a spot to stop the car. It was a no parking zone—he turned off the engine anyway. Ray only noticed he'd taken his hand away when he clicked his fingers to get his attention. He snatched them back as soon as Ray looked at him. "Ray? I'm sorry, I—I used the voice, didn't I?" Ray rolled his neck in the direction of his voice, dazed and a little confused. "Please tell me you are okay. I didn't realise what I was doing, you were just—your heart was going so fast and..."

Ray shook his head. His heart was calm now, steady and even, and so were his thoughts. "No. I mean, I'm fine." Sergi's pulse surged up, then started to slow, but he was still watching Ray like a hawk. "Seriously, it was... Well, it was like drinking too much, too fast. But I feel... relaxed." He tried to smile. "I'm sorry I didn't tell you about it being a girl."

"I don't care!" Sergi said, too quickly, then raised a hand and waved it like he could erase the words from the air between them. "I mean, I'm glad, but it doesn't... You didn't have to tell me. I get it, you were... Well, I don't know, are you happy about it?"

Ray slowly reached over and took his mate's hand in his, then brought it down to rest on his knee. "Yes, I'm happy."

Sergi glanced at their hands, then back at Ray's face. "Why are you not angry right now? Is it... Did I...?"

"Shut up a second," Ray asked softly. It did feel like being drunk and although he understood the idea of being angry, the emotion seemed out of his reach at the moment. "Tell me to stop being calm."

"Stop being calm," Sergi repeated a little desperately.

Ray rolled his eyes at him. "With *the voice*," he reminded Sergi.

"Stop being calm," Sergi repeated. The effect was as startling this time as the first: shocking like a blanket being lifted off his warm body and just as unwelcome.

Ray squeezed Sergi's hand in his, bending forwards a little as he dry-heaved, eyes clenched shut and skin breaking into a sweat. He breathed in and then out, concentrating first on the scents—his sweat, Sergi's creamy natural scent, the leather of the car's interior, the plastic still warm from direct sunlight—then the sounds—their heartbeats, the ticking of the car clock, the muffled sounds of traffic and birds from outside.

When he was ready, he opened his eyes. He watched his own lap for a minute, Sergi's darker fingers poking out from his own death grip. It took him a few moments to manage the wherewithal to loosen his grip. He felt Sergi's hand twitch in relief, but his alpha didn't try to take it away. "Okay, that wasn't a good idea," he decided. His voice came out rough, thready.

"Ray," Sergi whispered. He sounded so scared Ray had to raise his head despite how tired he suddenly was. "I—"

He shook his head. "No," he told him. "Don't..." He couldn't quite find the words, so he just squeezed Sergi's hand again. "It was a good idea, I was freaking out. Only... There has to be a way to come out of it that... I don't know, more slowly."

"But I'm not— You don't want us to use it. You said... I don't want to give you orders."

Ray struggled to order his thoughts enough to explain. "No, but you can. And... I trust you." Sergi swallowed thickly, eyes bright and face open and vulnerable. "I know you would only do it in an emergency. Only to help me."

"Ray, it was an *accident*," his mate explained, it sounded like a confession.

"I know that," Ray snapped, hands tightening. He forced himself to rub his thumbs against Sergi's skin gently instead. "I'm sorry, I just mean that you wanted to keep me safe and I was scared and you reacted instinctively to do that. And that's okay. You wouldn't use it to make me..." He glanced down.

"*No*," Sergi said at once. "I—I wouldn't. I don't even... I don't even want to do it for this," he admitted.

"Okay," Ray agreed, meeting his eyes. "You don't have to. But I'm not angry."

"I... I don't get it." Sergi still looked lost.

"Sergi," Ray said gently. "I can't be angry with you for being an alpha. It wouldn't be fair. If I... It's the same as if I had stumbled and you'd caught me. Should I be angry because you are strong enough to hold me up? Because you didn't think before you reacted to keep me safe?"

His mate was still frowning a little, but he was relaxing in Ray's grip. "You really... You really trust me that much? After..." He stopped, not just speaking but actually breathing and Ray let the silence hold, allowed him the time he needed. Sergi exhaled. "After what I did to you?"

"I... I probably should have talked to you about this, too," he admitted roughly. "It was... It was just really hard to talk about it with Josh, and... Well, Gabriel and Alec, too. I guess I have been putting it off because you seemed okay with..."

"I didn't want to ask for more from you," Sergi said into his own lap.

"Thanks," Ray responded. "I probably couldn't have... I needed the time. But, well, I'm just going to say it again, and then when... Not today, but, like, can you tell Iesu to talk to me about this too?" Sergi nodded. "Okay, so the way I see it: you asked if I wanted to be your mate and I said yes because I thought it was better than someone who wouldn't ask, and then... Then we all thought the sooner we got it done, the better. And that... that really screwed me up." He felt Sergi flinch at that. His alpha seemed to be physically restraining himself from pulling away. Ray opened his hands and let go and Sergi looked up in alarm.

"Did you know I didn't want it?" Ray asked him.

"No!" Sergi's eyes widened and he shook his head violently enough Ray thought it should have hurt.

"So you didn't know," Ray said firmly. "And you hurt me because you didn't know. And one of the reasons you didn't know is that I didn't know how to tell you. I decided it was the way things were, because of the wolves. I—I was not in a good place. But I should have known. I should have talked to you." He looked at his lap, swallowing down tears.

"No," Sergi repeated, more quietly this time, pained instead of indignant. "I could have asked. I should have asked, and I didn't. You are *not* blaming yourself."

"Okay," Ray agreed. "But you can't blame yourself either. Because... you didn't know. You didn't mean to. And I... I forgive you."

"*Fuck*, Ray," his mate said with feeling. Ray glanced up to see he'd buried his face in his hands.

"I think I should drive," Ray said after a moment. Sergi was breathing heavily, shoulders shaking a little. Ray was pretty sure he was trying not to cry. "We can pick up Iesu from his parents' place."

Sergi nodded, still into his hands, and Ray tentatively reached out and put a hand on his shoulder. "Or I could..." He tugged slightly, just enough for Sergi to feel it and Sergi collapsed forwards into his arms at once.

"I'm sorry," he mumbled into Ray's shoulder. He'd kept his hands against his own chest as Ray held him. Ray didn't tell him it was okay to hold him back, just shushed his apologies and rubbed his back.

There was no point in telling Sergi once again that he forgave him; it wasn't Ray's forgiveness Sergi needed. It was his own. And for that, he'd needed Ray to admit to how badly Sergi had hurt him. It was all Ray could do for him—to tell him he knew it hadn't been intentional and he trusted it wouldn't happen again.

He remembered that he'd worried about Sergi the most, and how attentive the alpha had been from the get-go anyway. And he remembered he'd chosen Sergi when he'd needed someone, and Josh had been too scared of hurting him to try to have sex with him. "You are okay," he said instead. "You know now, and I know you will be careful."

"I swear," Sergi promised in a strangled whisper, and Ray held him a little longer—until Sergi's phone went off with the Adam Lambert song Iesu had programmed as his ringtone.

Sergi straightened, face turning towards the sound. He looked calmer already—just with the song. "He makes you happy, doesn't he?" he asked.

His alpha looked up from the phone where he'd just hung up on his boyfriend. "Yes," he admitted. Ray had talked about this with Iesu several times, but not with Sergi. It surprised him to see him blush.

"Should you really hang up on him?"

"I'll call him back, and he'll... he'll get it. That I was with you and it was important."

"Well, I get it too," Ray pointed out. "That you are with him and it's important. Plus, Alec's cooking tonight and I don't want to be late," he added sincerely.

Sergi laughed, still a little fragile but more confident. "Okay, let me get out of the car."

Ray almost stopped him—but then again, why deny himself the pleasure? It was every boy's dream to get a boyfriend with a cool car they could borrow, right?

Ray's chest was a little sore from the milk pump but other than that, he was back to normal. With the help of a hoodie, he'd only really needed to miss college the first week after giving birth—thankfully, he was only going twice a week for two hours at a time.

"She's beautiful," Ray told Marisa. His sister smiled from the second armchair they'd set up on the porch, rocking the baby in her arms until she made a happy gurgling noise.

"Yes, takes after her aunt," she claimed proudly. Her eyes shone when she looked at Cali.

"You can... You can be her mum, you know," Ray offered quietly. He had never dared offer before. He'd stayed in his wolf form for the first week, afraid he'd not be able to feed the baby if he had to see her human shape. Marisa had picked her up right before Ray transformed to go have his well-earned shower and Ray had looked at the tiny fingers and plump cheeks, scanning for a sign, for... But, of course, there wasn't anything: he hadn't even been able to tell apart the babies he'd had with men he'd known for months. Cali was just a baby girl.

Marisa looked up, familiar brown eyes wide and the thought crossed his mind that he hoped Cali had those eyes, not the intimidating blue of Nicholas'. "Do you think she will care?"

He didn't know if she'd care about the words, but he did know she deserved to be loved, absolutely and without question. For who she was, not for where she came from.

He just wasn't sure he was strong enough to do it himself.

"Won't you care?" he asked his sister, because he had to remember Marisa too. Cali was his child, but he couldn't put her before Marisa's own needs either.

"I don't know, do you?" she asked in turn. "Do I have to call you something else for you to know what you are to me?"

Ray's breath stuttered, and he gaped at her. He'd helped raise Marisa from the time she'd been eight and he'd been ten when his father had died, but he wasn't her father. Except he was perhaps as close to a father as Marisa had really had—their own hadn't been around that long. "No," he admitted.

She smiled and nodded, looking proud. Of him, this time. "I want... I want to talk to mum about it, and Irina thinks..." She stopped, and Ray squinted at her. "Anyway, she's only little. It's too early for that. I'm happy right now, and she's happy too. That's what matters, right?"

Ray nodded, eyes travelling away from the baby and towards the wide field behind their house. He'd been sketching from memory—even taking photos would have been hard when the football match was played by werewolves. None of them were bothering keeping their speed to human limits. Irina had already taken out the net from mid-court once and the only reason their windows were whole was that Marisa had made them set up the goalposts a good hundred yards away. He could go and join them, but he didn't want to leave Marisa on her own, and he was fine, really. This early in the morning, the light was good for drawing, he was full of good food, and his children and his mates were safe and happy. He could play football tomorrow if he wanted—Monday was Irina's day off and she was always up for it, which meant Iesu could probably be riled into joining too. Josh would complete the team if Ray asked.

Alec blocked a shot and Ray huffed in disappointment, then shook his head at himself—it'd been an impressive catch, too, and Sergi was already running after Gabriel to try again. He had no idea which team was winning, and it didn't really matter.

"You look pretty happy yourself," Marisa said, sounding a little smug.

Ray shrugged, not looking away from Josh's blond head as he threw it back and laughed loud enough to be heard all the way across the open space of their backyard. "Yeah, I'm pretty lucky, aren't I?"

[End of book IV]

Shock Therapy

The Stars of the Pack – Interlude 4.1
N.J. LYSK

"Ray?" Sergi stared at him and Ray had to concentrate to keep his hand from shaking where he was holding onto Sergi's forearm. His alpha's eyes snatched on his hold before coming up his face. Ray could feel himself blushing. Sergi glanced at the drawing on the desk. "Did I smudge it or something?"

Ray shook his head. "I—I need..." Sergi's eyes widened but he didn't interrupt. "I want to be okay. I need to be okay. For..." He looked down. He didn't even want to *think* about heat, much less talk about it. "Can you...?" He pulled a little on Sergi's arm, not enough to actually move him closer but enough to be felt and understood.

"You want *me*?" Sergi asked, sounding shocked. Ray looked up. "It's just... I mean, well, Josh?"

Ray took his hand away and put it over his eyes, exhaling. Of course Sergi would ask about Josh.

"Josh... Josh is complicated," Ray explained, thinking of his best friend's combination of utter devotion and unshakeable belief that Ray needed to talk about what had happened to get over it. He didn't want to talk, he wanted to *know*. No, he *needed* to know. Because there was no way back, and what was it they said? The only way out is through. And Josh couldn't help him through this—he was too... too close, too involved. "And I—I can't trust myself right now, and I don't want to... Look, it doesn't matter." He met Sergi's eyes straight on—a challenge both for the man and the alpha wolf. "You said you wanted me, before. So..."

"I did—I do," Sergi said at once, like he was worried Ray would change his mind if he didn't make it clear at once. Technically, Ray had options. In reality, he had barely been able to bring himself to do this once. "But... What are you asking me, exactly?"

"Kissing," Ray almost spat. "I want... I want to see if I'm okay with kissing." And then, as if his brain had suddenly got turned on, he realised he'd forgotten a small detail. "Oh, is it Iesu? You think he won't—"

"Iesu?" Sergi interrupted, sounding almost amused. "No! We... Ray, he'll probably be jealous you didn't ask him." Now he sounded a little smug.

Ray raised an eyebrow at him. He was pretty sure Sergi was joking, but... "What if I ask you not to say anything?"

Sergi sighed, then shrugged. "Then I guess I'll have to take what I can get." He leaned towards Ray, bracing his left hand on the back of Ray's chair. He wasn't touching Ray at all but his dark eyes were so intense that it still made Ray swallow, a shiver running down his back. "Bit of a hardship, making out with a gorgeous guy, but I did sign up for it."

Ray's heart was going a mile a minute. He thought it was excitement and his dick seemed to agree, but he still couldn't forget why he'd decided to ask for this. "You have... I need you to be careful."

Sergi nodded. "No hands?" he offered.

Ray shook his head. "No, just... don't push me down." He'd looked away but he still felt Sergi flinch. He didn't comment. It was as much as Ray could ask for; maybe he'd been too self-involved to notice the alphas were freaked out by what had happened too but after seeing Josh almost cry... "And... I don't know, pay attention."

"Okay," his mate said, voice heavy and serious.

And Ray leaned in and pressed their lips together. His hand ended up pressed to Sergi's sternum, heart thumping underneath like it wanted to jump right into Ray's palm, and he put his other hand on Sergi's face to tilt his face a little. The surge of want that went through him at the contact almost shocked him into stopping, but Sergi's lips were already parting for his tongue and he was too distracted to be worried. Sergi made a noise into his mouth and pulled on Ray's chair hard enough to almost unseat him. Ray went with the move and climbed onto his lap, making him moan even as the chair he'd been holding onto clattered to the ground. Sergi was straining his neck a little—he was taller than Ray but not by enough to make this position comfortable for kissing—but what made Ray stop was realising he was the only one holding on.

He planted his feet on the floor more firmly before leaning back. Sergi's eyes fluttered open.

"You can touch me," he repeated.

Sergi was panting a little, but he nodded, keeping his eyes on Ray's face as he gently placed his hands on Ray's hips. Ray gave himself a moment but it was fine; he'd asked for it and he'd been ready. And he knew it would stop the moment he said so.

Sergi glanced down, licking his lips, and Ray squirmed a little. He wasn't ashamed of being hard—more like the opposite, when he'd been so worried he wouldn't be able to feel aroused at all outside of heat. But he wasn't quite sure he wanted Sergi to touch him there. Not yet.

"Um, I don't think this chair can handle this," Sergi said, turning to look at Ray's bed.

"Oh, okay, I..." Ray stood up, taking Sergi's hand from his hip and pulling him along towards the bed. "Just sit down there."

Sergi did as he was told, putting his palms down on the duvet and waiting patiently while Ray decided. In the end, he just walked up to him and straddled him again, bending his knees on each side of his thighs and curving his own back so that it wasn't such a strain for their mouths to meet. Sergi hummed his pleasure, then put his left hand on Ray's hip again. Ray tightened his legs and kissed him harder, chasing his tongue and... Sergi let out a little sound of surprise as he fell backwards. Ray fell right onto him, catching himself with his hands on his shoulders.

He was about to ask if Sergi was okay when his alpha started laughing. "Sorry, just..."

Ray rolled his eyes at him. "So much for having the strength of three humans," he commented wryly.

"Doesn't mean I'm not subjected to gravity!" Sergi protested, and then his eyes widened as Ray stretched atop him, pressing their groins together. He watched Ray like he thought he might have a weapon hidden somewhere. No, not a weapon because it wasn't fear on his face, it was *hunger*. Ray pushed his left knee between Sergi's legs, letting his weight pressed their cocks more firmly together. His alpha shuddered under him, letting out a half-swallowed whimper. He was beautiful like this—sweaty and a little desperate—and apparently Ray's wolf didn't give a fuck about proper omega behaviour at the moment. He didn't feel faint and loose; he felt powerful and electrified.

"Um, kissing?" Sergi asked, eyes fluttering open.

Ray smiled at him and licked his lips, rolling his hips and managing to keepi his expression neutral even as it sent a rush of ecstasy from his cock to his toes.

"You are not touching me," he pointed out, relishing how evenly he'd managed to speak despite how desperate he was to just go for it.

Sergi seemed confused for a moment and then his hands came around Ray to his hips, and, after a slight hesitation, slid down to cup Ray's arse and pull him closer. This time, they both groaned—Ray was too surprised to keep it back. He leaned in to kiss Sergi, burying the sounds of their pleasure between their mouths as their hips took up a steady if somewhat clumsy rhythm of their own accord.

Ray forgot to be afraid, too busy chasing after his climax and then he was there: Sergi's fingers digging hard enough to bruise his arse as he arched under Ray, all the world going white and electric for a moment. And then the sound of their panting breaths as he lay slumped on top of his mate.

"Fuck," Sergi breathed out. It took Ray a moment to realise he was trembling slightly but when he tried to roll off him, Sergi clung to him. "Ray," he said almost timidly. His hold went loose enough that Ray could have moved. He didn't. "That felt... It was like it was the first time," he said dazedly.

Ray was a bit out of it himself, but the words were too shockingly true to ignore. "Yes," he said into Sergi's ear and held back onto him. Because he wanted to. "It was."

- Interlude over -

Author notes: This is by no means advice on how to deal with sexual trauma of any kind (which, surprisingly, I'm not qualified to give). It is simply what makes sense for Ray in his particular circumstances, where the lack of control is a key feature of his trauma. I needed to write this scene after Josh refuses to be Ray's first alpha because I figured there was no way Ray was just going to wait around for him to change his mind, not when heat is coming his way sooner rather than later. This takes place between parts 1 and 2 of **"Beloved of the Pack"**.

Betas Aside

The Packs:

Gosden Pack Family Tree:
<u>Martha & Trevor Halley:</u>

- Raymond Halley (19)
- TJ Halley & Marisa Halley (17)
- Harold Halley (12)
- Anne Halley (10)
- Glen Halley (6)

Halley Pack Family Tree:
<u>Raymond Halley (omega mated to five alphas):</u>

- Michael Trevor Halley (by alpha Joshua Jeremiah)
- Sasha Halley (by alpha Sergi Somide)
- Maria Halley (by alpha Gabriel Gosden)
- James Halley (by alpha Alexander Aiken)
- Clara Halley (by alpha Iesuvel Ivanescu)

Ivanescu & Lupu Packs Family Tree:

<u>Gabriela & Ion Ivanescu:</u>

- Sorina Ivanescu Holmes
- Codrin Ivanescu
- Iesuvel "Iesu" Ivanescu

<u>Maria & Mircea Lupu*</u>: (*Living in Romania)

- Constantin Lupu*
- Mihai Lupu*
- Irina Lupu

Blurb:

When Marisa Halley's brother leaves their pack to start one of his own, she's frankly a little jealous. Children might be the last thing Ray wants, but Marisa has recently received confirmation she will never have her own. But as Ray's life rapidly descends into chaos, Marisa cannot do anything but offer her support by moving in with him to help bring up his children. But what's the price of giving everything to those you love?

Irina Lupu is adrift. She'd always wanted to travel and England is far away from her parent's expectations. But her new English pack comes with a lot more rules than she assumed, and as a beta with no important relatives, she has very little say in what those are. When her cousin asks if she'd like to cross the river and join his new pack, Irina doesn't hesitate. After all, what's a river after an ocean?

Marisa is young and ready to change her new pack into her perfect image. Irina is old enough to know that the best she can hope for is to find a place where she mostly fits... But no matter how different they are, they are newcomers to a pack recovering from an unimaginable tragedy and about to be struck by lightning for a second time. Can they band together to protect them? And can they go through it without seeing a lot more in each other than two women more than a decade apart in age should?

"Betas Aside" is a standalone companion novel in "The Stars of the Pack" series, contains spoilers for all other books and shorts.

Prologue: Irina

The Gosden pack had plenty of problems, but they also had plenty of land.

Land they had never sold no matter how much human investors offered. Land they were willing to share. It was a luxury Irina's own birth pack hadn't been able to afford and that had ended with several families leaving for greener pastures. Or wetter ones, in her case.

She glanced out her bedroom window and felt her shoulders loosen like she'd inhaled something a lot stronger than oxygen. To think she almost hadn't come.

Not across the river, that had been easy.

What was a river after an ocean?

She hadn't been forced to leave Romania; it wasn't anything tragic like that. Their territory had been cramped and the full moon had been getting more stressful, but she could have stayed and put up with it for a bit. For maybe the first time in decades, the pack had been large enough that her parents didn't mind that she was a beta and wanted to remain one—loved kids but wanted none of her own. Her brother had been more than happy to make up for the deficit with his young wife, so for the pack, Irina's role as a beta was as vital as it was meant to be.

But once Sorina's parents had announced they were going to England... it had been like a cord had been struck. She'd always talked of travelling. She'd closed her eyes at night and imagined just transforming and taking off in a random direction, seeing where she ended up. And coming back; she'd wanted to go back home, always, but she'd wanted to get somewhere else first.

It'd felt inevitable. What would have home been without half her family? Without her best friend? Sorina was technically an adult, but she wasn't going to let her parents and little brothers go abroad without her—she was the eldest and she took it seriously.

Sorina wouldn't stay, and there wasn't space to run, and so Irina had gone with them.

They had flown, of course, since having hands and pockets was handy to carry things like passports and money, but despite the plane and the absolutely revolting feeling of being off the ground and disconnected from not just her land but all land, it hadn't felt like her path back was cut off.

She could go back any time she wanted.

She'd told her parents the same thing every time they had asked when she was coming back. She'd repeated it when they'd started asking her to visit instead. She'd looked at tickets: plane and boat and long-distance buses that took the ferry across the channel. She'd looked at maps and planned the journey in four feet and two.

And she hadn't gone. Not even once. Maybe it was just impossible to imagine going back home and not staying. And, in any case, her parents had agreed to visit to meet

Sorina's children, and her brothers came every summer to work and send extra money back home.

She missed that land—her wolf howled for things it didn't even remember and only a small handful of the packmates howling back understood what those things were—but she loved this land too. It was fresh and new and strangely untouched, protected by human laws from humans themselves. It wasn't hers, but it welcomed her anyway; an endless expanse for running after prey that wasn't half-starved and half-domesticated, water that rushed free and wild and dangerous, a moon that shone pure, unhindered by the smoke of civilization.

Their adopted pack accepted them gladly, happy for the new blood and the extra bodies to protect what was theirs from human greed.

But they didn't truly belong, Irina could feel it. They all could. And then Sorina had presented as omega six months after their arrival and things had changed—because when she chose an alpha, she'd become pack. By blood. Not her own, but her children's. It was more than good enough.

Even though it had been her aunt's idea to come to England, she'd taken Sorina's engagement to William—and the promise of permanence it implied—quite hard. Irina got it: it was different to know for certain.

It hadn't taken long for Sorina to get pregnant—it never seemed to with omegas—and that had distracted her mother from her nostalgia. The future was bright, safe, green, and full of life; wild and domestic both.

Sorina had been distracted enough with a mate, and soon enough she had a baby as well. If Irina had been planning to leave at all, that would have been the moment to do it.

Except that, as a beta, Irina was expected to help with childcare, and she loved Andrei to bits. She missed being Sorina's main companion, but Codrin and little Iesu were around to play football—one of the few things her rudimentary English didn't make awkward with the local pack.

Her wolf relished the great expanses to run in, and so did her human side—finally free of the rather more antiquated expectations her original pack had had of a woman and her level of interest in sport past a certain age.

She couldn't say it had been easy not to leave, but it had been easy to stay too. So stay she had, until she'd made herself sit down with an English textbook and then attend the lessons at the local college for six torturous months, where she was reminded of every single reason she had ever hated school and discovered a few more the English had invented.

But at the end of it, she'd been okay. Okay enough she got the job when she applied to the local Decathlon, which was as okay as she was interested in getting. And after a day where the new sounds left her head buzzing and she learned she'd studied American English vocabulary and nobody actually knew what a 'monkey wrench' was, she'd got to go home, to the simple music of her language and her people, to the familiar scent of Andrei's baby skin and her aunt's cooking.

She was okay with staying, and then she'd met Alisha and she'd been a little more than okay.

Chapter 1: Marisa

Ray was still a wolf, but it wasn't like there was anything Marisa could do about it. She certainly didn't resent him taking the time off, but it wasn't like life had ground to a halt after his kidnapping—everybody ate, and after the first few days when he'd insisted on hanging around, even Josh had gone back to work. So naturally, there was laundry.

Laundry someone had fucked up.

Marisa didn't care how new they were at being alphas, they were all older than her and had been wearing clothes for most of their lives; how was it possible they did not know not to mix whites with colours?

She growled, hand clenching on the lovely baby clothes she'd personally chosen. White, because they weren't going to start putting the babies in gendered colours when they didn't even know what gender was. It was bad enough that the majority of omegas were female and the majority of alphas were male. That couldn't be helped, but fashion was optional.

Except now *all* the onesies were pink and Marisa was very close to homicide. It was lucky that the washing had erased the scents of whoever had put the load on or she might have been screaming at them already.

"You okay?" She jumped—she'd been too lost in her own thoughts to notice Irina come in. "Sorry, you smell like you are about to set something on fire."

Marisa shrugged, then waved at the clothes she'd put down on the table, mostly to stare at them in despair.

"Ah," said Irina sagely. "It can be fixed, you know."

"I *do*," she replied, maybe a little too testily. "I'm not useless, but I have better things to do than run after them and fix stupid mistakes like this. How do they not know how to do laundry?"

The other beta shrugged. "They are alphas, and they are men," she pointed out calmly and walked right in and started throwing the whites right back into the machine.

"I—I can't even." Marisa passed her one she'd missed.

"Then don't," Irina said with the same easy acceptance. "Don't let them do laundry. It's not like anybody argues with you about anything."

Marisa swallowed, feeling her face heat. It was true. She'd been a little unsure at first, but her brother had pretty much begged her to take over house-management for him while he dealt with his alphas and pups. Well, mostly with the alphas. Not that Marisa minded the babysitting, but she was a little worried about how overwhelmed Ray was being a parent—she supposed it was lucky she'd come over, and Irina.

Even if they had to share a room in the main house because the beta wing barely had walls.

She went to the shelf and got the white vinegar bottle, already pulling a face. "I guess it's better to do it once myself than to have to fix it every time they mess it up," she agreed.

Irina stepped well away from her as she went to pour the vinegar into the washing machine. "I think they can all cook, and they can definitely wash up, and that needs doing every day too."

She pushed the door shut, added some detergent, and started a quick cycle. "And this doesn't?" she asked sceptically. "Did you forget about the cloth diapers?"

Irina pulled a face. "Only in my nightmares," she said honestly.

Marisa smirked at her. "Well, we need to make some sacrifices for the land."

"I think that used to be blood," the other beta commented wistfully. "That must have been nice."

"Useless, but sure."

"You can check the schedule to see who was here this morning," Irina suggested with a wicked glint in her eye. "And make them wash diapers for a month."

"Wow, you are heartless," she said approvingly. She certainly didn't care if the diapers ended up pink, or neon, for that matter. "You're right. Maybe I'll let them do *some* laundry. I mean, otherwise, how will they learn?"

Other Books by N.J. Lysk

N.J. LYSK'S BOOKSHOP
WWW.NJLYSK.COM/SHOP

[1]

The Stars of the Pack:

1) **Omega for the Pack** – When Ray presents as an omega instead of an alpha, his life changes forever. As a male omega, he's expected to mate with a select group of alphas and start a pack of his own. **A/B/O, M/M/M/M/M/M, M/M, mpreg, dubcon.** *Also in German, French, Italian & Portuguese.*

1.1) **Simpler than Most** *(an interlude)* – Sergi has stopped lying to himself: he's had a crush on a guy for a while. But it turns out telling yourself the truth is just the first step of a long journey. *Also in Spanish, German, Italian & French bilingual editions.*

1.   https://readerlinks.com/l/3217648

2) **Alpha for the Pack** – Ray wasn't ready to become an omega, but he's come to accept his fate... until it seems the pack might need even more of him than he can give.

3) **Protectors of the Pack** – Alec and Gabriel are Ray's alphas first and foremost and nothing to each other. But three years ago... things were very different.

4) **Beloved of the Pack** – An omega is essential to his pack. But an omega is just a man. And a man needs to be loved. *Can you share your body and not share your heart?*

5) **Betas Aside** – Marisa never hesitated to go to her brother's aid—even when he has what she wants most in the world and can never have. But maybe where there's love, there is a way.

Or get the complete series with all extras here.

1) **Runt of the Litter** – An older omega who is ready to change the world, a young alpha who doesn't believe in his own potential; a love that's stronger than distance, age or inclination. **A/B/ O. M/M. Age gap. Long-distance.**

2) **Paper Kisses** – Abel's not the kind of alpha to make a fuss when his omega ex gets together with

someone else, but he's still lonely enough to seek out their kid's teacher to complain about wasting time to celebrate Valentine's day. He doesn't expect to find a lot more than paper hearts. **M/M. Age gap. Human/werewolf. Sweet.**

Rules to Break:

- **Not Destiny** – Thomas and Uriel were never meant to be together. If they choose each other anyway, can they beat the odds? **An Alpha/Beta romance.**
- **Cracking Ice series (7 episodes)** – Hockey means everything to them both... Until they meet each other. **An Alpha/Omega hockey romance.**
- **A Unique Perspective** (Coming soon) – Yadriel doesn't look like an omega, but to the eyes of a very interested beta photographer, maybe there is a lot more to him than his size. **A beta/omega BDSM romance.**

Standalones:

- **A Light in Winter** – Alone and trapped by a dangerous arctic storm, two young men have no choice but to confront their feelings for each other. **A/B/O. Cousins. Werewolves. Isolation.**
- **The Omega Sacrifice** - *Fate deals the cards, but you can still play your hand.* When a young omega is sent away to marry a strange alpha, he has no choice but to face who he is. **An arranged marriage omegaverse romance.**

- **A Bond Unbroken** – When Lia presents as an omega, her best friend offers her anything she needs. But Lia's been in love with Amira for years and whatever her wolf wants, her heart cannot take what's not freely given. **Best friends to lovers. F/F. A/B/O.** *Also in Spanish, German, Italian & French.*

- **Truth Unveiled:** When Kala comes out at work to spite her biphobic coworker, she ends up in need of a fake date for the Christmas party. Her best friend immediately offers to help, but for how long can they handle the pretence? **F/F. Shifters, not A/B/O. A best friends fake dating novella.**

- **Omega Under The Moon** – School is over and Cole is ready to take a break before adult life starts, but when a camping trip with his two best mates turns into something much wilder, it'll change his life forever. **A/B/O. M/M/M.** *Also in French, German & Italian.*

- **Omega On A Mission** - omegas are carers, not fighters, and Gabi is happy looking after his alpha. But when he comes across an animal in danger, his protective instincts flare up, and nobody wants to get in the way of an omega on a mission. **A/B/O.**

Intertwined Fates:

- **Not to be Borne** – When his twin brother presents as an omega, Michuá feels like the world is ending. In a way, becoming an omega himself seems like the only way to stay together... But Zybyn's new alpha wants a lot more than they have bargained for and in a journey towards a strange land, there is nothing to stop him from taking it. **Non-con, abuse, twincest, HEA.**

- **His, Truly** – When Shane unexpectedly presents as an omega during the full moon, his twin brother steps in to protect him from the alphas who'd claim him... But Tim is also an alpha. **A/B/O. M/M. Twincest. Also in French & German.**

- **The Realm of the Impossible** – The Queen is dead and Lorax is ready to take his rightful place when an intimate betrayal leaves him with no choice but to surrender his throne or lose his only remaining family. At this unbearable crossroad, Lorax can watch the new Queen lead his country to a war that will destroy it, or indulge his enemy's sole weakness: himself. **A Taboo M/M Royal Romance.**

Werewolves of Windermere:

1) **The Mating Habits of Werewolves** – Devlin is an omega with ambitions that have nothing to do with alphas, but when destiny comes calling, he may not have that much of a choice. **A/B/O, M/M/M, mpreg.**

2) **Alphas Alone** – An alpha werewolf has some responsibilities he can't ignore: finding an omega, protecting his pack, not falling for another alpha.

3) **The Parenting Habits of Werewolves** – With children in common, Devlin, Naveen and Rami know their fates are bound together, but can they find a balance beyond domesticity? And can they build a love that can last? **The conclusion to the M/M/M Mpreg Romance.**

Deep in the Dark – (Erotica by N.Y. Lysk):

- **The Weight of Duty** – Now that the twins are of age, their uncle takes them in hand to teach them their marital duties. But the experience will be very different for each of them. **Dub-con, feminization, medical body modification, abuse, group sex, arranged marriage, betrayal, incest.**
- **Soldier On** – When a humble young man is captured by the enemy lord during battle, he is expected to offer defeat to his captor by allowing him to bed him. But he is young enough that the act might unintentionally activate a hormonal process that will irreversibly feminise him. **Dub-con, Non-con, mpreg, feminization, debasement.**
- **The Will of Heaven** – Prince Hiram of Pradeira is deemed unfit to be king after his father dies. But as a direct descendant of the gods, only those of his bloodline can reign and so to avoid civil war, he agrees to have a child with each of the princes of the other noble houses of the kingdom so that his first born and heir can inherit the throne from whoever fathered him. **Dub-con, mpreg, feminization, medical kink, debasement.** *Also in German & Italian.*
- **His Brother's Dowry** – Tony agrees to accompany his brother to a new pack, knowing he will have to submit to alphas in the absence of omegas but willing to sacrifice his comfort to give Peter a

chance to find love. But his brother is already in love with an omega girl and he will give anything to get her. Even Tony. **Dub-con, non-con, mpreg, feminization, debasement, body modification.**

- **The Alpha Solution** – Junen will be the next alpha of his pack... until one day he's taken by a stranger—an alpha his father rejected and who's determined to use Junen to get to him. By making him his omega. **Non-con, mpreg, kidnapping, feminization, fisting, debasement, body modification, group sex, abuse.**

About the author

N.J. Lysk (pronouns: whatever) is a queer one—in almost every sense of the word—for whom stories have always been their one true home. She studied linguistics and literature (which is to say, someone offered him a genuine excuse to read professionally) and ended up teaching, but writing is their one true love.

Addicted to angst, enamoured of mpreg and always ready to try a new kink (in a book, that's it!) she became hooked into the omegaverse through fanfic (but he doesn't have the patience to write other people's characters) and has recently expanded from werewolves to hockey players.

If your heart veers towards the dark, look for the **N.Y. Lysk** instead & subscribe to the Dark & Taboo list[1] (these books all come with serious warnings!).

Join their mailing list[2] for book updates and free books, updates and more cool things.

Books can be acquired directly from the website at a reduced rate—new releases also become available there earlier.

---

1. https://readerlinks.com/l/3218963
2. https://readerlinks.com/l/3218944

www.ingramcontent.com/pod-product-compliance
Lightning Source LLC
Chambersburg PA
CBHW022141010726
47493CB00002B/295